THE FATED AND THE FALLEN

THE FATES OF AETHERIUM: BOOK 1

M. E. ALLQUIST

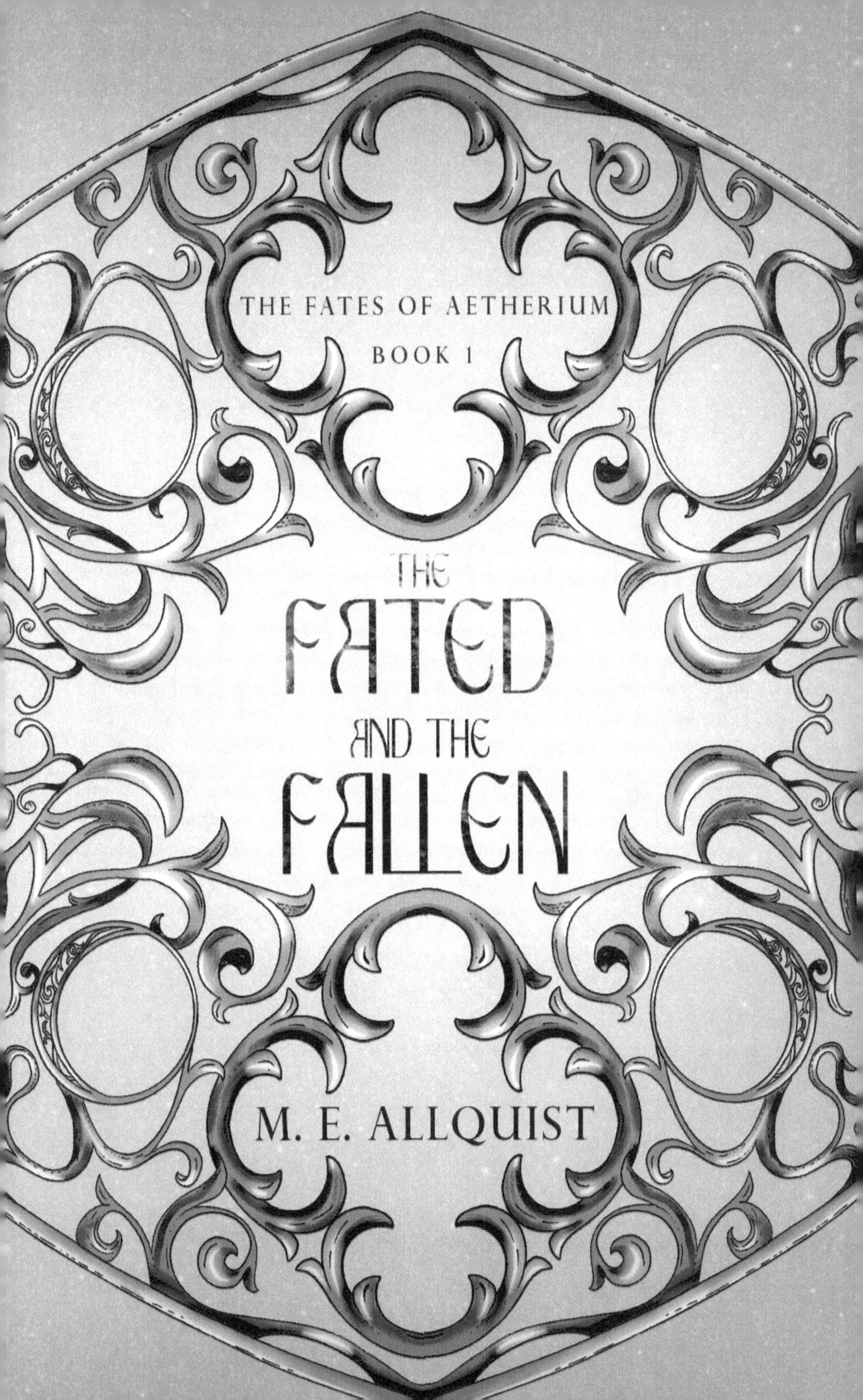
THE FATES OF AETHERIUM
BOOK 1
THE
FATED
AND THE
FALLEN
M. E. ALLQUIST

ISBN: 979-8-9945049-1-8

Book art and design by Rena Violet (@violet.book.design, coversbyviolet.com)
Map illustration by Milo, Stardust Book Services
1st edition 2026

To all who have ever struggled with their place in this world or questioned their self-worth, let this be a reminder that you are valuable, you are loved, and I'm glad you're here.

This one's for you.

THE WHITE SEA
AEROS
Mythranshara
MOONRUN
THE VALE
Thornwood
THE FJORDLANDS
THE RIFT
WESTERN WASTES
DRAGONS TEETH
NORTH HELM
THE ASHLANDS
GLASS RIVER
PORT HARUIDEN
SOUTH HELM
RED BAY
Mirror Lake
SQUALL'S END
Misty Willow Wilds
GLENN RIVER
STORMDRIFT
SAVAGE BAY
THE SOUTHERN EXPANSE

Kingdoms of
AETHERIUM
AEOS
INTER
ALL
STORMHOLD
The Kingswood
BONESPIRE
MOUNTAINS
ESWICK
RAVENHOLD
BLACK
ROCK
GULCH
SALT
FLATS
KINGS
CROSSING
MISTSPELL
BY-THE-SEA
ARKSRIDGE
BOULDER
MOOR
THE
DEAD
SEA
TUNSTEAD
MILL
Ironwood
Forest
IRON
GARDE
THE BONE GATE
SHADOW FEN
The
Dead
Wood
CIRCE'S
COVE
Wandering Wood
CAPE OF WRATH
KAEL'AETHES
AXIOS

Author's Note

The Fated and the Fallen is an adult fantasy story that contains dark elements and themes. It is intended for mature readers, as certain elements are not appropriate for people under 18. Readers who find any elements of the dark fantasy genre upsetting are advised to review the content advisory list, which can be found at the back of the book, between the Epilogue and Acknowledgements.

Your mental health is important to me above all else.

Take care!

Pronunciation Guide

You may find some names and places are difficult to pronounce and not intuitive. Some are pulled from Gaelic, others are Greek/Latin in origin, and others are completely made up. You may also notice the pronunciations here do not match the pronunciation in the real world (Aether and Aetherium, for example). Of course, you are also free to pronounce them however you like, this is but a guide!

Things and Places

Aether (AY-ther)
Aetherial (uh-THEE-ree-al)
Aetherium (uh-THEE-ree-um)
Aeos (AY-ohs)
Axios (AX-ee-ohs)
Aeros (AY-ros)
Anemoi (AH-neh-MOY)
Caelis (KAY-liss)

Names

Hazel (HAY-zel) **Callahan** (KAL-ah-han)
Ezekiel (Eh-ZEEK-ee-el) / **Zeke** (ZEEK) **Bertram** (BUR-trum)
Connall (KON-all)
Slaide (SLAY-d)
Elias (uh-LIE-us)
Magnus (MAG-nus) **Ragnaroth** (RAG-nah-rawth)
Phaedra (FAY-drUH)
Aisling (ASH-ling)
Mori (MOR-ee)
Roshi (ROW-shee) / **Roshiannagh** (Row-shee-an-uh)
Cailleach (CAL-E-yak)

Prologue

I WONDER if it will hurt.

Intimate thoughts of her impending death were a new normal for Hazel Callahan, but this time it weighed her down with a sort of finality she couldn't shake.

The hedge at her back slammed shut with an otherworldly groan, sealing her off from the brutish guards who'd shoved her inside only moments before. Hazel sighed, resigning herself to wondering not *if* she would die today, but whether she would feel it.

There was no sense in turning back. With the hedge closed behind her and the crowd gone, only the maze remained. Well, the maze and Hazel's fellow competitors, that is. And anything else awaiting within.

Moonlight vanished as though swallowed by the dense, living walls around her. Their enchanted boughs glowed faintly, providing the only light up the pathway before her. The air was oppressively heavy, carrying the smell of wet soil, damp rot, and decaying leaf matter—sweet, cloying, and *wrong*.

Survive. Get to the center. Drink the vial.

The instructions were simple, which scared her. Worse still, the rules were few; nothing of consequence was off limits—except quitting. Quitting was grounds for disqualification.

Hazel's thoughts shattered as a scream of agony rang out somewhere in the maze, sending a shiver up her spine. She took a deep, steadying breath, her hand rising to where her silver locket rested below her tunic. Slaide's words echoed in her mind…

Whatever you do, don't stop moving. The hedge feeds on stillness… and fear.

She took one step forward. Then another. Left. Right. Pause. Listen. It made for slow progress, but it was as safe as anything could be in this gods-forsaken hedge. A few more steps and she would be at the first intersection—and met with her first choice of this trial. Left or right?

The vines weaving overhead rustled, drawing Hazel's attention. All around her, the living hedge heaved as though breathing, and with each breath… the path forward narrowed. *Okay, fine. So, slow and steady is going to get me devoured by a bush. Got it.* But as she picked up the pace, so did the hedge. Its breathing intensified, matching the thunderous beating of her heart as she power-walked her way to the intersection.

Something burst forth from the hedge behind her, crashing to the ground in a heap of clattering armor. It was a knight, presumably a guard from beyond the hedge.

"Damn you, Perry! Let me back out this instant or I'll—" His words ended violently as a beast of smoke and shadow leaped upon him out of nowhere, engulfing every bit of the man with its incorporeal form. She couldn't see him, but his screams from within the ball of shadow told her enough.

Hazel backed away, afraid to turn her back on it or make any sudden movement that might draw its attention. It wasn't like she could peel her eyes away, anyway. She'd never witnessed something so foul, its shadows like Slaide's but moving of their own volition, no master to return to. Its body continually shifted, but there were no arms or legs to be seen.

She'd never claimed to be a graceful person, and unfortunately the threat of being in a life-or-death situation didn't change that fact. A twig crunched underfoot, and it might have been the loudest thing she'd ever heard.

Shit.

Time halted. The monster before her paused its feast before turning on her with agonizing slowness. Its murderous gaze landed on her, two haunting red orbs assessing as it stared her down.

All bets were off as Hazel spun on her heel, nearly tripping in her haste to get away.

Run, run, run. She dashed to the end of the aisle just as screams erupted to her right. Her locket warmed against her skin. *Left it is then.* She didn't stop, pivoting around the corner—

And slamming fully into a hedge wall. A dead end.

Hazel righted herself, pulling out of the hedge branch by branch, feeling the panic rise in her throat as each second ticked by that she wasn't free of its grip. And as the shadowy creature rounded the corner, her fear doubled. It crept forward in true predator form: slowly… and with malice in its crimson eyes.

As luck would have it, the hedge itself entered the fray, sending small snakelike vines to wrap around her ankles. The more she fought to get free, the harder the hedge pulled. But she wouldn't use magic here. Not yet. So brute force might be her best option.

It was, in fact, *not* her best option. Before she knew it, her limbs became fully entangled, the hedge pulling her in as if to swallow her whole. On the bright side—if there was one—the shadow beast stopped its pursuit upon seeing it had lost its prey to the bushes.

For a moment, only her face remained beyond the wall. But with a tug, Hazel found herself ensconced in darkness, pulled through a seemingly endless assault of boughs and branches.

This is it. She wasn't naïve. Hazel knew, realistically, she wouldn't make it out of this trial alive. She just hadn't expected to die so soon. When would the pain begin? Did the hedge have a stomach? Did its leaves produce human-digesting acid that would break her down bit by agonizing bit, slowly until there was nothing left? Would it spit her bones out when it was done?

Around her, the hedge shuddered and groaned. Then, all at once, everything froze. Even the hedge's breathing paused. Like it was thinking. Listening. *Checking to see if its prey is still alive, probably.*

A slender, serpentine vine slithered up to her face before wiping away a tiny droplet of blood where a thorn had scraped her cheek. She shuddered at the touch as the little vine retreated.

And then Hazel was moving again as another particularly ambitious vine yanked her abruptly by the ankle. Clawlike branches grappled with her leathers, seeking purchase against the smooth material and snagging at her auburn hair. They whipped and clawed across her face, making her eyes water.

Unexpectedly, and with a great heaving effort by the hedge, Hazel was expelled on the other side. She patted herself down in disbelief that she could be both alive *and* whole. But she was. It was all the encouragement she needed to get moving again.

Keep moving. Survive.

As she rounded the next corner, she heard a faint sound, unlike any of the screams or cries for help she'd grown accustomed to. No, this was a softer voice, more like a child than a man. But surely no child could have accidentally wandered in…

"Is anyone there?" the voice called. Unless Hazel's ears deceived her, a young girl had found her way into the maze. It didn't matter how, because the child didn't stand a chance and would more than likely suffer a brutal death within this hedge.

Hazel sighed. They'd tossed her into this trial with a bunch of selfish, ruthless men. The likelihood of even a single one of them coming to the girl's aid was slim. Was she foolish to involve herself? Probably. But she couldn't live with the vision of a child being mercilessly torn apart by monsters.

So, she turned toward the voice. As if on cue, the girl called out again.

"Hello? Is anyone there? I'm lost." She sniffled as though fighting tears.

Hazel ran toward the voice, which sounded closer the second time. But when she rounded the corner, she met another dead end, and there was no child in sight.

"Please help me," the girl called again. Only this time, the voice came from behind her. But… she could have sworn…

Damn hedges messing with my head. Somewhere, far too close, Hazel thought she heard a low, beastly growl. The hair on her arms stood on end and her locket warmed in warning, but she willed her feet to move. She might not be the only one hunting for the child.

Hazel doubled back in the direction she'd come from. But without warning, the hedge wall slammed shut before her, simultaneously opening an alternative path to her left. She did the only reasonable thing and changed course, pausing only to listen for the child… who'd gone concerningly quiet.

Frustrated, Hazel broke her own silence. "Hello? Are you still there? I'm trying to find you," she called. For a moment, it was eerily quiet.

Then, the girl cried out, "I'm over here!" sounding somewhere up ahead.

Hazel tore off toward the voice again, noting how the air grew cooler and heavier the further she pressed on. The walls were closer together too.

But she pushed on, turning sideways to shuffle through the narrowest parts. Eventually, the path opened into a small clearing. In the center was a crumbling fountain. And just beyond…

The crown of a dark-haired head peeked just over the stone rim.

Hazel almost leaped out of her skin with excitement. "Hey!" she called to the girl, more a whisper than a shout. "I'm here to help."

But the child did not respond. She didn't so much as move at the sound of Hazel's voice.

Perplexed, Hazel rounded the side of the fountain, carefully approaching the child's hiding spot. But what awaited her stole her breath.

A woman, not a child, sat before her, knees pulled to her chest. The woman's head hung low. She was rocking slightly… and humming. Her kohl-black hair was soaking wet as though she'd just crawled out of the ruined fountain… and she was naked. Completely, utterly naked, her sickly pale skin drawn taut over her bones.

Hazel recalled something else Slaide had told her earlier in the day: *trust nothing and no one. Your own senses will betray you if you let them…*

A chill crawled up her spine as unease coiled in her belly. She'd ignored the heating locket, assuming it was due to some other threatening beast lurking about. But something was wrong here.

"*Ruuuuuunnnnnnn,*" hissed a whisper-like voice in the breeze. But she had so many questions, and even though this wasn't the child she'd come for, she worried the woman still needed help.

Hazel reached out to touch her, to see if she was awake—or alive, for that matter. But before she made contact, the humming stopped.

She froze, hand outstretched.

The woman looked up at her slowly, her tangled black hair parting around her face. She was skin and bone, her sunken cheeks painting a portrait of a tortured soul.

Her eyes left Hazel speechless. Two milky, sightless orbs stared up at her with an eerie, unnatural awareness.

And then she smiled, revealing multiple rows of jagged, needle-like teeth.

Hazel had walked right into a trap.

The woman lunged for her, teeth gnashing just inches from her body. She stumbled backward and nearly fell, somehow keeping her feet beneath her.

And then she was running. Hazel ran like she should have the moment the strange feeling crawled over her. She made up for it by sprinting now, rushing around corners with reckless abandon.

She paused for a moment to catch her breath and check if she was still being pursued, only to hear the woman calling after her using the same childlike voice from before.

"Come out, come out. I just want to play," she called in a sing-song voice. "Won't you play with me?"

Hazel turned corner after corner, dodging vines and grappling roots as they tried to obstruct her path.

She veered right, peering over her shoulder as she ran, checking for any signs of the woman on her tail.

As she rounded the next corner, the sight renewed her hope. Just ahead, on a stump in the center of a glade, sat three glorious vials.

Thundering footsteps sounded behind her, urging her forward once more. She wouldn't have long before the creature was upon her again.

As she reached the vials, she found a piece of parchment nailed to the stump. A letter.

No, a riddle.

Shit. I do not have time for this!

But she read it anyway.

One vial glows with ruby light,
A single drop brings pain and plight.
One swirls like smoke, a candle's breath,

Its kiss is cold, its promise death.
One is plain and clear like glass
Still as frost on untouched grass.
Beauty lies and shadows cheat,
Only one will grant retreat.

She looked at the vials. It was simple enough. Too simple. One was ruby red. One was a swirling mix of gray and black, like someone had bottled a shadow. And the last one was perfectly clear, like water. She reached for it, her heart pounding in her chest.

But what if this riddle was designed to mislead? What if she drank the wrong one?

The monster burst through the hedge wall and ran for her, snarling. In a few good leaps, it would be upon her.

Hazel supposed it didn't matter if the riddle was a trick. She'd either escape, die of poison, or become dinner for a monster.

She grasped the vial of clear liquid with shaking hands, popping the cork. Just before she tipped it back, the entire labyrinth inhaled collectively as though holding its breath.

Hazel swallowed the bitter liquid, using everything she had not to spit it out. Around her, the walls exhaled a strange breathy sound, drawn out like a yawn.

Reeeee-aaaahhhhh.

A warning? Perhaps a name? Not hers, though, so it didn't matter. Unless it *was* a warning. Unless…

She shuddered, her vision tunneling. Stars danced across her eyes, and the sensation of floating overcame her. She was almost certain she'd chosen wrong. But she didn't care. It wasn't her problem anymore.

All around her, the world fell away, and everything went black…

ONE WEEK EARLIER…

Nightmares and Cat Hairs

AZEL should have known the day would be anything but ordinary the moment the spice jar threw itself from the shelf, shattering against the old plank floor.

She'd been scrubbing furiously at the soot-stained hearthstones in one of their unoccupied rooms, alone with her thoughts while Pa skewered the day's meat onto the spits out back. The inn's patrons were still asleep, and the tavern below was peaceful. It was her favorite time of day, and she didn't mind spending it on dirty work.

Today, though, Hazel couldn't pull her thoughts from the nightmares plaguing her. They'd began rather recently but with an intensity and frequency she couldn't ignore. Last night, her mind replayed the most recent nightmare it couldn't seem to let go of; the one where she was running through a dark castle corridor, never knowing from whom she fled or why. Despite knowing the long hallway led to a blood-spattered torture chamber deep within some clandestine dungeon, her feet—which she was almost certain were someone else's—always carried her forward of their own volition.

Her sigh evolved into a full-fledged yawn as she willed the memory of the nightmare to leave her alone. If Hazel bothered to care about her looks, she might have cared about the impact of these Helish dreams on her beauty rest. She snorted to herself at the idea. *Hazel the Nobody. And I wouldn't change a thing,* she thought.

Somewhere between the sloshing strokes of her stiff-bristled brush, a clatter arose downstairs, ending with the undeniable sound of breaking glass. She jumped, hand clasping at the locket dangling around her neck. In doing so, she elbowed the bucket of dirty, gray water, causing it to spill over the side, soaking her apron as she attempted to keep it from dumping its contents onto the floor.

Hazel blew out a breath and glanced at the soapy mess streaking down her apron. She didn't move otherwise, listening for any movement that might indicate she wasn't alone. But all was quiet. The guests were, gods willing, still asleep. In the distance, she could just barely make out the song Pa was whistling to himself outside.

No one else should be milling about Briar & Rose at such an hour. Even though she'd overslept again, most of their patrons wouldn't arrive for a few hours, around midday. Occasionally a local drunkard would drop in early to break his fast with mead or whiskey, but she'd either missed them in her own tardiness, or they too had slept in.

She stood and dropped her brush into the bucket, straightening her apron and the tunic beneath. Then she crept down the stairs, every floorboard announcing her descent. It was a good thing she wasn't worried about stealth.

"Hello?" Hazel called as she stepped onto the main floor of the tavern. She was unsure if she wanted anyone to respond, but thankfully, no one did. And as she stepped into the open dining hall, Hazel was happy to see she was indeed alone. Nothing was obviously amiss, so she set her sights on the kitchen.

With a sigh, she pulled her apron over her head and hung it on the hook beside the bar. Then, with what was probably more trepidation than the situation called for, she approached the kitchen door.

Pull yourself together, woman, she chastised herself. She knew she was being ridiculous, but figured it was the nightmares, surely, that had her so on edge. Why else would she feel so jumpy about something as innocuous as broken glass? More than likely, there was a completely logical explanation.

Hazel pushed open the door and immediately located the source: a medium-sized spice jar had taken a dive from the shelf, destroying itself. Its contents—a fine, ink-black powder—spilled upon the floor. Her locket warmed against her skin and she pawed at it absentmindedly.

As she stooped to clean the mess, she checked the glass shards for a label to identify the mysterious powder. But unlike the rest of the herbs and spices in their collection, this one was unlabeled. *Strange.* Surely, they would have noticed a missing label while inventorying their stores…

Curious, Hazel fetched a new spice jar to house the unfamiliar powder. She swept as much of it as she could into a dustpan and dumped it in unceremoniously.

She moved to pick up the larger glass pieces… and immediately sliced her finger open.

"Ah, shit," Hazel cursed at the sudden sting. She put her fingertip in her mouth to stop the bleeding. But when she looked down, the sight made her skin tingle.

A droplet of her blood was disappearing—having dropped into what remained of the black powder on the floor—sizzling and smoking into nothingness. Her mouth fell open, injury forgotten.

"What the Hel?" she hissed.

What the Hel, indeed. Within moments, the droplet of blood was gone, as though it had never been. She eyed the jar in her other hand suspiciously, two deep lines forming between her brows.

"What *are* you?" Hazel glanced up at the spice shelves, searching for an opening, the place the original jar might have been sitting before it took a tumble. But to no avail. There was no opening on the shelves. Everything else was in its rightful place.

Her mouth turned down at the corners as she popped a cork into the jar and slid it into the chestnut-leather satchel she kept in the corner for errands. She could ask Pa about it. Should ask Pa about it. But she decided to replenish the contents first and quiz Pa later. And she knew just the woman to replace what was lost. As she closed the clasp on her bag, Hazel made a mental note to ask her Aunt Agnes what it was used for.

She stuffed the bag back into the corner and left the kitchen, sparing only a brief glance over her shoulder as she pushed the door open.

As Hazel rounded the corner toward the bar to fetch her apron, she slammed into her father. Connall Callahan was a stoic, menacing figure of a man, with broad shoulders and musculature reminiscent of his years in the militia.

It was like walking into a wall.

"My girl!" he said, features softening. "I was about to send someone to check on ya. Thought maybe you'd taken ill on me and got to worrying."

She hugged him; his warm, firm embrace akin to hugging a bear—just without the claws. "No need, Pa. Just overslept is all. Was upstairs for a bit scrubbing the hearth." *Before a spice jar filled with black powder shattered on the kitchen floor.*

He eyed her curiously. "Again with the oversleeping? Listen, it's of no matter to me, but that's not like you at all. Are you sure you're alright?"

She shrugged him off, removing herself from the hug and moving toward the stairwell.

"I'm *fine*, Pa. Just not sleeping well. The roof sprung a leak again, and I haven't had a chance to fix it." It wasn't a lie. Not entirely. The thatch above her bed leaked when it rained.

But the real reason? She wasn't ready for that conversation. She hadn't told him about the nightmares or how she'd been waking up in the middle of the night in a pool of sweat, because he was the kind of father who would drop everything to fix his daughter's problems.

And she wasn't sure this one *could* be fixed.

"Why didn't you say so? I could have had one of the boys from town over to fix it if you'd have told me." She knew he'd do it himself if his old injuries would allow it. Connall Callahan was not prone to outsourcing work, but for his daughter, he'd set his pride aside.

"No need. You've raised me well, and I am sure I can manage it myself." She gave him a wink and nudged past him toward the stairs.

But Pa being Pa, he had to get one last word in. "What about that Ezekiel fella? I can send for him?" She could hear the ridiculous smile in his voice.

Hazel froze at the bottom step and rolled her eyes. "Really, Pa? Zeke might as well be a brother to me. You ought to know better." And he *did* know better. He also knew just what to say to get under her skin.

Ezekiel Bertram was Hazel's longest-standing friendship, and if she was honest with herself, the only real friend she had. Sure, there'd been a handful of female friends when she was a child, but none of them stuck to her quite like Zeke.

He was like a brother to her *now*, but it wasn't always that way. As teenagers, they'd grown a bit too close and wound up chasing feelings neither of them could quite sort out. A wild and intimate relationship developed between them, but like a flame, it burned out quickly.

They'd both moved on amicably, with the unspoken agreement that they wouldn't test those waters again. Even so, Hazel sometimes suspected Zeke *did* want to give it another shot. There were signs, albeit small ones; an "accidental" brush of her hand, a hug or stare lingering too long.

Connall was never privy to the details of their relationship, but he wasn't oblivious either.

Hazel shook her head.

"Can you blame an old man for trying?" he questioned through a smirk that stressed the lines around his eyes, scrunching his time-worn skin.

"Trying to what? Get rid of your only daughter?" She scowled. Though she knew it wasn't true. If Pa had wanted to pawn her off on someone else, he would have by now. Hazel knew she was in a rare situation, one where her father would cling to his only daughter, his only child, as long as he could. He would never force her to marry if she didn't want to, which left her as the oldest eligible woman in Larksridge.

"Never. I just don't want you to be stuck here with me forever. It's no life for someone like you. You deserve to see the world." He meant it.

Hazel rolled her eyes again. "We've been over this. I've no desire to see the world. Not now, not ever. The world has nothing to offer me I can't have right here at home. Plus, Larksridge has the added benefit of being *safe*. You know as well as anyone that the same cannot be said about out there." She nodded toward the open window.

Connall shifted his weight uneasily, relieving the strain on his bad leg. His eyes darkened as though his mind had wandered somewhere else.

It was something Hazel knew far too much about, having traipsed through her dreams a few too many times recently.

"*Anyway*," she broke the tension, "I am fine, truly. Now, if it's alright with you, I've got to finish up upstairs so I can get going on today's meals before the hungry townsfolk show up and burn the place down."

"Aye," he sighed, "I just want you to know, Hazel girl. You don't *have* to go anywhere if you don't like. I love having you here more than anything in the world. I just want you to be happy, be it here or somewhere else. The last thing your old man wants is to hold you back."

"I know, Pa. I know." She faked a smile. Not because he'd said anything wrong, but because he'd said everything right. They may not have had an easy life, but Connall would stop at nothing to see his daughter happy. Even if it was at his own expense.

She patted his arm with a gentle hand and kissed him on the cheek. "Love you. Duty calls."

Hazel finished refreshing the unoccupied room and stood back to admire her handiwork. She almost turned her back on the straw-stuffed mattress with its quilt folded neatly atop it when she noticed something peculiar. It was a long, orange cat hair. She plucked it from the quilt, silently wondering when she'd last seen someone bring an animal companion for their stay, let alone a cat.

As she turned to leave the room, Hazel glimpsed herself in the mirror and paused. Her wild auburn curls were as unruly as ever despite the kerchief she'd tied them back with. Her pale, freckled skin was dusted with soot. *Looking dreadful, Hazel Grace. What would Mother think of you now?*

And what *would* her mother have thought of her? Unmarried and with no prospects, Hazel lived a relatively solitary, ordinary life under her father's roof. She spent her days toiling in the garden behind the inn and helping with odds and ends around the tavern. Twenty-seven years under her belt and nothing to show for it.

Pa wasn't getting any younger, which was getting harder to ignore. If Mother could see her now—wherever she was in the great beyond of the Otherrealm—Hazel hoped she appreciated how her daughter looked after the doting husband she'd left behind. Regardless of her status in life. Regardless of whether she was far behind her similarly aged peers and deemed by most to be unsuccessful.

"I wish you were here," Hazel whispered to no one, pulling her locket from beneath her blouse. It was weird, missing someone she couldn't remember. Thankfully, Pa filled in the gaps, regaling Hazel with stories otherwise lost to the fog of passing time. But sometimes, she wondered if every memory was fabricated, something Connall had wrapped in a delicate package and handed to her. None of them *belonged* to her. As though all the memories she'd made had been erased. Her mind—much like the silver locket Connall had passed on to her on her sixteenth birthday—refused to open.

She was just a tot when her mother perished in childbirth. Hazel lost both her mother and sibling that day, and she often wondered what life would have been like were they still alive. Instead, all she had left was a useless silver locket hammered into the likeness of a quarter moon.

But she couldn't change the past. So, Hazel left her wandering thoughts behind and descended to the work awaiting her in the kitchen.

Before long, the kitchen was overflowing with delicious aromas. Hazel had prepared bowls of chopped leeks, turnips, potatoes, and carrots, along with a few small dishes of roughly chopped herbs. She had grown to love this time, just her and the quiet of the kitchen—the calm before the proverbial storm.

The gentle thump of her knife chopping against the wooden cutting board, the crunch of the vegetables, the incredible smells guaranteed to emanate from the foods before they were cooked… It was like magic.

And if Hazel was honest, she felt like a bit of a witch herself when cooking, especially when preparing a soup or stew. Perhaps it was a childish thing for a grown woman to enjoy, but sometimes she pretended she was crafting a brew or potion in the tavern's giant iron cauldron. After all, what was soup if not a potion to cure hunger? But each time she had those thoughts, Hazel scolded herself; an adult woman shouldn't be brewing imaginary potions in her father's kitchen.

In another world, another time, maybe. However, since the Dampening, all but the simplest of spells were nullified by the Border and its wards. Magic fell under an outright ban, even if the wards couldn't reach it. The Crown made it an act of treason to practice even the simplest, smallest practical magics. But Hazel could pretend—that in itself wasn't a crime. She didn't have access to real magic, anyway. Her blood was ordinary—they called it *pure,* but she despised the term—which was a relief and certainly one less thing she had to worry about. Though she had to admit she didn't understand the fuss about magic.

Hazel grabbed a shank of venison from the back table and, using her sharpest knife, removed the tendons and trimmed the sinew from the dark red muscle. It was a fresh kill; one she suspected the hunter had harvested that same morning. Connall had likely tossed the man a few extra coins for his trouble. Though they rarely had extra coin to spare.

After the venison, she added leeks, potatoes, carrots, and the herbs she'd chopped, along with a dash of salt and some whole peppercorns for flavor. While the stew simmered, Hazel prepped a childhood staple: her late Nan's sweetbread. It was a pillowy, buttery dough baked to perfection and topped with a cinnamon and sugar mixture. *By dinner, the entire town is going to be lined up outside the door, begging for a plate.*

Once everything was ready in the kitchen, Hazel stepped out back to toss some scraps aside in a crate for the farmers. Nothing went to waste if they could help it. Despite the seasons growing leaner and fewer farms continuing to raise livestock with each passing year, Farmer Albertsen still had a small hog farm just north of town, and his pigs loved food scraps of all kinds. He stopped by twice a week to pick them up.

She tried to ignore her satchel sitting in the corner beside the back door. To pretend it wasn't practically beckoning her to open it and take another look at the strange powder within. She pushed past it, finding herself released from its grip once outside.

Hazel next turned her attention to the spits, where Connall had skewered two hares and five hens. Their skin was browning nicely and would be decadent and crispy by the midday meal. She stoked the fire with some kindling, letting her mind wander. Just before she turned to go back inside, Hazel caught a flash of orange out of the corner of her eye. She turned just in time to catch the end of a cat's tail disappearing behind the old smokehouse.

Glancing at the spits, Hazel hoped the little beast would keep his paws to himself, however unlikely. Sighing, she shook her head and turned her back on the little scavenger she knew was waiting for her to disappear. As she crossed the threshold, she couldn't shake the ominous feeling climbing up her spine, as though she was being watched.

Her locket heated enough to garner her attention. She spared one more glance over her shoulder before going back inside, but no one was there.

The Butcher and the Barmaid

HAZEL spent the entire morning catching up on her responsibilities around the inn and tavern. And yet, despite her tardiness, she'd successfully prepped everything she and Pa would need to get a head start on their patrons, who'd since filtered in.

Mostly, she didn't pay them any mind beyond taking their orders and serving food and drink. Day after day, the routine was the same–barring any special festivals or events. As such, it was easy to get sucked into her own subconscious.

As she stood behind the bar pouring a mug of mead for a gentleman, she spied a young mother with two rambunctious tots in the corner of the dining hall. The woman desperately tried to keep them out of the aisles, an impossible task.

Yet, despite how taxing it likely was to be looking after them, Hazel envied the little family. She wondered if the children knew how special it was to have such a doting mother. Something she had yearned for as long as she could remember.

Watching them reminded her of the stories Pa told her growing up, about how Hazel was her mother's shadow as she cultivated her herbs in the garden. How her mother would sing to the saplings, encouraging them to grow, and how stubborn blossoms bloomed in the palm of her hand. And Hazel was there every step of the way, watching, learning.

It devastated Hazel that she could remember next to nothing of her mother. She sometimes wondered if none of it was true. Perhaps her mother would push through the front door of Briar & Rose any moment as though she'd never been gone.

She was jerked from her daydream by the splatter of mead onto the bar floor as it spilled over the counter's edge. In her absentmindedness, Hazel overpoured the drink without realizing.

"Stupid, witless fool," she muttered under her breath.

"Pardon?" a gruff man's voice called as she pulled herself out of her trance.

She blinked at him, slack-jawed.

"Miss? Did you say something?" He hunched over a bowl of fragrant meat pie, poised to take a bite, as though she'd interrupted his meal. Meaty broth dripped from his spoon onto the bar top.

"Oh, gods. No, I'm sorry, sir." She stumbled over the words and returned to the mess she'd made. *Get it together, Hazel Grace.* The bar. Her job. The customers. Pa would be in a fit of worry if he caught her in a daze at the bar and talking to herself, especially with so much work to be done.

While she scrubbed at a particularly stubborn spot on the bar top, Hazel smelled something burning. *Bloody burning gods! You're the one who prepped all of this, you twit... or did you forget already?* She was beside herself with anger at her carelessness.

"The sweetbread!" she hollered to no one in particular. Hazel began doing everything and nothing at once, as though each of her limbs was at odds with the others on how to fix this problem.

When at last she reached the oven, smoke was pouring from behind its door. As she opened it, a black, sickly sweet cloud greeted her as it billowed into her face. When the smoke cleared, only three charred braids remained.

Hazel had worked so hard to recreate the doughy delight from her late Nan's own recipe. Unfortunately, this marked the third time she had completely burned them to an unrecognizable crisp. And now there was no time to try again, not before the dinner rush. She sighed, tossing the blackened, crumbling sweetbread into the scrap food bin.

"At least the animals will eat well, I guess." She sighed. If nothing else, there was still stew and roast chicken to serve. Along with some rabbit.

She'd wanted to contribute something more, though, something the townsfolk would keep coming back for… something to remind them of warm hearthfires, cozying up with wool-lined boots, and easier times. Times when people were happy and neighbors weren't turning each other in on the suspicion of practicing magic. When children and their mothers weren't being stoned to death or beaten in the streets for suspected witchcraft. It didn't happen often, but it didn't need to. The threat of violence hung heavy in the air.

It was all hogwash anyway, the fuss about magic. No one in their town had seen so much as a lick of magic since the High King had banned its practice and sentenced all practitioners—mainly witches—to death.

The earliest years of the persecution had been harrowing, though if Hazel was honest, she had been too young to comprehend what was going on around her. Pa had protected her from experiencing too much of it and, until recently, things had calmed down.

There was a sixteen-year lull in the stonings, hangings, and pyres, and after the last one of record, the world had been set to rights for the first time in a long time. At least according to the King.

Hazel knew exactly one person who had access to any magical talents: her Aunt Agnes. But the old woman was a hermit and lived outside of town, so no one paid her any mind. At any rate, the gods of Caelis were pleased enough. *Praise be,* Hazel thought, with more than just a touch of cynicism. The gods were, after all, the source of more than their fair share of the problem.

"Aye, barmaid!" one of their regulars barked at her. Hazel knew who the voice belonged to, and she loathed him. Jonas the butcher was a sour sort of man who wore a permanent scowl on his scarred and pockmarked face. Forever smelling of smoked meats and stale ale, Jonas was the kind of man whose troubled past led him to believe the world owed him something, and he treated everyone accordingly. Alas, even when piss-drunk, he was the only person experienced enough to run the town butcher.

"I'll be with you in a minute, Jonas. And I don't think I need to remind you the barmaid has a name," she shot over her shoulder. He mumbled something incoherently under his breath, and Hazel was happy enough not to make out a word of it. It wouldn't have been anything pleasant, anyway.

She shook her head and reluctantly poured the man's drink. After returning the flagon to its home behind the bar, Hazel approached Jonas with a fake smile, ignoring the slight warming sensation produced by her locket. "Your ale, sir."

Without a word of thanks, Jonas tipped the entire pint back and drank it dry. Hazel watched in disgust, half wishing she'd have spat in it, as the amber liquid overflowed at the corners of his mouth, accompanied by his grotesque slurping. He drank as though he'd just finished a week-long journey through the blistering sands of the Western Wastes, the ale running through his beard and down to his stained apron.

When he finished, he slammed the mug onto the bar top. "Tastes like hot hog piss. Figures, though, seeing as this whole place has gone to shit since the old cripple put you in charge." Hazel winced at the insult, directed not at her, but at her father. And still, Jonas wasn't done.

He belched before continuing. "Any man who knows anything at all knows women shouldn't handle the ale, besides maybe serving it. Their womanly curse causes it to spoil." Rising from his stool, his whiskey-barrel gut butted up against the bar.

"Bet every drop in this place has gone sour in your presence." He spat on the floor.

Hazel knew one thing for certain. It was unwise to disrespect Connall Callahan. Or his daughter. Or his establishment.

Jonas went on ranting and raving as the rest of the tavern grew quiet, shifting uncomfortably in their seats. A large figure stepped out of the stairwell shadows, as though Jonas's actions had summoned him.

He approached the bar, his gait uneven and marred by a limp, but no less imposing. The silence was deafening as the man brought his calloused hand to rest heavily on Jonas's shoulder. Jonas flinched at the impact, glancing sidelong at his new company.

"Connall." He swallowed hard but kept his facial expression unflinching.

"*Jonas.*" Connall nodded, maintaining eye contact as he reached past Jonas to his daughter, who handed him the rag she'd been cleaning with. "Seeing as you'd *never* do that on purpose, go 'head and clean it up and we'll forget about it." He pressed the rag into Jonas's chest and patted him on the back. An unspoken warning. As Connall turned to walk away, Jonas tossed the rag to the ground.

"I'll do no such thing. Your disrespectful wench of a daughter can handle it. Could probably use a good whip—" Jonas's words caught in his throat as Connall snatched him by the collar and pulled him in close.

"Shall we head outside, then? Settle this like men?" There was fear in Jonas's eyes, sweat beading on his wrinkled brow. Connall smirked. "Surely you aren't afraid of an *old cripple*?"

Everyone in town, Jonas included, knew Connall's bad leg wasn't much of a hindrance to anything. What he lacked in mobility, he made up for in sheer ferocity and brute strength. He was a tall, broad man, whose hardened body represented a lifetime spent in the King's militia. It wasn't until his injury that he finally settled down, finding a new purpose as a family man. Later, his pride and joy became this very establishment, the Briar & Rose.

He may not be what he once was, but Connall maintained a reputation—one he wouldn't stand to have tarnished, especially not by Jonas. Disrespecting his daughter was disrespecting him, old-fashioned as it may be. It wouldn't do.

Jonas's gaze darkened as the two men locked eyes, but he broke first, as though realizing what was at stake. He rubbed the back of his neck and looked at the floor. Hazel watched as her father released his grip on the butcher's collar and folded his arms across his chest.

"Connall, I..." Jonas started, cheeks reddening.

"The *rag*, Jonas," Connall interrupted, uncrossing his arms to gesture in a sweeping motion at the floor. Jonas sighed in defeat, crouching down to pick up the rag. As he grasped it, a foot came to rest on top of his fingers. Jonas focused on the leather boot for a moment before his features scrunched and he closed his eyes, as though prepared to take the full brunt of the weight threatening to flatten his bones into the bar floor.

"The only reason I don't crush every bone in your hand right now is because this village relies on you for our meat processing," Connall spoke from up above him, voice grave and gravelly, heavy with the weight of his warning. "But let me be clear: you will *never* disrespect my daughter or this establishment again. Understood?"

Jonas whimpered his agreement, and Hazel almost felt sympathy for the man. Almost.

Connall lifted his foot, releasing Jonas. The butcher got to his knees, rubbing his hand. Connall outstretched his hand in offering. Jonas took it without another word.

"You're a better man than this, you old bastard, and I suspect you've had more than enough to drink tonight." Connall said. "Go home. *Straight* home. No detours. And get some sleep. We'll talk about this when you've cleared your head."

Hazel knew Jonas to be an abrasive man, but tonight he had acted different. She recalled how he had stumbled in despite the lack of alcohol on his breath. She'd just been too preoccupied to make much of it. If anything, it was unusual the drunkard *didn't* reek of drink, she remembered, frowning. She may not like Jonas much, but he and her father had a longstanding relationship she would never fully understand.

They'd served in the militia many moons ago and formed a bond like brothers, as military men often did. For reasons unbeknownst to Hazel, the two men had a falling out at the end of the war and went their separate ways. A decade passed without either of them so much as crossing paths. Then one day, Jonas showed up with his little near-starved family and begged for a second chance from Connall. Being a forgiving man, he welcomed Jonas with open arms and helped him find a respectable role in the village. Surprisingly, Jonas had a wife, though she rarely showed her face. Hazel sometimes wondered what horrors the woman had persisted through, and why she stayed.

Because of her father's relationship with the man, Hazel tolerated Jonas just enough to keep Pa happy. But she worried about keeping people like him around. Worried he would chase off other customers and cause Briar & Rose to lose business. Never mind the fact that Jonas believed most—if not all—women to be descended from witches, and the only way to ensure they stayed both compliant and subservient was to whip and beat the magic out of them. To keep the curses at bay, he said.

"What got into him?" She asked her father, who still had his eyes trained on Jonas. She hadn't noticed it in the middle of the commotion, but the remaining patrons had all gone. Jonas's departure left her and

Pa alone in the empty tavern. "Um, Pa?" When he didn't respond, she stepped into his line of sight. "Are you okay?"

He snapped to. "Fine. I'm fine," he muttered, though something clearly troubled him. "As for Jonas, well, I don't know, love. I don't know." He squeezed his brow between his thumb and fingers. "He's a complicated man."

As are you, she thought.

He eyed her thoughtfully. Then, changing the subject, he said, "So. Have a little mishap in the kitchen this evening, did we?"

She blanched.

He chuckled.

Connall grabbed an ale horn and started polishing it. "Do me a favor, love. Take some time off tomorrow morning and make a trip over to see Agnes. We are running low on tea at the house, and this old leg won't let me walk that far right now. I particularly need whatever blend takes the edge off my pain."

"No problem. Anything else?" She smiled, happy to have avoided a discussion about her ever-wandering mind.

He paused before returning to his polishing. "You ought to ask her if she has anything for those nightmares, too."

Hazel raised an eyebrow. *How?*

Connall just winked and gestured the polished ale horn in a mocking *cheers* motion. "A father always knows."

Aunt Agnes

THE next morning, Hazel set off to visit Agnes. *Aunt* Agnes, as she was lovingly known, held an honorary position in the Callahan family. As far as Hazel knew, Agnes had no true relation to their family. Regardless, Agnes had helped raise Hazel, coming into their lives after her mother's death.

Like a gift from the gods, she arrived just when she was needed the most, helping Connall get through a terribly traumatic time in his life and playing a critical role in raising little Hazel, who was too young to understand where her mother had gone.

Now, Hazel and Connall mostly relied on Agnes for her wonderful healing teas and her companionship.

The former brought Hazel to Agnes's corner of the world on a day when the air was heavy and warm, cloudy and gray. Connall's bad leg bothered him something fierce, and Agnes had a tea blend that helped stave off the pain. But they were completely out, so she'd set out to pay Agnes a visit.

It just so happened to be convenient that Agnes was also the most likely to have answers about what had occurred with the strange black powder in the kitchen. Try as she might, Hazel couldn't let it go. She patted her satchel, reminded of the unsettling substance she was carrying.

As she approached the clearing in the woods, a familiar buzz tingled along Hazel's skin. The slight metallic taste at the back of her tongue signaling she was crossing through Agnes's protective ward.

The first time she'd ever crossed through, it scared her so badly she refused to go back to Agnes's cottage for a fortnight. The next time she visited, Pa had escorted her, and they'd had a hushed, strange conversation about how Agnes differed from most townspeople, and why it drove her to live on the outskirts of town. She could do things others couldn't. Things others wouldn't understand. Pa and Agnes hadn't used the exact terminology for reasons Hazel now understood, but it went without saying there was a particular name for Agnes's occupation.

Witch.

Since then, Hazel had grown comfortable making trips to see her aunt in the woods. It was always a pleasant change of pace, especially with how time always slowed in her presence. There was nowhere else she needed to be and no reason to rush.

Once she'd passed through the wards, sunlight blanketed Hazel in warmth as it filtered through the canopy. The area smelled intensely of the oddest combination of tilled, wet earth and freshly baked pie.

As she approached, she could see through Agnes's front window. A broom swept the floor of its own volition, and a spoon stirred the contents of a cauldron hanging over the fire with no cook to direct it. The sound of soft humming drifted from within.

Enchantments. When Agnes sensed someone entering her wards, she usually cut off any magic currently working in and around her home. However, when Hazel stopped by Agnes always let her see some enchantments at work before cutting off the spells. Hazel delighted in seeing the wonderful things that could be done with simple magical housework. *I don't see what the purpose of outlawing this was. It's harmless, and if anything, it* helps *people.*

Hazel often imagined what life might have been like before the magic disappeared: an entire town of merry folk cooking with magical utensils and keeping their thresholds swept clean with enchanted brooms, looms weaving cozy blankets and sewing needles mending clothes. To her, magic didn't need to be feared. But something had made the High King feel otherwise.

She approached the door, and before she could knock, a soft voice came from inside.

"Hazel, dear! Is that you? Why, of course it is. Come in, come in!" called the cheerful, raspy voice.

Hazel pushed the door open with a gentle nudge. As it opened, it revealed the cozy interior of the cottage. Agnes was a simple old woman with very few needs. And with any needs she had, she could almost always make do with plants and such around her home. Anything else she might need, well, she just sent for Connall or Hazel, and they'd retrieve whatever she needed from town. She didn't consume any parts of animals, though, so there wasn't much in town she couldn't get elsewhere.

Mouthwatering smells overwhelmed Hazel's senses as she stepped inside. Though the magically imbued housewares had returned to their otherwise lifeless state, a cauldron of something delicious smelling bubbled over the fire in the hearth. The kitchen was quaint and decorated with many herbs and plants hanging to dry, jars of various seasonings scattered on the countertops. There was a loom and chair off in the corner beside the small yet comfy looking bed, a quilted blanket laid neatly across the top.

It wasn't much, but it was the most homey, welcoming place Hazel had ever been.

"So, tell me dear, what brings you out to see me? Finally going to let me read those palms of yours?" She winked and her round, tawny face drew into a wrinkled, nearly toothless smile. "But of course, I know why you're here. Sit, sit! I have a wonderful summer vegetable stew on. It will be ready soon, and I'll have more than enough to share. I insist." Her dimpled smile stretched so high into her cheeks it forced her silver eyes into a squint.

Hazel crossed the room to the small table set for two. "I would protest and insist I not keep you busy longer than necessary, but we both know I wouldn't win *that* war of wills. Besides, I've got nowhere else to be." She smiled warmly at Agnes. "I've missed you, Auntie. How have you been?" she asked, pulling out a chair.

"I'm as well as I can be. Nothing to report on in this old woman's life. No one comes to visit other than you and Connall. Therefore, no one bothers me, and I get to enjoy the company of the forest and the animals. Does it get any better?"

"For you, I suppose not." Hazel laughed. "I have to say it is much more relaxing here compared to town. Larksridge has been on-edge lately. I rarely feel like I can hear myself think."

Agnes drifted off in her own thoughts. "Hmm… I can imagine so," she said after a few quiet moments. Hazel was reminded of how much she truly missed her time with Agnes. Blood relative or not, she was the closest person Hazel had to a matriarchal figure.

Hazel thought about the times Agnes had wanted to read her future, only for Hazel to gently turn her down. On a whim, she decided today was the day.

"Tea or palm?" she asked with a smirk.

"What's that now?" confusion danced in her eyes, as though she hadn't expected Hazel to ever give in.

"Which reading would you prefer to do today?" Hazel clarified.

"You—you're sure?" *So you can't see the future directly*, Hazel mused to herself. *I'd wondered.*

"I am sure. Truthfully, I don't know why I've put you off on it all these years. So yes, why not?" A soft smile graced her features.

Hazel hadn't seen Agnes so cheerful in quite some time. But there was something else. Her mood shifted, if for only a moment, before she reclaimed her usual effervescence.

"My dear, I am glad you've asked. But if you're just humoring this poor old woman for the sake of it, we shouldn't. The thing with these readings… they depend quite a lot on the energy put into them. The reader and the participant must commit fully, and the ambiance in the room must be just so." She gestured around them. "It's quite alright if you still aren't ready. Someday, you will be."

"No, ma'am. I truly want you to give me a reading. I *am* ready," Hazel said with fire in her eyes.

Agnes eyed her lovingly, but with a wariness Hazel wasn't used to. "Alright then, let me put this tea on and we can chat."

She strode over to the hearth and checked the cauldron of stew Hazel had forgotten about. Surely by now it had burned and stuck to the bottom. Agnes took a ladle full and sampled it, remarking on how wonderful it was. But of course, an unseen enchantment kept it from burning.

What she did next was one of Hazel's favorite tricks. She gathered her kettle and two mugs for tea from her cupboard and brought them to the table. On the way over, she whispered something to the pot, and moments later steam poured from the spout. By the time she reached the table, the tea was at the perfect temperature and ready to enjoy. Agnes poured a cup for each of them and then sat down at the table herself.

"So, tell me," she began, "What has my sweet Hazel been up to these days?"

Hazel froze, knowing she should spill the details, but feeling woefully unprepared. As she began to speak, Agnes interjected. Hazel was grateful for the interruption… until she learned the subject.

"Any young men catching your eye?" Agnes batted her thinning eyelashes suggestively.

"Oh goodness, Agnes, can't we talk about anything else?" Hazel begged, her cheeks warming.

"You know I may not look like much now, but once upon a time I had to scare the men away to get even a moment's peace. Why do you think I took up witchcraft?" She whispered the last word and wiggled her fingers like she was casting a spell.

Hazel rolled her eyes. "I don't doubt that for a second. You're still a beautiful lady, Agnes. Everyone grows old. Not everyone does it gracefully."

"Not without magic anyway." She winked.

"You use magic to stay younger?" Hazel paused with the cup at her lips.

"No child, of course not." Agnes laughed. "I don't mess with the occult in that manner. Just cooking, cleaning, gardening. I'm a hearth witch; That's all my spells are good for. And the occasional protective spell, warding my home from evil and anyone who wishes me or my guests harm. That sort of thing. But I don't dabble in immortality, nor do I deal with the elements. That's what got us all into this mess anyway, you know."

Hazel sipped her tea and perked up at her words. She didn't know why magic had been outlawed, only that it was considered a threat.

"You don't know? I will have to talk to your father about that." She sighed. "Things used to be so different. Not too long ago, if you can believe it." She looked out the window longingly.

"What was it like?"

Agnes closed her eyes thoughtfully. Where to begin. "Such a loaded question, that one. Life was bright and full, the world was beaming with energy, and yes, like me, many folks used their enchantments to help around the house. A few, however, tampered with elemental magics, and that was where everything went downhill. It started innocently enough I suppose—simple experimentation. Then a couple of folks grew bored and bold, a dangerous combination. They messed with the weather, the growth of crops, the flow of our rivers… and well, it got out of hand. Before long, and as you might expect, that same group of witches became hungry for power, power they believed they could steal with this newfound magic."

Hazel was listening to a fairytale. Something so far from reality it simply could not be true. Magic was prevalent? She'd always imagined it a rarity, where every now and then someone was lucky enough to be blessed with it, as though the gods had chosen them for some higher purpose. This was a new revelation, indeed.

"Do you ever look around and wonder why our lands are the way they are? So decrepit and devoid of life? When you come here, child, you see what the lands could be. My wards allow it to be so because magic feeds the land, and the land feeds the magic. It is a beautiful, synchronous cycle. The two are… symbiotic you might say."

Hazel nodded thoughtfully, sipping the tea.

"When the High King placed a ban on magic and started wiping out the magic wielders, the lands suffered. The plants and animals withered and died. In his ignorance and arrogance, he refused to see the truth. He said we, the magic wielders, had angered the gods by tampering with the elements."

"But that wasn't true, was it?" Hazel wondered, setting her cup down.

"No, of course it wasn't. The gods did not react until *after* the land became unbalanced. The reason things are the way they are now, we don't entirely know. Something is likely amiss on the Aetherial Plane. That is where Caelis is located, the high seat of the remaining gods. All but the

Anemoi, the Wind gods, have forsaken us. The look on your face tells me you've heard none of this… hmm."

Hazel tried to fix her face. "No, I haven't. We don't talk about the gods much at home. But… I just don't understand. Why are the Four Winds the only gods who stayed for us?"

"For us?" Agnes scoffed. "No, child. The Anemoi have never been the most benevolent gods. Where the others saw a lost cause, those scavenging harpies saw opportunity." She started whispering her next words. "Don't for one second think they have our best interests at heart. While they were always one of the four main sects of Elementals—the others being Earth, Fire, and Water—they were never a top priority for any people, save for the sailors and pirates, perhaps. Those few folk who relied on the Winds for guidance and a push in the right direction were barely enough to appease the greedy gods. Whereas the Earth gods, Fire gods, and Water gods especially, were at the forefront of most peoples' minds each day. Not long before you were born, we prayed to them all."

Hazel's head was spinning. She brought her locket to her lips as the questions rolled through her. Why did no one talk about this? Why did people so willingly give up their way of life? "Agnes, this is so much to take in. Why wouldn't Pa have told me about any of this?"

"Don't fret about it. Believe it or not, Connall has good reason for doing most of the things he does, bullheaded as he may be. Maybe he just hasn't felt that the time was right. Or maybe, since you live among other people, he's worried someone would overhear any blasphemous talk." She nodded to the teacup. "How was it?"

Scratching her eyebrow in thought, she looked down, not even realizing she'd drank it all. "It was just what I needed, Agnes. Thank you."

"Still up for that reading?"

Hazel hesitated. No, she really wasn't up for a reading. She had so many questions swirling and buzzing in her head, and the last thing she wanted was anything else to worry about. She didn't even think she could go home to Connall and immediately volley him with questions.

Seeing her concern, Agnes withdrew. "It's alright, dear. We can do it some other time. Or not at all, if you prefer."

"No!" Hazel cut her off. "Sorry, that was rude. I just meant, well, I said I would do it, and I don't have any good reason not to. So yes, please, let's do the reading." She smiled reassuringly.

Agnes nodded, reaching for the cup. The old woman withdrew into herself as she pulled the cup in, sparing Hazel a quick glance before closing her eyes and seeming to go… elsewhere… again. After a pause—perhaps a silent beckoning to whatever gods she prayed to—Agnes opened her eyes again and peered into the cup.

There was no reaction. She didn't so much as flinch. She just stared at the bottom of the cup for ages. Hazel shifted uneasily in her seat.

She heard a breeze rustling the leaves outside. Perhaps it was her imagination, but she was sure there had not been a breeze when she arrived. Was the sky darkening as well? There hadn't been a cloud in the sky on her walk over.

Agnes appeared to return from wherever she had gone, looking around as if she had lost her way. She locked eyes with Hazel, brows furrowing slightly before her gaze shot back down into the cup. Hazel got an uneasy feeling in her stomach that something had gone terribly wrong. Like she was about to learn of some horrible fate awaiting her in the near future.

"Agnes?" She broke the silence, and Agnes looked as though she'd seen the undead. Then, as though it had never been, her clouded expression faded away.

"So sorry, dear! Sometimes I wander too far when I do these readings, and it's been quite a while since I've had someone willing to let me practice. Forgive me, please."

"Are you alright? I thought something terrible had happened to you."

Agnes tried to hide the flash of worry as it crossed her face, but Hazel caught it just so. She didn't mention it, but it was unnerving.

"Agnes, what's going on? What did the leaves show you?" Hazel leaned in closer. *Ask her about the powder.*

She sighed, pushing back her chair. "Nothing."

"That reaction was for *nothing*? I find that hard to believe."

Agnes shook her head. "Not *nothing* in the traditional sense. The thing is, Hazel dear, the leaves never show nothing. I am just not sure what to make of yours. It was… ambiguous. There is nothing distinct for me to work with. I was searching for something in a deeper place… *beyond.* But it is no matter." She waved her hand as if shooing the thought away. There was a shift in her tone as she stood up from the table. "It's no worry, child." She gathered the cups and kettle and turned her back on Hazel.

Something was off, but Agnes clearly needed some time to think about it. Maybe Agnes was just tired, and Hazel had overstayed. After all, she wasn't getting any younger. Hazel stood and gathered her things to leave.

But the presence in her bag weighed on her, its burden a boulder in her mind. She swallowed hard. "Agnes, I need to ask you about something else," she managed.

"Sure, sure," Agnes replied, too busy to turn around.

Hazel took a deep breath. "Something strange happened yesterday. A jar fell from a shelf in the kitchen, and when I went to clean it up, I didn't recognize the herb inside. Actually, I don't think it's an herb at all."

"Mmhmm," the old woman mumbled.

"I wondered if you might take a look at it and tell me what you think?"

"Sure, dear. Hand it here." Agnes reached back as Hazel pulled forth the jar, her heart thumping wildly as she did so. Agnes grasped the jar without looking and placed it on her workbench.

Without warning, she whirled on Hazel.

"*Where* did you say you found this?" Her voice was sharp.

Hazel recoiled. "I-It was in our kitchen. At Briar and Rose. Shattered on the floor."

Agnes's eyes grew wide then narrowed to near slits. Without another word, she spun back to her workbench, turning her back on Hazel. She knocked around her own glass jars of herbs frantically, as though looking for something specific. She dug around in her cupboard, grabbing things and mumbling to herself. When she turned around, Agnes had several small sachets of herbs, affixing them to Hazel's person and her bag. Hazel eyed them warily. "What was in that jar, Agnes?"

She fixed a pointed gaze on Hazel. "That is Witchbane powder, cultivated from Veilroot. Did you handle it? Did it touch your skin?" She glanced down at the bandage on Hazel's finger. "Your *blood?*"

"No," she lied. "I swept it up with a dustpan and dumped it into the jar. I cut myself with a knife while preparing the evening meal yesterday. Is it… Am I in danger?" She swallowed the lump in her throat.

"No more than normal, my dear," Agnes replied. Hazel found it less reassuring than she would have liked.

"What is it used for? Why are you worried about me touching it?" she blurted.

For a moment, Agnes said nothing. Then she gave what Hazel suspected to be a carefully crafted lie. It was too rehearsed to be the truth.

"Witchbane is exactly what it sounds like. In the decades following the Thousand Years War, during the first persecution of witch kind, Veilroot was ground into a powder, then steeped in tea and consumed by witches who wanted or needed to conceal their powers. Only in the last twenty-five years has it become prevalent again."

A manicured lie or a truth she lived through? Hazel wondered.

"I'm not a witch, Agnes," Hazel scoffed, "so why is it so important I don't handle it?"

Her weighted gaze lingered over Hazel before she answered. "Witchbane is known to cause childbearing issues in women. *All* women. And I'm not going to assume whether or not you want babes of your own, but if you envision that for yourself, you'll do well to stay away from it."

Fine. Hazel nodded and changed the subject. "And what's all this for, then?" she asked, gesturing to the herbs and trinkets Agnes loaded her up with.

"Hmm, these? Just some charms and small wards for you to take home to your father, along with the tea leaves he requested."

Hazel thought perhaps she'd had enough tea for a while, but she didn't say it aloud. She fingered through the herbs. Rosemary. Dried hawthorn berries. Bay leaf. Sage. Plants for protection, according to the limited herbology Agnes had taught her.

Her heart thumped a little faster. "Should I be worried?" *Should Pa?*

Agnes laughed then. "No, dear. And I am sorry to have frightened you. We will try again sometime, and I am sure we will have a more successful reading. As for the rest of this… it's nothing for you to concern yourself with."

Sure… Hazel was less than convinced but said nothing more.

They embraced, the tiny, hunched woman barely coming up to Hazel's chest.

"Love you, auntie." She planted a loving kiss on the old woman's wrinkled forehead before excusing herself from the cottage.

Hazel looked back one last time before she crossed through the ward again, waving to Agnes over her shoulder. As she stepped through, feeling the familiar buzz again, she thought Agnes's face darkened with concern. But then, she was on the other side and both the old woman and her cottage were gone.

A Weaver in the Wood

As she left the forest and Agnes's home behind her, Hazel pondered over the stranger-than-usual encounter. The unshakeable Agnes transformed into a hollow, unsettled version of herself during her visit. And while nothing was certain anymore, she suspected the tea leaf reading was the most likely source of her trepidation. At least she hoped.

All the talk about magic, witches, and how Larksridge had been one of many cities where magic once thrived had Hazel's mind swirling. It would have looked so different from the Larksridge she now knew, the place where she had grown up. The half-farming, half-merchant town would most certainly never accept a witch in their midst now. *Could you even imagine?* She laughed at the absurdity of the thought, though the reality was sad. Such a shame for people to be so closed-minded.

Amid her thoughts, she came upon a pebble on the path and gave it a little tap with her foot. Then another. She struck it once more, and it tumbled through the air before bouncing, skipping, and disappearing into the wood line.

Hazel scratched the back of her neck and brushed a rogue hair out of her face. Something caught her eye in the direction the pebble had gone.

What the…

Something was out there, glimmering and dancing in the tall grass at the edge of the wood.

Glancing around and seeing she was alone, Hazel went against her better judgment and left the path. As she stepped closer to the trees, she recognized what had caught her eye—creatures she'd seen before in Nan's picture books as a child.

A will-o-wisp. *A will-o-wisp*! *Of course. But… how?* Hazel had heard stories from Nan, Pa, and Agnes, but they were usually written off by most reasonable people as nonsensical fairytale creatures. The kind of stories meant to teach children a lesson or scare them into behaving, as most monster stories did.

Of course, wisps themselves were of the benevolent sort, appearing in stories when someone needed direction or answers. She rubbed her eyes in disbelief. *This is not possible. Is it?*

The little blue, flame-like creature bobbed and weaved, seeming rather keen to have her follow. Though she was hesitant, something tugged at her mind to follow the flitting wisp. Surely, she'd done crazier things in her nearly thirty summers. *Maybe.*

She followed it down a winding path, one she convinced herself hadn't been there before. Or maybe it had. The woods grew thicker the longer she followed her new little friend, its burning blue body disappearing and reappearing further up the fading trail. And the trail *was* fading. Before she knew it, Hazel had followed the wisp into knee-high grasses, which quickly became waist high and cumbersome to march through. Briars and stickers grabbed at her clothing, and sharp branches clawed at her face and hair.

The wisp charged ahead, nearly leaving Hazel behind. For a moment, she lost sight of the tenacious little thing. She spun around, looking high and low for its telltale blue glow. It popped up a moment later, barely visible between the trees, and Hazel dashed after it.

As she ran, Hazel was a haphazard mess, and her right foot struck a large root. She went flying, sprawling into a heap on the forest floor.

Now, was that really necessary? Raising her head, she noticed something that hadn't been there before. Or perhaps it had been. She did not know where she was and was certain she'd never been in this part of the forest before, even though, since she was a child, she'd spent more than her fair share of time romping in the withering forests around Larksridge. The trees were different here. And it was quiet. Too quiet for her comfort.

Hazel gathered herself and what remained of her dignity off the forest floor. She'd earned a tear in her tunic and a couple scratches on her knees, but otherwise, she was unscathed.

The wisp was gone, but as she dusted herself off, she froze, her eyes landing on a clearing up ahead. In the center of the little glade sat a cottage. Hazel stood up the rest of the way and brushed her unruly hair from her face. *What's this now? Am I dreaming?*

A strong wind blew at her back, urging her forward. Hazel tilted her head back in exasperation, and sighing, strode into the clearing. She approached the cottage warily. It was old, but maintained well enough; someone lived there. The closer she got, the more her locket made itself known, growing warmer as if in warning.

I wonder if the owner is home?

She heard mumbling from within and found herself wishing she hadn't.

Of course, someone is home.

Through an open window, Hazel spied the owner. An old woman sat within, weaving at a loom. The woman seemed peaceful enough, though Hazel was not at all interested in disturbing her.

She watched the woman a moment longer before she decided she would leave, will of the wisp be damned. The woman's hands as they handled the intricate work with ease despite being marred and misshapen by years of repetitive use.

The murmuring stopped, and so did her hands. Hazel watched in shock as the woman's face morphed into something… else. When the transformation was complete, her face was beautiful, youthful, feminine.

A heartbeat later, it transformed again. The process was grotesque, yet mesmerizing. Hazel found herself unable to look away as the flesh and bone rearranged, forming into something new. This time, the face took the form of a strikingly beautiful middle-aged woman who cocked her head and showed off a toothy, alarming smile. Hazel decided it was very much not a human smile.

Feeling overwhelmingly uncomfortable in her own skin, Hazel took a step backwards in retreat. Her foot came down on a stick and it snapped in half, the sound shattering the silence in the clearing.

The woman's head snapped up, black eyes landing like two knives as they pierced through Hazel, holding her in place. They were hypnotizing, just two black saucers of nothingness.

Hazel was not aware of having walked closer to the cottage, but somehow the woman had lured her in. Realizing she hadn't spoken a word to explain herself, she decided this was as good a time as any.

Perhaps the woman was simply surprised and considered Hazel a threat to her sanctuary here, hidden in the deep woods. Clearly, she was using some kind of magic, and like Agnes, probably desired that tidbit of information to remain a secret.

"I—I'm sorry to intrude," she stammered. "You'll probably find this hard to believe, but I wandered off the main path while I was… looking for wildflowers," she lied, feeling it necessary to omit the part about the wisp. "I got all turned around out there and literally stumbled into your home here," she said, recalling her less than graceful entrance.

The woman cocked her head, birdlike and unblinking as she evaluated Hazel's every word.

"So, you see, I truly don't mean you any harm," Hazel continued. "I wasn't looking for you or anything like that. I-I mean, I won't even tell anyone you live out here."

She swallowed hard, beginning to wonder what she could use to defend herself should she need to. Her hand went to her satchel as she remembered the protection herbs Agnes had loaded her down with. But she had no idea how they worked. Did their mere presence ward off evil? She wasn't sure the woman would harm her, but the hairs on the back of Hazel's neck stood on end.

Was she even making any sense to this woman? Could she hear her? Could she even see her? Those black eyes either saw everything or nothing at all by the looks of them.

Hazel's mind became foggy, as if she was trying to conjure thoughts in mud. The locket grew hot, drawing an involuntary hiss from between her teeth.

The woman-thing continued to stare. Hazel's skin crawled.

Who are you? came an otherworldly voice. Each word she spoke was drawn out, as though she were conversing with a snake. And, Hazel determined, it wasn't being spoken aloud. She was definitely hearing a voice in her head.

Why have you come? The screeching hiss rattled her head, dropping her to her knees.

Hazel noticed something then, a prodding in her mind. Something was tap-tap-tapping as though it wanted in. The shrill voice was enough to split her skull. She couldn't take it. She squinted her eyes and bared down, grinding her teeth to block everything out.

When she did this, the woman withdrew momentarily, hissing in pain.

Hmm. It bites back. You are not like the others. It drew out the last word as though it could remember the taste of a recent meal. *Interesting… Sisters, we have not seen one of these in ages.*

Sisters? She was still very much alone in this clearing with this… this thing. She was growing more confident it was not actually a human woman.

In response to her thoughts, the woman-thing threw its head back, a wailing banshee as bones snapped and flesh tore. Every fiber of Hazel's being screamed at her to run, but she was frozen in place, watching the horror unfold.

As the creature writhed and clawed at itself, a second set of arms burst free from its ribcage, spraying blood and bone fragments everywhere. Most of the hair was gone from its head, leaving wisps of sickly white strands poking out of its gray, wrinkly scalp. Its jaw dislocated with a sickening pop, and the teeth inside were now needle-sharp.

Talons formed where the fingers had been, some of them bent at unfortunate angles. This was another creature she'd seen in a fairytale, one that wasn't supposed to be real…

Striga.

Oh, Fuck.

Yes, it hissed, saliva dripping from its gaping maw. *See, sisters? It knows what we are. And we know what* it *is, too.* The entire clearing reeked of rot, and between the overwhelming stench and the war in her mind, Hazel knew she was going to pass out.

Another clawed mental finger caressed the exterior of her conscious mind. *What the Hel is this?* Hazel wondered. As it became more brazen and dug in its talon, Hazel did her best to repeat what she had done last time, baring down with all her might. It worked.

The mental assailant withdrew again, screaming in agony. The creature's physical form screamed in unison. Hazel was on her hands and knees, panting, certain she would black out at any moment. But something deep within willed her to have strength.

The Striga lunged, opting for a physical assault instead of a mental one. It was a snarling whirlwind of gnashing teeth and slashing talons. And it was upon her in a flash.

Hazel was knocked onto her back with a force that shoved the air from her lungs. The Striga landed atop her with all the ferocity of a pouncing helcat. It unleashed an otherworldly screech Hazel was sure would have her ears bleeding.

No. She would not die today. Not like this.

She mustered every bit of strength she had and let out a scream to rival the Striga's own. In desperation, she shoved with all her might, pressing into the monster's thin gray flesh. Something surged within her, and a vibration of energy zipped up her arms and into her hands. Those same hands glowed brighter than the sun itself before emitting a blast unlike anything Hazel had ever experienced.

The Striga catapulted across the clearing. It landed with a bone-crunching thud, but to her disbelief, the monster sat up, slowly popping its bones back into place. It was the most heinous thing she'd ever witnessed. At least until it stood back up and started toward her again, this time with vengeance.

And Hazel couldn't get up. Blood trailed from her nose, and her mouth tasted of scorched ash. Whatever she'd done to create the blast had left her utterly drained, still prostrate on the ground. She could barely will her muscles to move, let alone stand or flee, so fighting was out of the question. Whatever power she'd drawn on, she could no longer feel it.

She was completely and utterly *fucked.*

The Striga was nearly on top of her again, when movement in her periphery snagged Hazel's attention. Drained of all ability to move, she couldn't turn her head to see what it was. The creature before her was too busy deciding which parts of her it would tear off first to notice the disturbance.

Something burst in between them, a flurry of steel and… *feathers*? Hazel glimpsed a starch-white wolf's skull the newcomer wore as a mask, black leather armor and… yes, those were feathers at the shoulders. He moved with inhuman speed, battering the creature and beating it back. But the Striga was faster. She landed a vicious blow to the man's exposed side as he failed a thrusting lunge at her, and she ripped his armor to ribbons, exposing the mangled flesh underneath.

The follow-up strike disarmed him. But then, the man used magic—actual magic—and Hazel knew she was losing it. No one could use magic within the wards except the King's own mages. *Except that part where I literally just did.*

The masked man ripped the glove from his right hand, outstretched as if reaching to grab hold of the Striga. Tendrils of shadowlike black mist flowed from his hand, weaving in and out of one another.

The clouds overhead darkened the sky, and the soft breeze whipped into a whirlwind. His shadows ensnared the Striga, wrapping her body and squeezing it tight. His breathing was labored, but he showed no signs of relenting.

"You don't belong in these woods, Striga," he growled.

The Striga hissed, though it was unclear if she was in pain or simply pissed her meal had been interrupted. *Fallen-born scum! You belong here no more than I! We do as we are told. Same as you.*

"Who sent you?" he grunted through gritted teeth, his struggle to hold her captive growing more apparent.

We'll never tell! She cackled fiendishly, Helish creature she was. It made Hazel's hair stand on end. *Kill us and get it over with. More will return in our place.*

"You will leave immediately, Striga. Crawl back to your master and tell them that if you or any of your kind cross the wards into my territory again, they'll receive only heads in return." The Striga hissed angrily, eyeing her forgotten prize sprawled on the ground behind the warrior.

Holding it tight with his shadows, he glanced over his shoulder at Hazel, and then back to the Striga. "And you *will* leave the human girl alone. Not a hair is harmed on her head, or I'll remove yours."

Her gnarled face scrunched into something resembling confusion, and she sniffed the air. *Human, you say. Hmm… we think there is more to her than meets the eye, Dark One.*

"Don't call me that." He squeezed a shadow tendril a little tighter around her neck and she gasped for air.

That is enough! We'll let her go… for now… She turned her gaze upon Hazel, then. *Be gone, ill-fated spawn. My master hunts for you, and if you stay, he will find you. He will flay the skin from your very bones. Leave this place and never return!* The Striga's body and the incorporeal voice were at odds with this decision, the former still desperately wanting to make a meal out of her.

Through vision blurred by fading consciousness, Hazel watched as the Striga shifted again, her extra pair of arms wilting and shrinking back into her body, its bones cracking as they reshaped back into her human form while the warrior in black stood guard.

And then the world went dark.

To her horror, the strange male was still there when she came to. He sat with his back against a tree, picking his nails with a dagger. When he noticed she was awake, he stood abruptly, sheathing his dagger as he strode toward her.

As he stalked forward, Hazel fought to stay conscious. She tried to crawl away, but her limbs were weak, as though the magic had drained her.

"Please…" she begged. "Don't…"

He towered over her, a menacing figure. A visage of death incarnate. He cocked his head, drinking her in. Examining. It was animalistic, the way he looked at her. Perhaps he was another beast from beyond the Border and not a man at all. Perhaps he'd run off the Striga just to secure her prey for himself.

"Who are you?" came his gravelly voice.

Who am I? Not an unreasonable question. Up until moments ago, Hazel could have answered easily. But now?

He drew closer, so close Hazel could see the soulless black orbs where eyes should be. Not the slightest hint of white or color. She sucked in a quick breath.

She couldn't see his mouth beneath the mask, but when he spoke, the smirk was there in his voice.

"You should be more careful, sweets. Monsters roam these woods," he growled.

And she was looking at one. She was sure of it. Escaped one beast just to fall prey to another.

"You see, I'm looking for something. Or *someone*," he said, his gaze looming over her. He crouched down. "It's not by chance that I'm here. I have an acute sense for… certain things." He began circling her. "And those senses led me here. To this glade. I want to know why."

The magic. The magic. The magic. Hazel gulped. Her head was still swimming, and forming words was a foreign concept. Instead, bile rose in her throat. She kept her mouth tightly sealed as she forced the feeling back down.

"Well? If you're not going to tell me why this glade reeks of magic that most definitely did *not* originate from that Striga, you could at least thank me for saving your ass." He leaned in close, and Hazel watched wordlessly as his black eyes shifted to gold beneath the skull's bony sockets. Predator eyes, glowing in the shadows.

Hazel averted her eyes. He reached out and stroked her jawline before grabbing her chin and tipping her face toward his. Those yellow irises burned into her soul, locking her firmly in place. Her gut screamed *run,* but she couldn't even if she wanted to.

"Whoever it was, whatever it was," he began, letting go of her face and standing up, "they should know it's not safe out here. I was hoping to catch up with them and offer aid. I have connections. Resources that could help them, but you're clearly not who or what I'm looking for, are you?"

Hazel shook her head. No. She most definitely was *not* who or what he was looking for. Even if she was.

"Right. Well, I'll be going, then." He backed away several paces. The air behind him twisted and warped, as though it was melting. A flickering opening appeared, a doorway carved into the air itself, and with a half-hearted salute, the warrior stepped in. In a blink, the warped doorway was gone, and Hazel was alone once more.

Rumors Fly

Hazel remained seated for a few minutes, trying to make sense of what had happened. But her headache was unbearable and made it impossible to think. She pushed herself to her hands and knees, at which point the pain overtook her and she emptied her stomach into the grass.

She choked out a sob, squinting as her memory came crashing down on her. In a panic, she scrambled to her knees and tried to stand, but it was too much effort. She surveyed her surroundings from her knees.

There was no cottage to be found. Just a small pond in a clearing in the woods. Nothing ominous. And most certainly no Striga. But it had been real, hadn't it?

She backtracked through the forest as best she could. Like everything else in her fever dream of a memory, there was no path, though she could have sworn there had been one before. Perhaps she'd hit her head when she fell, and it had all been a lucid dream. That made more sense than the alternative.

After hours of fighting thorn and sticker bushes, she made it back to the main road.

Hazel dragged herself down the road, bone-tired and emotionally drained. Her head spun as she attempted to face the reality of what she'd experienced. What she'd *done*. She didn't dare say it out loud. But… was it …*magic*? No. It couldn't be. Because if it was, the consequences could be insurmountable. What if someone found out?

And *how*? She shook her head. This would mean someone in her immediate family had magic, and she knew Connall wasn't even a remote possibility. He'd served in the militia alongside men who could literally smell magical blood. He never would have survived.

But her mother? Unease roiled within her. She wasn't so easy to rule out. Almost everything she knew of her mother came from Pa, and he never mentioned magic. Hazel considered the possibility that she'd kept part of herself a secret.

Or maybe Connall had some explaining to do.

And if she *was* a descendant of someone with magic, why was it just now manifesting? She was almost in her thirtieth year. Wasn't this sort of thing supposed to rear its ugly head sooner in life, like some forbidden witch puberty?

Her thoughts drifted to the Witchbane powder, and she immediately regretted not pressing Agnes for more information.

She heard voices up ahead, which snapped her back to the present. She was happy to be amongst other humans again, damn near wanting to sprint to them and hug them. She took a deep breath. *Relax. You can worry about this later. Be… normal.*

A small group gathered about a wagon, chatting and carrying on. Dressed nicer than she was used to, they wore clothes without holes or stains. Travelers, perhaps. As she approached, they stopped talking. The one bearing a long, braided beard, possibly their leader, inclined his head out of respect.

"Hello, ma'am," he said. He eyed her up and down, his gaze lingering a bit too long.

For fuck's sake…

"Do you need someone to accompany you home? Where we're from, women don't travel alone. And from what folks are saying, it's dangerous out here."

Says who? I wonder if I'm not the only one to have crossed that Striga. Instead, she said, "No, thank you. I am headed home now, and I walk this road often. But thank you for your… *concern*."

His tone changed, then, becoming less pleasant and more demanding. "I don't think you heard me right, miss. Word on the street is there's a murderer about these parts. You really shouldn't be…"

"I said I'm fine, *thank you*." She turned away when a thought struck her. "Wait—did you say murderer?" It was the first she'd heard of such a thing, and she'd barely been gone half a day. "Who died?"

"Well, no one knows for sure, it seems, but word has it that the innkeeper over there had it out for the town butcher. Now, that butcher supposedly went missing under mysterious circumstances. As for us, well, we aren't from around here, and some would say we shouldn't speak about it as such. But from the sounds of it, they had bad blood and folks seem to think the innkeeper fellow might have finally done him in."

What the Hel? My father, a murderer? It was the first time she'd heard any of this. Her hand rose to the spot where her necklace rested beneath her tunic, fighting the urge to rub it between her fingers. She couldn't imagine any reason some random travelers would start a rumor about people they knew nothing about, which meant…

"Who's been saying these things? Where'd you hear about it?" She tried to control her voice. It wouldn't do to sound overly concerned.

The man gave her a perplexed look, one thick eyebrow raised. "The real question is, who isn't? Everyone we met back there at the market had something to say about it. Seems a shame of a thing to happen in this quiet town," he glanced around, gesturing with his hands. "But everywhere in this gods-forsaken kingdom seems to have issues these days."

Hazel nodded. "Thanks for the information. I need to be going. Better to be sure I'm home before dark."

The man shrugged in return. "Suit yourself. C'mon boys, we best be moving on as well." He and his friends said nothing more, letting her go without trouble. She wasn't sure she trusted them, but it was the least of her concerns at the moment.

Hazel had no desire to get involved in town gossip, but this was her father, and the allegations were serious. It was personal.

Jonas might have been a drunk and a massive thorn in their sides more often than not, but Pa wouldn't have *killed* him.

Ugh. She loathed gossip. Ignored it. But this time it meant her father's reputation on the line, and she would not stand around and do nothing about it.

She returned home to their cottage to find Connall already gone. She had hoped to talk to him about what folks were saying before he walked into town and found himself blindsided. But perhaps they'd keep it to themselves in his presence. He was, after all, far and above the most respected person in their village. But if this rumor caught on…

She ran into Ezekiel on the way to the Briar & Rose, as usual. It was one of his patrol routes.

"Hey, Haz," he said by way of greeting. His strong jawline was accentuated by his dimpled smile, a smile he reserved for her. Tan skin and dark brown hair drew in the sunlight as he approached.

"Hi, Zeke," she said flatly.

He frowned. "You okay? You seem off."

"I'm fine." *I am definitely* not *fine.* "Well… Honestly, I don't know."

"Is this about Jonas?" He was always so insightful.

She shrugged. *It most certainly has nothing to do with the earlier attack in the woods. Or that I might have used magic.* Instead, she settled on "Yep," as her response. Because between the two topics, it was far less risky to discuss the rumors around her father.

Zeke stopped her, placing a warm hand on her arm. "You can talk to me about it, you know." *No, I most definitely cannot talk to you about what happened in the woods.*

"What? Do you think I'm harboring some explicit secret or something?"

"No! Hazel, I just want to help. Why are you so jumpy?"

"He didn't do anything, Zeke!" She couldn't help it. The emotions came pouring out, and Zeke got to bear the brunt of it.

"What? I never said…" His face crumpled as his brows grew heavy.

She cut him off, wiping a tear. "You don't have to. Everyone else apparently is. I ran into some men on the road, not from around here. Even they knew."

"It will be fine. Jonas will turn up. Probably just wandered off in a drunken stupor and passed out. Once he's outslept his hangover, he will waddle home. Wouldn't be the first time, right?"

She sighed. "I hope you're right."

He tucked a hair behind her ear. "It's a matter of character. Yes, Connall and Jonas have their moments, but they also have a long history that means more than any minor squabble. People get too caught up in gossip. This will blow over, don't worry."

Hazel found it remarkable how his countenance rarely wavered. Was it for her sake, or did he believe what he was saying?

"I truly don't think it will. But I need to get going. I was hoping to catch Pa before he got to work, but he beat me to it. I wanted to give him a heads up that some folks are feeling a little extra *chatty* today…just, as a warning, I guess."

"Alright, well, I'll see you around?" It was more of a question than a statement.

"Maybe. It just depends on how the day goes. Could be busy, could be slow." *Could end in both me* and *my father being arrested.* She swallowed the thought down.

"I get it. I'll see ya when I see ya, then." He smiled, shifted his pack higher onto his shoulder.

Just when Hazel thought he would walk away, Zeke wrapped his strong arms around her and pulled her into an embrace. She caved, resting her head against his chest. The steady beating of his heart washed her in a sense of calmness.

"You know I am always here for you, Haze, no matter what. Anything you need, you always have me."

She pulled out of the hug, but he held her by her shoulders, forcing her to meet his gaze.

"I mean it. Anything."

Hazel nodded in understanding, and Zeke released her with a half-smile. She watched him as he walked away, his almost-black hair shining in the midday sun.

He could be right, I guess. I could be worrying over nothing. But she couldn't shake the feeling… something was different this time.

As she arrived at Briar & Rose, Hazel noticed a new piece of parchment nailed into the signpost out front, right on top of the help wanted and sales ads from the neighboring farms. Whoever had put it there wanted it to be seen and cared little whether they covered up the needs of other townspeople.

Then she understood why.

It was a royal parchment, stamped with the official seal of the High King. She plucked it from the board and read the announcement.

Citizens of Larksridge and Loyal Subjects of the Kingdom of Aeos:

It is with great excitement that His Majesty, the High King Magnus Ragnaroth, our Shield Against Darkness, announces the sixteenth year since the birth of His Son and Heir, Prince Tristan Ragnaroth, the First of His Name. In his Honor, your High King welcomes your presence at the First Annual Royal Tournament of Champions to be hosted at King's Crossing beginning on the eve of Summer Solstice. Events to include jousts, melee, archery, and more…

Beyond the call for competitors, it invited anyone seeking work to arrive on the eve of the tournament to be assigned a job, and for vendors and craftsmen to bring their finest wares and goods, with setup for the vendors' market beginning two days prior and no sooner.

But Hazel couldn't get past the idea of this being hosted on Summer Solstice, a holiday when the veil between this realm and the Otherrealm is said to be thinner. One that might draw out witches and other magical folk who dared to continue their practice. Coinciding with a celebration guaranteed to bring the King and his men in direct contact with them… It was too intentional for her liking.

"Ah, you've seen the posting, I see?" Connall, despite his size, had somehow snuck up on her. She jumped at the broken silence but was relieved it was just her father.

"Young fella stopped by just a little while ago and added that lovely thing right on top of all the others. You just missed him." She still held the parchment in her hands and glanced down at it, eyes scanning the words once more.

"I know what you're thinking. And while I'm not nearly as superstitious as you, I don't like it either. The way it's worded makes me think we won't have a choice, and shutting down the inn for more than a day or two… well, it's going to hurt us."

She hadn't even considered it, her concern lying with the timing itself. "Surely they can't expect business owners to close up shop for a glorified birthday party?"

Connall raised an eyebrow as if to say, *you know better*.

"Pa, this isn't fair. And since when are we calling Magnus the Shield Against Darkness? What in the gods was that all about?"

Connall chuckled. "I can't answer that. I suppose he fancies himself savior of the realm, what with banishing everything he disagrees with and calling it "darkness". Ah, well. At least we have a little time to prepare. I will ask around and if needed, I will have someone pen a letter to the King's handlers for me and see if we can't figure it out." He eyed her knowingly, because they both knew she would be the one to write it.

As the overworked son of a farmhand, Connall hadn't received much of an education. Life plucked him from one field and dropped him straight into another: the battlefield.

"Don't worry, love. Everything will work out."

Everyone was so gods-damned positive but her, which reminded her why she had raced over to catch up with her father.

"Pa, there's something else. I was hoping to talk to you before you made it into town, but…" her voice faded when she looked into his blue eyes, where she found but fatherly love. Not an ounce of concern.

"Yes, love, I know. I've already heard." He was calm; his face revealed nothing.

"You have?"

"Of course. And I've talked to a few folks who had concerns, snuffed out a few rumors—I think. We'll just have to wait and see what the coming days bring."

"Has there been any word?"

He sighed, shaking his head. "None. But now that you're here, I wonder if I might step away for a little while, see if I can't find that drunk bastard myself."

"Do you really think that's a good idea?" Hazel rubbed her arms nervously.

"Why not? Hazel, dear, it's not like I'm going to kill the man. And besides, if I did, then I'd just be confirming those rumors, eh?" *Joking.* Her father was making jokes about this whole ordeal.

And, as always, he was right. Regardless of the outcome, at least no one could say he didn't try. "Sure," she said. "I can handle things here."

"That's my girl!" He grabbed the parchment from her hands. "We will worry about this later," he said, bopping her on the forehead with the parchment lovingly. "For now, let's just stay focused, eh? We're running low on a few things in the kitchen. Mind running to the market?"

Though she loved the marketplace, the thought of being surrounded by more people made her want to crawl into a hole. But she wouldn't complain. "Sure thing, Pa. No problem. By the way," she added, fetching the sachets of tea leaves and herbs from her bag, "I stopped by to see Agnes this morning. Got the stuff you needed, and she sent me back with extra herbs." She thought about what happened *after* her visit, but it was a topic she wasn't ready to discuss.

"I knew I could count on you." He smiled, taking the sachets from her and sending her away with a nod before turning back to press the parchment back onto the signpost by creating a new hole.

After stepping back and rubbing his hands together in satisfaction, Connall Callahan grabbed his handaxe from its usual hiding place and strode off in the direction Jonas Gray had last stumbled off in.

Market Mishap

HAZEL trod down the dusty earthen path, thinking over everything she and Pa had discussed. It wasn't right for someone like him—someone who would give everything just to help another—to be in this situation. But maybe Zeke and Pa and everyone else were right. Maybe she was making something out of nothing, as she so often did.

The marketplace was bursting at the seams with townsfolk. More than any Hazel had seen gathered in one place for as long as she could remember, and soon it was clear why. A man stood upon a rickety pyramid of stacked wooden crates, dressed in obnoxious, frilly garb, announcing something and waving his hands dramatically. As she drew closer, Hazel understood what she was witnessing.

A herald from Ravenhold had arrived to relay a message. A message, she guessed, was likely the same one they'd found nailed to the sign board outside of the inn.

As folks were murmuring and shifting nervously, she was sure the consensus was the same. She was quickly reminded they were not, however, upset over the timing in relation to the Solstice. It was not in their nature to care about such things, especially since most, if not all, magic practitioners had moved on.

The herald wrapped up his speech with the usual call and response as dictated by the High Priests of the Wind. "We can do all of this because of the gods who make it so. The Anemoi provide all we need."

"And the Winds guide us," most of the gathered crowd chanted back. Hazel never returned the call when it was delivered. She wasn't sure what she believed in, and how could she return the call with words she didn't believe to be true?

According to what she'd been told, Aeos was a much happier, more prosperous kingdom when people celebrated the gods equally. When no one dictated which gods to worship. But when the rest of the Elemental gods disappeared, everything and everyone suffered. Hazel heard plenty of stories growing up; the landscape of their small part of the kingdom slowly died off, starved of magic and the gods who sustained life. The rest of the kingdom followed.

Famine led to disease among the animals, many succumbing to illness. As they were unfit to eat, farmers had to dispose of them in the only way they could: by burning them. Greasy, black smoke choked the sky for days on end, leaving nothing but bits of charred bone behind. It was something she was thankful she hadn't witnessed firsthand.

Hazel's attention was snared by the scent of smoked meats drifting over on the breeze. It was a wonder anyone could still enjoy the delicacy of meat, seeing as nothing had improved in her lifetime for the townspeople or the animals. In fact, they had less food and water each year. More famine, more thirst, more disease…and the High King sat in his castle worrying over whom or what his subjects *prayed* to. *What an obtuse prick,* she thought. *How can someone so detached from his people rule over them, and for so long?*

After refocusing on the market around her, she spotted a trio of men on horseback who had entered the north end and were making their way down the main aisle. Dressed as a living nightmare, the lead rider carried two daggers at his hip and wore a suit of boiled leather armor, dyed black. He wore no helm, his coal black hair pulled halfway into a bun on the back of his head, the rest spilling over his shoulders in curly, obsidian waves. The other men, his comrades, were clearly of the kingsguard—the Raven Blade—donning the King's black raven sigil on their tabards, with full sets of dragonforged black iron armor.

Hazel hadn't the slightest idea who the man in front was, but clearly, he held enough importance to warrant a guard. Yet enough skill to wear light armor. Hazel rolled her eyes at their audacity to ride into a meager marketplace on horseback when no one else did so. They carried themselves with such arrogance and inflated self-importance—turning their noses up as they passed the townspeople—that Hazel snorted.

Turning her back on them, she leaned over a vegetable vendor's table she'd been coming to for years, garnering his attention.

"Say, Mick," she started, "Any idea who those men on horseback are?"

Mick shook his head. "No, lass, but they're from the castle, no doubt. An' more will be crawling all over the place shortly, sure enough. Not good for business, that much I know. They make folks nervous, me included." He whispered the last part, shuddering slightly as he glanced in their direction. His eyes darkened as though their presence had taken him somewhere existing only in memory, but then Mick steeled himself, returning to the present. He scratched the back of his head. "Well, I suppose I'll see you around, then."

Hazel smiled and wandered off, pushing the King's men to the back of her mind.

A group of small, ragged children were playing a game with sticks and stones alongside the major thoroughfare, their laughter bringing a smile to her face. One child, an especially dirty, underfed youngster, started chasing the others around. They squealed and giggled, dashing about.

But then they darted across the road—right in front of the trio of mounted goons from the capitol. The small boy who'd been chasing them brought up the rear of the pack and he would not make it across.

Oh, gods. Oh, gods!

"Look out!" Hazel shouted, sprinting in their direction. Whether he hadn't heard her or just didn't care, the dark and broody stranger in the lead paid no mind to the child who was nearly underfoot. The boy was going to be crushed. But she was almost there. Just a little further…

Damning the consequences, Hazel dove to her knees, throwing her body between horse and boy. The movement was enough to startle the beast, causing it to balk and rear. As it did so, the beast struck her with a forelimb and sent her sprawling, knocking the wind straight out of her.

Fucking Hel! Hazel couldn't breathe, and she coughed, attempting to catch her breath. *Not dead, but that is going to leave a pretty bruise.*

The rider collected his horse and urged it on as though nothing of consequence had happened. One of the giant beast's hooves crushed a turnip.

"Hey!" Hazel shouted between coughs. "What the fuck is your problem?"

He ignored her and kept his horse walking. One guard sneered at her and the boy sitting beside her in shock. "Mind your tongue, girl, or you might have to show us what else it can do besides screech." He laughed at his own humor before spitting at her. "Peasant scum."

Hazel's face reddened as she watched them walk away. No one stepped forward to do anything. No one said a word. A combination of anger and embarrassment rose in her chest until she could no longer contain it—she exploded.

"Who the *fuck* do you think you are? Who died and made *you* King, you self-important son of a bitch? Yeah, I'm talking to you, you pig-faced bastard!" She wasn't even sure where the words came from. Hazel had never spoken to someone with such vitriol, and the words tasted sour, the verbal equivalent of bile on her tongue. Who did she think she was talking to this man in such a way?

Her words hit their mark as the man in black atop the thick-bodied, black-as-night warhorse turned his steed abruptly and walked in her direction. He moved slowly and with purpose. The little boy had abandoned her, the only remaining sign of him being the dust he'd kicked up in his escape. Hazel wished nothing more than to become invisible, to spare herself from whatever fate she'd just earned. The man walked his horse up next to her, dismounting wordlessly.

Hazel, you stupid fool. This is how you die.

He sized her up, his near-glowing, somehow not-of-this-world amber eyes so piercing she was left feeling stripped bare. She had no choice but to avert her gaze. It was too much. She stared at the dirt road as though it had become the most interesting thing in all Aeos. Then she heard the telltale song of sword against scabbard as he unsheathed the blade. *Oh, gods, I really* am *going to die. Fucking Hel…*

She supposed it wasn't a dishonorable way to die, protecting a child. Throwing insults at the King's men. It made for a good story, at least. Would anyone care to tell it the way it had happened, though? Probably not. Hazel closed her eyes, wishing she was anywhere else as the locket heated against her skin. She wanted to reach for it but didn't dare move. Sharp steel *squished* into something soft as though piercing flesh. Then, the tip of the sword was at her throat.

The man applied the slightest amount of pressure upward—not enough to break skin, but enough to *direct.* Hazel had no choice but to tilt her head up and look the stranger in the eyes again. In his off-hand, he held one of the turnips she'd bought earlier, split down one side where he'd stabbed it. "You dropped this," he said, tossing it to her where she still kneeled in the road. He kept the sword at her throat for good measure. "Was there something else you wanted to say? I thought maybe you'd want to say it to my face instead of my horse's ass."

She was about to shake her head no, but thought better of it, not wanting to risk beheading herself out of further stupidity. "No," she muttered. But gods, his gaze was distracting. Hypnotizing, even.

"Good girl," he growled, removing his sword from her neck, but keeping her frozen in place with his gaze. He sheathed it and mounted his horse again. Without sparing her so much as a parting glance, the man rejoined his comrades. Though she was too far away to hear them speaking, all three of them had a hearty laugh, presumably at her expense.

Once she was certain she could breathe again, she did so, letting out something between a gasp and a sob. Dragging her hands down her face in exasperation, Hazel surveyed her damaged goods. What a waste. And yet, she found herself more concerned with the man on the onyx steed. His unnatural amber eyes burned into her memory.

What Could Possibly Go Wrong?

HAZEL rose from the ground and dusted herself off. Well, that was humiliating… and terrifying. Who was that creep? She shook her head and brushed herself off, noting a few bruises blooming from the fall.

"Haze? You okay?" a voice called from behind her. She'd know the voice anywhere. It was Zeke.

"Yep, totally fine." *So* not *fine.* "Just hanging out on the ground in the middle of the road for the Hel of it." Her hand found the locket and pulled it from beneath her shirt. She flipped it between her fingers.

Zeke eyed her warily, his eyes falling to her hand on the locket. "Okay, so… you're not fine. Hazel, what happened here?" His dark eyes shone with genuine concern as he looked her over, in the fashion of a worried parent.

"Oh, this?" she asked. "Nothing." *It was definitely something.* "Just some castle prick trying to run over a little kid because he can, I guess. No biggie." *Liar. No biggie? You almost lost your head.*

"Hazel, don't you know who that was?" he asked, looking over her shoulder in the direction the men had gone.

"The biggest, most pretentious asshole in all of Aeos?" She crossed her arms in defiance.

"Hazel, I'm serious." He put his arm around her back and led her out of the road.

"So am I, *Zeke*. I seriously don't care."

He looked around as though worried someone would overhear, then grabbed her arm and pulled her close.

"Hey! Take it easy." She yelped, pulling away.

"Look at me." She did. "That was Slaide Elias."

"Okay… and?" Hazel all but rolled her eyes.

"You really have no idea who that is, do you?" He pinched the bridge of his nose and closed his eyes. Clearly this was more serious than she thought.

"Nope, and as I've already said, I don't care to." Hazel made to pull away from his grip again, but he held tight.

"Hazel." It was a command. "He's a witch hunter for the High King. In fact, he's *the* witch hunter. The best of the best." *Fantastic. Hazel Grace, you have impeccable timing with men.*

"Worst of the worst, you mean. He's a brute." *Even if he had incredible amber eyes. Stop it. You literally just pissed off the kingdom's most infamous witch hunter and you're fawning over his gods-forsaken eyes? He would kill you in an instant if he found out. Get a grip.*

Zeke sighed, realizing the conversation was going in circles. "Well, all I'm going to say is, it's best not to get in his way. He's not exactly forgiving. If rumors are to be believed, he's done some questionable things for the High King. Things that usually stay off record."

Well, consider her interest piqued for more reasons than one. "If it's off record, then how do you know about it, exactly?"

"That's why I was coming to find you, actually. I was promoted." His look of concern faded into a half smile, although it was clear he was still worried about her encounter. His face was riddled with a combination of concerns and secrets.

"What? No way! So, you won't be reporting to that dunce Carys anymore?" She asked hopefully. *Finally, some good news.*

"No, I won't. And what's even better is this promotion puts me in Collin's garrison. He's my immediate superior now." He was proud. She could see it in his eyes. "So, yeah, that's how I learned about some of the unsavory stuff going on. It's kind of unsettling, Hazel. I'm not sure I even want to know some things I've learned recently. If I could unlearn them, I would."

Her eyes rolled all the way back. "Spill the details then, Zeke. You sound like a little girl bragging about some boy she kissed without *actually* telling me anything."

"That's the thing. I can't. Not right now. There's some dark stuff going on in the background, but I promise if any of it concerned you or your family, I would let you know. It's just safer for you not to know right now."

Well, that's the least you could do. She huffed. "Can you at least give me a hint of what it's about?"

He hesitated but then whispered, "Witches."

She leveled him with a bombastic side eye and almost scoffed, momentarily forgetting Zeke wasn't aware of Agnes's… talents. Of course he would find the topic groundbreaking.

"I made the same face when I was told. But apparently there are some folks in the Outskirts practicing magic again. Either they're getting stronger, or the wards are weakening. And both are bad news for Aeos."

"Bad news for Magnus, you mean," Hazel quipped.

"Hazel." He shushed her. "You do not know how serious this is."

"No, I don't. How can I when you're keeping it a secret?"

"Trust me, please. It's better you don't know. Just trust me."

"I do. You should know that by now. But *witches*? Really?" She thought about Agnes and what this might mean for her. Agnes was, after all, a green witch. She was harmless, as far as Hazel was aware, her practice primarily aiding her around her home and in the garden. The most extensive magic Hazel had ever seen her use was the warding around her land, the one thing keeping her safe from outsiders.

Zeke knew about Agnes, but he didn't *know* about Agnes. Not in the ways that mattered. And despite trusting Zeke, she knew she could never really trust him with Agnes's secrets, especially not while he belonged to the King's army. As long as he took part in his duty as a man of fighting age, he was subject to her suspicions. If nothing else, he could be whipped or beaten for the information. And then what? No, it was better this way.

An awkward silence spread between them.

"Zeke?" Something crossed her mind. Perhaps it didn't matter, but she was curious. His alliances might be evolving the more involved he became with the High King's militia.

"Yes?"

"You have to report suspected witches, anyone suspected of practicing magic, worshiping the old gods, and whatnot, right?"

He raised an eyebrow. "I mean, technically, yes. I guess I do. Why?"

"No reason." *Definitely not because of some weird energy that exploded out of my hands in a fight against a monster from beyond the Border. Nope.*

"Seriously?" He raised a brow in question.

Yeah, that was probably a stupid thing to say. Now, salvage this, Hazel, because telling him is out of the question.

"Not so fun when the tables are turned, is it? Well, you're going to think I'm a stupid twit, but I was wondering…" she trailed off. *Am I really about to ask this? What if he figures me out?* She took a deep breath. "What if I was a witch? Would you turn me in?" *That was* so *not smooth.*

He rolled his eyes. "You're *not* a witch. So, it's a ridiculous thing to even ask me." *Erm… that was not an answer. Nice side-step, Zeke.* She swallowed hard, considering her next words.

"And if I was?" she pressed, curious now that his answer was uncertain.

"We'd find a way out." *We? What 'we'?* He made it seem so simple. As though it wasn't an act of treason to help a witch.

"You wouldn't report me?" The question was pointless, because of course he wouldn't report her. But hearing him say it aloud without any coercion on her part, she might be okay after all.

"How could I? If something happened to you because I turned you in, you'd surely haunt me from the Otherrealm." She punched him in the shoulder. "Ow! Hey, you asked the ridiculous question, not me."

She groaned obnoxiously. "Ezekiel Bertram, you take your job too seriously. You're not special, you know. Every boy who comes of age gets conscripted to His Majesty's militia. If anything, it's his pretty little spin on slavery. He puts you in a fancy uniform, gives you purpose." She shook her head. "Don't lose sight of what's really important."

Hurt flashed across his face.

Okay, that might have been a little harsh. "What I mean is, don't let them take advantage of you. You're a good person." She put a gentle hand on his arm. "I just don't want to see one of the few nice people left in this kingdom be destroyed by the sadistic assholes who run it."

"I know. I get it." He withdrew from her touch. Then, clearing his throat, he said, "Say, not to change this gods-awful subject, but did you hear about the Tourney?"

"Prince Tristan's birthday party, you mean? Of course I did. It's what got me into this mess. I came to the market to grab some supplies for the tavern kitchen while Pa…" She faded off there, unsure how much she should share. Zeke was the only trustworthy person she could confide in. Running her hand through her hair, she continued, "Pa went off to see if he could track down Jonas."

Zeke, to his credit, didn't look surprised.

"He said it didn't matter what people thought, but that the right thing to do was to find him." She sighed. "He's all I have, and he works too hard to have to go through all this trouble."

"If anyone will find him, it's your father. I just hope…" He didn't meet her eyes.

"Hope *what*? What are you not telling me?" She grabbed his arm so that he had to face her.

"Right now, it's not important. The only thing I can say is that it concerns the Border wards. My advice is to make sure you keep things locked up at night."

Weird. "Thanks? I guess." *Does this have to do with the Striga?* Gods, how she wished she could ask. But there were too many questions she didn't want to answer.

He cleared his throat as if to shift the subject yet again. "So, speaking of Connall, who'd he hire in your place while you come check out the Tourney?"

Hazel stopped walking. "What? I'm not going. We have way too much work to do and if I leave, Pa will have to close our doors for the duration of the tournament. If I stay, we have the chance to serve as an overflow from King's Crossing. There's no way the inns and taverns there have enough lodging and food for everyone. Briar and Rose will have to be ready. And since I was *also* promoted, I'm responsible for getting folks fed and passing out drinks. And cleaning rooms for visitors, and a whole host of unsavory things that out-of-towners will bring. I have to stay."

He frowned and then laughed at her. "That is the most ridiculous thing you've said all day."

Fair, I guess, since he didn't hear what I said to that Slaide character.

"You're going. This is the first tournament that has been held in years, and you can't miss it. Plus, I'm competing in the Champions Tournament since I was promoted. It would mean a lot for you to be there rooting for me." *So, no pressure then, great.*

"It's not that I don't want to. It's just… You haven't seen him lately. Getting around becomes more of a struggle every day. He hides it well, but it's there. It wouldn't be right for me to go play while he works himself to death."

If Zeke rolled his eyes any further into his head they would have stayed there. "You are quite possibly the most dramatic person I've ever met. Connall is built like an Axian destrier, even with a bum leg. He was running the place before you existed, don't forget. Pretending he is incapable without your help is an insult to his hard work."

Well, when you put it that way…

"And… I really don't want to ask someone else to go to the ball with me, so you'd be doing me a solid."

"Ugh, Zeke, you know I'm not cut out for high society events. I'll stick out like a sore thumb among the noble ladies."

"Just do me a favor and consider it." He could not look more sincere if he tried. *Damn it.*

She rolled her eyes. "Fine."

Reluctantly, Hazel approached Connall about attending the Tournament of Champions the following morning. And, as she'd predicted, he was more than eager for her to get out and "experience life"—whatever that meant. Only she knew how much life she'd incidentally experienced recently.

Between her run-in with Slaide Elias, nearly becoming lunch for the Striga, and then erupting in a blinding white light—she still couldn't admit it might have been magic—she'd experienced enough life for an eternity. And now, she would add the Tournament of Champions to that list.

But first, Hazel decided she'd pay Agnes another visit. She'd had too much on her mind lately. Too many loose ends needing tied up and questions begging to be answered.

Several times now, she'd thought about telling Connall about the day in the clearing. About the Striga and the mysterious stranger who swooped in to snatch her from certain death. But each time she approached the subject, Hazel couldn't bring herself to do it. Not for fear of repercussion, because Connall would never. She just couldn't stand the guilt of shouldering him with more to worry about.

On her way to Agnes's home, Hazel passed through town. Larksridge was abuzz with busy townsfolk as they prepared for the newcomers who would descend upon them, a swarm of flies to honey. The farmers gathered what produce they could from their fields and the best livestock would be brought in for slaughter. Everyone had a role to play.

And tomorrow, Connall would send Hazel off on the back of a wagon with a smile on his face. He'd already enlisted a couple of young men to assist him at Briar & Rose without a second thought, and she swelled with pride at the thought of not one, but *two*, people being required in her absence.

Before long, the noise and crowds were behind her, and Hazel was met with the quiet solitude of the lands beyond Larksridge. The forest grew thick around her, and the familiar tingle along her skin alerted her to her arrival at the wards.

Through the window, Hazel could see Agnes was busy, as usual. She made to clear her throat, hoping to gently alert Agnes to her presence, when the woman said without turning around, "Hazel! What are you still standing there for? Come in."

Hazel smiled. *Of course, she knew I was here.*

"Come, have a seat." Agnes turned, waddling over with two cups of tea. She sat and gestured for Hazel to do the same.

Hazel was surprised at the state of Agnes's home as she took her seat. She'd never been an organized woman, but her cottage was in an unusual state of disarray.

Animal bones and hides littered almost every surface, accompanied by stones and crystals, sachets of herbs, and an ornate crystal ball on her back table.

"It's good to see you, auntie." Hazel sipped from the perfectly heated tea. "What is all of this?" she asked, gesturing to the curiosities and trinkets scattered around.

A flash of orange outside the window caught her eye as a familiar orange feline sprang onto the windowsill. Realizing he had an audience, however, he let out a huffed yowl and leapt down. Hazel blinked her confusion away and returned her attention to Agnes.

"Hmm? Oh, that. I'm packing some goods for the vendor marketplace at that little brat's tournament. I don't fancy myself as a greedy woman, but a little spare coin hurts no one."

Hazel almost dropped her mug in shock. "H-how in all the gods is that safe for you? Going into the middle of a busy town so close to Ravenhold… it seems too risky. How will you practice without being caught?"

Agnes laughed her off. "My dear, this world will never be safe for people like me. But I won't be practicing any witchcraft. However, it just so happens that tea and herbs are not only highly sought after, but completely overlooked. Which tells me they haven't seen many green witches." She shrugged. "The locals eat this stuff up. Anything for a miracle cure. And if the rumors hold any weight, I'll be safer in plain sight than here."

Hazel frowned. It wasn't normal for Agnes to be so reckless. "What do you mean? What rumors?"

Something clattered outside, and Hazel thought she heard a hushed whisper. But Agnes hadn't so much as blinked in concern, so Hazel took a deep breath, willing herself to relax.

Agnes sighed. "Nothing to concern yourself with right now. Let's just say some of the King's dogs might come sniffing around, and I'd rather not be here if they do."

Hazel's eyes bugged, taken aback by Agnes's nonchalance. Yet she couldn't quite find the right words to express her concern.

"Say what you want to say, dear." Agnes gestured around her lazily. "No one can hear you out here."

She had a question brewing, but despite the warded cottage and its remote location, she couldn't bring herself to say the words out loud. Something was off. She couldn't shake the feeling they were being watched.

Agnes eyed her and lowered her voice just above a whisper. "It's all parlor tricks, my dear. None of these objects will raise enough suspicion, and tea leaves are for steeping and drinking. They soothe a variety of ailments from fever to body aches to watery bowels. Nothing to see here but an old woman with a bunch of herbs and 'useless junk.' No one here *knows* what I am or what I do. I'm assuming that answers what you're afraid to ask." Hazel nodded. "Now then, what brings you by?"

Truthfully? She was running from things she refused to acknowledge. Haunted by nightmares, attacked by a Striga, stalked by a witch hunter…

"Nothing in particular. I'm leaving for the tournament tomorrow myself and thought I would stop in and see how you're doing before I go." She smiled. *Liar.*

Agnes frowned, because of course she could see right through the farce. She'd known Hazel her entire life. She set the cup down and sat back in her chair, assessing.

"I see."

Hazel couldn't meet Agnes's intense gaze. "I… was wondering," she swallowed hard, "if you would have any tea to help someone sleep through the night? I'd intended to get some from you when I last visited, but it slipped my mind."

"Hmm." Agnes nodded thoughtfully. "I can certainly put something together." She stood then, moving back to her bottles and trinkets and talismans along the back table.

"And…" Hazel began again, tucking a hair behind her ear, "something to protect from harmful creatures."

Agnes kept working, but she asked, "What sort of creatures? Wolves, bears… exes?" She laughed at her own joke.

If Hazel was going to be honest with anyone, if she could trust anyone, it was Agnes. She took a deep breath then released it.

"No. More like… a Striga." It was such a weight off her shoulders, and yet, Hazel was going to throw up. It sounded so much worse said aloud.

The glass bottles clattered against each other and something crashed to the floor as Agnes visibly jumped at the mention of the creature. The old woman turned around in slow motion, fixing Hazel with a stare pointed enough to level an entire town. Abandoning the things she'd been working on, Agnes slid back into her chair, clearly shaken.

"Tell. Me. Everything," she whispered intensely. "Leave *nothing* out."

So, Hazel did. She thoroughly spilled her guts to the woman, sparing not a single detail. She even admitted to the possibility that magic *might* have erupted from her palms when she went toe-to-toe with the Striga. Agnes never interrupted, nodding occasionally and asking questions here and there.

When she finished and Agnes had run out of questions, they sat in silence. After a few moments, Agnes closed her eyes and sighed deeply. She stood from her chair without a word and walked to the front door. She locked it and proceeded to close the shutters. "We have a lot to discuss, and not a lot of time."

"So, you mean to tell me," Hazel said, "that the King struck some kind of deal with the Aetherial gods to protect us, but the lands had to be stripped of magic in return and we had to forsake all others? Who did we need protecting from, exactly?"

Agnes shrugged. "One of many questions I'm afraid we don't have the answers to. He declared the alliance was to protect Aeos from the Outer Kingdoms, claiming war was looming over us. But it made little sense. Aeos was one of the most magically adept kingdoms in the world. Few could have challenged us and posed an actual threat."

Hazel sat back in her chair and released a breath in an audible *whoosh*. "And our Border. It's made of the magic people have donated over the years, and it's weakening because there are fewer and fewer… donations. So that's how the Striga got through." She was trying to piece everything together. Pa had told her none of this, and her heart threatened to leap out of her chest. "Is-is that also why my magic is… manifesting? Because the dampening wards are failing along with the Border?"

Agnes nodded. "Possibly, but I do have another theory… About this magic of yours. Have you accessed it since then?" Hazel shook her head. "Want to try?"

"*Here?*"

"It's as safe a place as any. We don't have to, though." Agnes shrugged, feigning indifference. "I just thought I'd ask. I could likely help you, if you needed."

"I just don't understand how or why I have it. All my life I've been ordinary. I've stayed out of trouble and done as I'm told. Now, I've got this-this scar on my entire being… like some abomination." She dropped her head into her hands.

A warm, soft hand came to rest on her shoulder. She lifted her head.

Agnes's eyes were shining. "This is what you were *made* for, dear. You're the furthest thing from an abomination. And… there's something else you should know."

Hazel leaned in, eager to hear what would come next.

"I want to tell you about your mother. I wonder, how much has your father told you about her?"

"As much as he knows, I suppose? Which I would assume is everything. She was bright, kind, and strong. She was a steward of the land and had a way with plant life. I know she loved me, and even though she's no longer with us, I can still feel her presence." It made her feel warm inside to talk to someone else about her mother. A weight lifted.

But Agnes looked displeased, her lips slightly downturned. "You're not wrong, dear, but there was so much more. She had powers, Hazel. And she was both gentle and fierce, just like you."

Powers. Hazel shivered and her chest swelled with pride. She'd waited her whole life to hear more about her mother. She'd never expected Agnes would be the one to tell her.

Agnes continued. "When the pact was made, the strongest witches had to seek asylum elsewhere. This was prior to the Dampening going into effect, you see, so many of them could get out before the Border was strengthened. Your mother, however, stayed."

Something twisted inside of Hazel, wrenching her heart. *Witch.*

"She wanted to make sure you were safe and raised outside of the influence of magic. She thought she could pass as a normal woman. But we learned the King had sent his Bloodseekers to seek out magic-wielders in hiding and knew the risk was too high. He keeps fewer of them in his service now, but the Bloodseekers use magic of their own to sense wards and veils. It's a type of dark magic, truly evil stuff. Anyway, she couldn't stay. You would be safe because you were so small. No one knew if you were gifted, but even if you were, it would have been too little to sense. So, she was going to leave you with us."

Hazel's feet bounced nervously under the table. Control. She needed to control herself.

"She waited until they arrived to draw as much attention to herself as possible. We all watched in quiet horror as she mounted her horse and tore off toward the tree line, drawing them away from town and allowing the stragglers, ill, and elderly to escape to safety… and protecting you."

She couldn't. This was too much. But she steeled herself, biting her lip so hard she tasted blood.

"But what about the baby she had? Pa said… he said she died giving birth to my little sister. That neither of them made it. If what you're saying is true…"

Agnes watched Hazel quietly as she processed the information. Then she reached for her hands, cupping them in her own. "Connall Callahan was married to a woman named Briar," she said softly, "and she did die in childbirth. With a daughter he named Rose. But Briar was not your mother. And Connall…" Agnes trailed off.

Hazel could still feel Agnes's eyes trained on her, though. She looked up and found an expression full of fear and awe awaiting her. Her locket was so hot, she thought it might burn through her shirt… and was that *light* reflecting in her eyes? *Oh, gods, no.*

She looked down at her hands. She was glowing again. Except this time, she had nowhere to channel the sudden rush of power surging up from its source. It was begging for release. Her skin wanted to split from the building pressure and her head throbbed. She mouthed "help me" to Agnes, who, realizing how immediately dire this situation had turned, was already out of her chair and frantically searching for something in her wares.

The cottage erupted in blinding light as a powerful force tore free from Hazel. Agnes was knocked back against her shelves in the blast. Trinkets and talismans were scattered, the table overturned, and the crystal sphere was on the ground, split in two.

Agnes righted herself, visibly unharmed except for the slow trickle of purple blood coming from her nose. Hazel was on her hands and knees, completely drained and unable to stand.

There was a commotion outside, men shouting, and Agnes—suddenly very spry—flew into action. She wiped her nose on her sleeve and righted the table on her own. Then she grabbed Hazel's wrists and pulled her into the chair.

Something was wrong. Someone else was there.

"Hazel," she breathed, snapping her fingers. "Hazel, look at me. Come on. Come back to me. We don't have time. You broke the wards. We aren't safe."

She remembered what she'd been looking for then and dropped to the floor, searching. She found the small vial, and with renewed vigor, forced it into Hazel's mouth, draining the contents down her throat.

Hazel came to just as three fully armored guards busted down the cottage door and rushed in. Hazel recognized immediately they were not regular knights. These three were members of the Raven Blade. *Shit.*

Both women were instantly on their feet as the men surrounded them. Thankfully, Hazel no longer glowed with aetherial light, and there was essentially no proof they'd done anything wrong—if the guards ignored the trashed interior.

Agnes spoke first. "Can we help you, sirs?"

The first guard spat. "A bright light just exploded from within this cottage. Care to explain?"

"Oh, you saw that? Well, it's quite embarrassing! You see, this young woman came in seeking a fertility tea, but, well… I must admit in my clumsiness I knocked over a couple of mineral powders that aren't meant to be mixed. Now you see why, it seems." Agnes did her best to look bashful and ashamed. Her face was convincing. The story? Not so much.

The knight curled his lip in disgust. He grabbed the discarded vial from the table, smelling it. Hazel could see between the fear in her eyes and the way her already pale skin blanched, Agnes was worried about the vial. Before she could say anything, Agnes reached out to snatch it back.

But the knight was faster. He whirled on Agnes, sending her flying across the room with a backhanded slap—his hand encased in an iron-plated gauntlet.

Agnes slumped to the floor, bleeding from her eyebrow to her cheekbone, eyes beginning to blacken.

Hazel erupted with fury. "No! No, please!" she shouted at them. "She's a harmless woman, can't you brutes see that?"

They ignored her.

She shrieked, hurling herself at the knight. Surprising both herself and him, she landed a blow before he could react. But it only angered him.

The knight grabbed her by the neck and lifted her into the air as she clawed at the iron, to no avail. She tried to reach down into whatever emotional recess housed her powers, but once again, they were empty. Or perhaps the bitter liquid Agnes had forcibly dumped down her throat had something to do with it. Probably for the best in that case.

The other two knights approached, each grabbing one of her flailing, clawing arms. She was lowered to her feet. Then the first knight backhanded her the same way he had Agnes, and she was thrown to the ground, screaming in pain.

Please, please don't let me die like this.

As she rolled and writhed, a figure stepped over her, placing a steel-plated sabaton heavily on her chest. *He's going to crush me.*

Instead, another knight wound up his leg and kicked her square in the ribs with his iron-clad foot, causing her to scream again and cough uncontrollably. Blood ran from both her nose and mouth steadily, the warmth and sickly copper tang gagging her.

Through narrowing vision, she stared at Agnes's motionless form, still lying in a heap where the big brute had dropped her. She was so still. *Too* still. But then, there was the slightest flicker of her eyelids and the old woman's chest rose and fell, though shallow.

Hazel reached out for her with a shaking, battered arm. "Agnes," she gasped, barely over a whisper.

A barrage of kicks followed.

And again.

And again.

At some point, she went numb to it all, instead focusing her attention on Agnes's breathing. *Just hold on, Agnes. Just hold… on.* She wouldn't be able to live with the alternative.

In… out.

In… out.

In…

Then, everything faded to black.

The War Room

SLAIDE awoke to daggers of sunlight jabbing into his eyelids through the half-opened velvet curtains. *Who the fuck left those open?* He rolled over, groaning as his over-indulgence the night before caught up with him. He squeezed his eyes shut, willing the pounding in his head to cease.

Flashes of memory flickered behind his eyelids, reminding him of just how hard he'd *reveled* last night. Glasses of wine that never emptied. Naked serving women straddling him and feeding fruits and sweets to him like a god. Dumping mead down his throat and licking the streams overflowing from the corners of his mouth. The sounds they made… It was probably a great time, but he paid for it doubly in the form of a skull threatening to crack in two, and a stomach promising to turn itself inside out. "Fuck… me…" he groaned.

"*Again?*" Someone giggled, a seductive sound. Or at least it would have been if he wasn't so hungover. His eyes shot open, despite the searing pain. At the sight of the naked woman in his bed, Slaide groaned again and ran his hands through his hair. Apparently, he'd actually been inebriated enough to bring one of them home. *Oh, Magnus is going to love this.* He sneered at the thought, at the satisfaction he would receive from Magnus's displeasure.

"No," he mumbled. But then again…

The woman beside him—was it Marcella? Ariella? He couldn't remember and, frankly, didn't care—sat up on her elbow, gazing lustfully from below her lashes. He had to admire her, even if he was thoroughly disgusted with himself. She was a tanned beauty, with the softest skin imaginable. Her hooded eyes were a color he couldn't quite place, something almost unnatural, with a hint of purple. Her mouth was small and thin, but perfectly delicate… and functional, if memory served him.

She had a beautiful neck, which was now painted with marks of lust. Had he done that? His eyes traced her neck down to the soft lines of her collarbones, landing finally on her breasts, which he decided were in fact his favorite part about her. At least, his favorite part currently above the duvet.

Slaide reached for her, gently but firmly grabbing her right breast. He cupped it and ran his thumb over her nipple, finding it completely hardened and peaking under his touch. The woman let her head loll back as a moan escaped her lips. He too closed his eyes, his body remembering the feel of her, even though he couldn't recall a thing. He hardened at the prospect of having her again, and he dared not acknowledge that the ceaseless pounding in his head was quickly being replaced with the throbbing of his cock. *Fuck it. Why not?* He reached across her body and pulled her closer to him, putting her flat on her back as he did so.

Then Slaide's hands did what they did best. He traced a line from her breast with a featherlight touch, trailing down to her navel and then beyond, to the soft skin just above the apex of her thighs. Her back arched and her entire body shivered with anticipation and need. He growled under his breath, fighting the urge to thoroughly ruin her.

His contemplation was interrupted by a knock at the door, which then swung wide without allowing them even a moment longer to right themselves. Slaide's hangover returned immediately as his guard stepped aside to reveal Magnus pushing his way into the room. The woman scrambled, grabbing frantically at the sheets to cover herself before the King. Slaide just smirked and left himself completely exposed. He only bothered to brush a sweaty lock of hair from his face.

Magnus grunted at the sight before him. "You disgust me."

Says the pig, Slaide thought. "Am I not allowed to enjoy myself?"

"You've been doing too much of that lately. Get your shit together. We're meeting in the war room to discuss important matters."

"Which requires me because?" As far as he was concerned, he had much better things to do.

"It involves the future of this kingdom and your place in it. And because I said so." They stared at each other, two immovable forces, each in their own way.

And this is what happens when you give a spoiled brat the reins. "Sure thing, Magnus. But don't wait up. I'm not quite finished here."

Magnus's cheeks reddened, and Slaide thought he the spitting image of a tea kettle ready to scream. *Careful, Highness, we wouldn't want you to implode.* He opened his mouth to speak, but was cut off with a stern look that promised to rip his tongue out at the base. Slaide sighed.

"Right, right. Point taken." He turned to the woman. "Apologies, dear. It was lovely, truly, but you heard the man. Duty calls." She nodded obediently, but looked to the king, waiting for him to leave so she could gather herself. When Slaide realized what she was waiting on, he shooed the king out the door with an impatient hand motion. Magnus shook his head in disbelief, but turned in a huff and left, nonetheless.

As soon as the door closed behind him, the woman made haste, gathering her undergarments and clothes, though she simply wadded the former up in her hand and slipped into her dress with nothing underneath. *Well, I suppose that answers* that *question, then.* He'd been debating on whether she'd be expecting payment, and seeing as a common townswoman wouldn't have skipped putting on her underclothes, he figured he must have picked up one of the local Madames' girls in his drunken stupor.

"Here you are. My thanks, truly." She looked at the coins in his palm and smacked him firmly across his cheek. Slaide was dumbfounded. *Shit. Too little? I suppose it has been awhile—*

"I am *not* a whore!" she shouted at him. She grabbed what remained of her belongings and stormed out, slamming the door.

Slaide scratched the back of his head. "Could have fooled me."

As usual, he was the last to arrive. The war room was packed with far too many foul-smelling, sweaty men for his liking. *Let's get this over with.* While there were plenty of open seats to choose from, Slaide chose his preferred place against the wall, tucked into the shadows with his arms crossed.

The war room was one of the largest chambers in the castle. There was a hearth at one end and a giant carved table in the center detailing Aeos and the surrounding kingdoms. During wartimes, the map was used to track the movements of various armies and strategize against their foes. It was exquisitely detailed, featuring varying elevations in accordance with the topography of the land itself, which of course included the Bonespire Mountains to the northeast, the Dragon's Teeth to the southwest, the Western Wastes, and the Shadow Fen. Stormhold, the mage citadel, was the only other city given a dimensional prominence on the map. Others were dedicated with dots depicting their relative location.

A red dotted line comprised the Border. Cutting through Aeos and encompassing the mountain ranges as part of its barrier, it effectively divided the kingdom into northern and southern halves. The southern half had been forfeited to Axios because of the volatile nature of the lands below the Border, and the vast number of magical beings living in the fen and beyond.

As the meeting was called to order, the King's Hand made his usual introductory statements as though they hadn't had hundreds of these meetings in this same room prior to today. Magnus sat at the head of the war table in a chair upholstered in maroon velvet, wearing his standard, unamused scowl. A young serving boy flitted around the room, silently filling the goblet of wine before each guest. But Slaide went without. *Something tells me I'll want my wits today.*

"Well," Magnus began, clearing his throat, "The Champion's Tournament has garnered support from every corner of the kingdom, and is shaping up to be our largest tournament yet. Noble houses of the realm are sending their finest men to compete." He paused as though expecting a pat on the back for this. When he didn't receive it, he continued. "And I am proud to announce the Raven Blade Knights have already wrangled up a half-dozen traitorous magic-wielders. Your efforts made it possible."

The gathered lords clapped.

Slaide sneered, rolling his eyes. Half a dozen prisoners in one sweep would have been a disgrace once upon a time, when it was common to round up as many as thirty witches in a single raid.

"What is the plan with them, Your Majesty?" Lord Giles asked.

Courtland Rhodes, Chief Commandant of the Raven Blade spoke eagerly. "Public executions would serve as a good reminder to the populace that magic has consequences." A few of the nobles present mumbled their agreement.

Archmage Gammen stood abruptly. "Your Majesty, I must beg you to consider the bigger picture here. A quick execution, while effective in the moment, has less of a lasting impression than the other options we discussed."

"Yes," Magnus acknowledged, "I am well aware we have plenty of options. I am not concerned with making any decisions on them at the moment. We still have the tournament and celebrations to get through before their fate is determined. I may even let Tristan decide, as a gift from me."

No one spoke up this time.

"Now then, we'll crown our Champion from a selection of the finest men our lords send. But, I've added a new twist. To make things more interesting, I'm going to toss a few of our criminals in—for a chance at earning their freedom."

Murmurs rose around the room.

It was around then Slaide stopped listening. *I just want my bed, warm bread, and a flagon of ale.* So some whoreson would claw his way into the knighthood. Or a murderer. *Who cares?* He rolled his eyes. These things were always so incredibly boring, and apparently this meeting would be no exception.

As Slaide picked at his nail beds, the conversation quieted. He looked up, a bit surprised to find all eyes fixated on him. He straightened his posture against the wall. "Yes?"

"I was asking if you had a strategy for the first trial? You're meant to represent House Ragnaroth, Slaide. It is a position of honor, and you won't squander it. Many will bet good coin on your success."

"Maybe it's a good opportunity for them to learn a lesson, then." Slaide shrugged. "Don't bet on the horse who doesn't want to be there. C'mon, Magnus. You know I've never been one for the gallant knight charades."

"Slaide Elias, you never cease to disappoint me." He squeezed the bridge of his nose as though he could massage away the ceaseless headache that was Slaide Elias.

And yet you keep me around. "I only aim to please, *Your Majesty,*" he said, sketching a mock bow.

Magnus sighed. "As for our next order of business, there was a small uprising the day before last, on the outskirts of a small village. One of our men was struck and injured by a suspected witch."

Slaide sneered at the thought, rolling his eyes at their incompetence.

"A young, female witch," he added.

With this new piece of information, Slaide found himself much more interested. In his experience, modern female witches were normally of the docile sort, tending gardens and healing injured animals. Using enchantments to weave and cook. They rarely, if ever, fought back. *Good.* This, at least, made things interesting.

"She was apprehended in the end, along with her elderly accomplice. We believe the older woman was training the younger in her ways, though we've no solid proof yet. At any rate, the younger of the two is in the infirmary."

Slaide uncrossed his arms. "Why is a captive in the fucking infirmary?"

Magnus arched a brow. "That tends to be the outcome for those who dare lay a hand on my knights. She's lucky to be alive."

Is she though?

"And since we are discussing her fate, we need to decide what happens next. She is currently in the custody of my kingsguard, facing charges of unlawful use of magic and conspiracy against the crown, assault on a member of the knighthood… and so on."

The two sunken-faced Archmages to the King's left—Gammen and Oriss—sneered eerie, twin smiles that didn't quite meet their eyes. Slaide always found the higher mages unsettling, and they reminded him why. They were beyond unnatural.

Well, now. If the Magistry was interested in her, so was he. But he didn't know enough. Not yet. Time to play games of his own.

"So let me get this straight. You broke down the door of some girl and her grandmother based on, what, a hunch? In some small, seedy town no one who matters has ever heard of? And you really think you've accomplished something?" He pushed, hoping Magnus would take the bait.

Magnus did, sputtering in his fury. "One of these days I'm going to cut your tongue out. She's a grown woman who was accompanied by an elderly woman, in a cottage full of magical paraphernalia, on the outskirts of a town with a history steeped in magic. Where, I might add, there are rumors of their citizens growing emboldened and reverting to their old ways. So yes, Slaide, we had a *hunch*."

"Fine," Slaide grumbled. "I'll take her into my custody and interrogate her. See what I can learn about her powers, if she has any."

"You'll do no such thing. She's being turned over to the Magistry once she's fit to travel," Magnus commanded.

"On the contrary. I'll be taking her. When and only when I am finished with her can those freaks do what they wish."

"Master Elias, if I may," one of the Archmages interjected. "The Council will need to conduct a full investigation and interrogation of the subjects in question. Often, the most inconspicuous person has the most to hide. You might be surprised."

Slaide cocked an eyebrow. *He's giving these mages too much power.* Slaide had never been a fan of the kingdom's Magistry. They were mysterious, conniving, and since the Dampening, the only group of people allowed to use magic.

As far as Slaide was concerned, the creepy, beady-eyed men and women were monsters parading in human flesh. The Citadel of Stormhold—the Magistry's capital and home to every mage who didn't live in the castle—was an impenetrable fortress outsized only by Ravenhold. And that was to say nothing of the wards they erected to keep everyone out.

Everything about the Magistry and the mages who conducted business within the Citadel's walls was kept enshrouded in secrecy, from the way they educated their initiates to the contents of their sacred libraries.

He eyed the man. *Too much power.* "And what, pray tell, will you do if she *is* found to have access to magic? If indeed it was she who emitted the energy burst? Will you hang her? Burn her at the stake? Dissect her like your other *projects*?" He shot a glare at Magnus;. something unspoken passed between them. *No. If anyone is going to interrogate her, it is going to be me.*

"And why do you care, Slaide? Perhaps I need to keep a tighter leash on you after all." Magnus raised a brow, his apple-round cheeks reddening.

"I don't," he growled. "However, if you're accusing her of witchcraft, sorcery, demonology, necromancy, or *any* forbidden magic—which last I checked is all magic *they* aren't using," he said, nodding to the gray-skinned mage, "it falls under *my* jurisdiction and investigative responsibilities. Does it not?"

Archmage Gammen's grim face, for once, betrayed his emotion as panic flared in his eyes.

What are you hiding, mage? Why is this girl so important?

"Master Elias, I must insist! We don't know what she could be capable of. It would be safer for everyone in the kingdom if we have her taken to Stormhold, where she can be properly contained and observed," whined Gammen.

No, he would not lose this battle. If for no other reason than to keep her out of the Magistry's grasp as long as possible. "I'll make you a deal, Gammen," he said. "I will do the preliminary interview and interrogation. Should I fail or should she prove to be too much for me to handle, I will transfer her to the Magistry. Let's be real here: your order isn't exactly known for being personable. Someone who's just had their entire world upended won't give you what you're after if you lock her in a cell and poke her with a stick until she talks."

"You underestimate how *persuasive* we can be, I think," Gammen hissed. "However, I will agree to your terms with one condition. You will get her to reveal herself in three days. After, we will send someone to retrieve her."

Gods, he is insistent. But Slaide was struck with an idea. Whether ingenious or idiotic it was yet unclear. He looked at Magnus. "I've got a better idea. You said you're going to throw a handful of criminals into the tournament right? To make things—how did you put it—interesting? Enter her as a competitor. If she's truly so dangerous, you'll have yourself a new Champion in no time. If not, she dies and is no longer your problem."

Magnus sat there expressionless. "And what exactly is in this for you, Slaide? Because in the years I've known you, not a single plan of yours was not self-serving. What do you get if she wins?"

Slaide smiled. "My freedom."

Magnus tipped his head back and laughed heartily. "And what part of you is not already free to do as you wish? To fuck and kill who and what you please when the need strikes? I see no shackles, no chains. Freedom, ha."

But Slaide did not laugh. Instead, he leaned in closer. "You know *exactly* what I'm referring to, old man. And I want freedom from it. Permanently"

Magnus sat back, appearing deep in thought as his joke was turned on him. He glanced at his Cyrus, his Hand, but the man offered no words of advice.

"Fine," Magnus spoke at last.

Archmage Gammen was close to losing his composure. Oriss shifted uncomfortably but said nothing. Gammen turned to his king, as though to plead his case. "Your Majesty—"

"Or," Slaide interrupted, "Perhaps, Magnus, we should consider executing her. Tomorrow."

Gammen threw composure out the window and started sputtering. *Gotcha, you spineless worm.* They wanted her alive for some reason. But what?

"Enough!" Magnus pounded his fist on the table as he stood from the chair. "If I have to hear one more second of this bickering, I am going to throw both of you in a cell and leave you there to rot. Slaide gets the girl first. He will enter her in the tournament as his ward and be responsible for her training. Whatever happens after is determined by whether or not she survives. In the meantime, you're dismissed. Get out of my sight."

The two gaunt mages pulled their hoods up over their snakelike heads and bowed deeply before exiting the chamber, gliding along the stone floor, two wraiths in the night.

Their disappointment satisfied Slaide in a way he couldn't describe. He didn't care about the fate of the girl, but it brought him indescribable joy to deprive them of something they wanted so badly.

Once the doors closed behind them, Slaide turned to Magnus. "So, where's the girl?"

"Listen here, boy," he seethed, spittle flying. "I don't know what you're up to, but I *am* onto you. If this is another stunt of yours, I will not be as forgiving as I have been in the past. I am tired of the antics and games."

Interesting coming from someone who plays so many political games of his own. "I'm not up to anything, Magnus. I am only trying to do my duties as they were assigned to me. If you handed her over to your mages, there would be nothing left, and I don't think they would be forthcoming with their findings. The Citadel would swallow her whole."

Magnus stared at him with the intensity of a thousand burning witches. Without blinking, he said, "She's in the infirmary being looked after by the healers. It seems she suffered a head injury after the blast."

He didn't bother acknowledging the comment about the mages.

Slaide turned on his heel and marched to the door. The serving boy moved to open it when Magnus called out. "Slaide," came the emotionless voice.

And for some reason, Slaide paused, glancing over his shoulder.

"Don't fuck this up."

On the contrary, you bastard. Slaide smirked, turning his back on the king. *I'm going to fuck this up as much as I can.*

The Infirmary

When she opened her eyes, Hazel was deep in the bowels of the castle again, the telltale scents of death and rot and decay near suffocating. She stood in an arched doorway, iron dragon-head sconces lit on either side, casting eerie shadows on the walls. The room before her was dark, whatever secrets it held hidden in the shadows. Behind her, a winding stone staircase twisted up and out of sight. The sconces continued down every three or so stairs, likely lit by whoever or whatever had come before her.

Hazel looked at her hands and recognized she was in the body of the mystery person once again. She wore the skin of someone with dainty hands, whose slender, manicured fingers bore splendid rings. But Hazel immediately noticed something different. Her hands were shackled in iron manacles…

Her observations were interrupted by the sound of heavy footsteps up above. A jingle of keys and the click *of a lock being turned was followed by a sharp squeal of the door on its hinges as someone entered the stairwell. And she was somewhere she shouldn't be.*

She needed to move. Fast. Needed to find cover. And of course, her only option was to press onward into the darkness before her… and whatever else awaited her there. She cast one last glance over her shoulder to see the glow of a torch as its bearer descended the spiral stairs. She glimpsed a hulking shadow on the stairwell wall just before fleeing into the gaping maw of the chamber.

Hazel couldn't see a thing. She fumbled her way into the room, tripping and stumbling over obstacles she couldn't identify. She decided she would not get out of this alive by making so much noise and slowed herself down, giving her eyes—or whoever's eyes they were—time to adjust to the blinding blackness. As they did, she wished she could erase all of it from memory.

Both sides of the room were lined with makeshift cots. Some were completely soiled, the linens soaked with what she could only assume was blood. In some areas, the stains were darker… too dark to be blood. At least, too dark to be human *blood. A chill ran up her spine. Footsteps approached, the time between each stride an eternity.*

She couldn't breathe. Didn't dare.

She was completely exposed, too. There hadn't been enough time to orient herself to the strange room to know where she could hide. Hazel steeled herself against the fear within her, now bubbling to a primal level. But if she panicked, there would be no escape.

She heard the snap of fingers in the darkness.

The hallway burst to life with blinding light as the sconces re-lit themselves spontaneously. Two large braziers in the room followed suit.

Her company had arrived as a foreboding, godlike silhouette framed by raven-black wings, each tipped with a single, razor sharp talon. An angel, but so much worse. No, an angel of death.

The male figure relit his torch and held it before him, examining the room. Hazel took a few quiet steps back, taking in this creature before her.

Torchlight illuminated his body, revealing a bare torso and muscled arms riddled with scars. Was he a warrior? Or were those scars the memories left behind in his flesh from being whipped or tortured himself? Her eyes were drawn to his side, which looked to have been recently bandaged, blood seeping through the layered cloth.

He locked eyes with her then, and Hazel could not break free from her gaze. Where hers went wide, revealing the whites in her fear, his were solid black, endless, soulless orbs floating in the night.

The beast reached for her, and she found herself unable to move. A single, claw-tipped finger came nearer… nearer… so close to touching her.

She opened her mouth to scream, but nothing came out.

Hazel's eyelids fluttered, fighting against her will to open them. Brain foggy and vision blurred, she struggled to bring the world around her into focus. Lolling her head to one side, she closed her eyes and groaned from the pounding throb rattling her skull. But then…

It all came back to her in a blinding fury, her last waking memory assaulting her with a barrage of terror. Hazel thrashed, fighting the last enemy she remembered seeing. But her efforts amounted to nothing, as she found her hands were bound, restraining her from moving more than a finger's length.

She was completely tied down to a bed.

Hazel pushed up as much as her restraints would allow and pain seized her. It was a jolting sensation, the likes of which she'd never experienced. Her ribs were on fire. Lying flat once more, she tried to control her breathing through the intense throbbing between her ribs. As she attempted to wiggle her legs, Hazel discovered her ankles were bound in a similar fashion. Her pulse quickened, panic threatening to take hold of her senses. *Calm yourself. Learn as much as you can about your surroundings.*

Then it hit her. She recognized this room. *No, it can't be.* But it was. From the chandelier above, to the braziers burning at either end of the chamber, this was the room from her recurring nightmare. She may not have ever experienced it physically, but there was no mistaking this place for the same one she's been in half a dozen times now.

The domed ceiling, the windowless walls, and, worst of all, the infirmary beds all around the room. With a deep breath to refocus, she recognized the room was cleaner, more sterile—devoid of the blood and gore of her nightmares. Perhaps there were multiple chambers akin to this one. *Maybe this* isn't *the torture chamber from my dreams.* It was more of a healer's ward than the horrible place she was used to seeing. At least, she hoped it was. Hazel rested her head briefly, relaxing against the restraints and allowing her eyes to close.

Something moved by her feet, and her eyes shot back open. *What was that?* She lifted her head up again to see an enormous orange cat doing circles between her feet, kneading the blanket into the perfect bed. He plopped down and began grooming his paws. Well, at least there was one familiar face. Somehow, that brought her comfort, and she laid her head back down, feeling calmer than before.

Her moment of peace was interrupted by the thud of the hall's doors opening, the sound echoing across the large chamber. Soft footsteps padded across the floor as the visitor approached. A sense of foreboding washed over her, a bucket full of melted snow setting her nerves alight. She chanced a glance in their direction and found a plump, bald man bent over a workbench across the room, tinkering with something. A cork popped out of a bottle, and the sound of pouring liquid followed suit. Followed by something being stirred.

He stopped working and turned slowly to face her.

Hazel slammed her eyes shut, hoping he hadn't noticed she was awake. She heard him set the glass he'd been working with down and close a drawer. Her heart lurched to a gallop as his steps drew near. If he came any closer, pretending to be asleep would be futile. *Maybe I can talk my way out of this.*

She could sense the man at her side before he cleared his throat.

"Miss?" His voice was rugged but surprisingly soft. Almost gentle. "Are you awake?"

Hazel allowed her eyes to open slowly, hoping to create the illusion she was just regaining consciousness. "Hmm?" she mumbled.

"Ahh, shh. Shh." He comforted her. "It's alright, miss. I will not harm you."

"Wh-where am I? What happened?" she stammered.

"You were in quite the scuffle, young lady. Took a right beating, you did. Though, if I understand correctly, you put up a good fight." He smiled softly. It was disarming, his kindness. Hazel wasn't sure what to make of it, but his smile faded. "They were going to kill you for attacking an officer of the crown. You're lucky you aren't dead."

She tried to smile back and was met with more pain, turning her smile to a grimace. At the moment, she didn't *feel* lucky.

"Aye, suppose you're in a right bit of pain still, eh? Let me step over to my bench and get you something—"

"No—I mean, wait," she sputtered. The tang of blood indicating she'd broken open a wound of some sort in her mouth. "How long have I been here? Where's Ag—my aunt?" Her head was spinning, the pain growing more severe by the second. But she'd remembered poor Agnes piled into a lifeless heap on the ground in her tent. *No, not lifeless.* She recalled Agnes's shallow breaths before the armored guard had kicked her into oblivion.

"You've been out for a few days, miss. I've had to keep you under while the most severe of your wounds healed. But I assure you, it was for your own safety. Waking up before you were ready, well… you can see how much pain you're in now. It would have been tenfold, and quite dangerous, had I not provided you with a sleeping draught. And I give you my word, I have been the only one to attend to you. These are my chambers, and no one enters without my knowing." *Whatever that is supposed to mean. What good is the word of a stranger who keeps you tied to a bed and drugged?*

"I see," Hazel managed before breaking into a terrible coughing fit. By the gods, it was so painful she couldn't breathe. The cat jumped up and raised his hackles, alarmed by the commotion.

The stocky healer waddled over to his workbench again and gathered something from the cabinet beside it. He returned moments later with a dusky liquid-filled vial.

"Please, miss. Drink this for me." The cat hissed at him as he approached.

Hazel eyed him warily between coughs. Why should she trust him? Her body heaved, her abdominal muscles cramping with the exertion of each barking hack.

Wordlessly, he offered her the vial. She accepted it and, against her better judgment, tipped the whole thing back. It was surprisingly warm, quite viscous, and only slightly bitter. Her coughing subsided almost immediately.

"There now. That's better, isn't it?"

She nodded, half expecting to fall over dead any minute.

"It was just for the pain. I promise."

Judging by how he recoiled, Hazel knew her distrust was written all over her face, which was smushed into an accusatory scowl.

"Now," he continued, wiping his hands on a towel, "As for your aunt, you say? Yes. Well, I have little to report. She was brought to me the same as you but was released from my care within a day. I can't say for certain, but I believe she may be in the dungeons now."

The dungeons. My poor, frail Agnes. And it's all my fault. Hot tears welled in her eyes. "Take me to her, please," she begged, her strained voice barely more than a whisper.

"Oh, my dear. Would if I could. But I am afraid you won't be going anywhere for a while. You need to rest." He rested a hand on her arm and looked down at her. Warning bells pealed in her mind.

"It's time to go back to sleep, miss." His grip tightened around her forearm, and with his other hand, he drew another vial of clouded liquid. She tried to turn her head, but she couldn't feel… anything. Her eyes flared in panic, and she opened her mouth to scream, but the healer grabbed her face in his sweaty, meaty hand and dumped the vial down her throat. She swallowed involuntarily.

In an instant, a calmness overtook her.

He smiled at her. "That's a good girl. Get some rest, miss. We'll wake you when it's time."

Something Shady

SLAIDE stomped down the long corridor, his black cloak flowing behind him. He'd left the war room in a hurry, barely allowing the doors to close behind him before breaking into a brisk walk. He moved as quickly as he could across the worn stone floor, riding the line of drawing too much attention and getting to her fast enough. His gut told him he needed to beat the mages to the infirmary.

He wound down several hallways, each more secluded and emptier than the last. When Slaide reached the set of ancient double doors to the infirmary, he barged in without knocking. He opened his mouth to make demands, when he was cut off by the sight before him. Across the room, the healer Slaide recognized as Nemsen stood over the only occupied bed. And he was not alone. Gammen and Oriss huddled beside him, the former having lowered his hood.

Those beady-eyed pricks.

The doors slammed behind him, alerting the three men to his presence. Nemsen turned abruptly, clearly not expecting more company.

"Ah! Master Elias, good to see you," he said, closing the space between them. Slaide looked past him to where the Archmages stood, as though they were trying to absorb as much information as they could about this new pet before their little party was interrupted.

"Is that her?" Slaide asked, ignoring pleasantries.

"Who?"

"The girl," he ground out. "The girl accused of using magic. Don't play dumb. I've had enough of that today."

Nemsen reeled back as though he'd been struck by a snake. "Right. Well, yes. You see she's rather incapacitated at the moment. Really shouldn't be disturbed."

Slaide looked down at the short, bald man, rolled his eyes, and then shouldered past him, making for where the Archmages stooped. There was an oddly large orange cat sitting on her legs with its ears pinned flat.

He slid up behind them, casting a long, ominous shadow over the men and their subject. Oriss was the first to peer over his shoulder. He did a double take before subtly alerting Gammen to their visitor. Gammen turned slowly to face Slaide, his skeletal face devoid of emotion. *At least act surprised I caught you defying the King.*

"Ah, just the man I was hoping to see. You really should reconsider, Master Elias," he said. "One wrong move and you could unleash who knows what on this kingdom. Gods of Caelis, all Aetherium, even. Her kind are an abomination the likes of which only we have the means to deal with."

"Get. Out." The muscle in his jaw flicked.

"I can't do that, Slaide. Let us do the right thing—for everyone." Gammen was nothing if not persistent.

Slaide stepped forward, his eyes darkening. He was tall enough to look down at the Archmage. As their chests came to touch, grazing slightly, Gammen shifted his weight. He was uncomfortable. *Good.* "I said *get out.*"

Archmage Gammen inclined his head and stared into his eyes, as though trying to get a read on the man no one understood. *Good luck with that.* Then he submitted, bowing his head and replacing his hood as he stepped around Slaide. He and Oriss gathered their things and left the room without another word.

Slaide watched them leave, his eyes landing on Nemsen, who cowered slightly under his gaze. "Master Elias, I—"

"From now on, until she is well enough to leave this room, no one enters except you or me. That includes those two and their ilk. Do we have an understanding, Nemsen?"

"Yes, sir," he said. "Sir, if I may…"

Slaide shot him a warning glare but tempered his anger. "Sure, Nemsen. What is it? Speak freely."

"Well, it's just… she's in a rather delicate state at the moment. And while I wouldn't dare tell you what to do, I do hope you'll heed me when I say she shouldn't be moved or otherwise disturbed for a while." The man wrung his hands anxiously and avoided meeting Slaide's eyes.

Slaide sighed. "I don't know what they told you, and I don't know what they want with her. But I can assure you, for whatever my word is worth to you, I have no interest in those things. You've heard the stories. You know what I do. So, I am going to need you to just trust me on this."

Surprisingly, Nemsen nodded. "Master Elias, I don't want to overstep with what I am about to say. But… while we're on the subject of trusting one another, I wonder if you might have a moment to discuss some things going on around here… specifically in the lower dungeons? I haven't been down there personally, but a few of my colleagues have and the things I've heard are concerning. Disturbing, actually."

Slaide blanched. He did not, in fact, know anything about whatever was going on in the lower dungeons. He could be honest, or he could put on the face everyone expected of him. So, he chose the former. "I have no idea what you're talking about. But, I can address it with Magnus and—"

"No! No. It's not—no, that's quite alright." His brief outburst was disconcerting. "I figured you wouldn't be able to tell me even if you did know." Something had the healer out of sorts. "Do you… do you know about the salt mines?"

"I do."

"Well, my understanding is they—that is, the King and the Council—are wanting to expand production."

"They are, yes." He was growing impatient. "What does this have to do with the dungeons?"

"It doesn't. Well, not directly anyway. I overheard a conversation between two healers a few nights ago. They've been assigned to work on something down there. And they seem… different. Changed, maybe? Disturbed? Possessed?"

"Possessed? Nemsen."

"I know. I know. I'm a healer. A supposed man of reason. It sounds crazy, and maybe it is." He glanced around nervously, eyes rapidly shifting side to side. "Please, forget I said anything. If word got back to the King..."

Darkness crept over Slaide again. He wouldn't admit he'd sensed something was going on for a while now. And he certainly wouldn't admit he suspected he was intentionally being left out of certain meetings.

"It won't. Not from me, anyway. If you think your colleagues seemed *off*, and you suspect nothing natural to be the cause, I trust your judgment." Slaide considered his next words. "In fact, I think we could both benefit from this situation."

Nemsen arched a brow in interest.

"Until I learn more about her, I am interested in keeping this girl out of the Magistry's slimy paws. You're going to help me. You're also going to gather as much information as you can from your colleagues. Quietly. Discreetly."

His face reflected his thoughtful consideration as his lips pursed and brows dipped. He glanced at Hazel before continuing. "Can I ask you something, Master Elias?" He didn't wait for an answer. "You being who and what you are—and I mean no offense—you aren't going to just... kill her? It's just, if she's a witch—"

"Something we've yet to see with our own eyes. To answer the question, yes. If the time comes, I will execute her. But if you're worried about leaving me alone with her on that basis, you've nothing to fear. I'm not going to murder her in her sleep; you have my word." There was no sign of insincerity on his face.

Nemsen nodded, seeming to accept the answer. "Fine, then. So, you think whatever they're doing in the dungeons has to do with the Magistry?"

"I do."

"You don't like those mages much, do you?" Nemsen was nervously twisting a gold ring on his finger—a wedding ring. Slaide wondered if he had a wife and family who would miss him if anything happened.

"I do not." It didn't require further explanation.

Nemsen smiled and extended his hand in offering. Slaide grasped it, shaking his hand firmly. "I knew I liked you."

Silence passed between them as they stood over Hazel, still fully sedated. As he looked down at her, realization smacked him between the eyes. She was the same foul-mouthed peasant woman who'd nearly gotten herself killed over someone else's brat. And then had the balls to challenge him over it. And, if he was right about her, there was one other time, but… seeing her now, he couldn't imagine they were truly the same person. And yet… *What are you hiding?* He noticed her companion, then, keeping one eye on them both from where it was curled up on her legs.

"Nemsen, what's the deal with the cat?" Slaide inquired.

"I have not the slightest clue. He just appeared shortly after she was brought in and hasn't really left her side since. He doesn't bother anything, though, just seems to be keeping an eye on her."

Interesting.

Nemsen sighed. "Master Elias, if it's all the same to you, I was just finishing up for the night before all of this went down. I'll need to lock everything up for the evening and bring the lighting down before I head to my quarters."

Slaide eyed a chair in the corner. "If it's all the same to you, I would prefer to stay. In case she wakes up." *Or in case those sleazy bastards decide to come back.*

This would be the first test. How much did Nemsen really trust him?

"I—ah, alright then. I'll just bring the braziers down a bit on my way out. Please feel free to browse the library if you get bored. Though, I'm not sure you'll find the subject matter any more interesting than watching this one sleep. Either way." He turned to leave, waving a dismissive hand. "Good night, Master Elias."

"Nemsen." The man paused, turning halfway. "Call me Slaide."

The healer smiled halfway, then nodded graciously.

"Good night then, Slaide."

With the healer gone, Slaide turned to the cat and arched a brow. "I trust you and I will not have problems?"

In time, Slaide did in fact find himself excruciatingly bored. He wondered if the healers kept anything truly interesting on their shelves and crossed the room to investigate. Upon first glance, the dusty tomes appeared to be mostly compendiums of medical knowledge and herbal tinctures and remedies, but nothing of genuine interest.

His tired eyes danced across the titles one after the next, begging to find something unusual. And then, just when he was about to return to his chair to pick at his nails some more, he spotted a peculiar book. It was a history book, and it did not belong there. The world's written histories existed only in the sacred libraries at the Citadel… except this one. Slaide pulled it from the shelf, surprised to find it free of dust. It hadn't been there long. Its title read *The Rise and Fall of Magic: The Untold History of The Thousand Years War.* Slaide ran his fingers over the embossed leather. *Interesting to find this in the infirmary of all places.*

A cough sounded from behind him, followed by a groan. Slaide stiffened, the tiny hairs along his neck rising in alarm. He chided himself for his reaction.

It was just the girl, after all. For a reason he couldn't pinpoint, he wasn't ready for her to wake up. Sure, the sooner this interrogation got on with, the better, but this whole situation was messing with his head. There was so much more at play here than just finding out if she had access to magic. More, still, than just her success in the tournament.

Of course, he knew more than he was letting on and *of course* he wasn't letting anyone—not a soul—in on his little secret.

He'd seen things. If it was, in fact, this girl who'd used magic, then he'd witnessed it before. As soon as he took in her pale skin and auburn hair, he was sure of it. They were past the realm of coincidence.

He peered over his shoulder, expecting her to be awake, but found her very much still asleep. Snoring, mouth hanging open, hair in her face kind of sleep. He laughed to himself, shaking his head. *You need to get it together, letting one simple woman get into your head so much.*

But was she so simple? He noticed her cat friend had taken his leave and shrugged, not making much of it.

Slaide returned to his chair with his history book and began thumbing through the pages. Most of what he'd been taught was gained from the tutors he had growing up as part of his royal education—the same as all castle youths received.

They were expected to know the basics: the major wars, the allies, enemies, major battles… and as Slaide had taken an early interest in court politics and policies, he knew about the more minor wars and skirmishes throughout their history.

He'd memorized the patterns of the Sea Wolf raids and knew the relationship with Axios was tenuous at best. The Thousand Years War, well, it was simply a war from an age gone by. It was never discussed in detail, though admittedly Slaide hadn't given that a second thought. But now that he held this book in his hands, an entire written history of a war no one talked about?

Now he suspected it was more important than ever.

No Choice

As the last bits of drug-induced exhaustion faded away, Hazel finally opened her eyes, only to find her worst nightmare staring down at her.

"No! Get away from me!" she screamed through a painfully hoarse throat. She tried to thrash at him, but was quickly reminded her hands and feet were still bound. She snarled wildly, the very image of a feral, trapped animal, fully prepared to shred him with her teeth if it came down to it.

"Whoa, whoa. Calm down there, helcat." He put his hands up innocently. "I am not here to hurt you." *Yet.* He didn't need to say it.

If what Zeke told her about this one was true, he was more monster than man. And she was in no position to fend him off.

"Get. Away. From. Me."

The cat—having returned from his stroll—hissed at him as well, earning a glare from Slaide.

"Is that how you're going to treat the person who saved your ass? No, you wouldn't have a clue because you've been unconscious for days. Well, let me fill you in, sweets. You're in Ravenhold, currently a prisoner of the crown."

"I'm aware, thanks." *Prick.*

He raised an eyebrow and shrugged. "Good. That saves me time. Did you also know I'm the one who saved you? You should be thanking me, but I digress. You'll be happy to know it gets even better. How? I'm glad you asked. You're in my charge now." A sardonic smile graced his face, white teeth gleaming.

She wanted to throw up. Her already-pale skin blanched, and her nostrils flared. A noticeable absence of warmth against her chest had her heart racing. *No, no, no. Not my locket.*

He stepped toward her, reaching out a hand, and Hazel thrashed. Slaide retracted his hand. "Would you relax for two seconds? I was going to untie you. Or would you rather I just leave you here, tied and unable to defend yourself from the creeps in this castle who would do you actual harm?"

He says that as though he wouldn't harm me. As though he's to be trusted—and by me *of all people?* A laughable thought, considering his reputation. But she did as he asked and relaxed, allowing him to approach and untie her bonds. After all, what choice did she have?

"I know you know who I am, and I gather you've heard what I do. To be frank, I'm all you've got at the moment. So, with that said, I am going to make you an offer you quite literally cannot refuse. Here's the deal. The mages want something with you. Don't know what, and while I would love to know what they're up to, I don't really want to find out—catch my meaning?"

Hazel blinked. She'd heard rumors about the Magistry, and they weren't pretty.

"Good. So, unless you want to become one of the Archmages' new lab rats, I would suggest lending me your cooperation. First, King Magnus is hosting a Tournament of Champions in less than six days, and you've been granted the *honor* of participating. Ah-ah, don't interrupt." He held up a finger to her lips, and she considered biting him.

"While you've made it clear you would rather see my head on a pike outside the city gates than so much as be in my presence, I think we might have something in common. Intuition tells me you aren't exactly a fan of His Majesty. As it turns out, I'm not either." He whispered the last part, lest the castle rats be listening in.

Her face brightened, though she said nothing. Something fluttered in her chest, the smallest spark of hope. But she stifled it. She could not allow herself to fall for pretty words so easily.

"Thought so. You see, sweets, your participation in this tournament wasn't desired. In fact, I was laughed at, if you can believe it. And I'll be honest, while I'm sure you're a nice woman, maybe even a decent lay," he looked her over in a way that made her want to disappear, "I didn't choose you because I fancy you or think you've even got a shot at winning. I offered to train you solely to slight him, and it worked. So, he was furious. Tried to force my hand. *Really* wanted me to concede custody of you to the mages. But, he doesn't own me, despite wanting to convince himself and everyone around him of the opposite. *No one* controls me."

What is his obsession with the King? And what is the King's obsession with him? I don't get it... wait...

"Is Magnus your father?" She couldn't help it. She'd blurted the words out before she could think better of it. *Hazel Grace, you bumbling idiot. You just suggested he's a bastard, of all things.* Her cheeks flared with heat.

He blanched, eyes going wide in surprise. And then he laughed. Hysterically.

"My father? Not a shot. He wishes he'd sired someone of my abilities instead of mewling Prince Tristan. Though I suppose he feels I owe him something for allowing me to live this long." He shrugged carelessly, looking past her into some forgotten memory.

"Not sure what he thinks I should thank him for, anyway. I didn't share the same childhood as prince charming. As for being a bastard, I'm not the one who carries that title, though I'd be lying if I didn't acknowledge someone in that family had some explaining to do."

"Sorry, I—"

He waved her off with a dismissive hand. "It's not important. Made me who I am today, right?"

"Right." *Are we pretending that's a good thing?*

"So here's the deal, uh, Bella... Catlyn ...Margaret?"

"Hazel."

"Hazel." He smirked. "Alright, Hazel. We've only a few days to get you ready for this tournament. Lost an entire day to you lounging around. And before you protest again, I'll remind you the alternative is you being dissected by a bunch of creeps in hooded bath robes. So, I'm just going to assume you're in. And by the look of it, we've got a lot of work to do."

His gaze roamed over her, feeling far too intimate. Hazel grabbed at the threadbare blanket pooled at her hips. He cocked a curious eyebrow. "Can you even move?"

She shrugged, immediately wincing at the small movement.

Right on cue, the infirmary doors opened and Nemsen waltzed in. He balked, apparently forgetting he'd made a deal with Slaide to stay the night. Seeing Hazel sitting upright, limbs unbound, the color drained from his face.

The rotund healer scurried across the room to his workbench and frantically began preparing something. Glasses clinked, liquids sloshed, and before long he was shuffling over to them. Slaide instinctively stepped into Nemsen's way, barring his path to Hazel, forcing Nemsen to retreat a few steps.

"Master Elias—Slaide—the girl, she's awake."

"I have eyes. I can see she's awake. I was just explaining things to her. What's in your hands there?"

"I, well… You see, His Majesty requested she remain sedated. At least until we know more about her."

"Yeah, not happening. That may have been his prior direction, but she's my ward now." His next words were low and graveled. He spoke just low enough that she couldn't make out the words. "I can't exactly interrogate an unconscious person, can I?"

Nemsen shook his head. His fingers fumbled with the vial in his hands nervously, his internal struggle clear.

"No, sir. No, you can't." He sighed. "I know we talked about things, Slaide, but you'll understand why I still need to run this by the King. I can't lose my position here, much less my head, for disobeying direct orders. I have a family to feed."

"Do what you must, but in the meantime, no more drugs. No more sleeping draughts or poppyweed milk. I need her awake." He folded his arms across his chest.

Behind him, Hazel cleared her throat. "Not to intrude on your little conversation, but since it concerns me, I wonder if I might be included? Or at least know what in the name of the gods is going on here?"

Slaide turned to face her. "In time. For now, we need to get you into better quarters and cleaner clothes. When's the last time you bathed?" He scrunched his nose in disgust.

Hazel was aghast. She couldn't help the sorry state her body was in.

Slaide looked at Nemsen. "We're going to leave now. Do you and I still have an agreement? Or are you going to be a problem?"

Nemsen looked at the floor. "Yes, of course. It shall be as we discussed."

"Good. If Magnus has a problem, tell him to come find me himself."

Nemsen's eyes went wide, and he made to respond, but Slaide turned his back on the man. His heightened senses informed him of Nemsen's quiet departure, the doors hardly so much as creaking on his way out.

"Can you walk? Obviously, you've been bed bound for a few days, but can you try? I really don't want to carry you out of here."

Her mouth fell open. "You wouldn't dare."

"Better start moving." His grin was feral.

Hazel stared at him, unmoving. When Slaide sighed and moved toward her, she scrambled, attempting to get out of bed. Her erratic movements disturbed the cat, who yowled angrily at them both before hopping down from the bed and fleeing to a dark corner.

Once again, the pain in her ribs seared up her side. Her impossibly stiff joints protested and she winced. *Suck it up unless you want this monster touching you.* She slid forward, her feet touching the floor, and she braced herself as she shifted her weight onto her body.

And promptly fell to the cold, stone floor.

Slaide, to his credit—and Hazel's surprise—was immediately at her side. His face darkened as he looked her over, as though he was seeing how battered she was for the first time. Her infirmary-issued white tunic was askew, revealing the many hues of bruising covering her legs and arms. As he took in her injuries, something in the way he looked at her changed. At last, he met her eyes.

"Who did this to you?" The words were more growled than spoken.

She was startled at his change in demeanor, but as she thought about the actual question, she grew angry.

"You want to know who did this? Your people. Or at the very least, the people you work with. Work for. I don't know. The knights in their shiny armor? Yeah, them. Knocked an old woman unconscious and did *this* to me when I tried to protect her." She gestured to the length of her body.

Slaide tensed. She could see the anger in his eyes, in the way his expression changed. Perhaps she'd made a mistake speaking up, talking to him in such a way. Maybe this is how she would meet her end, escaping the clutches of one monster only to land in the lap of another.

He reached for her, and she cowered, closing her eyes. But the blow never came.

When she opened her eyes, Slaide was offering his hand, not reaching to strike her. Tentatively, she accepted it. His hand closed around hers, and it was surprisingly gentle. But when she attempted to pull herself up, her body faltered, and she collapsed.

Slaide caught her, bringing them face to face. There was that strange heat again warming her cheeks. This time, he looked away first, but not before conflict flashed across his features.

He stood, letting go of her hand. She watched him as he looked around the room, clearly thinking hard about something, the muscles in his jawline fluttering. Before her was a man fighting a very difficult internal battle, one Hazel wanted no part in.

She rolled to her knees, assuming it was now up to her alone to get to her feet. As she pressed her hands into the floor and attempted to raise her body, she found herself enveloped in muscular arms and hoisted—with overwhelming ease—into the air.

Hazel yelped. "Oof! Put me down! I don't need to be carried, and especially not like some fainting maiden!"

He looked down at her, and a coy smile spread across his face. "As you wish," he spoke as he pretended to drop her.

Hazel shrieked, expecting to crash to the floor. And then, much to her embarrassment, she realized he was still holding her. She let out a disgruntled *hmph* and folded her arms. *Sadistic asshole.*

"That was childish."

"No more childish than you refusing help."

"Is that what this is?"

He crossed his distractingly muscular arms. "Well, let's see. You are very much in pain and cannot stand, much less walk. The guest rooms in this castle are a *long* way from here, and we'll be taking many stairs. But please, by all means, I'll even race you there. But what we will not do is dawdle here any longer. I'm on a tight schedule as it is."

"I just don't understand why you're helping me. You're..."

"Not the helping type? Trust me, I've been waiting to come to my senses this entire time. But for the record, I'm not helping *you*. I'm helping *me*. Something about you has everyone in this castle up in arms, and that brings me joy. I thrive in chaos."

I was thinking more along the lines of a witch hunter who should probably have seen me executed by now, but sure. She simply said, "Charming."

"I try my best, sweets." He tossed her a sultry wink.

That gods-damned nickname again. Hazel curled a lip in disgust. "Well, what are you waiting for? I really *do* need a bath. Let's go."

"I thought you'd never ask."

Then, Slaide flung her over his shoulder like a rag doll, earning himself more than an earful of insults and expletives as he opened the infirmary door to the hallway beyond.

Clipped Wings

Being carted around by this brute was not her idea of a good time, but Hazel resigned to it despite her reservations. She'd spent too much energy trying to pummel Slaide into putting her down, and when he'd finally obliged, she discovered she was still in far too much pain to walk more than a few steps. So, she found herself in his arms again, much to her dismay.

They arrived at an archway with oaken double doors, which Slaide pushed through unceremoniously. "And this," he said with a grunt, "will be your home for the foreseeable future." He crossed the room to the wooden four-poster bed and tossed Hazel onto it as though he was offloading a sack of grain and not a woman.

"Hey! Take it easy!" she yelped.

"Says the girl who didn't want any help. Anyway, as I said, this is where you'll be staying. Phaedra will be attending you and is currently readying a bath."

Hazel was only half-listening as she took in her new surroundings. She flopped backward onto the thick, soft duvet and thought it must be stuffed with the most expensive down known to man, because damn was it luxurious.

"Are you even listening?"

"Hmm?"

"Fucking Hel, Hazel. I'm trying to give you some ground rules so you don't lose your head and you—"

But she was ignoring him again, cozying deeper into the covers and pillows. She was so, so tired. *I am* never *leaving this bed.*

"Ahem…"

Shit. Right. Currently in the same room—alone—with the most dangerous man in Aeos. "Err… Yes?" She found herself uncomfortable to be sharing this space with him. He could do whatever he wanted to her right now, and no one would know or care.

Apparently, he had a similar thought. "Witch or not, I'm beginning to think it really would be easier to kill you and be done with it. You're more trouble than you're worth." Slaide stalked toward her, causing her to slink up against the headboard, pulling her knees to her chest.

"Just stay out of trouble. Can you manage that? No, don't answer. Considering how you got here in the first place, I know for a fact you can't stay out of trouble. Keep in mind, I'll be around and checking in on you periodically, but I'm not always going to be here to rescue you."

Hazel rolled her eyes and pulled the covers back over her head without so much as another word. *You're the last person I'd want to rescue me, anyway.*

"Don't forget to bathe; you smell awful," he reminded her as he left the room.

Only when Hazel was certain the door had closed did she peek out from beneath her covers. For the first time since they'd entered, she was able to take in her surroundings in greater detail.

On the far wall to her right, there were two sets of floor-to-ceiling windows, each with a built-in window seat upholstered in red velvet. Heavy velvet curtains in a wine-stain red were pulled back on either side and tied with golden rope. Between them, a writing desk with a single drawer rested against the wall, complete with a small stack of parchment and an inkwell.

The four-poster bed was ornate, with whorls carved into the mahogany. The craftsmanship, though extensive, was exquisite and unlike anything she'd seen. Which, of course, was only fitting. She was in the home of the High King himself, after all.

Hazel's thoughts were interrupted by a tiny noise behind her. She turned to find a small yet statuesque woman standing there. No, not just a woman.

An angel.

She was curvy yet petite, with pinched features and much smaller wings than she would have expected. *Though I suppose that's fitting, seeing as absolutely nothing has been what I've thought it would be.*

The angel bowed low, revealing the intricate, delicate-looking wings on her back. When she stood, she spoke in a melodic voice the likes of which could only come from… well, an angel.

"Mistress, I am Phaedra. I do believe Master Elias told you I'd be attending you?"

"I—yes. He did. But it's alright, really. You don't have to worry about me."

"Worry, Mistress? I don't understand."

"Well, most people here don't trust me, and I can only assume Slaide—er, Master Elias—expects you to keep a watchful eye on me should I decide to do anything stupid?"

"No, Mistress. He said nothing of the sort. In fact, he told me you've had quite a harrowing few days and would need to be attended to until you are able to care for yourself."

Hazel didn't know what to say. Being in the presence of what she understood to be a supernatural being was disconcerting to say the least. But being waited on by one? No one talked about what went on in this castle, and they certainly never mentioned angelic servants.

"Mistress? If it's alright with you, I'll escort you to your bath now, lest it get cold."

"Oh, right. Thank you, Phaedra." She thought about attempting to cross the room to where Phaedra stood on her own, but seeing her hesitation, the angel appeared beside the bed.

"Please, allow me." She offered her arm. "I promise, I am stronger than I appear." There was a smile in her voice, but it didn't meet her face.

Hazel graciously accepted help, sliding from the bed and into Phaedra's arms. Despite her claims of being strong, Hazel noted the slight flutter of her wings as she steadied them both.

"I've got you, Mistress. Come, now. Let's get you to that bath."

Hazel desired privacy, but seeing as she couldn't maneuver her body quite right, nor lift her arms high enough to remove her shift, she found herself welcoming the angel's assistance. Sure, she'd shared her body with a couple of people in her lifetime, but she wasn't a fan of undressing in front of others. Despite her reservations, she supposed Phaedra was a woman in her own right, even if she was another species. And yet, she couldn't shake the overwhelming feeling of vulnerability roiling within.

As if sensing the tension in the room, Phaedra said, "It's alright, Mistress. You've nothing I haven't seen before." She smiled softly.

Hazel laughed awkwardly and swallowed her pride as the angel gently lifted the shift over her head.

And then there was the tub itself, fit for a king. It was porcelain, except for the gilded clawed paws on which it stood. A far cry from her former bathing experiences.

She tested the water and found it so hot it nearly scalded her skin. But she'd been caked in blood, sweat, and dirt for enough days she figured it was going to take the hottest water she could stand and a lot of scrubbing for her to feel whole again. Plus, hot water was a luxury. She'd only taken a few hot baths in her lifetime, and only when she'd fallen ill or injured.

And Phaedra was there, helping Hazel as she stepped into the tub, legs shaking like a fresh fawn in the spring. She held Hazel's hands and helped her lower her battered body into the steaming water.

Hazel hissed as she sunk her lower half in, the heat nipping at the sensitive skin. Though her cuts were well on their way to healing, the hot water made them feel torn anew. Her face pinched, eyes squinting as she tried to bear down and stay stronger than she felt.

"It helps sometimes if you breathe through it, Mistress. Deep, slow breaths."

Hazel did as she was told and though she was uncertain if it did anything to stave off the pain, it at least gave her something else to focus on. *Gods above, no wonder I was unconscious for so long.*

When she was finally resting comfortably, everything but her head below the surface, Phaedra retreated from the room without a word. Hazel opened her eyes, startled to find the angel gone. "Hello?" Her voice was so small, swallowed in the large bathing chamber.

Phaedra returned with a basket of what appeared to be soap, brushes, and vials of something. She smiled warmly. "Brushes, soaps, and scented oils, Mistress. For your choosing. I also have a few massage oils here that Master Elias delivered himself. The oils will help soothe the pain from your muscles and help them heal faster. There aren't many days until the trials start."

"I see. Well, thank you. You can just set them there beside the tub, and I'll pick one out."

Phaedra looked perplexed, as though conflicted on whether she really ought to leave.

Hazel sighed. "You're right. I'm not going to be able to do any of this myself, am I?"

"I suppose not, Mistress." She looked at Hazel with soft, pitying eyes.

"We may as well get to know each other then, eh? So. Which oil would you recommend?"

Phaedra, more than eager to help, jumped right into explaining the various properties and benefits of each herbal mixture, and once Hazel had selected one, she set it off to the side. Then, Phaedra grabbed a stiff-bristled brush and began working the goat's milk soap into it vigorously until it was frothed into a lather.

Initially, the bristles *hurt*. But as the scrubbing went on, Hazel found it almost calming. Phaedra was exceptionally careful around her cuts and bruises, or at least the more severe ones. To avoid them all would have meant neglecting to wash more than half of Hazel's body.

She next addressed Hazel's hair—the mangled, tangled mess of chestnut frizz streaked with mud and muck. Phaedra lathered her hair into a sudsy cloud and began working her fingers down to Hazel's scalp. *Oh, gods, this is incredible.*

Phaedra laughed softly, and Hazel wondered if she might have let out an audible moan. Her cheeks heated, though the color of her embarrassment was hidden by the pink flush from the hot water and intense scrubbing.

Once she was finished, the angel grabbed a small pail and began rinsing the soap from Hazel's hair and body. "There, now. Nice and clean." It was clear from her tone of voice Phaedra was proud of her handiwork.

The last part of this extensive, exhausting bathing ritual ended up being the most sensual, wonderful experience of her entire life. Phaedra set to work rubbing the lavender and lemongrass scented oil into her scalp and then moved down the back of her neck with strong fingers, driving away the soreness there. She did the same across Hazel's shoulders and back, careful not to get the oil into any healing cuts. Lastly, she pulled Hazel's hands from the water one at a time, patted them dry, and massaged the oil into them from her forearms to her fingertips.

At the end of it all, Hazel was as limp as steamed cabbage. Though her body was clean and invigorated, her eyes were heavy.

Phaedra helped her dry off and carefully escorted her back to the bedchamber. Once Hazel was situated comfortably, the angel made to take her leave. "Rest now, Mistress. I will return if you are summoned."

Fighting sleep, Hazel managed to crack one eye open. "Phaedra?"

"Yes, Mistress?"

"Thank you for your help," she said wearily.

"It is my pleasure to serve you, Mistress." She turned to leave.

"And Phaedra?"

"Yes, Mistress?"

"Please, call me Hazel."

Phaedra nodded. "As you wish, Hazel. Sleep well." She bowed deeply, and for the first time, Hazel noticed something unusual about the angel's wings. They were *clipped* in the same way a captive bird's would be. The thought turned her stomach sour and made her even more certain of one thing above all else.

The more time she spent in this castle, the less likely she was getting out alive.

Dinner Plans

She was so tired she didn't dream, and when she woke, Hazel found her hair was plastered to her face with drool. Overwhelmed by the urge to stretch her muscles, she elongated her limbs, a sea star reaching every direction on the ocean floor. She was surprised to find the stretch was far less painful than she'd expected. In fact, it was quite the opposite. Maybe there was something to those oils after all. The true test, however, would be in whether her body could withstand its own weight.

Hazel scooted to the edge of the bed, the task before her feeling as insurmountable as jumping off a cliff. She tempered her expectations. This could go very, very poorly. After all, it had only been a few hours, if the sunlight filtering in through the windows was any indication. The likelihood her body was ready for standing, let alone walking? Laughable at best.

She sucked in a sharp breath and held it, reaching for the floor with her toes. The process was painstakingly slow, her fear of the bone-jarring soreness gripping her wholly. She shifted her weight partially from the bed, allowing her body to be challenged just a little more. Her legs held. And the pain, though present, was duller than she anticipated.

Impressive.

Hazel shifted more and more of her weight onto her legs until she was standing on her own accord, half-expecting to collapse onto the floor at any moment. *Okay, so I can at least stand again.* And while it was no small victory, she knew she still had so far to go.

She let out a hefty breath and took a slow, hesitant step forward. Then another. The next step required her to remove her hand from the bedpost. No more safety net. She couldn't lie and claim it didn't hurt, because it did. But she could walk, even if her pace was slower than a garden snail.

Her next goal was the writing desk between the windows. If she could just make it to the desk, she could take a break in the chair. One foot in front of the other, over and over again, and before too long, she was there. It wasn't the worst thing she'd ever experienced. In fact, her body was a little less stiff after some movement. She'd be paying for it later, of course, but she allowed herself to enjoy the accomplishment for now.

The chair cushion was upholstered in red velvet. And she had to admit, it was soft. Not as soft as the comforting down duvet she'd left behind on the bed, but cushy, nonetheless. The desk was sturdy and crafted from white oak. Its surface was scratched and worn from use, marked with old ink stains, and watermarked with ringlets from a cup that sat in the same spot for far too long. She rubbed her hand across the surface, wondering what sort of scholars or noblemen had used this desk to draft their work.

Without warning or so much as a knock, the bedroom doors swung open, banging against the wall. Hazel whirled around to find Slaide standing there, mouth agape. He righted his face immediately, returning to his usual scowl.

He cleared his throat. "I actually wasn't planning on bursting in here like that. At least not right away." He laughed, and Hazel tried to figure out where the joke was. "Door was stuck."

She cocked a brow expectantly.

"So," he said, brushing invisible dust from his tunic, "I see you've managed to get out of bed."

He was pinned by her continued blank stare.

"Do we have a problem? I seem to remember pulling some strings earlier to get healing oils from the royal apothecary—at great personal risk, I might add. So, if you don't mind bottling that attitude back up and, oh, I don't know… trying the phrase *thank you* every now and then?

It won't kill you. Though existing in this castle without my help most certainly will."

"Do you often let yourself into women's rooms without knocking?" She crossed her arms over her chest. "I could have been changing."

"First of all, this is *my* room, sweets. Second, women *beg* me to come knocking. And third, I don't care. Unless you're hiding something unusual under that, which I very much doubt, you don't have anything I've never seen—or fondled—before. Anything else?"

Yes, for you to leave. "What do you want from me?"

Slaide stared at her pointedly. "You don't know what you are, do you?"

What was that supposed to mean? "I beg your pardon. I'm just a person. A human woman. What are you implying?"

"I'm not implying anything," he stated. "Just trying to see what you know—or don't know." He circled around her, each step more menacing than the last. "I'm trying to figure out how this foul-mouthed peasant brat from a backwater village ended up with such an enormous target on her back. Do you understand how many people want you dead?"

No. And I prefer it that way. She swallowed hard.

He ran a hand through his hair. "I figured as much. Here's the deal. You're going to do as I say, when I say it, how I say it. Got it?"

"But I—" Hazel protested.

"No." Slaide cut her off. "No *buts*. People with power want you dead. Worse still, some of them want to run tests on you, cut you open like an animal and see what makes you special."

Hazel averted her eyes. *Hel. I've landed myself in Hel.*

"Are you special?" he asked.

Hazel frowned. "What? No. You said yourself I'm just a peasant from a backwater town. I'm nobody."

"Right. Keep telling yourself that. But as long as *they* think you're somebody, you are. And that's not a good thing. Believe me when I tell you if given the option between their ministrations and death, you should choose death. Every time."

She sighed. This conversation was going nowhere. "Why are you so…" Her words trailed off as she tried to find the right way to describe him.

"So, what? Cheerful? Happy? *Handsome?*" Slaide wiggled his eyebrows.

"Impossible."

"Now, now. That's no way to talk to your savior. I still haven't heard a thank you, by the way."

"Thanks." *For nothing.*

Slaide uncrossed his arms. "We'll work on the delivery."

"Why am I still alive?" Hazel regretted the words as soon as they'd left her mouth. Something about his presence scared her less than it should. He *was* handsome. More than he had any right to be. But he was as deadly a man as she might ever come across, especially considering her newfound power. She could not let his looks disarm her.

He shrugged his shoulders. "Why not?"

Careful, Hazel. "Well, the King and damn near everyone else seems to think I have… forbidden magic." It nearly choked her to say those words aloud. "I've always understood this to be a kill first, ask questions later kind of thing."

Slaide laughed. "You're not wrong. Look at it this way. Consider me a cat and you a mouse. Maybe, like the cat, I just like to play with my prey every now and again. Haven't killed you yet—doesn't mean I won't." He winked at her.

"Reassuring," Hazel quipped.

"Well, what do you want from me? I can't have you thinking you're safe here."

"Oh, no. I think you've made that perfectly clear."

"Good. Now that we understand each other… ground rules."

"You mean there's more to this than just 'don't die'?"

"Such a loaded question. For now, let's start small. One: never leave this room unaccompanied. Two: do not under any circumstances try to escape. Three: always dress appropriately." He looked her up and down where she sat in the chair, eyes landing on where her shift was pulled up to mid-thigh. When he met her eyes, she blushed, looking away quickly. "Which means putting on actual clothes. Don't want to give anyone the wrong idea." He smirked.

Smug bastard.

"I had some clothes brought up while you were sleeping. Don't look at me like that. I didn't deliver them; Phaedra did. She's great, isn't she? As I was saying, she brought up a few things. Tunics. Dresses. *Underthings.*"

His grin was feral. "Though, you can always go without those. Up to you." He shrugged as though it wasn't the most inappropriate thing to say to someone he'd just met.

"And that brings us to rule four: be on time. Speaking of which, we're having dinner with your new dance instructor this evening, so do try to look presentable. I want to give Pimley some semblance of hope."

"Dance instructor?" she blurted. "You said I was going to be competing in some tournament. Not dancing. What are you going on about?"

Slaide smiled. "It's a week of fun and *entertainment* for the nobility, sweets. At the end of it all, we drink and dance and celebrate… and fu—"

"I get it. Thanks." Hazel cut him off.

"Of course you have to survive that long. Which," he looked her over in an assessing gaze, "let's just say I've got my work cut out for me."

Hazel rolled her eyes and scoffed at the absolute audacity of this man. *Barging in where he pleases and being a complete prick everywhere he goes.* But then a thought struck her. "Slaide," she began, "when I was… apprehended… I was wearing a necklace. A pendant from my mother. I was wondering—" she stopped talking as he reached into his pocket and pulled out something wrapped in silk.

She sucked in a sharp breath as he unwrapped it and held the delicate chain up before him, moon locket twisting gently in the air.

"I suppose you want this back?"

"Yes, I do. It was my mother's." So what if it also warned her when she was in imminent danger. He didn't need to know that bit of information.

His eyes narrowed. And then he stalked toward her, rolling his finger in a gesture commanding her to turn around. To *trust* this killer long enough to turn her back on him. She did, despite every fiber in her body screaming at her. Something told her if she'd been wearing her locket at that moment, it would have been very, very hot.

She heard his soft footsteps approach, warmth radiating from his body as he stopped behind her. Slaide loomed there for a moment, and Hazel closed her eyes, wondering if she'd made a mistake.

"Hair," he grumbled, voice gravelly and inconvenienced. Hazel gathered her copper locks with both hands and lifted it away, giving the monster of a man access to her neck. His arms reach around her then, one end of the fine silver chain in each hand. The quarter moon locket dangled in front of her. Without knowing why, she closed her eyes. Maybe it would be easier to die with her eyes closed?

Next thing Hazel knew, warm skin grazed her neck. It was slight, a featherlight touch. She stiffened and sucked in a sharp breath at the contact, and his hands froze in place. When his hands moved again, brushing the ultra-sensitive skin along her neck, the feeling spreading through her body was a rush of something else. It wasn't fear. It *was* confusing.

With deft hands, Slaide clasped the necklace. But his hands lingered against her skin for a beat longer than necessary—until Hazel turned her head enough to cast him a sidelong glance.

Slaide cleared his throat and stepped back from her, hands falling to his sides. His face flushed, and his eyes darted toward the floor for a moment. *Well, that was interesting.*

"Thank you," Hazel said, voice just above a whisper.

Just like that, the flush was gone, replaced by a predatory gleam. With a smirk, Slaide turned to leave her. As he closed the door behind him, he said, "Dinner is in half an hour. Don't be late."

She placed her forehead against the desk, heaving out a sigh she'd held in during the entire encounter. It was going to take some time to digest the information she'd just been given.

A *swish* came from behind her in the direction of the door, drawing her attention from the noise of her unpleasant thoughts. Hazel looked over her shoulder to find someone had slid something under the door.

She rose, slowly lifting her body out of the chair again, slightly annoyed that she had to move. As it had before, her body protested only slightly at the movement, stiff muscles complaining the most, and she was able to cross the room without much pain.

It was an envelope. She stooped to pick it up and was surprised to find it closed with the official wax seal. She carefully peeled back the wax, revealing the handwritten letter inside. It read:

Wear the green one.
- S

With a Side of Humiliation

Hazel stepped up to the doors behind her escort: a tall, broad-shouldered knight. She eyed his polished armor and the sword at his hip and wondered if his presence was more for her protection or everyone else's.

The man had hardly acknowledged her presence the entire exhausting walk from her room and ignored her few attempts at making conversation. The knight rapped his knuckles on the door twice to signal their arrival and palmed the iron door handle to pull the door on the right open. He nodded in her direction then, as if she was supposed to understand that to mean anything. When she just stared at him, he sighed audibly, making his exasperation clear.

"Enter," he growled.

She took a deep breath and stepped across the threshold, feeling much the same as a young girl playing dress up in her older sister's dress shoes. Except, she didn't have an older sister, and this was far from pretend play. The sound of her heels against the floor was jarring. She'd never worn high-heeled shoes. Never needed to, and she'd decided she could go her entire life without ever wearing them again.

After Phaedra had put the finishing touches on Hazel's hair and rouged her cheeks, she clasped her hands excitedly. When she looked in the floor length mirror, she could see why. It was a shocking transformation. Her skin was bright, bruises fading as the day stretched on. And despite wanting to do the exact opposite of what the note had suggested, she had to admit the green velvet, shape-hugging dress was the most flattering of them all. Clearly someone had good taste, as much as it pained her to admit it.

Hazel's wild mane had been tamed with Phaedra's help; the angel having teased the frizz out of it with some kind of floral-scented serum and then pinned part of it out of her face with an embellished emerald and silver hairpin—one that complemented her necklace. Phaedra smiled when she looked upon her masterful work, and it was easy to see why. She'd taken a plain girl from a meager village and turned her into someone who could just as easily pass for a nobleman's daughter. Maybe not quite a princess, but someone of higher birth, nonetheless.

The room was a quaint dining hall, clearly meant for entertaining a smaller, more intimate group of guests. Even so, the table at the center of the room had enough seating for eight people, though place settings had only been arranged for three.

Upon seeing her, a man she'd never met before—though it was easy enough to deduce this must be Pimley—rose from his chair abruptly, bumping the table and nearly knocking his wine glass over in the process.

Slaide laughed, apparently bemused by the show of respect. He grabbed his own glass and took a large swig before speaking.

"Settle down, Pimley, before you hurt yourself," he said. "Don't let the pretty outfit distract you from who and what she is. Need I remind you she is a prisoner here, facing potential treason charges? You don't need to stand in her presence."

Treason? It was the first time she'd heard the term thrown around.

"I—you mean—*this* is *her*?" He was baffled, expecting something else. *Charming.*

Hazel just stood there, hands clasped before her. She was a woman, not a broodmare at auction. Her locket was calm against her chest; warm, but not concerningly so. She ignored the urge to reach for it.

"The very same. Now sit. Both of you." Slaide gestured to the empty chairs.

Pimley sat, not daring to remove his eyes from Hazel. He was a small man; not only short in stature, but his fine-boned frame looked light enough to blow away in a strong gust of wind. And on top of it all, he was no youngster. Quite the opposite, in fact, if his wrinkled, sun-spotted skin and hunched posture was any indication.

Hazel approached the table and a serving boy appeared at her side to pull her chair out and assist her in seating herself. This was all so unusual to her. Of course, she knew it was expected in high society for men to stand when a woman entered the room, to hold the door for her and to pull out her chair… she'd just never experienced it herself. This was simply not the way she'd imagined it would play out, if ever.

No, she never expected a gallant knight in shining silver armor, nor some nobleman's son. She would have been happy enough with a kind gentleman who truly cared about her—even just a little. Unfortunately, she'd yet run across someone who did, outside of Zeke. These two certainly did not, even though Pimley had—however inadvertently—tried to show her respect.

Slaide grew annoyed. "Can we stop with the theatrics? Let's all make sure we're on the same page, yes? This girl is not a princess. She's not nobility. She's not even a servant here. She is a prisoner of the crown under my wardship. Moving forward, we will *not* be showing her the courtesies afforded to those women. Understood?"

Heads nodded.

As she took her seat, she noticed the servant boy's hand twitched as though his instincts wanted him to help her scoot her chair up to the table. But, per Slaide's demands, he refrained.

The place setting before her was overwhelming and unnecessarily complicated for… whatever this was. There was a large plate, a small plate, several spoons, forks, and knives, a napkin, and two drinking glasses. Hazel couldn't begin to fathom what all of it was for, but she was certain she was about to find out.

Slaide must have caught her gawking. "Overwhelmed by fine dining? Gods above, I really do have my work cut out for me."

Hazel tripped over her words, trying to seem as though she wasn't seeing all of this for the first time. "No—I just, well… we don't dine like this where I'm from. It seems like overkill for dinner."

"Oh, that's right! You see Pimley," he said leaning toward the man, "she's from one of those rural villages. You know the ones. Larksridge, I think it was? Not that it matters."

He said it as though it was inconsequential. And maybe it was. But he had remembered the name of her town, even if he did so in a backhanded manner. Despite being completely clueless as to what his angle was, he was paying attention. At least some of the time. *That should concern you, Hazel. It's not endearing.*

Their chatter was interrupted by the groan of the doors as they opened to a stream of waiters carrying silver platters of food. Wordlessly, three men approached the table and placed their platters along the center.

It was nothing short of spectacular. The sort of feast that would have been reserved for holidays and special occasions at home, and to be shared by far more than three people.

The heaped platters could have served all of Larksridge with some to spare. She couldn't even tell what all of it was, save for the obvious tarts, pies, and some sort of roasted bird.

As she was looking over the spread, another man entered the room and she gathered from his attire he must be the chef responsible for the mouth-watering meal before her.

He cleared his throat. "Gentlemen and… lady," he started, eyes shifting toward Slaide as he wrung his hands. Slaide rolled his eyes. "This evening's meal consists of three courses. The first course consists of our lighter fare: oatcakes, bone broth for sipping, sea-brined olives, pickled vegetables, and assorted cheeses. The main course includes rosemary roasted duck with a cranberry red wine reduction, sherry-braised venison shank, poached trout with pickled onion, potato and bacon pie, and summer mushroom pasty. Finally, for dessert, we have prepared for you a cream custard tart, cherry pottage, rose pudding, and buttercrust pastries filled with exotic dragonberry jam, drizzled with dark chocolate, and sprinkled with a pinch of salt harvested from the White Sea."

Gods above, am I dreaming? He'd said so many buzzwords, described so many delicious-sounding dishes, she couldn't think straight. *I'm either dreaming, or I'm dead.* She couldn't wrap her head around anyone feeding this sort of meal to a commoner, let alone a prisoner suspected of high treason.

"Thank you, Ernest," Slaide said.

Dismissed, Ernest bowed deeply and turned to exit the room.

Hazel was on the edge of her seat, a starving wolf ready to pounce on its first good meal in ages.

Slaide caught her ogling the food and sipped his wine. "Dining rule number one: don't drool on the food."

Hazel blanched, collecting herself and wiping at her mouth only to find he'd been teasing her. She scowled. "Is that what this is then, some kind of test?"

He dabbed the corner of his mouth with his napkin. "Not so much a test as it is the first of many lessons. Though if it was a test, I'd say you're not off to the best start. Unfold your napkin and place it in your lap. Now, bear in mind, most of this will be done on your behalf at the feast or the ball. However, if you're going to fit in with the attending nobility, you'll be expected to adhere to the high-societal rules for ladies. That means starting at square one. Do you understand?"

"I do, but—"

"No. No buts. You are either in, or you're out. Half-assing this won't work. You want to know something? Magnus and his vultures don't think you have it in you to do any of this. So, you either commit, or we're done here and you prove them right."

When had she signed up for any of this? Just days ago, she was supposed to be attending her first ever Tournament of Champions with hopes of exploring the town, tasting new food, meeting new people, and enjoying the exciting challenges and events.

Now she was a not-prisoner-prisoner being forced to learn and adhere to the rules and customs of high society by a man feared by most of the kingdom. And then, what? At some point she was expected to fight other competitors? Risk her *life*? She was somewhere she had no business being and had no way out.

"Well?" he asked as though she had a choice. Go to this ball or…

"Fine. I'm in. But don't patronize me; I'm not a child."

They held one another's gaze in an unspoken challenge, the heat of his molten amber eyes burning all the way to her core.

Pimley, forgotten, coughed rather intentionally from his side of the table.

The tension shattered, and Hazel looked at her lap as pink flushed her cheeks.

Slaide let out a breath, his shoulders visibly relaxing. "So. Let's start over, shall we? Hazel, this is Master Pimley. He's been the royal dance and etiquette instructor for longer than I've been alive. Usually, his time is spent educating our youth as they come of age and begin attending parties, so he is used to young, inexperienced students.

"Master Pimley, this is Hazel Callahan, hailing from Larksridge, a small village to the southwest of King's Crossing. While she is currently a prisoner of the crown, she is also my ward, and I alone am responsible for her for the duration of our training. She does not bite nor fight, though she stands accused of using unauthorized magic and attacking a knight. That is something to be wary of, though I've yet to see her use it or even consider using it. Frankly, I'm not convinced she can. Regardless, it would be wise to keep your guard up. Otherwise," he shrugged, "we'll just have to see how fast she learns."

Pimley—for the first time since she'd entered—smiled a broad, toothy smile at her.

Unsure of what the proper conduct would be, but certain she'd be corrected if she was in the wrong, Hazel stood. "It is both an honor and a pleasure to meet you, Master Pimley, and I look forward to your instruction." She then performed her best attempt at a curtsy.

When she rose, Slaide was looking upon her with raised brows, and Pimley's smile had doubled. He clasped his hands before him and rubbed them together eagerly.

"Hazel, my dear, the pleasure is all mine."

The meal was a disaster. Hazel apparently had not the slightest clue how to eat properly—according to Slaide, anyway—and it was a wonder she'd made it so far in life without his supervision and guidance. Pimley at least approached his corrections with sensitivity and kindness. Slaide, on the other hand, did his best to belittle and embarrass her.

Each time she moved to take a bite, reach for a new dish, or pick up the wrong knife, she was corrected by Pimley or chided by Slaide. She preferred the former and would have preferred even more if they'd both just let her eat. But, no. It wouldn't do to have some uncouth peasant spoiling the evening for the nobles with her lack of decorum. All she wanted was to stab Slaide in the eye with her fork. Didn't matter which eye. Didn't matter which fork, either. She reached for a slice of bacon and potato pie, glaring at him.

"Forgetting something?" he questioned.

Hazel rolled her eyes so far, it was a wonder they didn't get stuck. "Pass the potato pie."

Her demand was met with a raised brow, and no potato pie.

"Dear sir, won't you *please* pass a slice of that bacon and potato pie?" she asked in her most heinous impression of a whiny noblewoman.

"Better, but next time without the sarcasm." He reached across the table, handing her a lame excuse for a slice of potato pie. It was more of a sliver than a slice. And she loved potatoes. And bacon. And pie. She frowned.

"Hazel, dear, I think what Master Elias is trying to impress upon you is the… seriousness… of the situation you've found yourself in. Your beauty will unfortunately only get you so far among the nobility. They have expectations for how one, especially a young, unwed woman such as yourself, should behave. If you're found to be… under-performing… well, these people can be quite cruel. That's all." *Oh, just going to ignore the whole magic thing entirely, I see? As though my manners, not my powers, should be my biggest worry.*

She looked from Pimley to Slaide pointedly. "Is it really so hard to show some kindness? Maybe a little patience? Because clearly, *he* can manage talking to me like I'm a human being instead of a dog."

Slaide gave her a glance devoid of pity. "Actually, I'm usually nicer to dogs. But I *like* dogs."

Pimley dropped his head into his hands. Slaide laughed and swished his wine glass before taking another sip.

Hazel groaned. *Insufferable bastard.* She muttered something inaudible under her breath before stuffing her mouth full of pie. It was damn near half of the "slice" she'd been given.

"What was that? Couldn't hear you," Slaide commented.

Hazel went to open her mouth, but quickly closed it, remembering her manners for once. Back home where it was just her and Pa, she didn't have to worry about all these shitty rules. They'd laugh with their mouths full of food and mead, talk over one another, and belch loud enough to make a mountain troll blush. Gods, she missed him.

Her stomach twisted into a knot at the thought of her father, and though she'd barely eaten, her appetite vanished. One hand flew to the locket. With the other, she set her fork down abruptly with more of a clatter than she'd intended and dabbed at her lips with the napkin.

"Thank you, gentlemen, for this wonderful dinner. If I may, I will take my leave now." She pushed her chair away from the table without waiting for permission to leave.

"Whoa there. Slow down. What just happened?" Slaide asked, setting his glass down.

Despite Slaide's earlier warning, Pimley stood as she did. Slaide shot him an accusatory glare, and he sat, clearly flustered.

Hazel slapped her napkin on the table and spun on her heels, making for the doors. She nearly head-butted the door, half-expecting it to open on her behalf, but managed to thrust an arm out at the last moment. She shoved through the door, shocking the guard who simply watched her pass.

"Hazel!" Slaide called after her. "You're not excused!"

But she was out of earshot, her clopping heels echoing down the corridor.

Gossip

Hazel's feet ached. She just wanted to get back to her room, but her swollen toes made it more of a challenge than it should have been. Was she even going the right way? Fed up, she popped both shoes off, deciding instead to carry them. A passing servant eyed her, but said nothing. Hazel wondered if it was a crime to be without shoes in the castle corridors. She decided she didn't care.

As she padded around a corner, a door opened, and voices floated out from within. She slunk back around the safety of the wall, not entirely wanting to be seen in her current state. She decided to wait them out, but hadn't expected the ensuing conversation.

"And I just don't know if His Majesty is taking this as seriously as he should. The attacks are coming more and more frequently," came the first voice.

"Aye. And did you hear about the rumors coming from the Borderlands? Folks on the Outskirts have been reporting strange happenings. Some man came into one of the Outskirts villages looking for help, claiming his homestead had been ransacked by monsters." This man's voice was deeper, richer than the first, accented as though he were from another part of the continent.

"And what of that lass who used magic and tried to take down one of the kingsguard? Word has it she's here, right under our noses, and not even scheduled for execution!"

That'd be me, Hazel thought.

"But surely he has his reasons," uttered the second man.

"Hmph. If you say so. Between you and me, I think she has them all in her thrall. She's controlling them. Manipulating them with her mind, as witch-kind do."

This earned a laugh from the second man, who clapped his comrade on the back. "You've been reading too many children's tales, you ass."

She risked a peek around the corner. The men had their back to her for now. She suspected they were noblemen by their attire, the bold-colored fabrics trimmed in gold. She had no way of discerning which houses they were from, but it could prove useful as long as they couldn't hear her heart thumping against her ribs.

"Yeah, well, I also heard she's from the same town where a man was murdered. The butcher of all people, cut down in the street by some old man. Some say the old man was justified, that the butcher was possessed by some creature and attacking villagers and livestock. Seems far-fetched, but then again, very little seems out of the question these days."

The other man grunted his agreement.

Her blood ran cold. It couldn't be, could it? They were talking about Pa and Jonas. But *possession*? Was the Striga capable of such a thing? Maybe she'd returned to finish what she'd started.

Hazel backed away from the corner, hand covering her mouth to hide her shock. Her mind was racing laps, and her heart sank as both hands clasped the pendant. It was warm. The rumors were evolving, and they'd reached the capitol. *Gods, if anyone harmed him…*

She thumped into something solid, and a hand clasped her shoulder. Hazel shrieked, but another hand slapped over her mouth, cutting off the sound. She was whirled around by her shoulders and came face to face with Slaide.

For fuck's sake. "Oh, it's just you," she said.

"Lucky for you, yes. It's just me."

"I will consider myself lucky once I am out from under your thumb." She brushed him off.

"I've thought about you *under* a number of things. But I'll admit, my thumb wasn't on that list. However, I'm not picky."

She grumbled with disgust.

"Where were you going, anyway?" He was frowning. He was always frowning about something, if he wasn't laughing at his own stupid jokes.

"Back to my rooms. Where else?"

"Right. Well, I'd leave you to it, but you're in the wrong wing of the castle. Your rooms—*my* rooms—are in the east wing. You took a left when you should have gone right. So unless you were planning on eavesdropping some more, you might want to follow me."

"First, I wasn't eavesdropping. I was trying to avoid them, actually." She crossed her arms. "Second, I knew where I was going. I was going the long way." She most definitely did not know where she was going.

"Suit yourself. Just so you know, if you keep going that way, you'll end up somewhere you don't want to be. But hey, if you want to take yourself to the dungeons, I'm sure Magnus will be pleased. Saves everyone else the effort when he decides that's where he wants you after all. And... are those your shoes?"

Dungeons? Helfire... "Yes. They are. And they're absolutely dreadful. The real crime should be making ladies wear these around pretending they're happy about it. Men could never."

A small laugh escaped him, a smile just reaching his face before he shook it off. "No, you're probably right. The men around here could never. Speaking of which, who *were* you spying on?" He pushed past her, nosing just past the corner. "Ah, I see. Holden Marsh and Killian Giles. Two of the biggest gossips in His Majesty's retinue. Hear anything interesting?"

As a matter of fact... "What? No. I told you I wasn't eavesdropping. I'm going back to my rooms now." She turned, shouldering past him nearly making it out of arm's reach when Slaide snatched her by the wrist.

"Gods damn it Slaide, let me go!" she hissed.

"I'm taking you to your rooms, and you're going to tell me what's going on. Because *that* little stunt you pulled with Pimley wasn't cute. I worked hard and made promises I have no desire to keep in order to—"

Her eyes welled. "Have you ever stopped to think about someone besides yourself for even a moment? No. I guess not."

"Temper, temper. Better get it under control, sweets. Or else I can give you back to Magnus. Who will probably—no, gladly—hand you over to the mages."

She yanked her arm out of his grasp and turned away, walking in what she assumed—if Slaide could be believed—was now the right direction. After a dozen steps, it was evident he wasn't following her, so she glanced over her shoulder. "What're you—"

He was standing in the same spot, a thin-lipped smile drawn across his face. His arms were crossed, and he had his weight shifted to one side, ever the smug bastard. "Shh." He shooed her with both hands. "I was taking a moment to admire the view."

Hazel's repulsed groan could probably be heard three hallways over as she stomped off.

"For what it's worth," he hollered after her, "I was right about the green dress!"

Mirror, Mirror

When she arrived back at her rooms, Hazel wanted to collapse into her bed and stay there forever. Though the oils and tinctures were working something akin to magic on her injuries, she still found herself depleted after traversing the many stairwells and corridors. She stopped at the double doors and leaned forward, thumping her forehead against the wood. She huffed a breath.

Footsteps sounded down the hall behind her. Gods, she just wanted rest.

Slaide, unfortunately, wanted to talk. And she was in no shape to fight him on it.

She pushed one door in, stumbling into the room and just out of reach.

"Hazel," he grumbled. He'd been trying to chat the entire walk back to no avail.

A well-timed release of the door left it slamming in his face.

She limped across the room and plopped herself onto the bed, a sigh of relief escaping her lips as she sunk into the down-filled duvet. Her momentary bliss was interrupted by the doors crashing open, and she found herself sighing a second time, exasperated by his persistence.

"Hazel."

Maybe if I just lay here, he will leave me alone.

"I have all day, sweets." He plucked an orange cat hair off his jacket, pondering it for a moment before discarding it on the floor.

She rolled over, grunting her dismissal.

"Look. I don't know what happened back there, but I am trying to find out so I can… help you? So we can move on from this… whatever this is."

"Go. Away."

"No can do. Your leash may be longer than most, but make no mistake—you're still tethered to me." He crossed the room, approaching her side of the bed.

"Then maybe you should pull it a little tighter," she said as she rolled away from him.

The air was snatched out of the room, leaving a deafening silence between them. She turned to look at him, only to find his stare had darkened, giving him an uncomfortably feral expression.

"Say that again," he growled.

Nope. Not doing that. She rolled her eyes. "Fine." She sat up halfway, adjusting the green dress.

Slaide relaxed and walked over to the window, looking out over the stable yards.

Hazel took a deep breath. "All of the rules, preparing for this tournament, all the adjustments… it's just so much. I didn't ask for any of this." She looked at her hands. Cursed hands and cursed powers. She hadn't asked for any of it, and it was ruining her life. "I have always been a plain, simple person. A nobody. Pa and I lived on our farm forever. Our cottage and the inn are where I've spent most of my time, and up until a few days ago, I'd never been outside of Larksridge. My entire world has been turned upside down, and my own father doesn't even know I'm alive." She dropped her face into her hands.

"So, tell him," Slaide said as if it were really that simple.

She whirled on him, preparing to bite his head off, but he was gesturing at the writing desk and unused parchment there.

"I can write to him?" There was no way it was that simple. *Witch. Killer. It will mean the death of me if I forget that.*

"I don't see why not. Bear in mind it will be read by multiple people to check for code words or encryptions. You can't talk about anything you've seen or heard here, plan an escape, request a rescue… you get the idea."

Hazel considered it. She did want to ask him about the rumor she'd overheard, but perhaps it would have to wait. She sighed and slid herself from the bed, stifling a groan when her feet touched the floor.

"What would I even say? I have nothing to hide, and I've learned nothing about this place other than everything is a secret. I am just a daughter who misses her father. We are all each other has in the world." And… Agnes. Holy gods. The thought struck her harder than the guardsman the night she was arrested.

"Agnes," she blurted. "My… she… the other woman I was brought in with. What became of her?" Her heart was in her throat. She hadn't even had a moment to think about her beloved Agnes.

Slaide considered her for a moment. And then he looked as though a thought had hit him. "Ah. Was that her name?"

Was? Please, please let her be ok.

"She's been returned home, to the best of my knowledge. She took a hard hit to the head that night. Didn't remember a thing. Though, if what they say is true, you probably prevented it from being much worse for her." He eyed Hazel thoughtfully. "That was brave of you. Stupid, but brave."

She looked away, unsure what to make of the statement. Was it a compliment? Did she care? "I'm just glad to hear she's alright," she said.

Silence stretched between them.

Hazel pulled out the desk chair. She smoothed her dress and took a seat on the plush velvet cushion. She gathered the materials she needed to pen the letter, finding everything but a quill.

A hand appeared over her shoulder, holding a sleek, black feather. No, not a feather. A writing quill. She grasped it, meeting Slaide's gaze as he looked down at her, those golden eyes burning with the heat of ten thousand suns. "Don't mess this one up. It happens to be my favorite."

Hazel found herself giddy with childlike joy, smirking mischievously at the quill as she took it.

And then she began to write.

Once Slaide had taken his leave, Hazel's letter in hand, she collapsed into the bed.

Her body was tired, but her mind refused to turn off. So, she lay there, quiet and unmoving, hoping she could just… go to sleep.

Realizing her mind wasn't going to give in, Hazel climbed out of bed and decided to get to know her surroundings a little better. She grabbed the chamberstick and candle from the bedside table before slowly making her way around the room.

There wasn't much in the way of decoration. No family photos adorning the walls. No trinkets or personal items. In fact, besides the ornate bed and curtains, there wasn't much to say about the space at all.

Beyond the full-length windows overlooking the gardens and forest beyond, the bright moon began to peek over the treetops. It illuminated the room so fully, she almost didn't need the candle at all.

Hazel followed the light it cast into the room to where it met the floorboards. It was then she spied the tapestry hanging in a forgotten corner.

As she approached, Hazel discovered a depiction of their entire pantheon of gods, plus extra she didn't recognize.

In the middle, the elemental gods were represented—the ones she was familiar with. But below them… additional godlike beings took up residence in the Underworld. And above, a goddess with pale skin and flowing white hair was one with the moon, seeming to channel its power. Opposite her, a dark-skinned male figure was postured in the same fashion with the sun. *Celestial gods.* She wasn't sure where the name came from, but it fit all the same. She'd never seen anything of the sort.

A sudden draft sent chills up her spine. Gooseflesh pimpled her arms. But the windows were shut and so was her door.

Hazel frowned. But wait…

Carefully, she pulled the tapestry forward to peer behind it, finding nothing but a stone wall. Not that she had expected some long-forgotten hidden passageway that might spell her escape, but it would've been nice.

Across the room, the handle to her door turned and jangled, as though someone on the other side was fiddling with the lock.

Hazel's heart jumped into her throat as questions assaulted her mind. She should be sleeping, not snooping. But why was someone entering her room, knowing she should be asleep?

She blew out the candle and slipped behind the tapestry just as her door creaked open, silently hoping the room was dark enough to hide the obvious lump behind it. Her fingers itched to reach for the locket as it grew uncomfortable against her chest.

Whoever it was took three steps into the room before retreating back into the hallway. Hazel released a sigh of relief, relaxing her body into the cold stone against her back.

It shifted behind her with a click, groaning low like some awakened beast.

Before she could react, Hazel fell backward into nothingness, with nothing solid to grasp until the hard, dusty floor rose to meet her. She coughed through the cloud of dust as she righted herself.

But to her horror, the wall she'd somehow fallen through was already closing, sealing her off from her room and leaving her in darkness.

She pushed to her feet, lunging at the wall where the door had been moments before. She searched for anything, any way back in, but there were no loose stones, no hidden buttons. Clearly, she wasn't getting back the way she came.

Hazel turned to face the room she'd entered, surveying her surroundings once the dust cleared. She was in a small antechamber—high above her, a small, barred window allowed in a sliver of light. On the far wall, there was an opening about knee high.

After inspecting it, Hazel knew what she needed to do. It seemed safe enough, and her options were… limited, at best.

On the other side of the tunnel, Hazel brushed cobwebs away and dusted off her nightdress. This room was vast and long forgotten.

It was a library. An old, abandoned library, but a library, nonetheless. Notably missing… the books. Empty shelves filled the space, and the tables arranged near the looming windows were coated in a thick layer of dust.

Hazel walked down one dark aisle toward the center of the room. Something thumped to the floor several aisles up, and she froze, every fiber of her being on alert. *What in the gods…* Her locket *thrummed* against her skin, as if pulling her toward the sound. It had never urged her *toward* something; only warned against it. So, she obeyed.

As she peered from behind a bookcase, Hazel found the culprit: a small leather-bound tome. At first glance, the shelves had appeared bare, but perhaps someone had missed a book or two in their clean out

She picked it up, noting the ancient runes along the spine, etched into the leather. She couldn't make heads or tails of the symbols but thought the inside might hold more information. Except… it couldn't be opened. Not by her, anyway. It was bound by an obsidian lock with no place for a physical key. *Fascinating.* She'd heard of magical locks before, but seeing one in use was something else.

Hazel slid the book into the pocket of her nightdress, trying to ignore the way her locket damn near vibrated beneath her shift. Was it related somehow to the book? Maybe, if she was lucky, her magic would gain her entry beyond the dusty cover. But that was a problem for later. She still needed to find a way out.

The space was grand, and at one point, probably spectacular. The dark emerald velvet curtains were sun-bleached. The oak tables were scratched and worn from years of use, covered in cobwebs and a thick layer of dust. But there were no doors to speak of, at least not that she'd seen.

Walking along the empty stacks wishing she'd grabbed a shawl, a strange object caught her attention. In a corner ensconced in shadow, a cream-colored sheet loomed. It was nearly touching the ceiling and as she approached, she felt as though it could swallow her whole. She reached out to touch the sheet, and it fell.

Hazel yelped, unable to hold it in. But nothing could have prepared her for what was beneath.

It was a mirror, or at least looked as though it *should* be a mirror. Except there was no reflection. The glass was as still and dark as a motionless lake at midnight. Its frame was wrought from fine silver, with twisting vines and leaves so intricate they might as well be alive. Woven in among the vines were roses and briarthorn. Unable to resist the childish temptation, Hazel reached out to touch a silver rose petal and pricked her finger on one of the thorny stems. She recoiled, sucking away the blood that pooled immediately at her fingertip.

The mirror's surface came to life, rippling from the center outward as it formed her reflection. A visage drenched in moonlight, her hair was a wild, living flame as her gemstone eyes sparkled.

It spoke, then, in a language she'd never heard. Something visceral, vibrating down to the very marrow of her bones.

Then a booming voice came, deep and mysterious. Melodic and ancient.

"Who bares their soul to the Mirror of Truth?" the mirror asked.

What was she going to do, ignore it? It couldn't be talking to anyone else. "Hazel," she whimpered. "Hazel Callahan."

The mirror groaned. It spoke again with contempt in its voice. "Interesting. I wonder… does she lie to me… or to herself? I know no *Hazel Callahan*. But I do know the blood coursing through her veins. I have tasted it before. Hmm. No matter, though. I tell lies too."

Hazel gulped audibly.

"I am the Mirror of Truth. Though if I am honest, as a Mirror of Truth should be, I don't find my name all that fitting. You see, I don't *only* tell the truth. In fact, I promise to tell exactly one lie. Two truths and one *un*-truth. But I'm not going to tell you which. That's the fun of it. Though I suppose not everyone finds it enjoyable. In fact, I've driven a few mad over the years." Hazel was completely taken aback, wondering if it would be rude to ask the mirror who it was, or used to be. It was far too human to not be a cursed being.

After a few quiet moments had passed, the mirror spoke again. "Are you ready, Hazel Callahan?"

She nodded. What choice did she have? Besides, her locket was abnormally calm in the presence of this enchanted mirror. Perhaps it was harmless.

The surface of the mirror swirled, distorting Hazel's reflection until it was gone. "What you are about to see cannot be unseen. Two things are true, one make-believe, a glimpse of the past, or what is yet to be. Remember, the strongest are not those who can parse out the lie, but those who can live with the truth. And so, let us begin."

An image formed on the mirror then. A somber, rainy day where dark clouds blotted out the sky. Men and women dressed in black huddled together beside a giant pile of kindling. Upon the pile… a body. A mourning dirge rose up from the crowd slowly, amidst choked sobs and wails and Hazel understood what she was witnessing; it was a funeral pyre. She approached the women at the front but did not recognize them. Her eyes landed upon the deceased woman, taking in her too-young face, evidence of a life cut short. A face framed by kohl black hair streaked with white, the long strands draped delicately past her shoulders to lie upon her white gown.

A stunning woman, even in death.

Hazel's eyes snagged on a familiar face, and her heart fell into her stomach.

Agnes. Standing just to the right of where she rested, Agnes looked upon the woman with sorrow in her bloodshot eyes, wiping away a tear. She approached the woman and withdrew a small brown book from within her mourning robes, tucking it beneath the woman's clasped hands.

"Take this to the Otherrealm with you. Watch over us, especially your daughter," she whispered.

Holy gods. She heard the unspoken words. Somehow, as though the answer came somewhere from within her soul, she knew. It was her mother.

But it was no surprise to find out she was dead. Hazel had always suspected this, even when she thought Connall's late wife and her mother were one in the same. Both had met tragic fates, regardless. But the book… she reached for her pocket to find it was still there.

Witches gathered around the pyre and chanted, including Agnes. Between sobs, they conjured an enormous blue flame which was set upon the kindling. And moments later, everything was engulfed. Hazel watched as her mother's body dissolved into a million blue and white butterflies and disappeared in the column of smoke. And with them, the images dissolved and reformed into something else entirely.

That, Hazel decided, *was undoubtedly a truth. One down, one to go.* Perhaps this wouldn't be so difficult after all.

The new image formed slowly at first, then all at once Hazel was thrust into a fierce battle.

And in the middle of the fray was Slaide.

A caravan of wagons was ablaze and bodies were strewn about, some cut down by a blade, others by something else.

It didn't take long to see how they'd met their end. Slaide was outnumbered and should have easily succumbed to his foes. But Hazel watched in horror as he reached up and called lightning down from the sky upon his adversaries—completely obliterating them.

When the next round of enemies moved in on him, Slaide called forth his shadows and they bled from him in a hungry frenzy. They sought and destroyed everything they touched, leaving empty husks in their wake.

Another easy one. This is the other truth. Hazel was certain. This was the Slaide she'd been warned about: a butcher of men, women, and children alike.

But then… Slaide climbed into the back of one of the engulfed wagons. When he emerged coughing and sputtering, he cradled a young boy in his arms, unconscious from the smoke.

He ran the child's limp body to the edge of a forest, where he was met by a woman, who took the child into her arms before disappearing.

After handing him off, Slaide dashed back to the caravan, searching for more survivors. Each time, he carried them to the woods, where he was met by another man or woman, who would then carry or drag the person to safety.

Hazel scoffed. Clearly, she'd been too quick to judge this image in the beginning, for this was most certainly *not* representative of the Slaide she knew. The self-serving prick would never…

So the next vision she'd see would be a truth. It had to be.

As Slaide's rescue efforts faded into smoke and flame, a new one appeared. Hazel was looking at herself, asleep in her room back on Connall's homestead… tossing and turning mid-nightmare as she so often did.

The vision shifted, depicting a beautiful bronze-skinned woman approaching their cottage. Hazel stiffened. She'd never seen this woman before.

The woman crouched down, writing something in the dirt with her fingers, then leveling her gaze on their home. It was as though Hazel could feel the weight of that stare even through the mirror.

Within, Hazel could be heard mumbling something, attempting to shout at some unseen foe. The woman approached with caution, but with concern written on her face in the form of furrowed brows.

In a flash, she was gone, replaced by an oversized orange cat, who then hopped up onto the windowsill and into Hazel's bedroom.

What in all the gods. Hazel's face twisted. No. She was certain the orange cat she'd been accompanied by was nothing more than just that—most definitely *not* a human in disguise. That was ridiculous.

And yet, she was no longer certain of anything. Her mother's death was a given. Slaide was a bloodthirsty monster. And the cat was just a cat.

"You lied," Hazel said, voice wavering.

"Why yes, I did. But only once," the mirror replied.

"No." She took a step back. "More than one of those things was a lie."

"You're so certain?"

"I'm not playing these games anymore," Hazel insisted. On cue, the locket warmed.

"Oh, but on the contrary, my dear," the mirror crooned, "the games have just begun."

Under Pressure

HAZEL backed away and turned to run, immediately slamming into something solid.

No. *Someone.*

Hazel thumped off the wall-like body, landing on the time-worn floor with a thud. The impact forced the air from her lungs, and her chest heaved as she tried to regain her breath. But when she looked up, her heart skipped a beat.

Slaide towered over her, looking as unbothered as ever.

Hazel looked around the room, brows dipping in confusion. *But where…?*

"You look surprised to see me," he said, his smooth-as-whiskey voice washing over her.

"Of course I am," Hazel snapped. "How the Hel did you get in?" *And how do I get out?*

"You should know by now I have my ways. Besides, I live here. You think I don't know about the secret, walled-off library?"

Okay, fine. "Maybe, but did you know there was a secret passageway in your own damn room that dumps you in here if you lean too hard on the wall?"

Slaide's reaction was almost unnoticeable, just a shift in posture. But it said more than words ever could.

"It's better if you don't know the answer to that question, sweets." He smirked and broke eye contact as he bent at the waist to pick something up.

Hazel blanched when he stood up holding the leather-bound book in his hand.

"And stealing, no less?" He wagged a finger at her, stepping into her space and handing the book back.

She snatched it out of his hand and retreated a step. Sure, his allure was intoxicating, but she was on such dangerous ground here. A witch testing her luck with a witch hunter. Quite literally flirting with death.

Slaide noticed the mirror, as though it wasn't towering over both of their heads the entire time.

He side-eyed her through narrowed eyes. "Did you?"

Hazel shrugged, not wanting to reveal too much.

"Oh, ho, ho." A feral grin spread across his face. "The little witch is trying to get an early start on the trials, I see? Mirror, mirror, on the wall, who's the sneakiest of them all?"

She still maintained her silence, refusing to meet his gaze.

A finger curled under her chin, tipping her face upward so she was looking into his sinfully golden eyes. "Two truths and a lie," he said. "I wonder what it showed you."

"That's for me to know, and no one else," she snapped, jerking her chin away.

He slid his hands into his pockets but maintained a posture that made her feel small in his presence. "For now, maybe. But rumor has it this pretty little mirror will be brought out for one of the trials. It has this fancy little trick it does where it drives men into madness, so forgive me for finding it more than a little curious that you've engaged with the Mirror of Truth without losing your head. Though I suppose that bodes well for us, should it be used in the trials."

"Us? Last time I checked, you weren't competing." She scoffed.

"And last time *I* checked, Hazel dearest, I'm responsible for your performance. Staying alive is just as important as keeping your mental faculties intact to avoid disqualification. Forgive me for protecting my investment."

Gods, this man is as insufferable as they come. "What is your investment, anyway? Why me? Why do you care?"

"Care? No. I have a *vested* interest in your success, but don't get it twisted. Once you've won the tournament, whether through skill or sheer dumb luck, I could not care less what becomes of you."

It stung more than it should have.

Slaide stepped closer, looming over her. It was the first time she noticed his scent, that intoxicatingly earthy smell left to linger in the air just after a storm… petrichor mixed with something rich—something dark. Hazel's back bumped the bookcase behind her, and she sucked in a sharp breath at the realization she had nowhere to go.

He braced his arm against the shelf above her head as he leaned into her space. Shadows swirled around him with a life of their own, watching, waiting.

Hazel turned her head, not wanting to shrink in his presence but unable to meet his intensity. Her locket *burned*, but she didn't budge.

"Little witch, little witch, let me in," he growled. His shadows caressed her cheek, gently pushing her to face him.

"What do you think you're doing?" she asked, her voice betraying her feigned confidence as it wavered.

His free hand hovered below her chin, near her collarbone; his eyes devoured hers. "What do *you* think I'm doing?"

"Being obtuse, obviously," Hazel retorted.

He smirked down at her. "You're fascinating, Hazel. Since the moment we crossed paths in your town, you've wanted nothing more than to hate my guts—rightfully so, I might add. But look at you now, backed into the very corner you probably swore you'd never find yourself in. And yet, you don't tremble."

"I'm not scared."

His eyes traced the column of her throat, where her fluttering pulse betrayed her anticipation. A wicked smile curved his mouth.

"Oh, I doubt that very much, little witch. You're very scared. And you should be." He inhaled deeply, closing his eyes. When he opened them, they were no longer those molten amber pools. They were endless pits of darkness—the eyes of a hunter.

"Do you know what I like about you?" His voice grew gravelly, so low it made the hairs on her arms stand on end.

She wouldn't dignify that with a response. There was nothing he could or should like about her. They barely knew one another, and by nature alone they were enemies.

He grinned again, making Hazel wonder if she'd said those things aloud. Perhaps her silence said enough.

"It's the way you glare at me, as though you'd burn me to ash with a single look if you could." He brought his face closer to hers, his dark eyes searching as they flitted back and forth.

"You make me want to test you," he continued as mischief danced across his face, "physically and mentally. I want to explore what makes you tick and learn what sounds you make when you're unable to utter a single coherent word."

She swallowed hard, and her core betrayed her stubbornness at his velvet-wrapped words. Warmth spread throughout her body, forcing her to shove down the intrusive thoughts creeping in. To ignore how caged in she was by his body.

"I wonder how long I can hover here, tempting you with what you desire but can't have? Close enough to steal your breath, but never quite giving you what you want?"

"There is absolutely nothing you have that I want." *Liar, liar.* In reality, it was a good thing the library had been cleared out, because she was going to combust.

"Oh, I know. That's what makes this so much more fun. But mark my words, sweets. When I do take what I want, and I will," he brushed his thumb across her lower lip, "you'll already be begging for it."

Hazel locked her knees or else they would have buckled. *Fuck, he's good.* She reined in her focus, refusing to give him another ounce of satisfaction.

Slaide had the audacity to wink at her before pushing off the bookcase and turning his back on her.

"Come with me, little witch. The way out is right over here," he said, his voice aloft with sinful satisfaction. He gestured over his shoulder for her to follow.

And as she obeyed just one command, Hazel's throat bobbed, suddenly hyper-aware that she was at his mercy in more ways than she cared to admit.

Dance Lessons

N the following days, Hazel attended her dance lessons. To her surprise, they were quite literally dance lessons; it hadn't been quirky phrasing for swordsmanship or hand combat.

And while she cooperated, she didn't understand the necessity—unless one of the trials was a dance-off. Though, that was unlikely. Sure, there was to be a celebratory ball at the end of all this, but she had to make it through the trials to see it. If she was dead, no one would ever know she had two left feet and tripped more often when she was nervous.

Pimley, though kind, was vigorous and exacting in his expectations. His demeanor was gentle, though not to be confused with softness. He was not one for breaks and took no pity on her when she was exhausted, claiming she'd get no such reprieve on the battlefield.

Battlefield? Maybe the old man was going mad. Or perhaps it had been a simple slip of the tongue, and he'd meant "ballroom" or "dance floor."

"No," he spoke as he wrapped her ankles in a tight, stretchy cloth. "I meant battlefield."

Her shock must have been obvious on her face, for Pimley simply smiled and said, "No, I don't read minds. But I think you'll find the ballroom and the battlefield have a few things in common. Minus the bloodshed… ideally."

As usual, she was left with more questions than answers.

"Ask, child. If it is just you and I, nothing is off limits." He pulled the wrapping tighter, rounding her calf. She winced, the muscle still sore, and she wondered when her body would get used to this daily abuse.

"How long were you in the militia?" she questioned at last.

He stopped for a moment and glanced up at her. "Who said I was?"

"Well, no one, sir. I just—ah—you compared ballroom dancing to being on a battlefield."

He pointed at her shoulders, ignoring the question. "There. Right there. You see, you're too tense, Hazel. Especially in your upper body. You simply *must* release that pent up energy! Once you do, your body will flow and glide across the room like a fairy princess. Deep inhale… hold it… and exhale. Good."

She did as instructed, despite the nagging feeling she should be doing anything else. Although, she had to admit, she *had* been holding something in. Her feet carried her across the tile floor with greater ease, the movements smoother than she would have imagined herself capable of.

"That's better. Now to your question. No, I did not serve in the militia so much as alongside them. Since I was but a boy, my body has been cursed with a fragility that made me ineligible for the royal army. But since all men are conscripted at eighteen, they had to find it out the hard way. I broke so many bones trying to keep up with the other men in combat training. Eventually a kind healer noticed my ailment, having seen it only one other time in his entire career. So, I was given mess hall duty, serving food to the soldiers. As I learned names and regiments, I also noticed when men didn't return. The opponent was too quick, not only skilled in battle but generally stronger and faster.

"When I first offered my services as a potential solution, they laughed and sent me on my way. After enough men were slaughtered, they called on me. They were desperate. So, I got to work. I taught soldiers to use their agility and dexterity in ways they might not have otherwise. A twirl here, a spin there… it's not the kind of dancing you might imagine, no, but well-timed moves and strong, swift bodies can be the difference between life and death. The king and his generals appreciated the impact my training was having—namely increased survival rates of their men—

and, well, the rest is history, I suppose. Though I must admit I prefer dancing to fighting. Fighting is simply too messy."

He patted her leg when he finished. "There you go. Now, let's get to work. Start where we left off this morning."

They'd begun early each day, shortly after breakfast. After several hours of training, they'd stop for a brief lunch before continuing. This was followed by a break for tea and an afternoon snack after a few more hours. It appeared today would be more of the same.

Hazel was exhausted, but she stood anyway, accepting Pimley's hand when he offered it. After a few stretches, she fell into stride, gliding around the room almost as though she'd been doing it her entire life.

Hazel nearly tripped over her feet as she spied Slaide watching from the doorway. She'd been working hard and was feeling strong, but all her confidence flew out the window when she caught his stare. She almost didn't notice the warmth of the silver against her skin. Almost.

He strode across the room, unfastening his cloak as he moved.

Pimley noticed him shortly after and straightened his posture. "Master Elias!" he called across the room. "We weren't expecting your company today."

Slaide waved him off. "Had some time to kill and thought I would check up on my dancing prodigy." He smirked and tossed Hazel a wink, throwing his cloak to the floor. "I have to say, I'm rather impressed. Good work."

Hazel's cheeks bloomed a rosy pink. "Thanks, I guess," she mumbled.

She was countered by a scoff. "Oh, sweets, I wasn't talking to you. I was talking to Pimley. He's damn near worked a miracle getting you this far in so little time." She shrunk under his gaze, his words cutting more than normal. "But what I saw from all the way across the room was how stiff you are, like someone strapped a board to your back." He approached her, his formidable body towering over hers and making her feel like a mouse. He looked down at her, assessing. He leaned in and whispered, "Now, dance."

And then he straightened and backed away from her, returning to Pimley's side.

Hazel stood there, baffled, staring between the two of them. She didn't take orders from Slaide, did she? As if in answer, he gestured with a flick of his hand for her to get moving.

She sighed and fell into the routine she'd been practicing when Slaide had interrupted. She focused on the movements, trying to pretend she didn't have an audience. Occasionally, she glanced toward Pimley for his approval and was met with a nod, which bolstered her confidence if only temporarily.

She reached the climax of the routine, muscles aching and sweat beading on her brow. Each time she'd attempted this part of the dance, she'd failed spectacularly and found herself on the cold tile floor, staring at the ceiling mosaic. It happened so many times she'd committed the scene to heart: a broken, time-worn depiction of angelic beings fighting humans, the starbursts of color between them possibly depicting magic. It struck her as strange, though she couldn't pinpoint why.

Hazle regrettably spent more time than not adding to her collection of bruises. *Not this time*, she thought, heading into a twirl. *Confidence. Release your shoulders. Breathe.* Her steps fell into place one after the other, her body following, flowing more gracefully than ever. This was it. She was going to complete the routine and have Slaide choking on his words—

But Hazel's feet crossed up and the floor rose to meet her. She slammed her eyes shut, bracing for pain.

Strong arms caught her before she collided with the glossy tile. They hauled her up, where she was brought to face her savior wearing his favorite, smug smile.

"Careful," he said, "we wouldn't want to mess up that face of yours." He pulled her in close, and before she could protest, spun her into his body, her back to his chest. He whispered to her, his breath warm and sensual on her neck, "Dance with me, Hazel." Not a question. Not even a request.

He twirled her away from him, and when she was at arm's length, he bowed to her, still holding her hand. Then he brought her hand to his lips and kissed the back of it.

Her body caught fire, the heat of that small gesture coursing through her veins and warming her insides. Her cheeks pinked yet again, intensifying the blush Phaedra had tinted her skin with. Slaide stood, his expression darkening when he noticed how much his touch had affected her. She stared at a beast in a man's body. A predator sizing up its prey.

Lost in the moment, she remembered herself and dropped into a curtsy. When she stood, he pulled her in close, bringing them into a proper starting position as he placed his other hand at her waist.

She was going to combust. Why was he affecting her this way? She couldn't think straight. *Put your other hand on his shoulder, idiot.* Right. She placed her hand on Slaide's shoulder, trying her hardest to rest it there without feeling the warmth of his body beneath his shirt. Why was her mouth so dry?

"Ready?"

No. "Yes."

And then they were moving. Every step came so much easier under his lead. They spun and twirled and hopped about, waltzing across the room in perfect time. Pimley crossed his arms, looking pleased with the performance. Neither of them spoke, their bodies expressing more than words could. And Hazel was… loose… relaxed …the movements flowing smoothly even as they approached the most difficult part of the dance.

She became hyper aware of his hand as it moved to the small of her back, nearly melting into him. Everything about his touch, his movement, was disarming and comforting at the same time. She leaned into it, finding it hard not to savor the warmth at her back and the strength of the arms holding her.

She waited for her feet to get crossed again, but that moment never came. Instead, Slaide led her with confidence and grace, making her feel more secure than she ever had. She hit the steps perfectly and rolled into Slaide's body, falling into his arms as he dipped her low. He leaned over her, pulling her face closer to his. They were both panting, staring deep into one another's eyes. The look stretched on, perhaps a tad too long.

The locket was a steady reminder of the danger she was in, but Hazel ignored it.

Behind them, Pimley cleared his throat rather aggressively. "Ahem. Master Elias…"

Slaide nearly dropped Hazel on the floor as his senses returned. He bowed to her, stood straight, and retrieved his cloak from the floor as if *that* hadn't just happened.

Slaide clapped Pimley on the shoulder. "You're doing great, my friend. Keep up the good work. At this rate, I will have a competent dance partner by the ball, I'm sure."

"Of course, Master Elias. Good day." He turned to Hazel and smiled. "I think you've earned a break, Mistress Callahan. Please see you get something to eat and be off to bed at a decent time. I'll see you bright and early. You're dismissed."

Thank the gods. Because after that, she needed someone to dump a bucket of cold water on her head. Or perhaps she should just go jump in the lake.

Yeah, definitely the lake.

Sparring with a Monster

Hazel's bare feet padded across the cold stone floor. She flexed her wrists, feeling the weight of the iron manacles there. Between them was an iron chain, which led to the hand of her captor. She'd gotten used to seeing through these eyes that weren't her own and feeling with the fine, slender fingers belonging to someone of nobility.

Walking before her was the strange, winged man from the last nightmare. At least, he was a man in form, though his size and stature was somewhere between a god and a demon.

His raven-feathered wings were reminiscent of the storybook depictions of the mythical angelic beings she'd seen as a child, except for their color. The iridescent, oily black were unlike any known angel. Angel wings were almost always pristine white, sometimes golden, and rarely grey. Never black.

Wavy, shoulder-length black hair was pulled back in a sort of half-up, half-down fashion, presumably to keep the wild mane out of his face. He appeared unarmed, though the realization brought her less comfort than she would have liked. The only reason someone would go unarmed would be if they were lethal even without a weapon. Because they were *the weapon.*

The man paused and turned slowly to face her. For the first time, she recognized something about his face, but couldn't pinpoint it. His eyes were black orbs, and they stared at her blankly as though under a spell.

Hazel, he said.

Hazel.

Hazel.

"Hazel, time to wake up. You're snoring loud enough to wake the dead!" *Bang, bang, bang.* Someone pounded on the door. "Gods of Caelis, Hazel, please don't make me come in there."

When she didn't respond, her bedroom door burst open, revealing a disgruntled Slaide, dressed in fighting leathers. Hazel shot up at the commotion, clutching at the soft comforter and groaning when her unwelcome visitor crossed the threshold.

She pulled the cover over her head. "Go away," came a muffled demand. Her muscles ached from her hours on end spent learning to dance with Pim, and she was in no mood to get back to work.

"No can do, sweets. We're doing some off-grounds training today. The trials are fast approaching, and I'm not sending you out there unprepared. Get dressed." Slaide turned to leave. "Oh, and don't make me come back in here."

"Would a *please* kill you every now and then?" she asked.

"I don't beg," he said through a smirk, closing the door behind him.

THE RAIN SUBSIDED around midmorning though the clouds remained, casting the realm in a somber grey. Muddy puddles thwarted many a lady's efforts to keep their skirts clean, and children peeled away from their caregivers to splash in the largest ones, consequences be damned. Hazel smiled in spite of her own circumstances. Before her, Slaide led the way, completely silent except for his boots squelching in the muck.

Hazel followed close behind him as though they were linked by an invisible tether. It was strange, the way his presence both terrified her and made her feel secure—safe, even. For better or worse, she began to ignore the warning warmth radiating from beneath her clothes. It was clear more than a few castle inhabitants were wary of her, and several gave her the feeling they might cut her down where she stood if not for her escort.

And then there were the ones who would clearly devour her in another way entirely, undressing her with their eyes as she walked by. Somehow, those were worse. Hazel averted her gaze each time, choosing instead to stare at Slaide as though taking her eyes off his back would mean her immediate demise. Thankfully, all whom they passed gave Slaide a wide berth.

She caught whispers passed between the maids and servants. "*It's her*" and "*Witch*" were the most common. But two young children gawked at her as she passed and claimed in not-quite-hushed voices that she'd killed people with her magic. She laughed to herself, until she reminded herself it was a very real risk. Truthfully, she could no longer consider herself harmless. All because her mother was a witch and no one had thought to tell her.

After crossing the empty training yard, Slaide led Hazel alongside the path of wagon wheel ruts carved deep into the mud marking the comings and goings of soldiers and merchants. Before long, the sweet, earthy scent of horse hit her, and Hazel's spirits lifted. Up ahead, the royal stables awaited.

They entered to the warm greetings of the animals as they nickered upon seeing visitors. An enormous black steed grew antsy, dancing in his stall.

"Hey, Phillip, easy boy." Slaide approached the beast, speaking in a soft tone that didn't fit his demeanor. He withdrew something from his pocket and the horse, Phillip, accepted it eagerly. Hazel was seeing Slaide in an entirely different light. As if sensing her attention, he turned to her.

"Do you ride?" he asked.

"I—yes. Well, I mean I used to every day as a girl." *Before we had to sell them to avoid losing everything.*

She reached for the nearest horse, a chestnut brown beauty, and offered her hand. The animal nuzzled her affectionately, though he was probably expecting a treat. The inscription on the stall read *Sorrel.*

"Good enough," was all Slaide replied as he continued tacking up Phillip.

"Which one will I ride?" Hazel questioned, glancing around the barn.

He smirked at her suspiciously, then returned to the task at hand.

"You can't possibly expect—" *I am* not *riding double with him. Absolutely not.*

"Indeed, I do. And *you* can't expect me to trust you on your own horse. Hop on, sweets, we've got somewhere to be." He stepped back, offering her a hand up.

"I can do it myself," she snapped. And she could, maybe. As she approached Phillip's side, his withers impossibly higher than she expected, Hazel perceived just how much she'd underestimated his size. She tried to hike her leg high enough to reach the stirrup. On the third attempt, she got her foot in the stirrup but wasn't quite agile enough to pull herself up. Her body stalled out in mid-air before she fell back down—only to be caught by Slaide's firm hand. He grasped her leg just below her ass, and she yelped as he hauled her onto the horse's back with ease.

Sitting atop Phillip, Hazel scowled down at Slaide. "How dare you."

"You're right. Next time, I'll toss you over his back like a sack of potatoes. And I *won't* be as gentle about it," he snapped before hauling himself up behind her. He adjusted his seat and his hard body press into her back as he reached around her to take the reins. It was *very* hot in this stable.

The ride was, thankfully, uneventful. Hazel would have considered it almost pleasant, had her company been anyone else. The scenery and fresh air, combined with the sights and sounds that came with being on horseback again, were a welcome change. *I didn't realize how much I missed this.*

Even her locket remained relatively calm, maintaining the same level of warmth she'd come to associate with Slaide's presence; somewhere between danger and not, as though the pendant itself couldn't decide.

They arrived in a clearing among pines that reached for the cloud-laden sky, situated along a gently flowing creek. After they'd both dismounted, Slaide unsaddled Phillip and led him to the water. Hazel took the opportunity to stretch her legs.

When Slaide returned, he tossed a practice sword in her direction, and it landed at her feet.

"Something tells me we aren't dancing," she stated.

Wordlessly, he unfastened his cloak, discarding it into the grass, and then proceeded to roll his sleeves up to his elbows, revealing forearms tattooed a solid black, fading to his natural skin tone around the wrist.

"Pick it up." He nodded at the weapon.

Hazel stared at Slaide. Slaide stared back, unblinking. After a few moments had passed, she broke eye contact first, sighing in defeat. *Such a grouch.* She stooped to pick up the wooden sword, gripping the hilt with two hands and the picture of someone who'd never used a melee weapon in her life.

The corner of his mouth twitched upward, making Hazel's blood boil. Was she just entertainment for him?

"Are you going to tell me what we're actually doing here?"

Slaide ignored her. "Widen your stance. More. There." She complied, shifting her feet a little at a time. "Don't lock your knees out like that. Good."

He demonstrated a defensive stance, practice sword at a slightly upward angle before him, his feet planted just beyond his hips, knees slightly bent. Then he bounced with his knees a few times to show her the effectiveness of staying loose.

She watched his muscular form, admiring as he angled his sword in different directions, meeting imaginary blow after blow. His feet moved so effortlessly she almost didn't notice them as they skirted through the grass. He moved more quickly than Hazel would have imagined possible, demonstrating just how skilled he really was. *Showoff.*

Slaide composed himself abruptly, halting the demonstration. "Anyway, that's what it should look like. Takes quite a bit of practice and we are desperately short on time, but we're going to have to do what we can."

"First dancing. Now swords. What's next, breathing fire?" She was getting whiplash.

"Can you? Breathe fire, I mean." Hazel couldn't tell if he was serious or not.

"Of course I can't," she said. "So, what is this, Slaide? We've been practicing. I'd like to think I'm improving."

"You are." There was no mirth in his voice.

"So? Why the scenery change? What was wrong with my lessons with Pim?"

He rolled his eyes into the back of his head and pinched the bridge of his nose. "Nothing, Hazel. For fuck's sake. It was never about the dancing. No one gives a bog rat's ass if you have two left feet or not. But if you don't survive the trials, it won't matter anyway. Do you need me to spell it out for you? You almost died. You needed to build back some strength and coordination in your movement before we could move on. But the dancing itself? It doesn't matter."

She blew out a breath. "This is exhausting. Not the daily dance lessons that cause my bones to ache and my feet to blister and bleed. But you? *You* are exhausting. How am I supposed to trust you if you won't explain what the Hel we are doing?"

"I don't need your trust. I need your compliance."

"Well, what if I don't want to comply? I don't want to be part of any of these games or compete in trials. I want to go home, to see my father again and tell him that, despite everything, I'm alright. To see my patrons at the inn, smell the food and feel the floor, sticky with spilled drink. To sit in the quiet after they've all gone. You don't understand what you've pulled me from. I had a good, simple life."

"What *I* pulled you from? You're right. You wouldn't be here if not for me; you'd be dead. And believe me, I wish more than anyone that I hadn't intervened. But here we are. It seems to me *you* don't understand what lies ahead. This," he gestured around him, "is much bigger than you and I. Your prior obligations no longer matter."

Oblig— "My father is not an obligation! He is the only family I have left!" A single tear ran down her cheek, tracing a line through the dirt and sweat gathered there.

"Your father is a liar and a traitor to the crown, and damned lucky Magnus hasn't put it together yet. He's lied to everyone around him, including *you*. He knew you were wrong but said nothing. Told no one. He kept you drugged with herbal teas to stave off your powers manifesting. And then that hag showed up and helped him raise you, keeping her distance, but staying involved all the same. Your mother's coven sent her to ensure your father didn't fuck up, but he did. By lying to you *and* her, keeping you cloistered in his hovel in that backwater village, and hiding your true identity and purpose. Ah, there's the look. You didn't know any of this, did you, sweets? That's right. I did some digging. How does it make you feel, to know your father isn't your father at all, hmm?"

Rage was all Hazel knew then. White-hot, explosive rage. She could almost feel the power simmering deep within. But she understood what he was trying to do. He wanted to see her at her worst, and she wasn't going to give him the satisfaction. He wanted to see her magic.

Not today, asshole.

She steeled her resolve, choking down a sob and steadying her shaky breath. "Connall will *always* be my father, regardless of blood. He loved me and raised me with kindness and adoration for me as his own. I will always love him as such because he made me who I am today. So, not to steal your thunder, but I already knew he wasn't my *real* father. It doesn't change anything. I'd ask you if you understand, but no, you wouldn't know anything about that. You're a monster. No, worse than that; you're a bully and a coward."

In a flash, Slaide spun on her, his fury blinding and his speed incomprehensible.

The *oomph* forced from her was all the sound she could manage as the breath left her body.

He pinned Hazel to the ground, straddling her and pressing a hidden dagger to her throat without a second thought. His face was twisted into a snarl, teeth bared and face uncomfortably close to hers. It was reminiscent of a predator pouncing on prey. Anticipation and fear warred within her. He panted, something feral glowing in his amber eyes. She dared to swallow, the knot in her throat bobbing dryly.

"Is this a joke to you?" he growled. "Because if it is, I will throw you right in a gods-damned cell and leave you there to rot."

Wide-eyed and frozen, she didn't dare to move, much less speak. Too far. She'd pushed him too far. *Hazel Grace, when will you learn to keep your stupid mouth shut?*

He closed his eyes and sighed, seemingly composing himself. He sheathed the dagger and hopped off of her, walking away without helping her up.

Hazel pushed up onto her hands, dumbstruck by his absolute audacity to just… not give a shit. To act as though he hadn't just held a blade to her throat and growled at her like a wild beast. "Care to explain what that was about? Or are you just a moody, impulsive bastard all the time?"

Slaide turned around, his eyes darkening. He approached her again, this time slowly, menacingly, something about it much more terrifying than when he'd slammed her to the ground moments before. He stopped just before her, so close she could feel his breath. His form was tall and imposing, and he smelled of sweat, earth, and… rain? She should have been scared, should have cowered before him and begged for mercy. But she didn't.

Thunder rolled overhead.

"Pick up the sword," he ordered, kicking it with his foot.

Hazel did. Not because she wanted to follow his order, but because she wanted to smack him upside the head with it. She was surprised such a simple thing could be so heavy.

"Show me a fighting stance." If there'd been any mirth in his voice, it was gone now. He circled her, a wolf on the prowl, as she made a sorry attempt at a fighting stance.

Slaide sighed and with featherlight hands, he touched her shoulders. Her hands. Her hips.

She rolled her eyes and opened her mouth to protest but was cut off with a jab to her unguarded side that sent her stumbling.

"Hey, what the Hel!" she barked, mostly in surprise. "That wasn't fair."

"*Life* isn't fair, Hazel. Especially for you and I." His voice was cool. Impassive. "Never let your guard down and always be wary of your weak side, or it will get you killed."

Determined to prove him wrong, Hazel returned to her stance.

Slaide smirked. Then he struck.

Block. Parry. Strike. Repeat.

Minutes stretched into hours. The sky darkened with the threat of an impending storm.

Hazel's arms were shaking, her resolve about to give out. Sweat beaded her brow and matted her wild hair. Before her, Slaide looked utterly unbothered. His sword was still steady in his hands, eyes fixed on her in an expression she couldn't figure out.

"Again," he commanded.

She winced. "You're going to break me."

"Then become unbreakable," he snapped. "*Again.*"

She raised the sword high and put every last ounce of strength she had into her strike—only to have the blow deflected with ease.

Hazel dropped to her knees in defeat. *This is fucking insane.*

And if her battered body and ego weren't enough, the sky chose that moment to split open, a deluge of water dumping onto them. *Thank the gods. We can be done.*

Slaide walked over to her, his mouth tight, eyes sharp. Rain traced his jawline before dripping from his chin. "Get up."

Hazel's heart pummeled her ribcage, feeling as loud as the thunder around them. Her senses heightened, the most primal parts of her screaming *run*. The sharp sensation of true fear zapped through her body. Still, she got back to her feet.

"Stop. Holding. Back," he growled.

"I'm not—" Hazel's words were cut off by the slash of Slaide's blade.

She barely deflected it, the wood of her practice sword splintering slightly against the force of the blow. Any thoughts she had of complaining were washed away when she met his eyes.

Solid black eyes. Pools of the blackest ink. The locket heated.

"Maybe it's time you learn how it feels, Hazel. To be hunted by a foe that will *destroy* you. To be so outmatched your only chance of surviving is mercy."

A flurry of strikes followed, faster and more relentless, causing Hazel to stagger backward. Her breath came in ragged gasps.

"Slaide—"

"Block!" he barked, raining another blow down on her. "Move your damn feet!" Another blow. "*Survive*, Hazel."

His expression was as emotionless as a boulder. There was no prideful smirk as their swords clashed again, no teasing glint in his eyes. Just darkness and the promise of ruthlessness in his onyx eyes.

Hazel lost her footing in the fray and fell, mud splashing up her legs as she collided with the wet ground. The practice sword, barely holding itself together better than she was, flew from her hands.

She was disarmed, and her opponent was out for blood.

Big Bad Wolf

The locket *burned.* Slaide loomed over her, his chest rising and falling. His expression grew dark with murderous intent as he raised his sword once more. Lightning flashed, illuminating him like an otherworldly being. Like a god.

Hazel squeezed her eyes shut, fully convinced he would bring the blade down and end her. Slaide was done playing games and had, in fact, decided to execute her.

A moment of deafening silence passed, followed by a thud in the grass. Hazel opened her eyes, her breath hitching.

Slaide's sword was on the ground beside hers.

Anger welled within her, where gratitude should be. "What the Hel was that?"

He crouched beside her, raindrops carving intricate paths down his face. "That," he said, voice gravelly and low, "was mercy. And this is the *only* time you'll get it."

Her chest heaved in a futile attempt to catch up with her racing heart. Her eyes flew wide as she stumbled over her words. "That... you... you scared me." She admitted. "I thought..." She didn't need to say the rest. She could see in his eyes he knew damn well what he'd done.

"Good. Then you're learning." His stare did not waver. "In the upcoming trials, there's going to be a target on your back. You're going to be pitted against trained men at arms and hardened criminals. All men, to the best of my knowledge. It's going to take more than a pretty face and a smart mouth to survive."

Slaide leaned in closer to her as the air filled with tension, as raw and electric as lightning. His hand lifted, hovering at her jaw. When his fingers brushed her skin, an unfamiliar charge zipped through her body, pooling in her core.

Their faces were inches apart. Hazel could see the many shades of yellow, marigold, and orange combined to form his impossibly amber eyes. Eyes that dipped to her lips for a split second. Eyes that drew her in.

The storm cracked above them, a warning that the sky would soon be torn asunder. Hazel's breath caught in her throat.

"You're such a bastard." Her voice came out thick and low.

Slaide reached out and tucked a sopping wet curl behind her ear. "Oh, I most definitely am. But you like that about me."

She wanted to laugh, to roll her eyes, or spit back some witty retort. But her mind was erased by the weight of his gaze. His touch. Their faces were ungodly close. As her eyes flitted to his lips, a question formed in the back of her mind— curiosity. One she was *not* ready to give life to.

The corner of his lips twitched, and he pulled back.

Hazel blinked, trance broken.

Slaide stood abruptly, smirking down at her, but his eyes were heavy with something Hazel couldn't name. It made her insides twist, her cheeks flush.

Fucking Hel, Hazel, she scolded herself. "You're an ass and an idiot. I'm done here." The rain was subsiding. She could probably—maybe—make her way back.

His smirk turned down ever so slightly. "Listen here, sweets. I've told you before there are forces at play far beyond your understanding. Beyond mine even. In case you haven't noticed, I am the only person here willing to save your ass, so the least you could do is cooperate. You need me more than you realize."

She blanched, and something escaped her mouth resembling a scoff. "Save me? *Save* me? Is that what you think you're doing? I didn't ask to go to some ball with you, and I certainly wouldn't have thrown myself into this tournament. I didn't ask to be *saved.* What I need is to get back to my home. My life."

"That's not happening, so the sooner you get over it the better." He eyed the practice sword on the ground. "Tell you what. Let's try a different approach. You've got the violent part down, but I'm not sure you're ready for swordplay." He brought forth the dagger again and offered it to her, hilt first.

Hazel hesitated but took the blade, contemplating throwing it at his head. *Like we haven't spent enough time sparring today?* She was tired and completely drenched from the downpour. She wanted to plop herself before a roaring hearthfire with a mug of hot cider, and rest her aching bones.

"Do me a favor and keep in mind that is a real blade. So maybe try not to kill me just yet. I know it's tempting."

After what I just went through? No promises…

As though he could read her thoughts, he raised an eyebrow. "Right, well. First thing's first. You're not very tall. You're not very strong. And you're slow as shit. It's unlikely you're going to get a shot at your attacker's throat when he's coming at you, so you're going to need to focus lower."

Hazel watched in shock as he unbuttoned his shirt and let it hang open, revealing his solid, muscular chest that was tattooed solid black up to his neck. She knew she should look away, but she couldn't. She simply stood there, transfixed.

Slaide took a step closer and grabbed her free hand, placing it on his chest. He cleared his throat. "Now—do you feel this?" he asked, placing her hand over his breastbone.

Hazel knew he wasn't talking about the steady drum of his heart, but she could focus on nothing else.

"This bone is deceiving," he continued, dragging her fingertips down his chest to the tip of the sternum, where the bone gave way to cartilage. "You'd think it ends there, but it actually ends below this spot, here."

She knew she should be listening, but was distracted by the warm, tattooed skin over tight musculature beneath her fingers. This was without a doubt the strangest *dance* lesson she could have imagined, and she began to wonder what his motives were in all of this. He was certainly the most secretive person she'd ever met, if not the most temperamental.

Hazel registered that he'd stopped talking and was staring at her with the look of an exasperated parent. She was still standing there with her hand on his chest, gawking at him. Embarrassed, she moved to pull her hand away, but Slaide only tightened his grip.

"Focus." No calling her out. No belittling her. Just a reminder.

She nodded, desperately wanting the heat to leave her cheeks and hoping the pink flush wasn't noticeable in the moonlight.

"As I was saying, this soft piece here is tricky. It can be pierced, though with some difficulty, and even if you do manage to pierce someone here, you're going to find yourself without a blade." He moved her hand down to the left, tracing his ribs. "I'd also recommend you steer clear of the ribcage, but just in case, you should understand how they lie. Lots of folks think the ribs run perfectly side to side, but they don't. The ribs run in a slight diagonal from the center of your chest. It's important to keep in mind so you angle your blade correctly."

She swallowed dryly.

"Your best bet, since you're on the smaller side and inexperienced in combat, is going to be to insert the blade below the breastbone and ribcage. Even a well-muscled opponent such as myself has soft tissues there—below the hardened exterior." He pressed her fingers against his muscular abdomen, feeling the stark change between bone and belly.

"And lastly, you can always go for the groin."

Hazel stiffened, partially waiting for the end of the joke, the part where he'd try to place her hand in his crotch. *Not happening.*

Slaide chuckled, dropping her hand and running his own through his hair. "I didn't realize I was getting myself involved with such a delicate little flower. But you might want to get used to it, sweets."

I hate that nickname…

"In all seriousness, you never know when stabbing a man in the dick could save your life. And in some situations, it might be the only chance you get to get away. Now, let's practice."

"Practice?"

"Yes? Is that a problem?"

"You want me to *practice* stabbing you. No, it's not a problem for me. Feels like it could be a problem for you, though," she mocked.

"Of course I don't want you to stab me. I didn't realize that was something that needed to be said." He eyed her incredulously. "We are going to practice *location* and *angle*. No stabbing."

So, with shaking hands, Hazel stepped into Slaide and touched the blade against his skin, at the places he'd showed her. Each time he'd adjusted her angle slightly, to give the blade the best possible entry in a real fight. But overall, he looked impressed with her placement.

"I'm going to turn around now, and you can practice the spots I showed you on the back. Same rules. No stabbing."

But this time, with his back turned, the temptation was real. They were in the middle of nowhere. Maybe she could incapacitate him and get far enough away. Sure, he'd kept her alive so far, maybe even kept her from a worse fate, if he was to be believed. Her eyes traveled from the blade to the spot on Slaide's back he'd explained was the location of the kidney.

"I don't recommend doing what you're thinking about doing," Slaide tossed over his shoulder.

She paused, lowering the blade. "How would you know what I'm thinking?"

Slaide laughed. It was a surprisingly warm, homey sound. "You're a captive of the crown, you despise me, I kicked your ass in sword training… you're thinking what any desperate person would be." Something changed in his voice. "Actually, you know what? Do it. I dare you. No one will mourn my loss. I doubt anyone would even come looking." He crossed his hands behind his head to give her full access to his back.

Hazel looked down at the glinting steel in her hands. At the intricate swirling patterns in the blade, the hand-carved, wooden hilt wrapped with supple leather cording. How many lives has this dagger claimed at his hand? How many innocents bled under its edge? And she held it in her grasp. She could put an end to one man's reign of terror. *No*, the voice in her head said, *you aren't like them. You're weak and feeble both in mind and body*. And it was right. She was in over her head.

As though he'd sensed the change in her, Slaide turned around, finding she was no longer poised to run him through. Instead, she stared at the grass, blade arm limp at her side, her mind lost to thoughts of things she'd been torn away from.

His brow furrowed. "Hey." His voice softened. "What's going on in that head of yours?" He grabbed her chin and tilted it up to look at him, but she wouldn't meet his eyes. "Well, well. Aren't you a pretty, broken little thing?"

She shoved his hand away. "I am not broken."

"Yeah, sure. Neither am I," he deadpanned.

"You don't know anything about me," Hazel hissed.

"Well, there's something we can agree on. You aren't much of a talker so…"

Her eyes shot daggers.

He put his hands up defensively.

"Can I go home?" Her eyes shimmered slightly, the angry mask she put on faltering.

"No." Slaide folded his arms.

She examined the dagger again.

"Changed your mind about stabbing me that quickly, eh?" He was smiling broadly. *Idiot.*

Her face was stone cold, but the fire in her eyes could have melted every last inch of ice and snow from the twin peaks of The Sisters. "I never said I wasn't going to stab you. It makes little sense to do it when you're expecting it."

He chuckled softly. "Something tells me I will always need to expect a knife in my back as long as you're around."

"Who's scared now? Careful, we wouldn't want anyone to find out the big bad wolf is actually a timid kitten," Hazel jeered, ignoring the warmth blooming against her skin.

He stepped into her, closing the space between them. "You talk a lot of shit for someone who can't back it up. And you flinch like someone who has something to hide." His eyes shifted to something predatory, feral, and he crouched down to meet her gaze.

"And you look at me like you hope I'll break."

"Not hope, Hazel. Expectation."

Before she knew it, his hand was around her wrist, causing her to flinch at the sudden tension. His grip didn't quite hurt, but it was most definitely too tight. His entire demeanor changed, and she was pretty sure this was no longer a playful game. Hazel glanced at her wrist, and then back to Slaide, the dagger falling from her hand.

His eyes had melded into a sinister pitch black again, the golden irises completely devoured by an endless void. And when he spoke, the air trembled, the ground beneath her feat carrying the vibration. Clouds were closing in, blanketing the starry sky in darkness.

"You're right," he said, his face far too close to hers. "I'm not the big bad wolf." His grin was sinister, teeth—and fangs—bared. "I am the monster before which the big bad wolf cowers."

Slaide let go of her then and took a step back tilting his head up to the sky and spreading his arms wide. Lightning struck all around him, leaving nothing but charred, black earth in its wake.

And then enormous, onyx-feathered wings unfurled from his back, and he launched into the air, disappearing over the treetops.

Sylvie

HAZEL stared up at the sky to the place she watched Slaide's winged form take off and disappear, finding it hard to form even a single thought as shock wracked her body. All this time she'd thought Slaide was human. But he wasn't, was he? *Where the Hel was he hiding his wings?* Her thoughts were swimming, and she needed answers.

Night was upon them, and she was not looking forward to being outside the castle walls by herself in full darkness. With no time to lose, she mounted Phillip and charged off in the direction Slaide had headed.

She urged the horse to the forest's edge and to his credit, he didn't protest. When she dismounted, he was content with being left to graze.

As Hazel walked down the path, the damp earth soft beneath her feet, thunder rumbled overhead. A warning of another storm, she concluded as she glanced up to see clouds sliding in from the western skies.

A twig snapped beneath her feet, startling her and sending her heart into a gallop as she remembered Nan's stories about the monsters roaming the Borderlands.

The fact this forest was here, that it was as thick and overgrown as it was, was evidence enough of the magic in this place. And where there was magic… She shook off the thought. Those were just stories. So what if the Striga happened to be real?

But as she trudged on, she was hounded by a feeling she just couldn't shake—someone was watching, following. She paused abruptly and heard footsteps that weren't hers. She picked up the pace, her head on a swivel, determined not to be caught unaware. A chorus of howls went up in the distance. *Far enough away for now, but for how long?*

Hazel rounded a bend in the forest path and came to a halt when her eyes landed on the silhouette of a creature sitting in the middle, unmoving. It was a… cat? And a very large one at that. Hazel cocked her head as it approached her, stalking slowly on giant furry paws. As he approached, she noticed the orange fur and ethereal green eyes. But it couldn't be.

He padded up to her, sat at her feet, and proceeded to groom himself. Hazel squatted down beside him, admiring how his coat stood out so brightly even in the fading light. She reached out to pet him, but he froze, eyeing her suspiciously, body tense.

"Right. I'm not allowed to pet you, am I? Well, in that case, I'd better be going. Good seeing you, Cat." She stood and dusted off her pants.

The orange cat approached her and arched his back into her shins, his tail curling around her calf with a mind of its own. Hazel smiled, happy to still have some piece of home there with her, even if it was a strange cat she'd only recently become acquainted with.

He walked a circle around her before trotting off in the direction she'd been walking. As though he sensed she wasn't following, the cat paused and looked over his shoulder, waiting for her to follow.

She considered for a moment, but decided to follow him since she was headed in that direction anyway. He trotted onward, tail held high, looking back at her every so often as though to make sure she was still there.

As they crested a hill on the forest path, the cat paused and sat on his haunches. He began grooming his paws again, and Hazel wondered if she'd been a fool to follow a cat through the woods.

But then she looked up and found he'd led her to the end of the path and the edge of the forest. She'd successfully left the howling beasts and dark corners of the wood behind. And that wasn't all.

Well, I'll be damned.

Up ahead near a small lake, the ground rose sharply into a cliff overlooking the calm waters. The moon had risen in the sky, bathing everything in its milky white light. And at the top of the ridge was the silhouette of a winged man.

She'd found Slaide. The *cat* had found Slaide.

When she looked back, the cat was gone without a trace, as quietly as he'd arrived.

As Hazel took in his Slaide's form sitting on a boulder near the cliff's edge, she sighed. She had so many questions she wanted to ask, and not one of them was appropriate to lead with. The pendant was warm in her fingers, though she didn't remember reaching for it.

Not wanting to disturb him, Hazel approached quietly, uncertain how best to get his attention. After a few moments in silence, she cleared her throat.

"I'm not going to apologize for what happened back there, so if that's why you're here, you're wasting your time," he started.

She jumped, taken aback; so much for being civil. "Good thing I don't want your apology then. You do, however, owe me an explanation as to where you've been hiding *those*, and why you didn't tell me you had gods-damned wings."

"Didn't exactly come up in conversation," he quipped.

"Well, no, I should think not, seeing as they were hidden. I don't know what kind of conversations you're used to having, but where I'm from, we don't exactly walk up to folks and check them for hidden wings."

"Alright, smart ass. Calm down. Yes, I have wings." He flared them for emphasis. "As for why you've never seen them, I keep them veiled. No one sees them unless I allow them to. And before you ask, yes, Magnus and his inner circle all know about them."

"But, how…" she faltered.

"Hazel, I'm not… like you." He didn't meet her eyes.

"No shit, Slaide. But something tells you're meaning something more than skin deep. So, what, are you going to tell me you're not human?"

When he met her eyes, she got all the confirmation she needed. Of course he wasn't human. She should have known.

She backed up a step, shaking her head in disbelief. He really was a monster, and he was having difficulty controlling himself.

"Hazel. This doesn't change anything," he said, but his words were hollow.

"What are you? I mean, if you're not human, just help me work through this, please." She was ready to beg. For her life, if need be.

Slaide sighed, hanging his head. He spread his wings wide, as though that was supposed to answer her question.

And then it hit her. Perhaps he had answered her after all. "You're… an angel?" she stuttered, unable to believe the words coming out of her own mouth.

"Yes and no. It's not that simple."

Of course not. Nothing ever is. "Well thanks, that clears it up."

"The problem is, I don't entirely know what I am myself. I wasn't born into a loving family, or really any sort of family. I was bred to serve a purpose—to be a mindless, ruthless killer—and my mother was discarded after my birth. I don't know who or what she was, other than a slave. My sire was one of the Fallen. Beyond that, even I don't know. I've heard them describe me as *Nephilim*, but I've never figured out what that meant. Never cared to know."

He had warned her it was complicated, hadn't he? But she found herself with more questions than answers. He was right about one thing: she was in way over her head. A change of subject was in order.

"Can I ask you something?"

"You just did," Slaide pointed out.

"I'm serious." Hazel crossed her arms to emphasize just how serious she was.

"If I say no, is that going to stop you?" Slaide cocked his head to the side in question.

"Probably not." She shrugged. It was something she'd wondered about since getting dressed.

"Go on then." His expression rested somewhere between boredom and annoyance. The face of a parent dealing with a petulant child.

"It's not overly important, but curiosity is getting the better of me."

"Out with it." He sighed.

"Fine. Where did you get fighting leathers in my size? I mean, it's not a perfect fit, but it's close. Did you get my measurements from the tailor? It's impressive considering the short amount of time you've had to work with."

Slaide's gaze melted into a contemplative stare, rolling over her from head to toe. "No, I suppose they aren't a perfect fit." He poked at an anthill between his feet with a stick, sending the ants scurrying in alarm. "I wouldn't expect them to be, because they weren't tailored for you."

"Whose are they then? Do you just go around raiding women's closets?"

"Bold of you to assume I *took* them from anyone, especially without their knowledge." He waved a dismissive hand. "These are borrowed. From a… friend."

It wasn't lost on Hazel how Slaide had tripped over that last word, as though friend wasn't the term he was searching for.

"She no longer needs them."

Sure, she'd seen a couple of those women in the training yard. But not a single female warrior she'd observed shared her body type. They were all tall and broad-shouldered, thickly-muscled, ferociously badass women. They were everything she was not, and their fighting leathers, no matter how fitted they were, would have sagged off her worse than a burlap potato sack. So instead of quelling her, his response had piqued her interest even further.

"That doesn't explain where this came from, though," she said, gesturing to her attire. "I know you think I'm gullible and stupid, but we both know I wouldn't fill out a true warrior's fighting leathers. So, whose clothes am I wearing?"

And his eyes were once again ablaze with unspoken rage. That question, and pushing for an authentic answer, had crossed a line. She should be used to this by now.

"Someone who would be insulted to see you wearing them while insinuating she couldn't possibly be a warrior due to her size. But you know what? You're right. You don't deserve to stand where she stood, playing dress up in her clothes. She'd kick my ass for even considering it."

After getting that off his chest, his gaze cooled and he looked almost remorseful. *Almost.* He returned to his quiet, brooding demeanor then, pivoting on the boulder and turning his back to Hazel.

So that was it then. Big bad Slaide Elias, witch hunter and monster slayer, had taken a lover and something had befallen her. His mood was understandable, and pity bloomed in her chest. But was it too much for him to just be up front about those things?

They sat quietly for a while, accompanied only by the evening chorus of crickets and bullfrogs in the nearby marsh.

It wasn't long before Hazel couldn't take it anymore, and she broke the silence. "I'm sorry for offending you. It's obvious you cared deeply about her." She took a step closer. "Would you care to talk about her? Tell me what she was like?" She knew she should just let it go, but she couldn't find it within herself to do so. How long had it been since anyone asked about her?

Slaide shifted, but didn't speak.

"Can you just tell me her name? Is-is she alive?" she prodded.

He tilted his head to the sky and ran a hand through his hair.

"Sylvie," he ground out. "Her name was Sylvie. And no, she isn't. At least not here in the physical realm. I try to keep her memory alive as much as possible. It's… difficult. They expected me to just move on. To forget her as they did. But I didn't. I can't."

"I'm sorry. I can't imagine."

"No, you really can't. No one can. We were soul-bonded—two halves of the same whole. Those who care to remember say the entire continent shook when her soul was torn from her body. The only thing that keeps her tethered here is the small strand of her being living within me."

Hazel had heard of bonds and tethers to the soul before, though she admittedly had never thought much about it. Most humans didn't have those sorts of connections with one another. Some of the fae and other magical creatures were said to take mates instead of spouses, and while it was much the same concept as a marriage, it was on a deeper level. The souls of mates were destined by Fate, and once the bonds were acknowledged, the souls became tethered for eternity. So, maybe…

Hazel took another step forward and raised her hand to place on his shoulder. "Was she… your mate?" she asked tentatively.

That *almost* got a laugh out of him. More of a choking-scoff, but she'd take it.

"No. No, it wasn't like that. She was more than that. Closer to my own soul than any mate could ever be. She was blood of my blood, as they say. My twin sister. She was murdered."

Oh, this was so much worse than she'd thought.

"I-I'm so sorry. I just thought… never mind. Did you find the person responsible? I'm assuming they've been dealt with?" He shook his head no. "But Slaide, she was the only family you had. And they just… got away?" She shouldn't care. This wasn't her problem. Pleading with him was more dangerous than playing with fire, but she couldn't stop. Common sense and her warming locket be damned, she reached for him.

Slaide's body rumbled with a sinister growl as it rolled through him, and Hazel's hand froze in midair.

"And why do you care? You just want to go home, remember? Not only are you unskilled, untrained, and utterly useless, you're clueless as well. You don't seem to get it. We *can't* avenge her. Perhaps someone else could. Come to think of it, maybe they should. But *I* can't."

"Maybe I don't understand having my family murdered, but I can understand having your life turned upside down," she snapped.

He spun on her, rising and putting his face mere inches from hers, eyes burning with the heat of a thousand suns and the sorrow of a thousand and one deaths. He was so tragically handsome.

"You have no idea what you're talking about, Hazel. There are forces at work here far beyond your wildest nightmares. Maybe I was foolish to think I could help prepare you against them."

Defeat and heartbreak carved their way into her soul. Strong feelings for someone she barely knew. And if it was a ploy to gain her sympathy, to let her guard down? It was working.

"You're so intent on forcing me to face my fears, but you're too scared to face your own. Hypocrite." The words were out before she could stop them.

In a flash, his fangs were bared and hovering at her neck, just above her collarbone. The amber in his eyes had given way to those endless pools she'd seen once before. He sniffed up her neck and along her jawbone, stopping at her ear. She didn't dare move. Hardly chanced breathing for fear he might snap.

Nothing could have prepared her for what he said next.

"You want to know who did it so you can, what, help me avenge my sister?" he whispered against her ear with hot breath that made the hair along the back of her neck stand on end. "Then take this dagger and plunge it into my heart. Avenge Sylvie and right the wrongs I've done in this world."

The confusion written into her features must have been question enough, for his next words were in answer to that which went unspoken…

"It was me."

The Test

Hazel recoiled as though she'd been slapped. *No, that's on me*, she thought. *I should have seen this coming. He's a dangerous monster. This is what he does, and I let my guard down.* She backed away from him slowly, hand rising to touch the locket.

He grabbed her other wrist and held firm. It didn't hurt, but she yelped, nonetheless.

"I'm not going to hurt you. Just let me explain." His eyes were remorseful, but once again, her mind was screaming at her to *get away*.

How? How does one simply explain murdering their own sister? She said nothing aloud, only stared into his eyes, fearful and searching.

Slaide's grip slid down to her hand. Hazel glanced at their clasped hands, her insides roiling with conflicting emotions. When she looked back up at him, his eyes were pleading, so she offered a silent, consenting nod.

He walked back to the boulder overlooking the lake, tugging her gently behind him. He sat facing her and pulled his hand from hers.

"I never meant for it to happen. If you understand nothing else I tell you tonight, please believe me when I say that." Slaide released her then.

He ran his hands down his face.

"As far back as I can remember, they've been telling me I was special, filling my head with delusions and making promises that would never be fulfilled. I entered combat and weapons training from a younger age than you can possibly imagine."

Hazel crossed her arms over her body, cradling herself.

Slaide continued. "I spent my entire young life as the bastard. The weapon. The beast. The odd one out. It became unbearable." He looked into Hazel's eyes, his own glassy and full of sadness. "I fought tooth and nail against what they were trying to turn me into. I was just a boy. I wanted to play with the other boys in the castle yard, harass the young maidens as they often did, and practice sword fighting. But I wasn't allowed to be normal.

"I tried—on more than one occasion, I tried to escape this fate I've been dealt, this life I've had no choice in. I thought if I could just remove myself from this world, then I could undo some of the harm my existence had caused. And do you know what I learned? I can't even die like a mortal. I'm blessed, so they say, with advanced healing capabilities. Some blessing that is, when you don't want to live."

Hazel's heart was ripping in two. This man was dangerous. He was a trained killer who'd shown no remorse for his victims. However, hearing him admit he couldn't continue on, that he'd rather die at his own hand than face what the future holds? She wondered if maybe he wasn't as hardened inside as he'd led everyone to believe. That perhaps he showed them what they wanted to see while he suffered within.

"My life improved for a bit when they introduced me to Sylvie," he said. "I'd had no idea I had a sister, let alone a twin. They'd kept us separate to prevent us from forming a bond as siblings do, insisting this would be a hindrance on missions. Which was laughable at best because when I met her, the connection was immediate. Her presence lit a long-dormant beacon in my soul, one I always knew existed but never knew how to light. All they'd managed to do was to delay the inevitable. She was not just the only family I had, but my other half. The missing piece of my soul. I finally had someone who understood the struggles of being what we are. For once, I wasn't alone. We shared in each other's hardships and burdens, and having her in my life made the days seem just a little bit brighter."

He took a deep breath before continuing.

"It was short lived. The rest is a blur, except the bits and pieces that are burned into my memory. The Magistry cooked something up in the Citadel. A potent serum that causes the user to return to their base instincts and magnifies any special abilities, be it magic, strength, or ferocity. The Archmages paired this with a magefire-infused obsidian collar—one they could control with a flick of their fingers—and it gave them the ability to wield powerful beings like weapons.

"Sylvie and I were used for late-stage testing. I remember seeing Gammen's smug face as they led us into an arena and forced us to slaughter scores of men. They'd forced us both to take the serum. I never tired. Nor did she. But then it was just us remaining… and I… I didn't have a choice. She was Hel-bent on killing me and if not for the serum… I would have let her. But I couldn't."

He was staring at the ground, but Hazel heard the choked sob in his voice. Her eyes welled, too.

"She smiled at me just before she went limp in my arms. No one rushed to us or offered help. They just watched from the stands like they were watching a couple of caged animals fight."

Hazel's eyes spilled over, and when Slaide looked up at her, a single tear ran down his cheek. She stepped forward and cupped his face, brushing the tear away with a swipe of her thumb. He grabbed her wrist and held her hand in place.

"You needed to know. I saw the look on your face. The fear. It fits the narrative, doesn't it? Slaide Elias, the monster. And you know what? They're right. I am all those things and more. Because after Sylvie's death, I made a choice. I became everything they feared I would be. Every whispered rumor, every assumption made behind my back. I brought it all to life. I altered my entire essence to become their nightmare, and I never looked back."

He looked up and Hazel stared at him as though she could see into his soul. And after he'd laid himself bare, maybe she could. She watched his eyes follow a lone tear as it traced a line down her pink-tinged cheek, and then he was moving, pulling her close. She didn't balk at his firm touch, didn't pull away. Instead, she stepped in to Slaide and swung her leg over his thighs, straddling his lap.

He reached up, hand trembling, and cupped her cheek, wiping the tear away with his thumb. She closed her eyes at his touch and her cheek warmed under his caress, the pink in her cheeks deepening.

She opened her eyes again and let out a breath before reaching up and covering his hand with her own.

"I see you, Slaide Elias. I see there is more to you than meets the eye. More than the rumors and the assumptions and the horrible things they've made you do. I am sorry your childhood was stripped from you, and that you've been forced to live your life as a monster. But you are more than the skin they've forced you to wear."

He closed his eyes and Hazel watched as a layer of the barrier he'd built around himself came down. How long had he waited for someone to tell him it was okay? To validate his suffering? To give a name to his inner turmoil?

She leaned in, bringing her soft lips to his cheek, laying a kiss where the tear had been. Slaide flinched, and his eyes shot open, wide with disbelief. Hazel pulled back and ran a hand through his hair. This wasn't lust or some feral hunger. It was something completely different. Something new. A tender touch for a broken soul.

"I don't know why the Fates insisted we cross paths," she said, "but I'm starting to believe it was for a reason."

All he could do was stare into her eyes, shining more green than brown in the pale moonlight.

Another otherworldly howl shattered the otherwise silent night, interrupting what was quickly becoming something Hazel couldn't put a name to. She was almost grateful for the distraction. Slaide, however, bristled. She watched as his pupils dilated in an animalistic manner, his features scanning, searching.

"Uh, Slaide?" She questioned uncomfortably, shifting from his lap.

"Shh." He stood, slowly.

"Mind telling me what's going on?" She lowered her voice to a whisper.

Slaide ignored her, walking to the cliff's edge and staring out over the lake. Hazel followed, keeping a respectful distance. She stopped beside him and watched as he looked out over their surroundings. He tipped his head to the sky and closed his eyes, letting the soft breeze blow over him.

When he turned to face her, she noted how he fixed his expression, masking the concern that flickered there.

"What is it?"

"Something that isn't supposed to be on this side of the Border. It's… nothing. But we should go." His voice was laced with concern, something Hazel wasn't used to hearing. And to make matters worse, her locket's warmth was noticeable again.

"Doesn't sound like nothing. Why can't you just tell me what it is?"

"Because I don't know what it is. You need to stop talking, and we need to head back. Speaking of which, where'd you leave my horse?"

She shrugged. Admittedly, she had forgotten about Phillip, but she was sure he was fine. *I hope.* But she pushed those thoughts down, instead saying, "Phillip is in a glade in the forest, probably still grazing. That boy doesn't miss an opportunity to eat."

"No, he doesn't." He began walking down the hill, Hazel taking her cue to follow.

"So, you're not going after it?" She asked, a little too eagerly. Was she enjoying the danger? Or was it the proximity… the opportunity to get to know this not-so-deadly witch hunter?

"No." He huffed.

"And why not?" She tried not to sound too disappointed.

"Because *you're* dead weight."

Rude. But for once, she wasn't in the mood to argue. It was getting late, dark, and they had a long ride back through the forest while the night's creatures began their haunts. She found herself sidling up to him.

He glanced down at her as they walked, a smirk crawling across his face. "You're not *scared*, are you? The infallible Hazel Callahan. You'll take me on, but you're afraid of the dark?" He put his arm around her then, pulling her a little closer.

"You know as well as anyone it's not the dark I'm afraid of. It's what lurks in the shadows." She frowned up at him.

Slaide let out a *hmph* in response. "You've got a lot to learn if you think your only enemies are the ones hiding in the shadows. Sometimes the ones who don't hide are the most dangerous of all."

Hazel didn't think they were still talking about wild beasts in the night or the monsters crossing the Border. His gaze lingered over her for a moment before he looked away.

They rounded a bend, and sure enough, Phillip was right where she'd left him. Still eating. Much to Phillip's dismay, Slaide put an end to his extended mealtime and pulled the stubborn horse from his grassy buffet.

Things were almost too quiet on the ride back.

"You know," Hazel started, breaking the silence, "you're not the only one struggling with who and what you are. I've never felt so lost and alone as I have these past few days. My life was turned upside down before I landed here, after I battled a Striga, of all things."

He perked up at the name of the monster. "Striga. You're sure? They generally don't come that far beyond the Border."

"I am. And if I wasn't, the man who showed up and drove her off confirmed it."

Hazel thought she heard him scoff over her shoulder.

"You don't believe me."

"It would be a lot more believable if you were dead. You used your powers, didn't you?"

There was no sense in lying about it anymore, was there? "If I had these powers everyone claims I do, wouldn't I have used them by now? Wouldn't I have obliterated you during our fight? Used them to escape?"

For a moment, Slaide said nothing, and Hazel enjoyed the satisfaction of shutting him up for once.

It was short lived.

"Probably self-preservation," he replied at last. "The same reason you're lying right now."

Hazel stiffened.

Slaide chuckled softly against her back. "Fine then. Keep your secrets."

She scrunched her face. "The only thing I know for sure, and *you* know for sure, is that my mother was more than likely a witch. And while I don't understand it, I'm not denying it. I just…" her words trailed off. "I don't know what it means for me. I'm trying to wrap my head around Connall and Agnes both lying to me for so many years. My *entire* life has been a lie."

Silence spread between them again, the clopping of Phillip's hooves on cobblestone the only sound. It was as though Slaide was giving her space to process.

"Searching for answers is how I ended up in this mess, you know. I don't have a single memory of my mother, and if that wasn't bad enough, the associations I'm forming around her now… well, they're not great. I was hoping to find out she was a good cook, perhaps a talented seamstress, or even a healer of some sort." She didn't need to clarify that she meant the non-magical variety.

"Well for what it's worth coming from a witch hunter," Slaide said, voice low, "your worth isn't limited by who or what your mother was. All that matters is how you choose to move forward."

Her heart skipped a beat. Maybe two. Because there was absolutely no way Slaide was being nice to her.

But she didn't have the energy to argue. Hazel was so tired, the weariness seeming to catch up with her out of nowhere. The side-to-side rocking and dipping of Phillip's stride reminded her of Nan's old rocking chair, lulling her in as the day's events caught up with her.

Slaide's chest was a warm, solid wall behind her, his breaths coming in a steady rhythm, his heart thumping in time with Phillip's hoofbeats. She leaned into him involuntarily, but Slaide didn't protest. For the first time all evening, she let her guard down and closed her eyes, replaying the gentle words of a man who should have killed her by now.

The Kingswood

Sunlight filtered in through the paned windows, falling over Hazel in a warm caress. She groaned, rolling over and seeking the cover of the duvet. Why weren't the curtains closed?

Wait.

She sat up with a start, jolted by the realization that when she'd last been awake, she was astride Phillip—with Slaide. And she… Oh gods. Had she fallen asleep on him? She brushed the wild, unruly strands of hair from her face and attempted to reorient with the world.

She glanced down and was unsettled by the discovery of a night dress, and not the clothes she'd last had on. Her cheeks heated. Had he…?

"Phaedra's work again, sweets, not mine." Slaide's voice shattered her inner monologue. "I have my issues, sure, but messing with people while they sleep isn't my thing." He was sitting backwards in the chair at the writing desk, his arms folded over the chair back. He feigned disinterest and picked at his nails with his dagger. "You sleep like the dead, by the way."

Hazel rolled her eyes. "So how did I get in here?" She had an idea but wasn't in love with it.

"I carried you." *So matter of fact,* Hazel thought, *as though I should just* expect *that from him.*

"Why?"

"Would you rather have slept in the stables? Phillip is great company, but when his gas gets going, he's nearly lethal." He shrugged. "But if that's what you'd prefer…"

"No—I… It's fine. I just… thank you." She rubbed her arms, not meeting his gaze. "I don't know what came over me to fall asleep like that."

Slaide laughed softly. "Generally, exhaustion will do that to you. Believe it or not, I do acknowledge you've had a trying few days. And I understand this has been a big change for you." He waved her off. "I did try waking you but…"

Then it was her turn to laugh. "I guess I really do sleep like the dead." Then she cleared her throat, suddenly very aware of Slaide's presence and her lack of clothing, a blush warming her cheeks.

He smiled. "It never does get old, watching you squirm." He sat up then, dismounting the chair and straightening his shirt. "Anyway, I have some business to attend to out in the Wilds today. Want to join?"

"Are you actually giving me a choice in something?" She was only half-teasing. Up until now, no one had given her a say in what her next move would be. She fluffed the duvet, if for no other reason than to have something to do with her hands.

"It seems I am. So, what do you say?" The way the sun was hitting him caused the amber flecks in his eyes to turn to liquid gold. It was mesmerizing.

"Ahem." He was staring at her, one corner of his mouth lifting.

She'd stared too long. "What? Oh." She scratched the back of her head and tucked a loose hair behind her ear. "Yeah. I think I will."

"Good. Now get dressed and meet me downstairs in half an hour. It could be a long day, so we need to grab a bite to eat before we head out." As he turned to leave, a knock sounded at the door.

"Expecting company?" Slaide asked pointedly.

She shook her head. She wasn't, but maybe Ezekiel had finally tracked her down? She found herself missing his company.

Another knock, more forcefully this time. Hazel's hand flew to the locket, finding it warm to the touch.

"Slaide!" came a voice that sent shivers down Hazel's spine. Not Ezekiel, then.

"*Fuck,*" Slaide hissed. He looked back at Hazel. "Don't move." He cracked the door open and said, "To what do I owe this visit, Your Majesty?"

Hazel gulped. *He's probably wondering why I'm not dead.*

Slaide slid out between the doors, leaving them slightly ajar behind him.

The berating started immediately.

"Slaide Elias, you'd better tell me the gods-damned rumor I just heard isn't true." The King seethed.

"Depends on the rumor, I guess. You'll have to be more specific," Slaide joked in his particularly nonchalant way.

"Don't toy with me, boy. You're letting her sleep in your gods-damned quarters. I knew you were stupid. But this… She's meant to be in a cell, you fool! Locked away like the prisoner she is. What are you thinking?"

"I'm *thinking* she'll be more likely to explain, cooperate, Hel, even show me what secrets she's hiding if she's comfortable here. She needs some reassurance that death isn't looming around every corner." She heard Slaide say plainly. She pictured his crossed arms, his feigned boredom.

"But death *is* looming around every corner, Slaide. Especially for her. She's not a guest here. Imagine how ridiculous I looked this morning when I learned from Lord Giles of all people that the bitch wasn't locked up in the dungeon! When I said you could oversee her interrogation and training for the tournament, I didn't mean she could roam the halls!"

Was this it? Would Slaide relent and she'd be forced to be back in the depths of the castle?

But she heard the smile in Slaide's voice when he responded. "To be fair, Lord Giles is the Lord of Gossip. He could tell you when you're going to take a shit before your bowels so much as grumble."

"This isn't a joke, Slaide. Mark my words. You will pay for this." The last Hazel heard of the King was the sound of his shoes clopping down the hallway.

"I look forward to it," Slaide muttered in his wake.

After the abrupt intrusion, Hazel and Slaide met for an uneventful, silent meal before making their way to the stables. Despite the recent rain, the previously squelching mud had mostly dried up. Impressions of wagon wheels and horseshoes were hardened into the ground, which was much easier to traverse this time around. No boots getting sucked into the muck, no splatter from the wagons as they rolled past.

The sun warmed Hazel's face, and she could almost feel her freckles threatening to pop up in its embrace. A few of the horses were in the paddocks grazing, and she spied Phillip among them.

When he saw Slaide, he whinnied and trotted to the fence. Slaide pulled half an apple out of his pack and handed it over to the eager beast, who crunched happily. Juice from the apple spritzed Hazel's face, and she laughed. She wiped her cheek and caught Slaide staring down at her.

He shook his head as though trying to shake off the grin growing on his face before turning from her and entering the stable. Phillip took his cue and walked to the paddock gate and back into the barn to meet them.

The barn smelled of freshly oiled leather, alfalfa, and horse. The grooms and stable hands took meticulous care of the animals and grounds, but Hazel noticed none of them ever touched Phillip. She pondered that for a moment, when she discovered a second set of tack sitting beside Slaide's. Hazel's insides flipped in excitement, glad at the prospect of riding again—and not having to ride double. Slaide handed her a stiff bristled brush and nodded toward his horse, who was now munching hay in the stall.

Hazel approached the midnight black gelding with a beaming smile on her face. Phillip paid her no mind, continuing to munch on his meal as she entered and approached him. Only when she reached his flank did he lift his head in acknowledgment before returning to his business.

Slaide observed from outside the stall, arms folded as usual, and Hazel was beginning to think it was the only way he knew how to stand.

She started brushing Phillip with short flicks of her wrist, dislodging loose hairs, dander, and dried mud. She had to admit, the animal was far less dirty than his stablemates, as though someone had already groomed him. *So, then why am I doing this all again?* She cocked a brow in Slaide's direction.

"Something the matter, sweets?" he crooned.

"You groomed him already." Not a question.

His eyes widened, and then he uncrossed his arms, placing his fists on his hips. "So, what if I did? I wanted to see something."

"Well, are you satisfied? I was under the impression you had some important business to get to today. I see no reason to groom Phillip twice, even if he is a total sweetheart. You could learn a thing or two from him, you know."

"It's *unofficial* business. Nonetheless, we should get going, yes." He nodded to the stall next to Phillip's, where a fat flaxen pony was crunching on grain. It had a thick, black and white double-layered mane that stood on end in a permanent bad hair day. A black dorsal stripe ran down the center of its back to the base of its tail, which was as multicolored as the mane. The lower half of its legs were black, like tall socks, and its neck was obnoxiously thick. Hazel thought it was clearly a cart-pony or pack-pony.

"Him?" she asked Slaide. "He's so… stout."

"*Her*, you mean. And yes. That's Nanna." Hearing her name, Nanna lifted her head and snorted, ears pinned.

That's a mare, alright.

"Hey now. Knock it off, you old nag. Your boyfriend likes her, so lighten up." He pulled something out of his pocket and offered it to her. She accepted the treat greedily. "Nanna puts on a big show, but she's actually a loving old soul. That's not to say she won't bite you in the ass sometime today just to make a point, but it's part of the fun with her." He winked.

Hazel moved to the front of Nanna's stall and the old mare turned away from her, leaving Hazel to stare at the pony's rump. Behind her, Slaide chuckled under his breath. "One more thing," Slaide said as Hazel prepared to mount Nanna. "Do not run." His voice dipped dangerously low. "If you run, I *will* catch you. And while I'll thoroughly enjoy what comes next, I won't be happy about deviating from my plans to chase you down. Understood?"

Her throat bobbed in response. She nodded her agreement, ducking her head behind Nanna to hide the blush creeping into her cheeks.

Oh, today is going to be eventful indeed.

Slaide and Hazel made their way down a heavily trodden path which Slaide had said would lead them to the Kingswood, a sprawling woodland in the Wilds butting up to the Border on the eastern side of the kingdom. The Kingswood was vast, Slaide informed her, indicating they likely wouldn't cross its entirety on this trip, but would need to see where the day took them. To Hazel, that sounded promising, and not in a good way.

As they entered the Kingswood, Hazel thought it was one of the most beautiful forests she'd seen. Due to its proximity to the Border and the magic beyond, the Kingswood was lusher than those back home. Tall, white birch trees towered toward the heavens, and the forest floor was a mix of lush moss and dark, fertile soil. Mushrooms and other fungi littered the underbrush, and new growth, well, it actually existed here. Hazel imagined that this must be how all forests looked, once upon a time.

"So," Slaide began, "Phillip has taken a liking to you."

Hazel wasn't sure why this was something to comment on. In her experience, if you treated an animal with the respect it deserved and paid attention to its body language, it wasn't terribly difficult to get along. Though, she'd always had an easy relationship with most horses. Even the difficult ones. She shrugged. "He seems easy enough to get along with."

"Phillip has never let anyone touch him except me. Until you came along."

"Seriously?" She whirled on him from Nanna's back. Nanna didn't appreciate the movement and huffed her disapproval.

"Seriously. He has a sad history. One where he was overworked and abused. And because of that history, I am the only one he has ever trusted. He's bitten, kicked, maimed, and damn near killed people for trying to do what you did today. Most horses take issue with him as well.

The only stablemate he puts up with is Nanna. He picked a fight with her once, when they were first introduced. And boy did she put him in his place. They've been inseparable ever since." He smiled at the memory, then frowned. "Magnus despises him, though, and once threatened to have him carved up for the royal hounds. Needless to say, he's never made *that* threat again."

"Wait. Were you trying to get me killed?" Her eyes bugged.

Slaide laughed. "No. I told you. I wanted to see something. And I was mostly confident he wasn't going to act out. After all, he did let you on his back once already."

"Yes—with you. Who's to say he would have allowed that if you weren't also there? He could have turned on me today, and you didn't bother telling me."

"I seem to recall you riding him by yourself last night without issue," he reminded her. "Look, Hazel. This animal has a way with people. It's as though he can read someone's true intentions… maybe even see their soul. Animals do have a sense for those things, you know. And after all he went through, I would say he's especially attuned to the intentions of those around him."

"Are you certain? He likes *you*, and I'm fairly sure 'good intentions' are not associated with your name."

"I saved him, remember? I earned his trust. And besides, have you ever considered that my intentions and my actions are two totally different things?" He rode ahead of them slightly and looked over his shoulder.

"Maybe you should be less of an asshole every now and then, if you want to make your intentions clear," Hazel retorted.

"Or, maybe *you* need to stop taking things at face value all the time."

Hazel pulled back on Nanna's reins softly, momentarily stopping them. She watched the swaying of Phillip's steps and the swishing of his long black tail. How Slaide sat lightly on the horse's back, despite his size. And how the two worked synchronously, one body instead of two. Her hand found the locket, and she worked it between her fingers as she watched them.

She clicked her tongue at Nanna and the pony got moving again, trotting briefly to catch up with her friend.

Maybe he's right. It certainly gave her something to think about.

"So," he spoke, changing the subject. "The first trial is tomorrow."

Nausea overtook her, and her grip tightened on the reins.

Slaide looked over his shoulder. "Stunned into silence?"

"I don't know what to say. I thought we—I—had more time. I don't feel ready." She wanted to crawl into a hole.

"The fun could only last so long, sweets. But, look on the bright side. You've got me to tell you what the trial is and what to expect."

She cocked an eyebrow.

"We really need to work on your thank-yous. Mind you, no one else gets this information ahead of time."

"Whatever. What's the first trial then?" she asked.

"An enchanted labyrinth. No rules. Nothing is off the table. The only task is to survive and get out."

Something was far too easy. She could feel it in the marrow of her bones and her locket warmed in confirmation.

I'm going to die tomorrow.

The pair trekked for half the day. It was uneventful—peaceful even—and for that Hazel was grateful. The tension eased out of her. The horses were less uptight as well, their bodies relaxing under their riders, even Nanna.

Hazel took the time to enjoy the sights and sounds the forest offered, trying to ignore the proximity of her demise. Birds chirped and squawked in the canopy while crickets chittered and frogs sang their songs along the forest floor. A pair of fox-eared squirrels darted across their path, causing Nanna to snort her aggravation.

She had no idea who or what Slaide was searching for, since he'd evaded her attempts to get those answers out of him. She grew suspicious that he wasn't hunting for anything at all, but instead using this as an excuse to get out of the castle walls. And who could blame him? He wouldn't hear a complaint out of her. She didn't even mind *his* company at the moment.

Slaide came to a stop without warning. Well, he had warned her, she just wasn't paying attention. After almost running Nanna into Phillip's backside, Hazel became aware of Slaide signaling their halt silently, with his fist in the air. Hearing her *oomph* behind him, he darted a disapproving glance over his shoulder. And that was when she noticed it…

When did the forest get quiet?

As if in answer to her thoughts, something whizzed past her head, nearly grazing her ear. She turned to see what it was, only to find an arrow lodged into the tree across the path from her. Her stomach roiled. That tree could have been her head.

"GET DOWN!" Slaide shouted, rolling Phillip back with a tight rein to give Hazel some cover. All at once he was grabbing his hunting bow and leaping from Phillip. He tackled Hazel from Nanna's back in one swoop. The ground drove the air from Hazel's lungs, and she'd inadvertently struck Slaide in the belly with her knee, causing him to gasp as well. But he recovered more quickly, hauling Hazel to her knees and forcing her to crawl to the cover of the bushes. With a sharp whistle from Slaide, Phillip took off for his own safety, Nanna close behind.

When the dust settled, it was quiet, save for Hazel's panting—which felt louder than it probably was. Her eyes were wide as saucers, her face saying what her mouth didn't dare.

What. Was. That?

Slaide didn't answer immediately, steeling his gaze on the path before them. He was preternaturally still, the very picture of a helcat stalking its dinner. She watched as his eyes transformed into their other form: those dark, obsidian pools. She was quite certain she could drown in them, even if they were fearsome.

As she watched him, her gaze drifted and she noticed something that caused her to freeze. Slaide had an arrow shaft protruding from his calf.

"You're hit!" she hissed.

He turned to her, face contorted as though not understanding.

"Your calf. You were hit with an arrow!" It was everything she had to keep her voice low.

As the realization washed over him, Slaide rotated to look back at his leg and sure enough, there was an arrow taking up residence where it didn't belong. He sighed as though this was just another inconvenience he was used to facing. He worked himself up to a seated position, then without warning, he grasped the shaft and yanked the arrow free, hardly wincing as the arrowhead ripped through his flesh again on its way out.

Hazel, on the other hand, balked when the arrow was torn free. She watched as Slaide examined it in its entirety, going so far as to sniff the feathered fletchings.

"Fucking gobkins," he muttered. Meanwhile, blood dripped steadily from the untended wound on his calf.

"What's a gobkin?" Not that it mattered in the grand scheme of things, but she was curious anyway.

Slaide was digging for something in his pack as he answered. "They're… uh… you've heard of goblins, yes? Shit… where did I put it? So… they're like goblins… except… there it is…" He withdrew a roll of cloth and began wrapping his leg. "Like I was saying, they're nasty relatives of goblins, but smaller and cleverer." He held up the arrow. "Their weapons-craft is superior to most lesser beings. Combine that with their ability to actually *use* them? Well, this is what happens. Oh, and they're particularly skilled… in… poisons." He winced.

And then he toppled over.

"Slaide? Shit! Slaide, get up!" She was no longer being quiet.

"Can't… poison… arrow. Magic… blocking." His voice was strained, barely above a whisper. And somehow he managed to convey his annoyance just the same.

No no no. You are not leaving me here alone like this. "Slaide, I need you to stay with me and tell me what to do. Please!"

Something moved in the brush across from them, and she froze. She'd ignored her locket's prior warnings, but now it was unmistakable: danger lurked nearby. In the tall grass, a small form moved, two grotesque yellow eyes blinked. They were staring.

At her.

Think, Hazel. Think. She didn't have any weapons with her, but Slaide did.

She dove toward him and heard the gobkins burst into movement behind her. She tucked into a roll and grabbed his ashwood bow and three arrows from the ground. By the time she was standing, the bow was drawn, string taut and prepared to fire. Her toad-like adversary was nearly upon her when she released, sending the arrow through one too-large, sickly-yellow eye with a squelch. The beast reeled backward with the force of the blow, flopping twice before it went still.

Another arrow flew past her head, and Hazel whirled to find her assailant posted on a boulder at least fifty paces away. In an instant, she sent an arrow back at him—while dodging his second shot—and thumped the gobkin in the chest, knocking him from his perch. Two down. But how many were there?

A gurgled cry sounded from above her, and she looked up just in time to see a third gobkin diving toward her from a tree limb, daggers outstretched. She dove just out of reach but quickly realized her mistake as she righted herself.

They weren't after her; they were after Slaide.

And she'd given the beasts exactly what they wanted.

Secrets

HAZEL stared in horror at the gobkin before her, his wart-riddled skin and horrendous underbite stealing the show as he snarled at her. Large tusks protruded from his lower jaw, and she shuddered at the thought of those tusks ripping into her flesh. Or Slaide's.

Slaide was still laying on the forest floor, nearly paralyzed. The gobkin turned from Hazel and approached Slaide warily, as though he knew what the man was capable of. Hazel wondered if this had been a planned ambush. Either Slaide and these creatures had a less than pleasant history, or they were going to pounce on the first unsuspecting travelers to ride through this territory, no matter who they were.

Regardless, she needed to move. He was still far enough away from Slaide that she wasn't overly concerned with skewering the wrong target with a wayward shot, so she made her decision and nocked her last arrow. As she steadied her breath and prepared her shot, something rustled behind her. Before she could so much as peek over her shoulder, something barreled into her, causing the arrow to loose prematurely, finding itself embedded in a nearby birch tree.

She rolled over, grappling with her gobkin attacker in order to get onto her back, where she could better defend herself. The beast lunged, claws swiping and teeth gnashing as she tried to push it away with her feet. But it was relentless, taking blow after blow to its face and soft body, completely unbothered in its pursuit of destroying her.

Deep down, Hazel was losing control, panic and uncertainty creeping in. She no longer had the upper hand in this fight. She chanced a glance at Slaide and found the other remaining gobkin still circling him, taunting, playing with its food. Slaide's body was twitching, his feet trying to move as though the poison was slowly wearing off, but they were both running out of time.

Pain lanced through her forearm, her thoughts cut short as the gobkin clamped down on her. Flesh and muscle gave way easier than wet parchment, and she was certain the bone would soon snap. She would not die this way. *Could not* die this way. Then something occurred to her: she had another weapon at her disposal.

Hazel didn't know what she was doing, but she had to try. She closed her eyes and focused inward, trying to find that deep, warm light she'd gathered in the past. She pushed past the pain of the gobkin above her, shredding her arm to get to her face and neck. *Focus.* She dove deeper and deeper into her mind, wondering if it was possible to get stuck in one's own self-conscious.

And then, like a beacon of hope, there it was.

Hazel grabbed it fiercely, a fine thread of power, and began her ascent toward the surface. As she drew the power upward with her, it grew in size and strength until there was no more room. Nowhere for it to go.

She erupted into a ball of light, all the energy she'd built up blasting outward from her body. The gobkin was caught in the blast and thrown against a nearby tree, where she heard his body crack before he fell into a limp pile on the ground. It hadn't occurred to her to check Slaide's proximity to the blast before she'd essentially detonated herself, but she was pleased to see she hadn't obliterated him.

Better still was the sight of Slaide—mobile enough to finally be able to fight for himself—landing a killing blow to his assailant. He drove his dagger in hard as the gobkin's body came down upon him, spraying him with black blood. Its form went limp against Slaide's chest with a gurgle. Trapped under the corpse, Slaide coughed and gagged at its stench.

Hazel tasted the familiar burnt flavor of charred ash, just as she'd experienced in her previous magical outbursts. She righted herself and made her way over to Slaide. She grabbed hold of the dead gobkin by its shoulder, trying not to breathe in the reek of rotting flesh emanating from its body as she lifted it off him.

"Gods, I hate those things," he groaned, taking in large breaths of untainted air. "More a nuisance than anything, but they're full of tricks." He looked up at Hazel. "And specialize in ambushes."

After a few more moments and with Hazel's help, Slaide scooted back to the base of a tree and rested his back against it. As she was aiding him, she caught Slaide staring at the torn skin along her forearm. At how the injuries were less severe than they should be.

She expected to see bleeding, torn flesh. Instead, she found an injury that appeared several days old. *What in the name of the gods… I'm healing?* She met Slaide's eyes with her own, and a smile slowly formed on his face.

"Well, that's certainly interesting."

"Mhmm," she mumbled. *Time to talk about something else.* "So," she said, eyeing his immobile legs. "How long until the rest of this reverses?"

His gaze was burning a hole in her arm, apparently reluctant to let this go, before he sighed and accepted her change of conversation. "Any moment now, if the rest of me is any indication. Those buggers must have developed a new formula; I've never had it last this long."

Hazel's eyes shot open. "You mean to tell me this has happened before?"

"First, pick your jaw up off the floor. Not *that* surprising, is it? Second, yes. More times than I care to recount, much less admit to. Always minor, though. While we're waiting, I think I'm the one who should be questioning you."

Oh, this will be good. She folded her arms. "Go on…"

"You can shoot. Quite well, in fact. You never said you could shoot."

"You never asked." It was her turn to smirk at him.

"Really? And why would I? You didn't exactly strike me as the kind of woman who would be able to draw a bow, much less pick off our enemies."

"What was it you said to me before? I need to stop taking things at face value all the time? Maybe you should take your own advice. My father taught me some basic survival skills, should I ever need them. Plus, our farm is on the edge of town, half a day's ride from the market. It's just easier to source our meat from the woods when we need it. And he and I enjoyed the occasional target practice duel. I only beat him once, and I'm still not convinced he didn't let me win out of pity."

"Huh. Well, I guess I'm glad he did. Wasn't planning on giving away a life debt anytime soon, and especially not to you, but I wasn't getting out of this mess in one piece if you hadn't been here."

Hazel blushed and averted her eyes.

"And on that note, I guess I should thank you for coming. Had you stayed in bed, I would probably be a dead man." There was no sarcasm. No ire.

Compliments from Slaide made her uncomfortable, and she couldn't pinpoint why. Was it the questionable authenticity? The way his compliments made her feel warm inside when they absolutely should not? She cleared her throat, ready to change the subject.

"So," she said, gesturing to the corpses around them, "I'm assuming these are what you were hunting?"

He shook his head. "I wish it were that simple, but no. That was just a chance happening, though if I'm honest, ambushes aren't all that uncommon out here. What I'm searching for… It's not any sort of beast or creature."

Hazel kept her eyes locked on him, waiting for him to explain. She was growing tired of his cryptic half-answers. As though feeling the weight of her stare, he looked up from where he was watching his still-motionless legs and caught her gaze.

"What?" he questioned.

"What's going on? What are you looking for out here?"

"I've already said more than I should have." He rubbed a hand down his face. "Someone, something, is tearing rifts in the Border. I've been—unofficially—tasked with tracking the rifts and closing them when possible. Usually, there are signs of increased magical creature activity near these rifts. That, or the beasts themselves."

"And the gobkins?"

"Shouldn't have been on this side."

"There's a rift nearby?" Hazel thought she might be catching on.

His demeanor shifted, and he chewed on the inside of his cheek, mulling something over. "Possibly. Listen, Hazel. I should probably take you back. This has already amounted to more than I was expecting, and my mistake could have cost you your life."

"Why do you care? I'm honestly surprised you've let me live this long. Seems it would be easy enough to let me fall prey to something like this." She nudged the smelly creature with her boot.

Slaide shrugged. "I find you interesting. Most people with power chase it. Use it. Bleed kingdoms with it. You're dangerous, Hazel, but you're an enigma. I can't figure you out, and *that* interests me."

"You're a shit witch hunter," she shot back, instantly regretting it.

"You're probably right," he said, staring at her a moment too long before letting out a sharp whistle.

He was answered by the thundering of hooves pounding the ground, and Phllip and Nanna came charging around the bend. She turned to face Slaide, then, and found him maneuvering his legs, attempting to pull them under himself. *Stubborn ass.* She rolled her eyes and stepped in to help.

And despite his burning pride, he let her. By the time the horses had settled, he'd nearly regained his strength. Still, Hazel doubted he could sit astride Phillip without falling off. He could hardly stand.

"I don't think this is a good idea." She put her hands on her hips.

He waved her off. "This boy takes good care of me. I've had less control over my body returning home from a long night out than I do now. He makes sure I get home in one piece."

"And how, exactly, do you plan on getting up there?" Hazel questioned, hands on her hips, a parent watching their toddler about to do something reckless.

He patted Phillip on the shoulder. The gentle giant responded by bending one foreleg and bowing low, giving Slaide easier access to the saddle. When they'd righted themselves, the pair turned to face Hazel. "Any more questions?"

Wordlessly, Hazel mounted Nanna before addressing him. "Just one. What now?"

"Follow me."

Finally happening upon the sundered section of the Border was… anticlimactic. If Slaide hadn't pointed it out, she'd have been none the wiser.

"This is it?" she asked, her anticipation fading.

"This is it. Sorry to disappoint."

"No—it's just… Well, I was expecting a giant torn hole and scorched earth. I can't even tell what I'm looking at here." She cocked her head to the side.

"Do you feel it? The Border?" he asked.

"Is that what it is?" Something was buzzing in her ears. In her bones. It was reminiscent of visiting Agnes's cottage and passing through her wards, but stronger. More dangerous somehow. As usual, the locket thrummed with nervous energy, growing warmer the closer they advanced.

"Yes. And that's just the edge of it. It's stronger the closer you get. Generally, it only affects magic-wielders, though some don't feel it at all. And For others… it can be rather unpleasant. Are you still feeling ok?"

"I am. So, where's the hole?" There was no sign of one, and she was growing more curious by the minute.

This earned her a childish smile from Slaide.

"Seriously? Grow up." She shook her head in disbelief, though she wanted so badly to laugh. He wouldn't get the satisfaction.

"Right, then. This way. Let's leave the horses here for now and go on foot. It won't be far."

"Should I expect any surprises this time?" She raised a brow.

"You're in the Wilds. You should always expect a surprise, because then nothing will catch you off guard."

"Wow, you're quite the philosopher, aren't you?"

Slaide snorted and dismounted Phillip. He draped the reins over the horn of the saddle and gave him a pat on the side. Hazel followed suit, sliding off of Nanna's broad back. It wasn't much of a distance to the ground, but the pony's width added some difficulty to the dismount, requiring Hazel to swing her leg quite a bit further. She grunted, barely landing on her feet, and Nanna looked back at her in disapproval before dropping her head to the grass.

Hazel followed Slaide between the trees, the tingling sensation growing more intense as they pressed onward. She was wondering when they would arrive at the actual Border. Surely something so widely known, revered, and feared would be easy to see as they approached. Up ahead, the forest path widened into a clearing. To her dismay, that was right where they headed. She was tired of glades and clearings in forests. They never held anything good.

As if on cue, her line of sight opened up to reveal a new addition to her list of *probably-not-good* things.

"What is that?" she gasped.

"What is what?" He asked without looking back at her.

"That *thing!*" She pointed out in front of them at the giant pillar in the center of the clearing. It was…vibrating? Could he feel it, too?

"Oh, that? That's just an obelisk."

Oh right. As though she should have just known. Stupid uneducated girl from her stupid backwater town. *Of course, it was an obelisk.*

"And what do obelisks do?" Because it was making her stomach want to turn inside out just looking at it. Slaide turned slightly to look at her, but before he could so much as open his mouth, she cut him off. "I don't need to be patronized. Just tell me."

He sighed. "The obelisks are crucial to the stability of the Border. They work kind of like a fence post, an anchor point for the anti-magic wards that stretch between them, fencing magical things out. The field that makes up the Border itself lies between each obelisk. They provide grounding and a backup source of power should the wards themselves ever fail."

Interesting indeed. "Is it the obelisks that are failing or the wards?"

"We don't know." She could see how it pained him to admit it. Slaide, who prided himself on being right. Slaide, who always had an answer.

"I see. So how do we find the break in the wards?" She was happy to have a distraction, and glad he had one, too. The less he focused on her and her abilities, the better.

"Normally, I start near one of these obelisks and work my way out. When the sensation decreases at an odd rate or an unnatural part of the

Border, it means we're close. This time, though, it's not going to take that much effort."

"How do you know?"

"Because we're almost there," Slaide said plainly.

Sure enough, as they approached the obelisk, the tingling, buzzing sensation faded. "Is it normal for the Border to be weaker near these pillars?"

"No. They should be strongest here." A look of concern grew on his face, brow furrowing. As she walked to his side, he stuck a protective arm out, blocking her from taking another step. "Stay behind me. Touch nothing."

Well, that's less comforting than it should be. But she obliged him, if only because she didn't want to lose her head.

The base of the obelisk was broad. It towered over them, reaching twice as tall as the tallest tree. Slaide looked up at it, then at its base, running his fingers through the grass, looking for something. Wordlessly, he stood and walked toward the broken portion of Border.

While he busied himself with his search, Hazel approached the obelisk. From a distance, its surface looked so plain…just black. But up close, it was spectacular. The stone was almost glossy, its smooth surface dotted with speckles of gray, white, and silver. It reminded her of the night sky back home. The same sky she used to lie under and count the stars with Zeke—when life was simple. His invasion into her thoughts startled her. Where *was* Zeke? Why hadn't he come to check on her? Did he know she was in the castle? Did he know she was alive?

While her thoughts wandered, she reached out to touch the stone. It was cold; so much colder than she'd expected and she drew her hand back in a flash. But then she reached out again, feeling the coldness, embracing it. Just above head height, a blue glyph appeared from within the stone, as though the stone itself was glowing. It was blue, glowing so bright it almost looked white. She stared at it with the cluelessness of a child staring at the sun, ignoring the warning that flared beneath her shirt.

Slaide looked over his shoulder in time to find Hazel with her hand against the obelisk and the blue glyph glowing on the stone surface, indicating the pillar was still active.

He was on his feet in a flash, charging toward Hazel, yelling at her to back up, but she couldn't hear him. The world around her buzzed louder. Louder.

The glyph morphed into an angry red. Even with his unnatural speed, he would not make it to her in time. The world around them slowed to a crawl. Tendrils of smoke and shadow leaped from him and made a beeline for Hazel. He threw as much force into them as he could. His shadows barreled into her the very moment the obelisk erupted in light, throwing them both on their asses several yards away.

His shadows withdrew into him as he ran over to her. She was lying on her back panting, eyes wide as dinner plates and hands gripping the grass at her sides.

"Spinning?" He asked.

She barely glanced at him before squeezing her eyes shut.

"That would have killed you." He scowled. "*Should* have killed you."

"What was it? Why did that happen?" She was out of breath, a combination of having the wind knocked out of her and being scared half to death.

"That, my dear Hazel, was the Border demonstrating how it works. Except it failed, since you're not a pile of ash. You're welcome, by the way."

She tossed him one of her now-signature *go-fuck-yourself* glares. "That just makes us even."

His laugh sparked something she chose to ignore. "Fair enough."

"Well," she said, standing and dusting herself off, "clearly the obelisk is functioning."

"Indeed. Better than I'd expected. But while you were playing the game of touch-stuff-and-die, *my* investigation turned up something interesting." He held up his open palm.

"What is that?" She moved closer. There were fine black granules in his hand.

"It's salt."

Salt and Stone

"SALT?" She grabbed a few of the granules from his palm and rolled them between her fingers. "But it's black."

"It's not *that* kind of salt. This is, as its color indicates, black salt. Some people call it obsidian salt because it comes from the same mines as obsidian stone. But the salt itself isn't obsidian at all."

Hazel nodded in understanding. "The way things have been going I probably don't want the answer to this, but what is black salt used for?"

Slaide sighed. "That's the problem. It's extremely versatile. It is good for protection and magical cleansing in small spaces. Some people wear it in its granular form, usually in glass vials. Others imbue it into small trinkets or jewelry."

"I thought obsidian was used for protection against magic?"

He nodded his head side to side. "It is, and it is far more potent for that purpose than black salt. Obsidian isn't entirely practical for personal use, though. Its anti-magic properties are far reaching, which is why it was chosen for the obelisks all those years ago. It does a better job of amplifying anti-magic spells and warding on a grand scale."

"What else is the salt used for, then?" Slaide looked at her, appraising. The unspoken words were written on her face: *why was there salt sprinkled at the Border?*

"Black salt can temporarily amplify certain spells… and nullify others. It's as powerful as it is brief. That being said…"

"It could last long enough to get someone through the Border?" she finished for him. But something wasn't adding up. "Where does this kind of salt come from? I always thought salt was deposited near coastlines by rain and sea air. We aren't even remotely close to a coastline."

"No," Slaide said. "We aren't." His face darkened.

Slaide looked out at the Border, and she noticed how his shoulders tensed. He turned back to her with a crease between his eyes, apprehension clear on his face. "Come with me. There's something you need to see."

The pair led their mounts quietly back through the Kingswood, hoping to avoid any further surprises. The only sound they made came from the plodding of horse hooves into the dirt path.

After a while, they reached an area where the grassy plain rose slowly into a hillside. Without a word, Slaide brought Phillip to a stop and dismounted, and Hazel took this as her cue to do the same. She crossed the few paces between them, leading Nanna by her reins.

"We'll leave the horses here. They'll be too easy to spot from the hilltop," he said, turning his back on her, black cloak billowing slightly behind him as he started up the hill. She followed, wishing she'd worn more than her borrowed leathers. The higher they climbed, especially now that they'd left the protection of the trees, the more blustery the wind grew.

As they approached the crest of the hill, Slaide crouched and signaled for her to do the same. He stared straight ahead as he spoke.

"What you are about to witness is something few know about and even fewer have seen. There's a reason for that, which you'll soon understand. Before we move forward, I need you to understand me. You *must* keep your head down. While this is the best vantage point to what I am about to show you, it's also more exposed than I like. If you sit up too high, you'll give us away."

Well, that isn't unsettling at all. "I understand," she whispered.

He spared a moment to glance at her before crawling forward, and she followed despite the growing warmth of her locket. They crested the hill, where Hazel found it wasn't a hill at all. It had been the rear slope of a cliff. The drop was devastatingly sharp, but that wasn't what took her breath away.

Below them, in a crater carved deep into the ground, people bustled about. The rim was dotted with caves with people going in and out. Wagons and wheelbarrows were overflowing with minerals or ore, she couldn't tell. It was a mine system, larger than any she'd ever heard of. Practically its own town.

"Welcome to Blackrock Gulch," he spat as though the words soured his mouth.

She was dumbfounded. A place of this enormity would have taken years to carve out. Thousands and thousands of hours of work. Countless workers and horses traveling to and from…

"How?" Hazel asked. "How does seemingly no one know about this place? This must be the biggest, best-kept secret in Aeos. But I don't understand how it could stay hidden in plain sight like this."

"Until recently, I didn't know much about its origin. I just assumed it was a natural cave that the Kings of the past dug deeper over time. But I now have a book in my possession that has made everything a lot clearer. Sometime in the years before The Thousand Years War, the angels fell from the heavens. Based on location descriptions given in the old text, I believe Blackrock used to be the crash site known as Angelfall. Which may have something to do with why the harvested ore is so powerful; it was imbued with Aetherial energy."

Gods… but then that would mean…

An air-splitting snap tore her from her thoughts. Screams followed.

No. She searched for the source of the sound.

Thwack. The sound lashed out again, and Hazel's gaze landed on it. A man was on his knees in the mud, arms stretched above his head, where he was tied to a post. A whipping post. The color drained from her wind-lashed cheeks as her stomach turned over on itself.

Crack. She watched the knotted leather cord cut through the air. Watched as it made contact with the already bleeding flesh. Watched as it tore a new gash through skin and muscle, spraying blood and gore. Watched as the man vomited before going limp against the post. Watched as the overseer lashed into him again.

Hazel buried her head, desperate to block out the scene. Why had he brought her here? She could still hear the whip as it continued to sound despite covering her ears. Bile rose in her throat.

She brought herself to look at Slaide. Had he known? The answer was etched into his features, guaranteed by the guilt shining in his eyes. Of course he had.

"This isn't just minework. This is slavery." She choked on her words, trying to whisper but wanting to scream.

Slaide said nothing.

Anger boiled within her. "Take me there," she demanded.

"I'm sorry, what?" He nearly choked.

She looked at him with fury burning in her eyes. "I said take me there. Take me down there." She looked back at the crater. "Take me, or so help me, I will go on my own."

"That's madness, Hazel. I know this is upsetting, but we are not going down there. That's worse than hand delivering you to the Magistry's gates. Because this?" He gestured to the mine below them. "This is where you go when they're done with you. This is where they send people to die. You want to know why the public hunts and executions have stopped almost entirely? You're looking at it."

Her eyes welled with tears. She imagined her peaceful life, growing up with Connall, with only the Briar & Rose to worry about. Meanwhile, people from all ages and walks of life were dragged here, to their eventual demise. *How could this go on, and no one speak out about it?*

He grabbed her hand. "Come on. Let's go."

She ignored him, unable to peel her eyes from the horrors below.

"Hazel—"

"You knew about this," she seethed. "You've always known, and you've done nothing to stop it. You may not carry the whip, but you're just as complicit in this as they are. And here I was starting to… I thought…" She didn't finish the sentence. She didn't need to. Her insides were igniting. Her power bubbled within, promising to erupt again if she didn't control herself.

His face flashed with hurt, with shame, and she was glad for it. Her words had hit their mark, and she was not the least bit sorry. Something about that small victory quelled the bitter, boiling rage.

But then his expression shifted to anger, twin lines furrowing between his brows, his eyes darkening. She wondered which part of what she'd said had crossed a line.

"People *do* know, Hazel. Trust me when I say they make *very* calculated moves behind the scenes and are near impossible to track."

Hazel locked eyes with him, refusing to accept that as an answer.

Slaide accepted the challenge. "Why don't *you* do something about it, then?" He nodded toward the crater below. "Light it up. Put an end to the suffering."

She flinched. They'd tiptoed around this subject until now. He'd called her out. Acknowledged what they both knew.

"I'm not interested in murdering innocents, Slaide." She turned her back on him and started in the direction they'd come from. "And if you're so certain I can, then arrest me. Gods know you can't have a *witch* wandering around the kingdom."

He followed her silently.

"Make no mistake," she whirled on him, stopping him in his tracks, "I *will* put a stop to this. I don't know when, and I don't know how. But when I am finished, no witch or magical being will ever be in chains again."

Before she turned around, the corners of Slaide's mouth tipped upward, hinting at a smile.

Not another word was said as they returned to the horses, leaving the horrors of Blackrock Gulch behind.

Once they were out of sight from the gulch, Slaide brought the horses to a stop and dismounted, making his way around to Hazel. He offered her a hand down, but she ignored him and managed on her own.

Slaide stood there, hand still outstretched as she walked past him.

She walked a few paces away and then got down on her hands and knees, her body immediately racking with sobs.

Slaide walked up behind her, and she looked up at him in disgust before averting her gaze.

He knelt beside her and placed his hand gently on her back, though her body flinched at his touch.

Without warning, she whirled on him and clocked him in the nose.

"Gods damn it, Hazel!"

She mounted Phillip and raced for the Kingswood while Slaide tended to his nose. She was going not just to the Border, but through it. She was going to leave all this behind.

The Border Wraith

PHILLIP charged headlong into the woods, spurred on by Hazel's urgent commands. She chanced a glance over her shoulder, fully expecting Slaide to be on her tail, but was surprised to find he wasn't. She took the opportunity to slow the horse down and take inventory of her surroundings.

The forest was thick and dark here. The trees pressed in closely, and the path had grown almost nonexistent. The evening had been drawing close, but she could no longer see the sky through the canopy to tell how late it was. The air was heavy and cool, almost damp.

She led Phillip aside and dismounted, walking alongside him briefly before deciding to continue on foot, even if she knew she was safer atop the giant horse. He would draw far too much attention when what she needed was stealth. So, she left Phillip to his grazing and walked on alone.

As the forest grew thicker, the air stirred. A familiar buzz passed over her, similar to the one she'd experienced coming and going from Agnes's warded home. And yet, it was different. The pressure on her head was nearly unbearable. Her skin tingled, the locket warmed, and the hair on her arms stood on end. She was pimpled in gooseflesh as the sensation rolled over her. It was cold. So cold. Someone called her name in the distance. It might have been Slaide, but she wasn't sure. Her hearing was muffled and her head was a bog.

She remembered his promise. His *threat. Go ahead and run, little witch. It will be that much more fun when I catch you.* She pressed on anyway. Let him catch her. She was done caring.

Hazel knew in her bones she'd reached the Border. The magical palisade between Aeos and everything Beyond. She didn't see the obelisks, but there must be one close, given the vibrations in the air. She just needed to make it through, and then past the restricted zone beyond.

She came to a halt, head pounding, and seemingly out of nowhere, Slaide caught up with her. He must not have liked what he witnessed.

"What did I tell you about—shit," he said, moving to her.

"Slaide?" she asked, the world around her growing hazy. "W-what's happening? I feel…" She spilled her guts then, vomiting what was left in her stomach onto the forest floor. When she sat up, a trickle ran from her nose.

Slaide's eyes went wide. Had she ever seen so much surprise in his face before? Such concern?

She wiped her nose on the sleeve of her leathers and it came away blood-streaked. Her eyes met his. She was so light, a feather that might float away.

He lurched to her side, catching her just before she could hit the ground.

Hazel giggled, trying unsuccessfully to push his hands away. "S-stop. That… tickles."

"Hazel, stop." His words were muffled as she shoved her hands in his face, her fingers smashing into his lips and mouth. "I'm… trying… to help… you," he got out while attempting to fight her off. He finally got a grasp on her wrists and held tight, pushing her to the ground.

She laughed again, bucking her hips and kicking wildly. Much to her surprise, Slaide straddled Hazel, pinning her wrists to the ground above her head.

"I knew you liked me," she slurred. "I never thought you'd be so direct, though."

A sinister expression overtook his face, as though a war waged within. His grip tightened on her wrists, and his eyes began to darken. But as quickly as it had come on, the feral beast shrunk away as Slaide shook his head, seemingly trying to clear his mind.

"Hazel. Hazel, look at me," he commanded. When she didn't listen, he let go of one wrist and grabbed her chin. He turned her head, forcing her to look him in the eyes.

Weightlessness overcame her and Slaide's touch was hardly noticeable as he shook her.

"Snap out of it, Hazel. Come back." But she didn't respond.

All she could do was watch as Slaide started rummaging through his pack. "Gods damn it all. Where is—gotcha!" He returned to Hazel, still lying on the ground where he'd left her. He sat her up slowly and her head lolled to the side. Try as she might, she couldn't control her neck.

She couldn't decide if time was moving both unusually fast or painstakingly slow, but Slaide was moving in slow motion as he grabbed the cork stopper between his teeth and pulled it from the vial. When he cringed at the smell, she tried to laugh at him. The joke was swiftly turned on her when he shoved the vial under her nose without warning.

Hazel came to in a violent fit of gagging and coughing, followed by a heave of bile into the grass. "What. The fuck. Was that?" She spat.

Slaide chuckled, and she glared at him after wiping her mouth. "Welcome back." He brought forth a waterskin and offered it to her.

While she drank deeply, Slaide said, "That was Border sickness. And this," he held up the vial, cork replaced, "just saved your life. Hartshorn salt. Potent, unpleasant stuff. Better than being dead, though, which is where you were headed."

She stared at the vial and the white powder within, stomach roiling in response.

Something in the distance cried out, a mix between a howl and a scream. Judging by Slaide's reaction, it wasn't some simple wolf or were-cat.

"Do I even want to know?" she hesitantly questioned.

Slaide bristled, his entire body fraught with tension.

"Slaide?"

"Shh!" he scolded her. "Border wraith." As though that was supposed to answer her questions.

Border… what? "Excuse me, what now? What's a Border wraith?"

He grabbed her by the wrist and began dragging her. "Trust me, it's not worth finding out. We need to move. Now."

Hazel pondered the urgency. It hadn't sounded overly close, but… As if on cue, a second screeching wail tore her from her thoughts. Whatever it was, it was closer than before. Much closer. The hairs on the back of her neck stood on end the way they always did before something ominous happened.

The air grew cooler, the temperature dropping unnaturally fast as though something had sucked the warmth out of the atmosphere.

Slaide was moving before she had time to recognize anything was happening. She didn't see him move, but he barreled into her, forcing the air from her lungs and slamming her to the ground.

"What in the name of all the gods. Slaide!" She huffed. "Get off!"

Instead, Slaide slapped a hand over her mouth and shimmied himself so that his body almost completely covered hers. "Shh," he whispered against her ear. "Don't. Move."

She was staring at the sky, watching the clouds slide across the moon and stars. A breeze caressed the trees, and the crickets still sang around them. Aside from that, the world was completely silent.

And then it all stopped. The chirping. The rustling leaves. The soft breeze. If the world could get any quieter, it did.

A feeling crept over Hazel that made her want to shrink down even smaller than she was and hide herself completely under Slaide's form. Her silver locket was hot against her skin.

Something was wrong. So wrong. She squeezed her eyes shut, as though that could offer more protection than leaving them open. Slaide's breathing was so slow and shallow in comparison to her own. Too loud. She was breathing too loud. Her heart thumped against her ribs, betraying her as she willed it to be quiet.

It came into view then—an eerie, ghostly presence. A cloaked figure walked toward their hiding place in the tall grass, just off the path. No, walking was the wrong way to describe it. It was floating, gliding through the air, its tattered shroud billowing behind it. Its face, if it had one, was cloaked in shadow and covered in a hood. Sleeves draped down to its long, spindly fingers, bone-white in the moonlight.

The smell hit her before it reached them. Rot and decay, but not the earthy, loamy kind. This thing polluted the air with the stench of a days-old corpse left to bake in the summer sun. Her stomach rebelled, and it took an extreme mental effort not to gag.

Slaide's words echoed in her mind as it grew closer. *Don't move. Don't move. Don't move.* It floated so near she wondered how it hadn't seen them yet. But some things were better left unanswered, and this she quickly learned as the wraith pulled back its hood, revealing a corpse-like face—or at least what was left of one.

It was then she understood why they'd been able to hide in plain sight: it was blind. Well, not just blind, but lacking eyes altogether.

The Border wraith had gaping black pits where its eyes should be and two dark slits for a nose. When it opened its mouth, she was met with a view of two rows of needle-sharp fangs. It was gliding close. Too close.

She was sure this thing could hear her every breath, if not her telltale heart. It could probably smell her, too, because the amount of stress she was feeling was without a doubt seeping through her pores.

As if on cue, the wraith tilted its head back and sniffed, something akin to a wild beast on the hunt. Its slitted nostrils flared wide as it sampled the air around it. Then it opened its mouth and panted before licking its lips greedily.

Oh, they were so dead. Maybe. Hazel had not the slightest clue what these wraiths did and made a mental note to ask Slaide later.

"Sslaaaide," came a voice, dragging out his name in a hiss. "You're not supposed to beee heeere." The wraith looked over them slowly, its eyeless gaze dragging so painfully slow that Hazel wondered if perhaps it did have vision after all.

"I can sense you, Slaaaide. You *and* your friend. And oooh, she smells exquisite." Its face twisted into something reminiscent of a smile, but with more teeth. "She's special, Slaaaide. But you knew that, didn't you. Just like you knew better than to bring her into our domain. Why don't you reveal yourselves? Any friend of Ssslaide's… will make an excellent sssacrifice."

The pressure against her skull grew. Claws ran down the edges of her mind, reminding her of the Striga, but heavier, more foreboding. And yet it was somehow soothing, beckoning her to come out of hiding. Promising no harm. Her head was foggy, her mind slogging through mud to form a single thought.

Yes, I should stand up and reveal myself. Say hello. Why not? Slaide's grip on her tightened, as though he could sense her thoughts. His hand was still over her mouth. He clamped that down tighter as well.

"Where aaare yooou?" the wraith sang. "You can't hide forever. I can feel your little pet's mind. We could aaall have so much fun. All you must do is show me where you aaare…"

Yes, Hazel thought. *It's not going to hurt anything.* But Slaide was pressing into her like their lives depended on it. *Why is he doing that? Maybe I should bite his hand. Yes, I should. Then he will let me up to say hello.*

Hazel chomped down on one of Slaide's fingers. His body tensed against hers as he cringed against the pain. But he didn't release her or utter a sound.

"C'mon, Slaide. Won't you let your pet come play? She absolutely *reeks* of magic. We could change the world with her, Slaide. Make them bow to us, the creatures they've too long scorned. It's unfair to keep her all to yourself. Didn't your mother teach you to share? Oh, wait. That's right…"

Something screamed in the distance, and Hazel watched as the wraith's head snapped in its direction. The scream was clearly human. Someone else was trying to cross the Border. The screech that followed was indication enough: the unfortunate soul had crossed the path of another Border wraith.

Their own undead stalker friend sniffed the air again and let forth a blood-curdling call that snapped Hazel back to her senses. Then it looked in their direction and sighed, defeated.

"Pity. Duty callsss. I'll be back for you, though, Slaaaide and pet. I'll beee back…" Hazel watched in silent horror as the wraith dissipated into nothing, no more than smoke carried away on a breeze.

When enough time had passed, Slaide finally pushed away from her enough to look down upon her, his face drawn into an angry scowl.

She frowned back, mouthing, "What?"

Slaide lifted his head to survey their surroundings. Satisfied the wraith was gone, he pushed off of her and onto his knees. He held up his hand, middle finger swollen and marred with a deep, almost penetrating bite imprint. "What. The fuck. Was this?"

Hazel looked from Slaide's accusatory gaze to his hand.

"Did… I do that?"

"Yes!" he hissed. "You almost broke the skin, you animal. Why did you bite me?"

"I have no idea! It wasn't… I don't…"

His brow knitted in thought. "Shit." He scrubbed a hand down his face, dragging the scowl with it. "He was in your head, wasn't he?"

It was her turn to scowl. "How would I know? All I remember is hearing nothing as it approached, then that chill passed over us, and then my head felt like I was wading through a marsh."

"What else did it tell you to do?"

"I wanted so badly to stand up and say hello, but you wouldn't let me. I guess he was trying to get me to reveal where we were."

"Compulsion," Slaide explained, as if that meant something.

She stared at him, blank faced.

"The wraith was using compulsion to try and find us. He knows me from… past encounters. But you…" He trailed off.

"The magic."

"Yes."

Hazel shrugged. "Alright then. Well, I'm sorry for, uh, biting you. And for nearly getting us eaten."

Slaide laughed. "Under different circumstances, I'd say you can bite me all you want, Hazel." His voice was deep and his grin feral. "As for being eaten, well, Border wraiths do far worse than eat people," he taunted, circling her. "They tend to play with their food, slowly sucking your soul from your body," he pulled her in close, his breath hot on her neck, his fingers caressing down the side of her face. "Until nothing is left but an empty husk where your body used to be. But as long as I'm around, you've got nothing to worry about."

Hazel looked up over her shoulder at him, his darkened eyes and stern expression picking up where his words left off. She got the feeling that they weren't talking about Border wraiths anymore. Something deep within her warmed, the sensation spreading through her body, heating her core. She could get lost in those dark, amber eyes.

Slaide moved slowly, wrapping his arms around her stomach, her waist, pulling her in tight to his body where he stood behind her. She felt his chest expand as he inhaled deeply, and her eyes fluttered closed.

"I warned you, little witch, of what would happen if you ran." He reached up into her tangle of auburn hair and tugged her head back ever so gently, the movement sending sparks through her mind.

"You disobeyed me. And I don't appreciate it," he growled into her ear. Then Slaide brought his mouth down to her exposed neck, pressing his lips to the sensitive skin with a butterfly-soft touch. Not a kiss; a warning.

He grazed his lips along the base of her neck to the ticklish spot just below her ear. And when he stopped there, he whispered, "Do you have any idea what you do to me, Hazel?"

He nipped her ear before working back down her neck. When he got back to her shoulder, just above the dip of her collarbone, sharp fangs brushed against her skin.

She stiffened, and Slaide chuckled against her skin. "Relax. I'm not going to eat you." He ground his hips against her backside. "Unless… you want me to."

He spun her around to face him. *Gods… he is handsome.* Her thoughts were racing to places they shouldn't go. Not with Slaide, and especially not here. And yet, something had set itself aflame in her chest.

Her thoughts were interrupted by his gaze. His smile. "What are you thinking in that pretty little head of yours, sweets? I want in on all your secrets."

Hazel's eyes shifted to his mouth, but something was holding her back. When she met his eyes again, there was a hunger she'd never seen before, and it was clear he felt it too. She wondered if the same war waged within him.

"I don't have any secrets," she breathed, unable to break eye contact.

"Oh, I think you do," he insisted, voice low.

Before she could respond, another desperate, ear-splitting scream rang out in the distance. Hazel shuddered from her toes to her shoulders, sobering her right out of the moment.

"Better them than us," Slaide offered with a sigh before reaching for her hand. "Let's get out of here."

"For once, I won't make you ask twice," Hazel eagerly replied, grasping his hand.

Candlesticks and Things That Go Bump in the Night

AFTER tucking in for the night, Hazel lit a candle and fetched the small book she'd *borrowed* from the hidden library. She spent far too long fiddling with the lock, but it didn't budge, and there wasn't a slot for a key. As she originally suspected, it likely opened with magic and magic alone. Something she had no control over, as if it mattered. It was unlikely her magic was what was needed to unlock the tome, anyway.

She ran her fingers across the runes etched into its surface. They were familiar somehow, as if she'd once known what they meant but long since forgotten. Though she supposed she shouldn't be surprised. Witches dealt in the runic language, and considering her mother, well…

It was disconcerting that a book such as this would be left behind in a castle library, in a kingdom that looked upon magic as a sin. Considering runic language was steeped in magic, she had no doubt the book had been stolen from its original owner. Or perhaps left behind in haste.

She sighed, setting the book aside. She knew she should be sleeping with the first trial just hours away, but she couldn't quiet her mind. All of this was for her mother. *Because* of her mother. Because of powers and Witchbane tea and people near and dear who'd decided lying was safer than the truth.

She'd only just closed her eyes when a knock sounded at her door.

Hazel jolted upright, and realizing it was still dark outside, grabbed the nearest thing she could to defend herself with: a brass candlestick.

The door handle jiggled, and the person on the other side cursed under their breath. When nothing else happened, Hazel loosed a breath in relief.

But then the door burst open, and a body landed just inside the door, still muttering curses.

Hazel raised the candlestick again, and when the intruder stood to their full height, she launched it across the room.

It hit its mark.

"Gods of fucking Caelis!" came the first in a slew of additional curses. A voice she recognized. Slurred slightly, clumsier than normal, but…

"Slaide?" she asked.

"Depends," he groaned. "If I say yes, are you going to throw something else?"

Shit. She hopped out of bed, crouching beside where he sat on the floor. "Are you…" she caught herself, realizing the pitch of her voice made her sound far too concerned. "Are you alright?"

Slaide rubbed his head, scowling at her. "I'd be much better if I hadn't been hit with a candlestick. But I'll manage. Good aim, by the way." It wasn't lost on her that he was slurring his words.

"Wouldn't have had to do it if you didn't scare the shit out of me." She crossed her arms over her body.

"Shhhh… you're being too looouuddd," he complained.

Hazel rolled her eyes. "Where were you, anyway? Why are you drunk?"

"I'm not drunk," he insisted.

"Slaide."

He sighed, hanging his head. "I don't even know where to begin."

"Start with why in all the gods you're in my room in the middle of the night," she said.

Slaide looked to the window as if wanting to confirm the hour. "Right. Well, I was at my favorite seedy pub, uh, taking the edge off, and on my way back, was jumped by two men."

"Gods, Slaide! Why didn't you start with that?"

He shrugged. "Because they're both dead in the bushes. That's not the point. When they thought they had the upper hand, the one man said something about buying the other's time." His eyes flitted to hers. "No one else has been here?"

"I—no? Slaide, what is going on?" she pressed, helping him stand.

"Evidently, someone wants you out of the running before this even starts," he managed.

And maybe she should have been more surprised by that. But she wasn't. She'd known all along she was on borrowed time, and that someone would come for her throat eventually.

"And you're drunk because?"

"Am I not allowed to drink?" he answered, swaying a bit on his feet.

"Drinking is one thing. Coming back completely inebriated, hardly able to stand, and busting down my door? I know you don't think I'm that stupid."

He rolled his eyes in irritation, but relented. "Fine. If you must know, I'm… apprehensive about sending you into the competition tomorrow. I just—"

"You doubt my ability to stay alive," she deadpanned. Though if she was honest, she doubted it too.

"No, it's not that. Okay, well… a little. But only because we haven't had enough time. Not because you haven't proven yourself capable."

Fair enough. It stung, but he wasn't wrong. They'd had mere days for something others had used a lifetime for: honing their skills and bodies, perfecting their swordsmanship and training in combat…

But his honesty was disarming.

"And it's not *just* that. I'm dealing with some personal demons I'd rather not get into right now. It's just… sometimes it helps to drown one vice with another."

Hazel didn't press him but made a mental note to ask about it later.

"So," she began. "Any idea on how I'm supposed to get some sleep without worrying about getting stabbed before morning?"

He didn't answer. She watched as Slaide stumbled over to her bed and snatched one of the down pillows. He crossed the room, stopping before her as he tossed the pillow onto the floor, never breaking eye contact.

"Absolutely not," Hazel exhaled, realizing what he was doing.

But Slaide ignored her as he lay down on the floor between the door and the bed.

"I don't have any say in this, do I?" she asked, already knowing the answer.

"Not if you want to stay alive."

Hazel sighed quietly to herself, leaving Slaide on the floor in favor of her bed. Just before she closed her eyes and tucked into the covers, she whispered, "Good night, Slaide."

But the only response she got was the sound of him snoring.

Hazel sat up slowly, stretching her limbs and letting the shafts of early morning sunlight caress her skin. And it hit her, the alarming sensation she'd forgotten something important.

A loud, grating snore reminded her she wasn't alone, and her conversation with Slaide the night before came flooding back.

She slid out of the enormous bed and found Slaide curled up on the hard floor. He had the pillow wrapped in a bear hug, and his wings draped over himself in place of a blanket. He looked almost innocent, if she ignored what he was capable of.

His wings were captivating now that she had the chance to see them up close. Feathers an oily black, their sheen in the sun catching deep purple and blue hues.

Watching as Slaide's chest rose and fell, Hazel had the urge to touch his wing. Maybe if she was careful, if she was gentle…

She leaned in, arm outstretched.

"I don't recommend that," Slaide mumbled, eyes still closed.

Hazel startled, stumbling backwards and falling hard on the floor beside him.

Slaide laughed, peeking through one eye.

"That wasn't necessary." She frowned.

"Neither was you deciding to touch my wings without asking. Not just without asking but while I slept? I didn't know you had it in you."

"I wasn't trying to do anything nefarious. I've never seen wings like yours up close."

"And I've never seen hair like yours up close. Would you be happy about me caressing it while you sleep?" He tilted his head to the side.

"No," she conceded. She hadn't thought of it that way.

"Plus," he continued, "wings are, by nature, only the *second* most sensitive part of our bodies. So much so that I will not be held responsible for my actions if you try that shit again." She heard it in the tone of his voice; it was a promise, not a threat.

"Fine. Point taken. I'm sorry," she resigned. "So, what's the plan for today?"

The "festivities" weren't set to begin until later, starting with a commencement ceremony and dinner. Then, the real fun would begin.

"I figured we would take it easy. I want you to save your energy for the trial tonight, so beyond making sure you eat and drink enough today to keep your energy up, I have nothing planned."

Great. Looking forward to twiddling my thumbs in boredom awaiting my death.

"In the meantime, I have a few meetings today. If I learn anything else about tonight, I'll relay that information." He stood and stretched before opening the door to leave.

"I know I don't have to tell you this, but do lay low for once. And if anyone tries to get to you… blow this place to Hel."

And with that, he closed the door behind him, leaving Hazel alone in deafening silence.

Phaedra came and left a few times throughout the day, offering Hazel various foods and refreshments at Slaide's insistence, books to cure her boredom—though nothing of great interest outside of an old romance novel—even offering her company at one point, which Hazel gratefully accepted.

Later, Phaedra drew her a magically-warmed bath filled to the brim with fragrant suds. The bath included a tantalizing massage from her scalp to her toes. If nothing else, Hazel figured this was the best last bath she could have asked for. But she quickly shrugged off the thought. She had to start thinking positive, or her thoughts might become reality.

As Hazel finished dressing for the evening's event and Phaedra put the final touches on her long braid, a knock sounded at the door.

"Come in," Hazel called.

Slaide let himself in, dressed in his signature black-dyed leather armor. His hair was pulled back into a half-ponytail with his daggers sheathed on either hip and a long sword strapped across his back.

Hazel addressed him over her shoulder from where she sat in the writing chair as Phaedra fastened some loose ends.

"Here I thought I was the one fighting for my life tonight. Any reason you're dressed for battle?"

"Because it pays to be overprepared rather than underprepared and I don't trust anyone. Any more questions?"

Hazel was jarred by his edgier-than-normal response, but shook her head.

"Good," Slaide remarked as he walked a circle around her, looking her over from head to toe. "You know, you don't look completely useless today. Some might even think twice about the target they've put on your back." He turned to the angel. "Good work, Phaedra."

She bowed deeply in response.

Slaide paused in front of Hazel and unsheathed one of his daggers from his belt. He offered it to her hilt first, just as he had during their training. *But this time, it's real.*

"Thank you," she said.

"Take good care of that," he countered, voice low. "These were Sylvie's." He patted the dagger's twin on his other hip. "But they're still sharp as shit and deathly accurate when thrown. Which we didn't work on, but considering how you tossed that candlestick, you'll probably be fine."

Probably.

"So, we're ready then?" Slaide asked.

"As ready as I'll ever be." *To face death.*

With that, Slaide led Hazel from the room, the beginning of a long, silent walk to the dining halls.

To Hazel's dismay, the competitors were separated from their trainers—if they had them—for dinner. Slaide had warned her this might be the case, but as she was one of the last to arrive, all eyes fell on her as she entered the space. She would have done anything to have him at her side as she walked to one of the last open chairs at the long table, especially as her pendant warmed angrily. Not that she was surprised. She'd known there would be men here who wished her harm. Without Slaide, though, she was wholly exposed. *And this is just dinner…*

Their meal was meager and uninspiring. Nearly-stale bread was served with a communal dish of liquid that looked to be somewhere between a broth and a gravy. The men squabbled over it, though whether that was because it was a delicacy or simply because it softened the bread into an edible state, she couldn't be sure. Whatever it was, she chose not to partake, instead breaking off tiny pieces to spare her teeth.

Apples were provided, and Hazel managed to find one without marred flesh or signs of rot. Even so, it tasted off. She sighed, waiting for something more substantial.

A few of the competitors of noble houses complained about being seated and fed amongst the rabble, but they were quickly reminded that their participation was voluntary—if they didn't like it, they could leave.

Without warning, a behemoth of a man, still in chains, rose from the table and turned on his handler. The heavy iron cuff struck the man upside his head, rendering him unconscious. The beast in chains roared at the onlookers, daring anyone to move.

One knight thought to approach from behind, slinking beneath the table for stealth. To Hazel's surprise, he leapt for the giant's shoulders, but he was too slow. In an unnatural burst of speed, he whirled on the knight, catching him in midair and spiking him to the ground with little effort. The knight didn't move.

But all it took was a well-placed arrow—*several* well-placed arrows—and the angry man-beast was put down. A collective sigh of relief spread through the dining hall when it became clear he would not rise again.

And just like that, dinner was over.

A Living Nightmare

SLAIDE watched from his seat as the competitors filed in, listening to the names as they entered. When at first he didn't see Hazel, he worried she might have already gotten herself into trouble.

But at last, he spied the top of her auburn head bobbing as she brought up the back of the line. It was shocking to see such a stark difference between her and the men that surrounded her. They were so much larger, so much more intimidating than she was. He hoped she would remember to use that to her advantage.

The announcer called her name as she walked into the makeshift stadium the king had set up in the tilt yard. Of course, the men around him were quick to comment on things that set his pulse pounding.

"Hazel Callahan… of Larksridge… representing—no, that's not right, excuse me. Participating as a captive of the crown, held on charges of… conspiracy and unauthorized magic use… as well as assault on a knight of the King's guard."

Murmurs rose in the crowd, and Slaide watched as her opponents glanced at one another. It would be a double-edged sword, but one they could hopefully use to their advantage. For on one hand, the target on her back became exponentially larger for those who wanted to remove her expeditiously. On the other hand, more than a few of them would likely steer clear of an accused *witch*.

He was counting on the latter.

When her gaze met his, it wasn't lost on Slaide how her posture changed. She relaxed, if only for a moment. He lost sight of her again as she took her seat among the others.

The briefing was quick. Painfully quick. The rules were laughable, in that there were almost none. He'd half expected a rule against magic usage, under the guise of it providing an unfair advantage. But then again, Magnus still wanted to see her powers for himself. He needed solid proof.

The pair was reunited briefly on the way to the castle gardens, where the hedge maze awaited.

"Well?" Slaide asked by way of greeting.

"Dinner was awful. They killed one of the competitors. Granted, he killed two men first…"

A moment later Slaide discerned why she trailed off. The gargantuan hedge loomed before them, stealing her breath. He'd almost forgotten most people hadn't seen such a thing before.

"Hazel," Slaide started, grabbing her arm, "you can do this. Don't worry about what anyone else does. Lay low, stick to the shadows, and keep moving no matter what."

Her face twisted in an expression he couldn't read as she looked over his shoulder.

"Hazel, look at me. Look. At. Me." She did.

They were nearly to the hedge. Most of the competition had already entered, and the crowd was thinning.

"Worry about no one but yourself. Do not under any circumstances help anyone. Do not trust your senses, for they will likely betray you. And for the love of all the bastard gods, Hazel, do not stop moving."

Still, she said nothing. What he wouldn't give for any sign of confidence out of her, something to show she hadn't given up.

At last, they faced the labyrinth. He stood behind her, one hand on her shoulder. Two knights approached, pushing him back from her and stepping between them.

She finally looked back at him, eyes glistening as the living wall behind her shuddered and groaned.

"Give 'em Hel, Hazel," he called to her. "I'll see you on the other side."

The knight to her left gave a brutal shove, and she fell to her knees just within the hedge.

And then it slammed shut, sealing her out of sight.

Every scream and wail grated on Slaide's nerves. Most of them sounded masculine, but who could really say, when a person was facing their death? The labyrinth itself was sinister enough without the addition of men who would gladly see Hazel dead. He could only hope that she would trust no one, nothing, and keep her feet moving.

The labyrinth fed on fear and stillness. The moment she stopped moving, she'd become prey.

"What did you think about the announcer's addition of her charges?" came a voice from behind him. *Magnus.*

"Completely unnecessary, since you're asking. Made the target on her back bigger than it already was, so if that's what you were going for, then congratulations, you succeeded."

The High King looked taken aback. "Careful, Slaide, or I might think you're growing too attached," he warned.

"Attached? Why, Your Majesty, you *wound* me. How can I not be concerned with her success? Her survival? Need I remind you, it's personal for me. I have a lot riding on this." Slaide folded his arms in an attempt to bolster his appearance of indifference.

"Indeed," Magnus growled. "Well, in the meantime, your little underdog is making me a pretty amount of coin. It's a win-win for everyone, really. Not her, of course, but the rest of us. Our coffers will get nice and fat from bets placed on her, you'll get your freedom if she wins, *and* I get to execute a powerful witch when all is said and done. I have to say, Slaide, this has been one of your more profitable ideas."

Slaide stopped listening then. When he'd made the deal, he didn't know Hazel. Knew *of* her, sure. But it wasn't his concern whether she lived or died beyond his need of her. But now…

"Slaide? Did you hear what I said? Listen when your King is speaking, boy. I asked you what your thoughts were on bringing the mirror out of retirement for the second trial." Magnus snapped his fingers in Slaide's face, and Slaide fought the urge to snap the man's wrist.

He feigned a smile. "An excellent addition, my King," he lied. "Now, if you'll excuse me." He made to step around Magnus, but the King stepped in his path.

Their gazes met, and the King's eyes roamed Slaide's face as though he could find some unspoken truth written there.

Without breaking eye contact, Magnus grabbed Slaide by the hand—by the fist, really—and placed something in his palm before closing his fingers around it. Not a single word was spoken as he turned and took his leave, his cloak the color of dried blood billowing behind him.

With Magnus gone, Slaide looked down at his hand, unfurling his fingers to reveal what the King had left him, though deep down he already knew.

A vial of black liquid Slaide was all too familiar with.

The Black Draught. Serum Noctis. Fellblood. It was known by many names across the alchemical community, but for Slaide, it represented the bane of his existence. His vice.

He hadn't asked to be introduced to the life-altering substance. Hadn't had a say at all. And now, he was a shell of himself without it.

The Magistry hadn't known about dependency as a side effect of long term use. Or if they had, they hadn't cared. And now… it was the one thing keeping him tied down to Ravenhold. To Magnus. Because Serum Noctis wasn't available anywhere else in the world.

And while it wouldn't outright kill him to go off of it completely, Slaide worried he would slowly lose control of his faculties. That his sharp mind would begin a slow descent into madness.

The High King's act of placing the small vial in Slaide's hand wasn't a gift of goodwill; it was a reminder that Magnus owned him. A reminder of what Slaide stood to lose if he left.

Hours went by with no sign of Hazel. Admittedly, Slaide found himself worrying for her safety and regretting forcing her into this. Witch or no, she was still a person in her own right, one whose company he didn't entirely despise. But it was just too soon. How could he have thought he could prepare someone with no combat experience, Hel, limited *life* experience for the tournament's trials—in mere days at that?

Idiot. You've cost her her life and any shot you might have had at your own freedom.

Cheers arose behind him, tearing him from his wallowing. He sprinted to where they were coming from hoping, however unrealistic it was, that Hazel had been teleported out.

But as Slaide pushed through the crowd, he was almost annoyed at the presence of a greasy, middle aged man, not Hazel. The man was trembling, nearly foaming at the mouth as he ranted and raved incoherently about something he'd experienced within.

Something bright flashed over his shoulder, but Slaide ignored it as he tried to listen to what the rambling man was saying. Perhaps with any luck, he might find out what had become of her.

Someone coughed and sputtered behind him, and when he turned to see who was causing the ruckus, Slaide almost collapsed to his knees.

It was Hazel. Tattered, battered, and clinging to consciousness, but alive.

"Gods above, Hazel!" he shouted as he dove for her, cradling her weak form.

She could only groan in response, as if caught between this world and another.

Nemsen and a couple of other healers Slaide didn't recognize rushed over, shoved him out of the way, and without a word, carted her off.

Before Slaide could comprehend what had happened, a heavy hand clasped his shoulder.

"Well, I suppose congrats are in order," Magnus jeered. He was joined by Courtland Rhodes, First Commander of the Raven Blade. Slaide straightened slightly. He didn't care much for anyone who kissed the King's ass in the name of status, but Rhodes had at least earned his position.

"Congrats?" Slaide asked.

"Your little witch managed to survive the first trial. The crown earned a pretty penny off that, I must say. Many, many people expected her to die. Myself included." He said it with a smile on his face, as though they weren't discussing someone's life.

"Yeah, that's great," Slaide said, voice purposely lacking excitement. He looked to Rhodes. The man didn't just make appearances. Something was amiss.

"Ah, right," Magnus said, as though suddenly remembering. "Rhodes received some disturbing reports from the competitors. Apparently, instead of simply fighting the labyrinth's tricks, several of them were attacked by monsters."

Slaide didn't let his face betray his surprise. What had he sent Hazel into? What did she have to face?

"And these monsters *weren't* part of your plan?" Slaide pressed, skeptical.

"Master Elias," Rhodes interjected, "the men who survived have described things that are almost unbelievable. If it weren't for the issues with the wards—"

Slaide interrupted him. "You think they were beasts from beyond the Border." Not a question.

Courtland Rhodes shot a cautionary glance to Magnus, then nodded.

"Slaide, your skills are needed in the labyrinth. Besides retrieving bodies, I need you to see if you can figure out how they got in. We can discuss this further when there aren't so many listening ears around," Magnus grumbled.

Fantastic. So seeing Hazel would have to wait then.

"Well," he said, "this could take all night, and I'd rather it didn't. We'd better be going."

Rhodes nodded his agreement, and the two of them approached the massive living hedge, which opened briefly just before swallowing them whole.

Not Dead Yet

Hazel slept the entire following day, and Slaide, despite his earlier agreement with Nemsen, wasn't given leave to visit.

The other healers, Nemsen had explained, weren't privy to their discussion, and Nemsen wasn't comfortable exposing himself in such a way that might cost him everything.

Fine. Slaide supposed he could respect that. Even if he did smash a potted plant on the steps leading out to the gardens to vent his frustration. It was that or Nemsen's head.

He took his meals in private, half expecting her to walk in the doors at any moment. At this point, he would just be grateful for her to regain consciousness before the next trial.

They had less than twenty-four hours. Magnus had confirmed in private that he was in fact bringing out the Mirror of Truth, and Slaide desperately needed to form a game plan with Hazel. He needed to know how the Hel she'd kept her wits during her first encounter and what it had revealed, though he wouldn't bet his life on her sharing the latter.

Would it show her the same truths and lie? Would it concoct entirely new ones? Would she succumb to madness this time?

And yet, the most important question of all remained to be answered: would she even be awake by tomorrow evening?

Slaide took dinner by himself in the small dining room, the same room he'd teased Hazel about her manners until she left the room crying. He could almost see her sitting across from him, reaching for a slice of potato bacon pie before he'd scolded her. He'd been too harsh. He knew it then, and he knew it now. But she was too soft. She needed to learn that no one would coddle her there. Didn't she?

Appetite lost and questioning everything, Slaide pushed away from the table and stalked to the window, fighting the urge to put his fist through something again.

As he overlooked the gardens, he was haunted by the things he'd uncovered in that gods-forsaken hedge. The body parts strewn about, the blood splattered leaves, the corpses sucked completely dry with only husks remaining… but no monsters.

The signs were there. The competitors surely didn't do those things to each other, and the living labyrinth didn't act alone. And yet, despite the carnage, there was no sign of their coming or going.

Except the black salt, but Slaide had kept that bit to himself.

Half the competition had been wiped out one way or another. Some died, some forfeited. And somehow Hazel had made it through. He wasn't sure she deserved this anymore.

"Why here, Hazel? Why now? Why couldn't you just have—"

"Am I interrupting something?" a soft voice from the doorway interrupted.

Slaide nearly jumped out of his skin as he spun around. "Hazel? Gods, I-you-you're alive."

"It seems that way, yes," she said with a hint of mirth in her voice.

Conflicting feelings raged within him. One, the urge to run to her and squeeze her tight. The other, the voice of reason, told him to stay calm and collected. The end result was somewhere between a hop and a skip that left him feeling mortified.

For better or worse, it made her smile. And in that same moment, it occurred to Slaide that she'd never smiled in his presence that he could remember. And he *would* remember.

"Are you okay?" she asked after a few moments went by. "You're acting weird, er, weirder than normal."

He snapped out of it. "Fine. I'm fine. I-are *you* alright?" After all, it wasn't he who had just been through Hel and back.

Her eyes glossed over for a moment before she spoke. "I think I am. I'm not dead—not yet, anyway. A little sore and my head still feels weird, but I'm—" The next sound she made was an *oomph* as Slaide scooped her into a hug and pressed her tight against him.

It wasn't until she squirmed in his grasp that he came to his senses. *Get your shit together, stupid. She's a means to an end, nothing more.*

"Maybe I should go get Nemsen," she suggested. Reaching for her pendant as he so often caught her doing.

"No, really. It's fine. I'm fine. See?" He held his arms out to the side as if that was supposed to prove something. "Please, Hazel, sit. Eat something. I feel we have a lot of catching up to do."

It was late when Hazel stretched and yawned in her seat. Slaide was unaware of how much time had passed until he noticed her struggling to keep her eyes open.

Recounting the trial in grave detail was probably almost as exhausting as living it. Especially after learning she'd survived not only the labyrinth itself, but a shadowkin called a Tenebris, and a siren-like water wraith known as a Nixie. Two creatures that weren't supposed to be there, Slaide explained. He didn't feel it was necessary to tell her she was lucky to be alive.

"I think that's about enough for tonight." Slaide stood and moved to help her out of her chair. Yes, the same Slaide who had previously barked at Pimley and the servants for doing the same. He convinced himself this was different. Plus, that was before he'd gotten to know her. Even if it had only been a week.

"We'll talk more tomorrow after you've had time to rest."

She wavered slightly as she rose.

Perhaps being awake in time for tomorrow's trial shouldn't have been his only concern. Though, the mirror should be more mentally taxing than physical. He'd been so immersed in his thoughts, it thoroughly shocked him when Hazel's thumb grazed the corner of his mouth.

His thoughts raced. *When did the evening take this turn? Did I miss something?*

"Relax, weirdo," she said, removing her hand. "You had sauce on your face."

He blinked. *Sauce. Right.*

"You know," she continued with laughter dancing in her eyes, "you're kind of cute when you're flustered."

Cute. He wasn't sure if he should be flattered or offended. Slaide Elias, witch hunter for the High King, should not be seen as cute.

He raised a brow. "You should be getting to bed. Another big day tomorrow."

"Ugh. Don't remind me." That she had the nerve to act inconvenienced by her mandatory participation in a tournament that could easily mean her death was something new to Slaide. In her short time as a prisoner, she'd changed.

And he was glad for it. The Hazel he'd met mere days ago was a shell of the one before him. Apparently, she just needed the right encouragement.

They walked back to her quarters in silence, though Slaide's mind was anything but quiet. He wanted to press her for answers to his burning questions so he could stay up and form a plan for the coming day, but it wasn't the time.

Before they reached her door, he finally broke his silence. "Hazel," he spoke, "tomorrow's trial… we really need to talk about your previous interaction with that mirror." *I don't know if you can withstand it twice.* But he kept that part to himself.

She yawned rather dramatically, to the point where Slaide wondered if she was being intentional. "That's a problem for tomorrow me."

He frowned. "Indeed. And tomorrow *me*."

"Oh, for crying out loud, Slaide. Not everything is about you. If you're so worried, why don't *you* face the mirror?" She grabbed his wrist and smacked his palm against hers as though they were clapping hands. "There, I tagged you in. You're up, tough guy," she chided.

"I don't mean that, smart ass," he snapped, stepping into her space. "You know damn well you had no business surviving that first encounter. But you did, and your success tomorrow depends on me knowing why. So I can help you."

"You're insufferable," she said, glaring up at him.

"So I've been told."

They had a momentary standoff at the door before Hazel opened it just enough to slip through and disappear inside.

Slaide looked at the ceiling, exasperated. He needed to get things back under control before she got herself in trouble. Well, more trouble.

"I know you're still there," she called from within. "Good night, Slaide Elias."

He couldn't help the smirk that formed at the corner of his mouth. "Good night, pain in my ass," he yelled back.

Morning came sooner than Slaide might have liked. But his wakeup call came in the form of a boot in his ribs, and it was difficult to ignore. He groaned as he rolled over, his entire left side numb from sleeping on the hard floor outside her room. Despite her insistence on him leaving, he'd decided against leaving her door unguarded. It was woefully uncomfortable.

"Go away," he grumbled, eyes still closed.

The foot bumped him again.

"If that foot touches me again, I'm going to tear it off." He popped one eye open to see who his assailant was and if they dared try it again. He really didn't want to have to make good on his threat. But when Slaide discovered who loomed over him, he considered making good on it anyway.

Archmage Gammen.

Something akin to a snarl tore from Slaide as he got to his feet with inhuman speed, coming nearly chest-to-chest with the slender man. Gammen, to his credit, took a step back.

"Must you be so violent all the time, Slaide?" he crooned.

Slaide looked at Gammen as though his eyes were daggers and he could cut the man's heart out where he stood. Damn shame it wasn't that easy.

"I see you're not willing to be civil this morning. No matter. I'm not here for you anyway," he said as he made to step around Slaide toward the door. Slaide, of course, blocked his path—and the door handle.

"I don't believe there's anything in there for you," he growled.

"Oh, cut the territorial beast act, would you? It's not convincing anymore," Gammen remarked. Slaide considered bleeding the seedy mage out where he stood, then tossing his corpse out the nearest window.

"You need convincing? That sounds like an invite to a party you don't want to attend, mage."

"Except you won't touch me. You can't. Besides, I'm here on orders from the healers." The bastard mage was up to something, Slaide was sure of it.

"I don't deal with the healers. I deal only with Nemsen. Where is he?" Slaide questioned.

"Who could really say? I haven't heard a word of him or from him since he was detained yesterday." Gammen had the nerve to smile, knowing damn well he was delivering news.

Detained. Slaide hid his surprise and feigned disinterest. "I guess it's true what they say, then. You really can't trust anyone," he replied, keeping his voice even. "Which is precisely why you won't be entering this room." He crossed his arms.

The door creaked behind him, and Hazel peeked her head out. "Can you keep it down? I'm trying to—" She stopped talking when her eyes landed on the mage, but her hand flew to that damned necklace again.

"Close the door," Slaide barked over his shoulder. Hazel obeyed.

Gammen appeared to grow flustered, his cheeks flushing. "You have my word. She won't be harmed."

Slaide scoffed. "Your word? That's worth about as much as a pile of Phillip's manure, maybe less. The answer is still no."

"Fine. Have it your way," Gammen warned as he turned on his heel, cloaks billowing around him. "We'll see what His Majesty has to say about this!" he hollered over the sound of his clopping shoes.

An empty threat. Slaide didn't give two shits what Magnus thought. He knocked on Hazel's door twice. "You can come out now. He's gone."

She poked her head out, clearly unconvinced. "Why was *he* here?"

"Hel if I know. I haven't seen any of them in several days, which leads me to believe they're up to no good. He didn't come to wish you good luck, that I can guarantee you." For a moment, they just stared at each other. "So… can I come in?" Slade finally asked.

Hazel rubbed her hand down her face. "I guess getting more sleep is out of the question?"

"That would be correct. We have a lot to go over today," he reminded her.

"Fine," Hazel mumbled, opening the door all the way. "Come in."

Slaide stepped past her, making his way to the writing chair. After she locked the door against unwanted guests, Hazel crawled back into bed.

"Tell me about the mirror," Slaide demanded, cutting to the chase.

"I slept great, thanks for asking," she responded, voice drenched in sarcasm.

"Hazel," he warned.

"Fine. Gods, you're so pushy today. What do you want to know?"

"Everything, Hazel. Every detail about your first experience with the mirror. How you managed to keep your wits when grown men rarely do."

"Well, for starters, I'm not a man," she said without a trace of her prior sarcasm. "Maybe he doesn't like men. After all, men are the ones who use him and shove him in abandoned libraries to collect dust."

"It's an enchanted mirror. It's not sentient—wait, did you say *he*?"

"Yes."

"What in the name of the gods makes you think the mirror is male?" Slaide was truly baffled. A rare thing.

"His voice? His demeanor? Why don't you talk to him and see for yourself," she challenged.

Talk? She'd talked to it?

"I said something stupid again, didn't I?" she asked unironically.

"Not stupid. Something I've never heard. The mirror doesn't converse."

"But it does. It talked to me. It told me my blood tasted familiar, and when I told it my name it said I was wrong. Which I thought was weird, but what can you expect from a senile mirror? Anyway, I found him to be chatty. Maybe that says more about others who have faced it than it does about the mirror. Or me." She shrugged.

Could she be right? The mirror had been used to serve the selfish purposes of noblemen and Kings. Some went mad in the process, but each time, the mirror was tossed back into storage. Had anyone else *tried* talking to it? Or was it that she'd triggered something in the mirror no one else could?

"Maybe," he said, not entirely convinced. "Do you want to tell me what it showed you?"

"No. It's personal."

"Of course it is," Slaide pushed, "that's the point. The mirror uses your blood to see your fate. But it only shows you two true things. The lie is based on what it sees, but it twists the images into something loosely based on the truth. Regardless of truth or lie, everything the mirror shows you—shows anyone—is personal."

"You first, then." She folded her arms across her body.

"*Me?* No. Not the time or the place for that," Slaide said, realizing the hypocrisy as the words left his mouth. "Fine. The first thing it showed me was images of myself, but in a female form. Mind you, I didn't know about Sylvie's existence yet. Thought that one was a lie. The next two were strange for me. The first... showed my death. I died defending Magnus from a powerful witch attacking the throne room."

"And the last?" she pressed. "You only gave two."

Slaide sighed. "You."

"What?" Hazel asked, her confusion apparent by the dip of her brows.

"You. The mirror showed me you. A woman with fiery red hair burning enemies to ash with power unlike anything I've ever seen. Freeing the oppressed and destroying anyone who stood in her way. Tearing down this world as we know it and building it anew."

He could see in her face that she was trying to figure out which one the lie was. It should have been obvious. She knew now that Silvie was real. He would never stand with Magnus—couldn't she see that? Had he not made it obvious how much the King's voice made him want to gouge out his own ears?

He could understand why the vision involving her was jarring. Even understand why she would refuse to believe it. But in the short time he'd spent with her, he knew it could be no one else.

She sat up, pulling her knees to her chest and resting her chin on them. "Why are you telling me this?"

"Because, Hazel. You're not an ordinary woman. I knew it from the moment I met you in Larksridge. But I ignored everything within me screaming that it was you. So Fate literally tossed you at my feet where I couldn't ignore you any longer." He ran his hand through his hair, eyes closed.

"So," he continued after a moment, "I've told you mine. Care to share yours?"

Hazel appeared to ponder it for a minute before speaking. And then she told him everything.

The Games Kings Play

By mid-morning, they had a plan. It was far from foolproof, but it was the best they had. In a few hours, they would put it to the test.

"Slaide," Hazel began, "what happens when everything is over? Assuming I survive, I mean. What's next for us?" She fiddled nervously with her necklace. Did she realize how often she did that?

For us. Gods. How could he tell her there was no *us*? How could he tell her that she'd survive this tournament only to be handed back to the King? She wasn't the one earning her freedom. He was.

She was being bargained into a lifetime of servitude.

"Well, there's the ball. We can dance and get drunk, but I'd wager you're not asking about that. I suppose you'll be able to do whatever you want," he lied. She'd never really asked what was in this for her beyond surviving her execution. He hoped she wasn't about to start now.

"Did you mean what you said, about me freeing the oppressed? I'm assuming you were referring to the slaves in Blackrock?"

"Yes, I meant it. And, sort of. I mean… you absolutely freed them and made sure no one would ever be enslaved there again. But you didn't stop with the slaves."

She nodded. "That's good. I-I don't know how—if it was me, that is—how I'm supposed to help anyone when I can't even help myself. When you took me to the gulch… when I saw what they did to those people and the conditions they were working in…"

"Do you understand why I took you there? It wasn't to hurt you. It was to motivate you. Everyone loathes the King, but only those who truly know what he endorses *hate* him. Unfortunately, hate isn't enough. Hel, if hate alone could kill him, I would have taken care of it long ago."

"So, what do we do?" she asked sincerely.

"We start with a conversation. It probably won't get us anywhere, but we can at least let him know how bad the conditions have become."

"You don't think he knows?"

"I'm certain he doesn't. He hasn't been there in years." A truth-wrapped lie. Magnus knew. But even Slaide had been taken aback by the extent of the violence.

It would be a hard, ugly conversation, though it was a long time coming. He was tired of the games. The charades and secrets.

"Let's go." He grabbed Hazel's hand. "No time like the present to get this shit done."

She yelped when he pulled her arm, but quickly fell into step behind him.

Magnus may be the High King. He might be the most powerful man in all the land—politically speaking, anyway—but it was time for him to answer some questions. Slaide charged down the main hallway toward the throne room with Hazel in tow.

They arrived at the throne room doors, where two Raven Blade Knights stood guard. Slaide pulled up, nearly skidding to a stop when he noticed them. *Knights? On guard for a meeting?* The guards stood statuesque, choosing not to acknowledge Slaide and Hazel's presence. That was, at least, until Slaide stepped forward.

Without a word, the knights shifted, crossing their spears before the doors.

"I suppose that's on me, for thinking you'd let me waltz in. His Majesty is expecting me, though, so step aside."

One guard eyed him from behind his iron helmet. He lifted his face guard, and Slaide recognized the man from his missing left eye. *Oswald. Not a shot in Hel he's letting me through.*

"As a matter of fact, I have strict orders to keep these doors barred until the meeting concludes. No one in, no one out. Including you, Slaide Elias. *Especially* you."

"Aw, good. You do remember me. I was beginning to wonder if you'd already forgotten all the good times we spent together. Good to see you in good spirits and that you've managed to keep at least one eye."

"No thanks to you, bastard." He glowered.

"No, I suppose not. Anyway, it's been great fun seeing your ugly face again, but we've got an urgent meeting with Magnus."

"I said His Majesty is busy. You know better than to play the fool with me, Slaide. I learned my lesson. Never again." He crossed his arms.

"That's a shame. I was just thinking I'd get a chance to add your right eye to my collection, too."

Hazel leveled an incredulous look at him. And he wasn't sure why. Surely by now she'd figured out that his middle name, if he'd had one, would have been *Despicable*. Or perhaps *Depraved*. Or *Wicked*. He had a penchant for harassing and taunting his adversaries, and Oswald was no exception.

After all, it had been Slaide who'd relieved Oswald of his left eye in the first place. The two had scrapped after an exchange of words turned violent in the middle of the banquet feast celebrating the Midsummer hunt. To this day, Slaide found himself laughing at the memory, how he'd popped Oswald's eye right out of the socket with a soup spoon—no sooner than the toasts had been finished—and launched it across the room. The eye had rolled across the packed dirt floor and came to a stop before the paws of one of the King's hounds.

The hound, of course, inhaled the eyeball without so much as a second thought. Horrified screams had gone up around the banquet tent, and one obnoxious woman had shrieked just before fainting. He laughed at the memory, earning a scowl from Oswald.

A knock sounded from the other side of the doors, ending Slaide's romp down memory lane. Oswald one-eye and his partner stepped back, each grabbing a door handle and pulling their respective door wide.

A few nobles and council members filtered out of the throne room, followed by two more guards. Hazel stepped slightly behind Slaide, probably trying to stay out of the way.

As they passed, neither the noblemen nor the council members paid her any mind. The first guard walked by without incident. The second guard stopped to peer around Slaide for a glimpse of her.

"Hazel?" the guard asked. She glanced around Slaide, who looked between the two of them with narrowed eyebrows. "Oh, right," he said. He slid his eye guard up, revealing dark brown eyes set into a tan face. "Better?"

Slaide watched as she squinted at the man. There was no way she—but he saw the recognition the moment it hit her face, her eyes lighting up.

"Zeke? Ezekiel Bertram. Is that you?"

Zeke lifted his helm off and tucked it under his arm. "The one and only. Gods of Caelis, Hazel, when I heard the news… I can't believe it—the things they're saying you did. But it will all get straightened out, you'll see. And you're…" he glanced over at Slaide, "You're okay, I take it?"

Slaide stepped forward. "Is there a reason you felt a need to look at me before asking her if she's okay? Because unlike you, I've been keeping her alive."

Zeke bristled. "Are we pretending this situation is *good* for her?" He gestured between the two of them. "She stands accused of using magic, which is *crazy* by the way, and you're King Magnus's own witch-hunting dog. No one actually believes she's safe under your watch. Plus, you entered her into the tourney as your little pawn. But go on."

Slaide stepped into Zeke's space, which apparently triggered something in Hazel.

"Hate to interrupt this pissing match, but stand down, both of you. This is completely unnecessary. Slaide, meet Zeke. Zeke, Slaide. Believe it or not, you're both on the same side. Sort of. At any rate, I'm unharmed, see?" She held her arms out to the side and spun around.

Zeke had the nerve to look unconvinced.

"Zeke. I know Slaide has an unsavory history, and I'll be the first to admit his methods are… unconventional. But, walking around with him is like walking around with a helhound. It's rare for anyone to so much as look in my direction."

Zeke rolled his eyes.

"And Slaide," she continued, "this is my best friend since childhood, Ezekiel Bertram."

From beside her, Slaide grunted.

Hazel shot him what he figured was meant to be a warning glance.

"Not to ruin this sweet reunion, but we've got things to do, remember?" he chided.

"Wait, you're working with him?" Zeke looked at her in shock.

Slaide flung his arm over Hazel's shoulders and pulled her in close. "That's right, pal. She's helping me with an important *personal* project, and you're currently keeping us from a meeting with the King." He didn't need to emphasize the word personal, but the way it made Zeke flinch was worth it.

Hazel tried to pull out of his grasp, but he held tight, a saccharine grin stretched across his face. She elbowed him.

"Knock it off. Yes, Zeke. Slaide and I are, as of today, working on something. I think. And we do have to discuss something with His Majesty. We can catch up later though, okay?"

His brow furrowed. "Yeah, okay. Good seeing you, Hazel." He glanced at Slaide before adding, "Stay safe." He placed his helm back upon his head and closed the visor.

The guard announced their arrival after the King returned from his brief break between sessions. Slaide knew their time was limited, as a second military advisory session was set to convene shortly. They had to keep this brief.

"Your Majesty, you have visitors. They claim it is urgent."

Slaide walked in before Hazel. He sketched a full bow, and Hazel followed his lead.

Magnus squinted at Slaide as though he could see his true intentions. He then looked at Hazel, who bowed far longer than she needed to.

"Well, is one of you going to start talking or are you just here to waste my time?" he grumbled.

"No, Your Majesty. We do not wish to waste your time." The words choked out of Slaide. He rarely had it in him to address the King appropriately and with such decorum, but they needed Magnus to hear them out.

Even though he knew this was likely a futile effort, they had to try. Slaide knew Magnus was aware of how Slaide felt about enslaving people. Slaide also knew Magnus was well aware of what would happen to his kingdom if his subjects ever learned the truth.

"I hope," King Magnus began, "you've come with good news about my prisoner, there. Need I remind you that the next trial is tonight? Wouldn't want you to forget about our little deal." The venom-coated words dripped from his tongue.

Slaide balked at the mention of the bargain. *Now is not the time for this…*

"On the contrary, I come to you with information that I—that *we*—feel is of the utmost importance. It is in regard to…" He looked over at Hazel, unsure what the King would think about her knowing he's keeping slaves. *This could end poorly…* He cleared his throat before continuing. "There seems to be a lack of proper training and oversight at Blackrock."

Magnus sat up straighter, eyebrow cocked in apparent curiosity.

Well, that piqued his interest. Here goes nothing, Slaide thought.

"And what, pray tell, seems to be the problem?" King Magnus leaned forward in his obsidian throne, resting his elbows upon his knees. He placed his hands together, aligning his fingertips in a way that suggested he was already thinking he knew where this conversation was going. Probably contemplating their demise.

"Your Majesty, with all due respect, the guardsmen, foremen, and overseers at Blackrock are running the workers into the ground. There isn't enough for any of them to eat, their sleeping quarters are cramped, generating unsanitary conditions, and that's assuming they get to sleep at all. They're being worked to the bone, quite literally, and beaten when they take a break. While we were there, a man received ten lashes—"

"And *why* were the two of you there in the first place?" He glared.

Choose your words carefully, Slaide. "This one has been tough to crack," Slaide responded, glancing at Hazel, hoping she would go along with it. He was walking such a dangerous line. "She's… not giving me much to go on, and I thought I could scare her into submission by taking her there. But the conditions… Your Majesty… they are unacceptable. They are being treated worse than animals, let alone workers."

"I think you'll do well to remember that those are *prison* workers. No, they did not choose to work for me in my mines, but why should they? Each of them has been charged with a crime against this kingdom, be it treason or supporting a traitor in some way or another, amongst other crimes. They are criminals and will be treated as such, not given posh amenities with their every whim catered to."

Slaide's polite façade began to crack. "While I do understand your position, Majesty, I *insist* you see it for yourself if my word is not enough. Consider what kind of message you're trying to send."

Slaide's temper was rising. If word of this got out, the reign of Magnus Ragnaroth would come crashing down around him. And the man didn't even pretend to care.

As expected, Magnus only shrugged and sipped from his goblet. He set it back down before speaking again. "You know as well as anyone, Slaide Elias, how hard I have worked to get this kingdom under control. To make it a more prosperous, habitable place where people can raise their families."

He looked directly at Hazel, then back at Slaide. "Preventing and punishing magic usage is one of the ways we keep this land safe. You of all people should understand, considering it is you who does most of my bidding. Does your little pet know her knight in shining armor is really a bloodthirsty demon in disguise? Does she know she's befriended a monster who will sell her secrets to the highest bidder?"

Slaide's face flushed with anger and a touch of embarrassment, of uncertainty. Without saying anything at all, Slaide had effectively said too much.

"Oh, ho, ho," he crooned. "Don't tell me you're falling for the magical little bitch? This is too good. Too good, indeed. Well, I hope she gives you a good lay before tonight. There's a good chance she won't even recognize you after the mirror is done with her. Don't forget the Archmage expects to receive custody of her after the entertainment ends, whether that's with her losing—or by some miracle she wins—per our agreement. He says the Prime Magus is most intrigued with her. And I have to admit, I am as well." He smiled down at her, his wine-stained teeth stretched into a suggestive smirk.

Well, since it had been brought up, Slaide might as well set the record straight. "No, our agreement was that I was going to find out if she can truly access magic, and if so what kind, while preparing her to participate in the tournament. Only if I failed was she to be handed over to those bloodlusting basilisks. If I didn't fail, and if she were to be successful, she'd have a shot at becoming your champion," Slaide growled. He did not want to have this conversation in front of Hazel.

"And so, you mean to tell me you *haven't* failed? You should have led with that." Magnus scowled.

"I haven't failed until the night of the ball comes to pass and I come up empty handed. So, no."

Hazel looked from Slaide to Magnus and back to Slaide again, fiddling with that pendant around her neck.

His heart sank, but part of him wanted to scream at her for being so foolish. She shouldn't have been surprised that Slaide had made a bet on her life. Used her as a bargaining chip.

He could see it on her face as clear as day, the betrayal. The broken trust. The realization that all of this actually meant nothing to him; he was every bit the monster he claimed to be.

"I wonder," Magnus said with mischief gleaming in his eye. "How much does she know about you, Slaide? She seems far too comfortable with you to know the truth. The *whole* truth, that is. Does she know your past? Does she know how far back your history with her *really* goes? Oh, yes. So, you've pieced it together too, I take it? The Fates are fickle beings, aren't they?"

Slaide took a step back as though he could back out of this mess. Yes, he had pieced some things together over the past few days he'd spent with Hazel. He couldn't tell her, though. It would ruin the progress he'd made in getting her to let her walls down. He'd seen her magic multiple times and probably had enough information to make Magnus happy. But he'd also learned more about her.

In ways he hadn't thought possible, he appreciated the existence of Hazel the woman, not just Hazel the ward. She was the first person he'd connected with in a very long time. Revealing what he knew would destroy everything he'd been working toward.

"Yes, your face says enough." He smiled again, gulping down more wine. "Well since we're all here right now and we're already spilling each other's secrets, let's keep this little game going, shall we? Slaide has revealed a secret project of mine, and I am fairly certain we all know *your* little secret." He pointed a finger at Hazel. "So that just leaves Slaide's hidden past. Do you want to tell her or should I? No, never mind. It's only fair that I do the honors.

"As you already know, Slaide has been my loyal dog for quite a long time. His entire life, actually. See, you may not know, but he was born and bred here. Slaide is a product of a little side project I've been working on with the Magistry, at the behest of the Anemoi. That's right. A task appointed to me, High King of Aeos, handed down by the gods themselves. Great, isn't it? It really is. And they really couldn't have chosen someone better and more driven to get this done. Anyway, Slaide, you might have guessed, isn't human. In fact—"

"I'm well aware he isn't human, Your Majesty," Hazel interrupted. "I'm also aware that you cut the wings of your angel slaves so they can never leave the palace walls. Just as I know he only carries out your bidding because he has no other choice."

Slaide's eyes nearly popped out of his head hearing her cut the King off mid-sentence. He wanted to laugh and scream at her audacity at the same time. He was oddly… proud of her.

Magnus, however, did not appear amused. "You may want to mind your tongue when speaking to your King, woman, otherwise you will find yourself without one. The decisions a King must make are for the good of all people, even if they can't recognize it at the time. A time will come when my subjects will turn to me for protection, and I will be able to protect them only because of the actions I am taking now. They may seem cruel, but in time, it will all make sense.

"As I was saying, my dear boy Slaide is, as you know, not human. Instead, he is the bastard son of a Fallenborn angel, and his mother was some unfortunate witch whore. She wasn't pretty, but she was powerful. We kept her and a few others shackled in our breeding cells at the Citadel, closely monitoring the bitches for signs of pregnancy. We let our Fallenborn have their way with them each and every night. But most of the whelps were born disfigured or stillborn. We were running out of hosts to breed with our Fallenborn warriors. And then this one's mother was captured.

"She was a particularly nasty wench, killing a score of men before we were able to trap her. As punishment for her behavior, I let all of the beasts have at her at once, instead of making them take turns. Not a shot in Hel of figuring out who *his* father is!" He erupted in raucous laughter, as though he'd told a joke.

Slaide's fists were clenching at his sides. Magnus settled himself before continuing.

"He had a sister. A twin. They both survived infancy and were the strongest, most superior soldiers I've ever seen. But we needed truly superior genetics to continue the breeding program, so we gave them a special serum the Magistry concocted which amplified their skills. Worked them into a frenzy and then pitted them up against each other. It was spectacular. A shame to lose the female's genetics, but Slaide's were clearly superior."

When the King paused, Hazel butted in. "Your Majesty, if I may, why are you telling me this? Why now?"

His grin was pulled straight from the depths of Hel. "Because, my dear. Slaide has been capturing witches and sorceresses from all over Aeos and hand-delivering them to me for participation in my experiments for his *entire* life. The ones that put up a fight are selected for breeding. The ones who don't… well, they're disposed of. No reason to keep lackluster genetics in the gene pool. But that's not Slaide's big secret, no. You want to know what it is? Come closer," he beckoned her with his finger.

Hazel obliged him, stepping up to the dais. Slaide could see how much it scared her to do so, to get so close to the real monster in the room.

Magnus towered over her. Slaide knew his nasty scent by heart, how he reeked of wine and stale bread. And he knew damn well she could probably see the ugly, unruly hairs sprouting from his nostrils.

"Do you know who the first witch was that Slaide took down? The first one he ever brought to me like the well-trained, well-bred hunting dog he is?" He sneered.

Hazel swallowed hard. Slaide flinched as she shook her head, for he knew what came next.

"Your mother."

Missing Pieces

HAZEL glanced between Slaide and Magnus, the shock and horror written plainly on her face. *Her mother?* Other than Agnes, no one bothered to tell her about her real mother. No. It couldn't be. Yet… the pieces were all falling into place.

And now she was supposed to come to terms with the fact that the one person she had slowly come to trust, the only person who routinely dragged her out of harm's way, had been the cause of her mother's death.

Slaide looked at her with eyes full of regret, and in his face, she knew it was true. He didn't attempt to deny it. Hazel backed up slowly, looking between the two monstrous men. She needed to get away. Needed the safety and sanctity of her rooms. Her locket burned.

"Oh, now now. See what happens when you withhold the truth, Slaide?" Magnus teased. "You deceive people. And then when they find out the truth, it can be devastating. I recommend you *don't* deceive people. Especially me."

"Hazel, I can explain. I—" Slaide reached for her.

"What could there possibly be to explain, boy? Directly or indirectly—and I'd personally favor directly—you're responsible for the fate of her mother. A mother who was never there to raise her because *you* got to her first." The bastard smiled.

"You've said enough, Magnus. I think she gets it," Slaide snapped.

"Do I need to remind you not to talk to your King in that tone?" His face grew a deep red.

"Hazel, please," Slaide begged.

But Magnus went on, smiling at the chaos he'd sown. "She whisked you away with her blasted portal magic and then somehow managed to hide you from me all these years. And for what? For you to end up at my gates? Don't look so surprised. Archmage Gammen was a tremendous help in acquiring a sample—just a strand of hair, don't worry—for testing in the labs at Stormhold. Imagine my surprise when the results came back. The witch that got away delivered herself back to me."

Slaide blanched.

Had he known?

"And what's even better," Magnus continued, "is that Slaide had the nerve to approach me to strike a little bargain. Did he tell you about that? No? Well, then let me fill you in—"

"Magnus!" Slaide shouted.

"Quiet, boy, or I'll have you thrown into the dungeons for insubordination!" the King spat. "As I was saying, Slaide wanted a deal. You'd participate in the tournament, somehow manage to win, and Slaide would be free of his service to me. Your life against his freedom. He was never your friend, my dear."

Hazel shook her head slowly as if fighting an internal battle. She wanted to lash out. To scream. To punch something. To run away. None of them, though, were viable options. The walls were closing in, constricting. She was trapped here, in a place where people like her were dealt horrible fates and none made it out alive.

But not her. She decided then and there she would make it out. For her mother. For herself.

She backed into the doors and felt for the latch behind her. She fumbled with it unsuccessfully and then knocked instead. Three raps on the wooden door and it was pulled open by an awaiting guard. Hazel ducked under his arm and into the hallway beyond.

Hazel didn't slow down until she'd reached her rooms, at which point she slammed the bedroom door behind her and allowed her body to slink to the floor. She pulled her legs in tight and tucked into herself, resting her head on her knees. It started with a single tear running a ragged path down her cheek, and before she knew it, she was sobbing.

At some point, she'd drifted off, exhausted by the sadness. She was awoken by a light shuffle of feet outside the door, followed by a soft knock.

"Go away!" she scolded between sobs.

There was a pause before they spoke. "I am terribly sorry, mist—Hazel. I do not mean to disturb you. I will just slide this under the door. It came for you today."

There was a scraping at the underside of the door, and then a piece of folded parchment poked out on her side. She eyed it suspiciously before grabbing it from the floor.

The seal on the letter was already broken, indicating the contents had been reviewed prior to it being delivered. She wiped her eyes as she unfolded it, then let her eyes drift to the bottom, curious who it was from. Connall Callahan. Her father had responded to her letter.

She was on her feet immediately, throwing the door open. "Phaedra! Wait!" But the angel was already gone. Not a trace of her in the corridor, as though she'd never been there.

Instead, she came face to face with Slaide. Her rage returned in an instant, and she slammed the heavy wooden door in his face. Or she would have, had Slaide not caught the door before it closed.

"Hazel."

She leaned against the door, tears welling in her eyes again.

"Hazel, please," he begged again.

"Get out of here. Leave me be, please." Hazel choked back a sob.

"Please, just let me in. Let me explain."

"I *did* let you in, Slaide. I trusted you, and it was the worst thing I've ever done in my entire life. Congratulations, asshole."

"I deserve that. I do. But you deserve so much more. Starting with the whole story, not just the half-truth that Magnus regurgitated."

"I'm done here, Slaide. I'm done complying. I'm done playing your games. I'm done. I'm not participating in this tournament any longer, and I'm most certainly not going to the stupid ball. You can find someone else."

He recoiled. "Hazel, you… you have to. It's not just because I *want* you there, which I do. Truly. But if you don't show up, you'll be escorted away by knights of the Raven Blade and handed over to the Magistry.

They'll take you to the Citadel, where you'll become another test subject. Is that what you want?"

"It's been proven time and time again that what I want here doesn't matter. What I *want* is to go home. And I can't. At this point, I will go willingly into the arms of the mages, because at least I know what they're all about. They're not going to act like something they aren't." Her voice was full of vitriol and spite. "Get out of my sight, Slaide. I never want to see or talk to you again."

He stopped pressing against the door, allowing it to slam fully in his face.

She listened closely for any sign that he was still there and was met with the sound of his retreating footfalls. She breathed deeply, sinking back to the floor and closing her eyes.

The piece of parchment crinkled in her hand, reminding her it was there waiting to be read. She unfolded it and ran her eyes across the ink, written by her father's own hand. Parts of it were nearly illegible, marred by what were likely dried tear stains.

My dearest Hazel Grace,

I am so relieved to have received your letter, and I hope this letter still finds you well.

I assume you've heard the news. Jonas returned, or what was left of him. Something was wrong. He was out of his mind as though possessed. He attacked neighbors in the street like a rabid dog, and I had no choice but to intervene. I regret that I was unable to subdue him without lethal force. I will live with his blood on my hands for the rest of my days, but I wanted you to have the truth of it from me.

Lastly, I owe you an apology. I am sure by now you have discovered the truth one way or another, and I am sorry that I did not tell you sooner. I am sorry that I suppressed your powers and kept this a secret from you. I understand if you feel let down or betrayed, and I do not blame you if you never want to speak with me again. I did what I thought was best for you at the time, with Agnes's guidance. Though I must admit she did not know about the Witchbane. That was my doing, and she was beyond cross with me when she found out. I regret it with my entire being, all of it. I thought I could get away with maintaining that you were mine and I was yours, and that was all we needed to be.

I now see it was selfish of me to hide you away as though I could cheat Fate. You were always destined to be more, and the world needs that now more than ever. Be the light in the darkness ahead.

Love forever,

Connall Callahan

By the end of it, the words blurred and Hazel's tears joined the ones Connall had left. She wanted nothing more than to hug him, to tell him there was nothing in this world that could turn her against him. And yes, she was deeply hurt that so many around her knew she had magic-tainted blood, knew that she wasn't his by blood and said nothing. But that did not, could not, change the fact that he was everything a father should be. No blood relation could change that.

She reread the part about Jonas, and her heart sank. She twirled the locket in her hands, knowing what he said was true. Sure, Jonas was a pain in the ass at times and would fight at the slightest provocation. But picking fights and outright attacking people were two different things. What Connall described wasn't normal.

He was probably possessed, she thought. Possessed? Connall had suggested as much. With everything going on around her, it was fitting. She made a note to look into creatures with the ability to possess someone and control their actions.

Hazel strode over to the writing desk and set the letter down. It was late, and the day had been physically and emotionally exhausting. She didn't even want to think about what the coming evening might bring. She just knew she needed to get out of this god's damned castle before anyone else could dig their claws into her.

She decided to prepare her own bath, not wanting to bother Phaedra after her earlier outburst. *Let the angel rest.* She could handle this on her own. Besides, she didn't want to talk to anyone. Didn't want anyone else to look upon her with pity in their eyes. She just wanted to sink into scalding hot water and be carried away by the lush, scented soap they kept stocked for her.

As she sank into the bath, Hazel hissed, the hot water stinging her chafed thighs. All the recent horseback riding had taken its toll on her skin. But once she was submerged, she cleared her mind of the thoughts that had plagued her. Tried to, anyway.

Sitting in the quiet bathing room without anyone to attend to her proved to be a lonely experience. Her thoughts wandered over the previous day's events, specifically the part where Slaide's mouth had brushed her skin and the conflicting emotions he'd invoked. Her body heated in response to the memory, to the thought of his lips on her neck, the brush of his fangs that sent a shiver up her spine. She sank deeper into the water, wanting to dissolve in the warmth.

But she caught herself mid-thought, just as her hands had begun to roam her body beneath the water's surface. *What am I doing?* Slaide was a dangerous, traitorous monster that she did not need to further entangle herself with, not even in her fantasies.

She spent the rest of her bath scrubbing every inch of her body furiously, as though she could remove the memory of him on her skin. By the time she was finished, the water had grown cold and her skin was raw and angry. She wrapped herself in a linen towel that had no right to be as soft as it was and padded barefoot across the room to fetch a nightdress from her armoire.

Then she grabbed the letter off the writing desk and carried it to bed with her. She climbed up into the over-sized, ultra-plush mattress and snuggled into the down-filled duvet. She read the letter repeatedly, her father's words bringing her comfort until sleep finally came to claim her.

Hazel was startled awake by a rapping knock on her door, light yet firm.

"Hazel?" called the voice. She slowly recognized it was Phaedra. "May I come in?"

"Sure, Phaedra, come in," she called back.

The door opened cautiously, and Phaedra peeked her head in.

"You can come all the way in," Hazel said. "I won't bite."

Phaedra entered the room looking as though she'd been scolded. She carried a tray with a steaming teapot and small cakes. She didn't meet Hazel's eyes.

"Mistress Hazel," she said quietly while pouring tea, "I've come to help you get ready and escort you to the next trial."

Hazel's demeanor shifted, as she comprehended why the angel was so gloomy. "Then you're wasting your time. It's not your fault, Phaedra, but I'm not going."

"But Mistress—"

"Please, Phaedra. Don't. I've come to terms with the fate that awaits me, and it's the only real choice I've had since I've been here. Let me have a say in just this one thing, please," Hazel insisted.

The angel nodded and walked to the window. "I understand as much as anyone what it is like to have no say in life. And I'm sorry you've had to experience it."

As Hazel watched her, she noticed the clipped wing tips again. And then she noticed the marred flesh across her back. Fresh, angry red wounds layered atop old ones, scarred pink. Her alabaster skin was a portrait of suffering.

"Phaedra. Your back," Hazel managed.

Phaedra shrunk as though struck, turning her back away. "Oh, it's nothing, Mistress. Please don't worry about me."

"No. No, I most certainly will worry about you." She hopped out of bed, crossing the room to where Phaedra now stood, nearly trembling. The little angel wrapped her arms around her body defensively.

When Hazel reached her, she wrapped her arms around Phaedra in a tight embrace, careful not to put too much pressure on her wounds.

This was her fault, she knew it. She'd thrown the King's mistreatment of his slaves in his face, specifically commenting on the wings of his angel slaves. And while Hazel had been wallowing in her sorrows, taking a scalding hot bath, and slinking into a cozy bed to cry herself to sleep...

Phaedra was being whipped.

"I'm so sorry," Hazel whispered into her hair. "I'm so, so sorry. This shouldn't have happened to you."

The angel squirmed in Hazel's embrace. She wiped a tear from Hazel's cheek. "Please, Mistress. Don't weep for me." She grabbed Hazel's hands. "Win for me instead. Don't give up now. Don't let Master Elias's shortcomings, or the King's brutality, or their limited expectations of someone they've written off as less-than get in the way of what can be. What *should* be."

Hazel froze, struck by the feeling of being caught in a dream.

"Instead, let it light a fire within you. For you. For *us*. Because it's not just me cheering for you behind the scenes, Mistress. You've brought light into a dark place. Don't let them put it out. Let them burn."

Her eyes shone in a way Hazel had never seen. Gone was the timid angel. This Phaedra was fierce in mind if not in body. And she was speaking the words of someone ready to fight.

And Hazel decided then that she wanted to fight, too.

Merrill

PHAEDRA walked Hazel as far as she could, which was the last archway before the grand hall.

Slaves apparently weren't allowed outside the main halls—something about being a bad look for the King. The grand hall, throne room, and ballroom were reserved to a higher class of servant. The lessers—angels like Phaedra, among other beings—were required to use a tunnel system behind the castle walls, deemed too unsightly for the public eye.

Rules be damned, Hazel gave Phaedra a hug before her departure into the enormous hall.

"Be strong," the angel whispered in a voice so soft and melodic Hazel thought it might break her. Phaedra's grip on her wrist tightened momentarily. "You can do this," she said before letting go.

Hazel had the overwhelming feeling of being the smallest fish in a big pond, and the many eyes trained on her the moment her feet hit the tile did not help.

Let them look. For once, Hazel didn't shrink beneath their stares. She didn't wish herself invisible. She didn't reach for the locket's comfort.

She simply walked in and found an empty seat at the long dining table. No theatrics. No interactions. She would not give them what they wanted today.

At least, that had been the plan she'd formulated with Slaide. She tried to ignore the pang of sadness that struck her, the wound left by his betrayal still fresh.

He might have put her life on the line to spare his own, but the plan was likely still solid. After all, sabotaging her wouldn't have done him a lick of good.

In spite of herself, she looked for him. Some deep seated longing for his familiarity drove her to seek his face in the makeshift stands. She was disappointed to find him absent.

Fine. It was fine. She didn't need him to be there in order to succeed.

Above all else, she planned to face the mirror just as she had the first time. If it revealed anything damning, so be it. She would keep a straight face, betraying nothing.

That was the plan. But things so rarely went to plan, as she would soon find out.

She was one of the last competitors to test their mettle against the mirror, and it didn't bode well for her nerves.

Especially since several men had, in fact, lost their wits due to things the mirror showed them.

One man was shown an image of himself reunited with wife and children, when in reality, they had died earlier that spring in a terrible fire at their home. Visibly confused and distraught, he ran from the hall yelling something indiscernible about "coming for them."

Another man was shown his death at the hands of a fellow competitor, who then went on to take his widow for his own.

A fight ensued, and to nearly everyone's surprise, the mirror had been correct. The man did die at the hands of his fellow competitor… albeit sooner and in a more gruesome fashion than predicted.

And of course, as her luck would have it, Hazel was next.

"Step forward," the guard beside the mirror said.

Hazel did.

"Must I spell it out for you, girl? Do as every man before you has and offer it your blood. The trial will commence henceforth." His foul temper left her wondering who had peed in his porridge.

Hazel pricked her finger on a thorn, just as she had before, and blood welled from the tiny hole in her fingertip. She waited an ominously long time before the mirror finally spoke into her mind. And that in itself was jarring.

We've met before, he said.

Hazel wasn't entirely sure how to speak from one mind to another, but she gave it a shot. *You said that the last time*, she responded.

No, I said I've tasted your blood before. But you… I would remember you.

You're the first to find me memorable, Hazel admitted.

I do not believe that to be true. And you lie, the mirror accused.

So do you, she said a little too quickly.

Indeed, my dear. So. You've come back. The voice was thoughtful, considering.

Yes, she said, trying to stifle her impatience. *Can we wrap this up? They're staring at me.*

The mirror ignored her. *Why have you come back? Did they not tell you I usually drive men out of their minds with madness or sadness?*

Hazel tapped her foot. *Yes.*

And still you came back. An observation.

I did.

Why, I wonder? Is she driven by greed? Didn't like what she saw?

I wasn't given a choice.

Hmm. She could almost feel him appraising her, even without eyes.

Hazel's heart raced as the entire room focused on her. *Please, they're going to suspect something.*

Do they not already? he asked.

Mirror! Please! Hazel begged. *I don't have much time.*

He went quiet.

Mirror?

I have a name you know. His voice was quiet, almost a whisper.

She shifted her weight. *I-you do? What is it?*

He was clearly toying with her, right? Perhaps this was what drove men to madness. Obscurity and nonsense.

Oh, sure. Now she cares. And now the mirror had developed an attitude.

She frowned. It wasn't lost on her that perhaps this being was exceptionally lonely. Something she could relate to.

I do care. Won't you tell me?

Magnus cleared his throat in a way that suggested he was losing patience. Onlookers mumbled under their breath.

Hazel begged as much as she could through thought alone. *Please—*

Merrill, he said.

Merrill? Hazel asked, immediately regretting her tone, and the fact that she'd nearly laughed.

Yes. Is there a problem? He'd sensed it well enough.

Merrill the Mirror, she said. *No. There's no problem.*

You laughed. She pictured a young boy pouting with his arms crossed after having his feelings hurt.

I did not. Well, okay. It's a bit unusual…

Unusual is being a bard cursed to live out his days as a dreadful mirror such as this. My name is all I have left of who I was. So, excuse me if I seem attached to it. It was my father's name and his before him, he offered in a dejected tone.

Hazel truly wanted to know that story, but now was not the time.

Merrill is a wonderful name. I just hadn't expected it. I would love for you to tell your story when we have more time. But I fear if we do not get moving, His Majesty might put me to the pyre and have you melded down into something he finds more useful, she explained as kindly as she could.

I feel like I should be insulted.

Perhaps you should, but not by me. It is not I, but the King who uses you for personal gain, Hazel reminded him.

Your blood on my thorns suggests otherwise, little witch, Merrill countered.

Hazel froze. *I-what did you just call me?*

If Merrill had eyes, Hazel imagined he would have rolled them. *I told you. I've tasted your blood before. Your kin, perhaps. A grandmother? An aunt?*

My mother, she guessed.

Ah. All these images make so much more sense now, Merrill said thoughtfully.

Will you show me? Hazel asked. She was so close. So close to getting the mirror back on track.

Fine, then. You know the rules, he conceded.

Wait! Merrill?

Yes? He sighed.

Hazel grimaced, wishing she didn't have to reveal so much. *They... can't know. They can't know I'm related to her. Or any witch for that matter. My powers. All of it. It's not safe.*

I can't promise you will find comfort in what I show you. But I will try not to get you into trouble. That was the last thing Merrill the mirror said before her reflection began to shift.

Hazel's palms were sweating.

Two truths and a lie. You can do this. Phaedra's words echoed in her mind. She just prayed Merrill would be merciful. That if he witnessed anything damning, he would twist it into something else.

The smoke and shadows bent and swirled within the mirror, and then an image formed.

Hazel sucked in a sharp breath. She was on a battlefield. Bodies were strewn about, the metallic stench of blood a heavy assault on her senses. A flash of motion caught her attention and there she took in the vision: Slaide, cutting down man after man without a second thought. Fury in his eyes, a beast that only sought destruction.

Truth. Her mind warned her. Everything she knew, everything she'd learned, supported this narrative. Slaide was a butcher. He was and always had been a cold-blooded killer. Doubt crept into her mind. Had anything he'd said been real? She'd trusted him.

Hazel took a step backwards, slowly shaking her head. She didn't pay any mind to who they were. Did it matter? Future or past, Slaide killed and would continue to kill. He didn't slow, he didn't pause as if weighing the consequences of each life he took.

But she did. Hazel tore her gaze from the mirror, and when she looked back into it, the horrors were gone, a new image forming in its place.

It was again a visage of Slaide. He had a woman by the hand, dragging her behind him. But as Hazel looked closer, she determined the woman wasn't resisting. She was running with Slaide, a banner of raven-black hair flowing behind her. Her face was otherworldly—maternal, but fierce. And he was leading her somewhere.

Shouts arose behind them, and Slaide's eyes flew wide.

"Now?" the woman asked, voice laced with panic. Hazel watched, realizing this apparent escape had just evolved into a dangerous pursuit.

"Not yet," Slaide called over his shoulder. "Not yet." His face was much younger, less haunted.

They were crossing a field on foot, headed toward a dark forest past the castle grounds. To a land beyond the influence of Ravenhold.

But the thunder of hoofbeats threatened to cut the race too short. They wouldn't outrun the Raven Blade, even with Slaide's inhuman speed.

"Now?" the woman asked again, nearly begging.

"No! We must get closer!" he shouted. "If we do it too soon, you won't make it across!"

A few moments later, though, Slaide pulled her hard, slinging her in front of him as he released her hand.

"Now!" he shouted, tossing a handful of black powder into the air ahead of her.

The woman's arms moved erratically, as though she was writing invisible words with her hands. But then those motions created runic inscriptions in midair—not unlike the glyphs Hazel had seen at the Border obelisks. They glowed blue, followed by a bright white she could barely stand to look at.

A rift opened in the fabric of the world itself, a circle burning along its edges. It was suspended in midair, just large enough for her to fit through, and in the blink of an eye, she was gone.

The image in the mirror faded, replaced by the whorls of black and gray smoke.

For a moment, nothing more happened. The crowd began to whisper. Magnus shifted in his seat.

That was two. Where was the third?

Merrill? She tried to reach out to the mirror. Initially, it did not respond. *Merrill, are you there?* Hazel couldn't explain the way the energy in the room was off.

Little witch, Merrill said at last. His voice was strangely quiet, a rasping whisper.

What's going on? What happened to the third vision? she asked.

You asked that I not show anything damning. But your future is too intertwined with the Dark One… witchkind… and the fall of this kingdom. I have seen more than I wish to share, for I do not wish to harm the only one who has shown me respect.

Hazel's breath hitched.

I have seen too much in my time trapped here. Things I cannot unsee. Realities I cannot undo. I do not wish to serve this corruption any longer, so allow me to take the only stand I can in this form… as my first and final act of service to the future Queen of the Realm.

Before Hazel could speak, before she could process what he'd said, Merrill's mirrored surface morphed into a masked face, half-smiling, half-crying.

A gasp moved through the crowd. Magnus stood.

"Mirror!" he shouted. "I order you to finish your task!"

"High King Magnus Ragnaroth," Merrill began, "for years I have served this kingdom and done the bidding of the men who have stood where you stand. For too long, your line has driven this kingdom into the dirt while making yourself fatter and richer—"

"Mind your tongue! There are consequences for speaking to your High King in such a manner!" Magnus spat.

"I will no longer be silenced. You are a walking contradiction. You denounce magic, but keep the mages close. You blame the turmoil of this land on the departure of the gods, when it was the mages misuse of the world's mana that drove them out in the first place—"

"I said SILENCE!" Hazel had never heard Magnus so furious.

But Merrill would not stop. He continued, even as a nearby guard wielding a mace approached with the threat of violence in his eyes.

"You sentence half-breeds to death while creating your own monstrosities in the Citadel's dungeons. I don't need to see it with my own eyes, because the men you trust the most come to me when they seek counsel. In doing so, they reveal your secrets, not realizing I listen. I learn. I know. And I know that if any one man had committed half the crimes you have against your own people, he would be executed."

Hazel looked from Merrill to Magnus. The latter was an overripe tomato, cheeks flushed red with anger.

"You are a tool, nothing more. Easily destroyed, easily replaced. Keep spouting nonsense, and I'll demonstrate for the audience just how fragile you are," Magnus warned.

The mace-wielding knight took another menacing step closer, patting his hand with the weapon. It was everything Hazel could do not to scream at them all to stop being so stupid.

And still, Merrill went on. "The aforementioned crimes barely scratch the surface of His Majesty's transgressions against his own kingdom. Which is why, as of this moment, I am renouncing my allegiance to the Ragnaroth line, swearing it instead, henceforth and forevermore, to the woman before you, the future Queen of all Aetherium. Long live the Queen."

The moments that followed were a blur. Magnus's gaze trained on Hazel, dark with the promise of death. The audience was on their feet, some shouting accusations and obscenities at the King, others defending him.

Someone slammed into her, grabbing her hand as they went by, and Hazel found herself dragged away from the commotion. When she managed to get her bearings, she discovered it was Pimley hauling her to safety.

"Keep moving, Hazel. We need to get you out of the line of fire," he insisted.

But as he pulled her from the grand hall, the shattering of glass could be heard above the din, and with it, the deepening crack in Hazel's heart. She didn't need to see the shards littering the floor to know Merrill was gone.

Love, Mother

THE following morning, Hazel sat alone in her room. Again.

Since the truth had come to light and Slaide had, to her surprise, taken his banishment seriously, Hazel had found herself with nothing but time. Time to let her mind wander. To read. To grow bored. To regret that everyone she crossed paths with ended up hurt or killed.

She was shocked he hadn't attempted to stop by and harass her about how she could have possibly survived the mirror a second time. Or how that event resulted in the mirror's demise.

But he didn't.

And it was in those boring moments that Hazel found herself thinking about him again. It was a dangerous path, for she kept going back to one of the last things Slaide had said. Magnus was full of half-truths. So why had she been so keen to believe them?

She sat in bed, surrounded by the fluffy, cloud-soft duvet, with the strange book set before her. Her kitty companion was curled at her feet, snoring.

It was the first peace Hazel had to herself in days, and she was about to ruin it by messing with her magic. The locket thrummed in anticipation, much to her annoyance.

Hazel pressed her palm into the book's cool leather surface, feeling its bumpy grain beneath her hand. She ran her hand over the divots made by the etched runes, wishing she knew what they were.

Relax, she told herself. *Clear your mind.* After all, she wanted to open the book, not destroy it. So far, channeling her magic while upset had devastating consequences.

She took a deep breath and closed her eyes. As she exhaled, Hazel dove deep into her subconscious… and found nothing but darkness. The well of power wasn't present, not even a thread.

Hazel opened her eyes, sighing, and found the cat on high alert, staring at her with his bright green eyes.

"Don't worry," she said, "nothing will happen if I can't reach my magic anyway."

His tail flicked in response.

She closed her eyes once more, determined to try again. She dove deeper this time, searching desperately for any sign of the power she knew swelled there. Still there was nothing.

Panic crept into her veins and her breathing intensified, so Hazel backed out quickly. As her frustration boiled over, she picked the book up and threw it against the opposite wall—and immediately regretted that decision.

"Shit," she muttered to herself, scrambling out of bed. *What have I done?* She might have destroyed the book. She might have broken its spine or damaged the age-worn pages.

When her fingers brushed the cover, though, a zap ran through her arm. She recoiled, looking at her hand in confusion. For a moment, bluish light filled the runes across the cover, and as the light faded, Hazel rubbed her eyes in disbelief. She made to repeat the action, and the cat mewled sharply over her shoulder. But Hazel ignored him.

She touched the cover again, slowly allowing more of her hand to make contact. She received the same shock as before, but it was less jarring since she'd expected it. After the initial shock, the feeling leveled out into a vibration, spreading into her hand and up her arm… into the locket.

And that was when a possibility occurred to her… perhaps it wasn't her magic that was needed to force open the book.

Perhaps it needed a physical key after all. And maybe the locket was… she shoved down her excitement as she pulled the pendant from beneath her clothes. It bounced excitedly on the chain as she unclasped it and lowered it to the cover.

For a moment, nothing happened. Hazel braced for impact, expecting the book to revolt against her or otherwise injure her for trying to get to its secrets.

Then to her surprise, the runic inscriptions began to glow again. Bluish at first, then lighter until they were such a bright white she could barely stand to look at them.

Out of the corner of her eye, a disappearing flash of orange told her the cat had hopped down and scurried beneath the bed skirt out of harm's way.

Once the entire book was aglow with ethereal light, it pulled against her grip, trying to break free. The leather grew hot, as though she was trying to hang onto a burning star, so hot that she had no choice but to let go.

Both book and pendant should have fallen to the floor. But they didn't.

Instead, they levitated before her, still glowing. Then, the glow faded away and the book and locket thumped to the floor.

Hazel heard the click of the lock before it really registered. It hit her as she watched the lock fall open.

After all this time spent fighting this ancient tome, willing it to open, she'd been wearing the key. *Go figure.*

She picked it up, afraid to open it. What if the binding failed? What if the pages turned to dust?

But she thought about what had got her into this mess in the first place. She was searching for answers about her mother. This book had called out to her in a locked, abandoned library she stumbled into by chance. And now, the book had responded favorably to a locket she'd inherited from her mother.

No, it couldn't be chance. It was *Fate.*

Hazel inhaled sharply as she opened the cover.

Everything was written in the runic language. An ancient, dead language, forced out of use when the witches were pushed into exile beyond the Border.

A forbidden language.

The language of magic.

She carefully turned the page, and to her horror, a page fell out. It fluttered to the floor like a dying butterfly before coming to rest at her feet.

Shit. This was exactly what she'd hoped to avoid. But when she stooped to pick it up, Hazel's heart stopped.

This page wasn't written in runes. And it appeared to be a letter.

My dearest daughter,

If you are reading this, it means you've taken up the chase, just like I always knew you would. I did my best to leave you breadcrumbs, with the hope that we would be reunited someday. Though I fear some will be lost to time or mice before you find them. My time here is growing short, so I leave you with this: never stop seeking the truth. You are the light in the darkness. Do not let them snuff you out.

I'll see you on the other side.

Love,

Mother

Hazel collapsed to her knees, unable to comprehend what she'd read. Holy gods. Her mother. Her mother had been here. And she'd been alive long enough to explore the castle. To leave notes in strange books and lock them with magic.

Her heart yearned to tell someone. But there was no one to tell. Slaide came to mind, but she couldn't trust him. Zeke? It probably wouldn't be safe to tell him either, not as long as he continued chasing fame among the knighthood.

Hazel wouldn't risk telling Phaedra, lest the angel have the truth beaten out of her. Hazel had no doubt the angel would keep her secrets, but at what cost? No, that wasn't fair.

She flipped through the book, checking for clues. While there were none, she did come across illustrations depicting angels, witches, humans, and kings. Times of war and times of apparent peace. And through those illustrations, Hazel understood what she had in her hands.

A history book.

Her thoughts flitted to the pendant, having forgotten it in her haste to open the book. It was resting on the floor where it fell. And it was open.

She picked it up, expecting to find something life-changing within.

But it was empty.

She spent hours in her room, alternating between rereading her mother's note and examining the illustrations throughout the book. Even without reading the words, there was so much she'd never known. So much most of the kingdom probably didn't know. Books like these were removed from the public eye. If they existed at all, they were in the Citadel's forbidden libraries.

She glanced occasionally at the empty locket, now resting on the bedside table. Her disappointment at it's barren interior had left a sour taste in her mouth. What was the point?

A knock sounded at the door.

"Come in," Hazel called. By now she'd come to recognize Phaedra's knock. It was very specific to her in a way Hazel couldn't begin to explain. She tucked the book beneath her pillow, just as the angel opened her door.

"Evening, mistress," she spoke softly.

"Hazel, Phaedra, please. I can't have you using honorifics to address me. Not when it lumps me in with the monsters who hurt you. Just Hazel."

"I am terribly sorry. It's just that… if they hear me being too informal with you, well, it could be dangerous for both of us," the angel explained.

"They really monitor everything you do, don't they?" Hazel didn't mean it as a question, but Phaedra nodded in answer.

"Never mind me, then," Hazel said. "Can't have you getting in trouble on my account." She smiled at Phaedra, hoping to relieve some of the tension.

"Thank you, mistress." She set down her usual tray of tea and cakes, the aroma of baked oats and warm honey floating over Hazel in a cozy embrace. "I come bearing news."

"Oh?" Hazel asked as she made her way to the oatcakes.

"Yes, well… There's no easy way to tell you this, but they've moved the last trial up."

Crumbles of oatcake fell into Hazel's lap as she stopped chewing mid-bite. "Dare I ask when?"

"Tonight. In just a few hours, actually. I thought perhaps Master Elias would have informed you by now, but I didn't know the two of you were still not on speaking terms. I came as soon as I realized." She looked sheepish, embarrassed even.

Leave it to Slaide to let me find out on my own. Asshole. Hazel caught herself frowning.

"Right. Well, do we know anything about this trial? Did Slaide at least relay anything of importance to you?" She tried not to sound too hopeful.

"I'm sorry, mistress. He did not. Though I must stress it was not for his petty tendencies that he doesn't relay the information. It's because none was given." Sweet Phaedra, always protecting those she cares about.

"A surprise trial, then?" Hazel asked. She didn't love that.

"It seems that way. Mistress, I must insist you use caution moving forward. I sense something is amiss. Most of the slaves have been extra quiet today, even in our common spaces. Whispers in the halls indicate something insidious happening tonight. That the trial might test one's morality and allegiance to the crown."

Right. Because in the end, that's what this was. A tournament designed to test the mettle, wit, and allegiance of the King's prospective champions.

This didn't bode well for her.

"Alright. That's that then. How the Hel do I dress for this when I don't know what the trial is?" Hazel wondered, her blood pressure starting to rise.

Phaedra shrugged. "I suppose you should dress for combat. Something you can move freely in. Just in case."

Hazel eyed her wardrobe. She could almost see Sylvie's battle leathers within, mocking her with their existence. She truly couldn't escape Slaide's influence, no matter how hard she tried.

She heaved a sigh. "Combat it is then, I guess."

The competitors were rounded up just before dusk, the setting sun painting the sky in a myriad of pinks and oranges. On any other day, in any other place, Hazel would have found it beautiful.

But as they gathered in the courtyard awaiting the announcement of their fates, Hazel found it foreboding, as thought the sky was already ablaze with wildfire.

As she shifted from one foot to the other, she caught Slaide staring out over the crowd with a scowl smudging his features. He was looking for someone.

For her, probably. *If he truly cared, he wouldn't have betrayed my trust.* It was an important distinction, and once she came to terms with it, moving on was easier.

When his gaze passed over her, he froze. The heat of those twin molten-amber pools flowed into her even from a distance. It caused her to reach for the locket that she's chosen to put back on, hoping it had retained its magic. When her eyes locked with Slaide's, Hazel forgot everything in an instant, at least until someone shoved her forward.

"Keep moving," a gruff, unshaven man mumbled. So she did. When she stopped again, she found Slaide once more. But the man beside him sent shivers down her spine and boiled her blood equally. It was the King.

She'd expected Magnus's presence, of course, but to see them standing almost shoulder to shoulder… It hurt somehow. So much so that she wondered if he was standing there against his will. Especially when she noticed the Archmage, Gammen, on the King's other side.

Magnus stood, and a hush spread over the crowd. Though she supposed it wasn't much of a crowd anymore, seeing as there were fewer competitors left than guards.

He scanned the faces, stopping when he landed on her. An ugly, evil smirk stretched across his face. To her surprise, the locket warmed on her chest.

Slaide didn't budge. Didn't show any emotion whatsoever.

"Welcome, competitors, to the final leg of the tournament!" Magnus shouted, voice unnaturally loud. Leave it to the anti-magic King to use his own mages' tricks to amplify his voice…

"The ten of you have proven yourselves worthy of being here, one way or another. Even if some of you have hung on by the skin of your teeth," he continued. Laughter filled the void left when he stopped speaking.

Ten. She was one of only ten competitors left.

"So far, you've overcome two trials. One designed to test your stamina, dexterity, adaptability. The other was designed to challenge your mental fortitude and ability to withstand pressure. All of these attributes are things we look for—require, even—in our Raven Blade Knights. So to be considered as the Champion of Ravenhold, you must be all of those things and then some. Unfortunately for some of you, survival is no longer enough as of tonight." He paused to look directly at Hazel.

"Tonight," his voice boomed, "we have a special trial. One intended to test your willingness to do as you're told without question. A trial that will test your undying allegiance to your King and kingdom. Because above all, you must swear your life to upholding our laws at any cost. Even if it means doing something that challenges you to your core."

Hazel swallowed hard. Unnerved and uncomfortable, she looked to Slaide for comfort but received none. His eyes were wide, and his nostrils flared in that animalistic look he got when something deeply worried him.

Her heart raced beneath the heating locket. Something was wrong.

Somewhere across the courtyard, a door groaned on its hinges and the scraping of chains on stone could be heard. An almost rhythmic pattern of two marching footfalls followed by the scraping chain marked the approach of a group of people. But Hazel couldn't see them over the crowd.

That was until the men around her parted, making room for the line of prisoners to file in.

Shock rattled her as a line of ten disheveled women were dragged before them, shackled and connected to one another by iron chains. They were bruised and bloody, with matted hair and rags for clothes.

As she connected their arrival with what Magnus had said during his announcement, Hazel fought the urge to falter. To run.

Moments later, Magnus confirmed her fears.

"Tonight, ladies and gentlemen, we're killing witches."

Which Witch

CHEERS rose around her, but Hazel wanted to slink into the shadows. To be forgotten about. Or at the very least, to wake up from this nightmare.

And didn't they suspect her of being a witch as well? What did this mean for her? She had a bad feeling she'd find out all too soon.

The commotion died down as the crowd and competitors settled back in. She heard Magnus's booming voice droning on and on about something, but she couldn't hear him. Everything sounded too far away. Her head swam. She needed grounding, so she looked for Slaide.

But Slaide was no longer beside the King. He was nowhere to be seen.

For reasons she didn't want to acknowledge, Slaide's absence was what made the bottom drop out. She couldn't do this. She had to get out…

Retreating backwards, she stepped on the foot of a brutish man, who growled and shoved her. Before she could catch herself, Hazel slammed into the back of another man, who turned to glower at her.

Murmurs rose in the crowd, men started to shift angrily, and the tension around them grew.

Hazel never thought she'd be grateful for the man's voice, but it was Magnus's next announcement that saved her.

And doomed her in one fell swoop.

"I'm sure each of you are chomping at the bit to slaughter one of these demon spawns yourselves. But there's no need for this preemptive violence—I've brought a witch for each of you. I will, however, accept volunteers. Who would like to draw first blood?"

A few of the men before her stepped aside, clearly not wanting to draw attention to themselves. Someone toward the back hollered that he would do it. But Magnus ignored him.

Instead, his eyes trained on Hazel, who found herself wholly exposed after the two men in front of her stepped out of the way. He smiled.

"Well, would you look at that? Nothing like a knife into the back of your own people! Ladies and gentlemen, it seems in a stranger turn of events than even I could have orchestrated, the competition's only witch has volunteered to kill one of her own. Dedication indeed."

Raven Blade Knights approached her from either side. She should have fought. Should have done literally anything. But she froze, too shocked by this sickening scene.

The sky revolted as clouds moved in to shroud the courtyard in darkness.

The men coaxed her forward, hovering but not touching her as though afraid she might harm them. Reluctantly, she went along.

"I'll even give you the first pick. What do you say?" Magnus teased as though he were offering his weight in gold and not a choice in which woman she murdered.

In the distance, thunder rumbled.

They walked her before the line of women, and none of them met her eyes. Not until she reached the end of the line, where an old woman stared straight into Hazel's soul. Her skin was tanned and time-worn, her hair a tightly curled smattering of salt and pepper hues. She smiled softly at Hazel, thin lips pulling tight, wrinkles forming in the corners of her eyes. The woman reminded her of Agnes, and it hurt.

She couldn't do this. She didn't recognize a single face, but that didn't make it any easier.

When the woman made the faintest nod, Hazel wasn't sure if it was real, or if she was seeing things.

But then she tipped her chin high, exposing her throat.

Lightning split the sky, and the immediate crack of thunder announced the storm's arrival.

Grown men scattered at the unexpected change in weather, and horses reared against their ties. Magnus had the audacity to look annoyed.

"Get it over with already!" he yelled. "We don't have all night!"

One of the knights beside Hazel offered her a piss poor excuse for a dagger. She'd seen sharper butter knives.

She reached down into her boot and to the shock of those around her, withdrew a dagger of her own—Slaide's dagger.

"Oh for the love of the gods! Enough playing around!" Clearly she was getting under Magnus's skin. And for a moment she thought she might be enjoying it.

But the task at hand remained. She looked to the heavens as though someone would answer her, and was instead smacked between the eyes with a large raindrop.

Hazel stepped up to the woman, trembling, dagger held loosely in her hand. She knew the woman hadn't chosen this fate, but clearly she'd accepted it.

Hazel would do no such thing.

She dropped the dagger to the dirt.

And all Hel broke loose.

Out of nowhere, seven masked horsemen infiltrated the courtyard, rushing into the crowd from different angles. The slaughter began almost simultaneously.

There he was—the familiar figure like a vision from her past—leading the charge, the Wolf Mask. He cleaved a knight in two just as another tried to cut him down. In an inexplicable burst of speed, Wolf Mask ducked, spearing the man in the gut with a hidden dagger. His assailant doubled over as the dagger slipped between the links of chain mail, and Wolf Mask brought his broadsword down into the man's neck.

Hazel cowered in fear as she took in the horrors around her, but then she witnessed something that changed her perspective.

Wolf Mask's six accomplices dashed down the line and scooped up each witch in turn, using whatever means necessary to break their chains and cutting down all who stood in their way. The women were tossed into the saddle, handed the reins, and given a command in a language Hazel didn't recognize. But the horses did, and they bolted for the courtyard walls.

It wasn't an ambush. It was a rescue.

With only six horses and ten women needing rescue, several of them were doubled up, but not a single steed balked at the additional weight.

Their riders continued the assault, but as Hazel watched, she determined they only went after the knights and any others who attacked them first.

People do *know, Hazel. Trust me when I say they make* very *calculated moves behind the scenes and are near impossible to track…* The rebels. She knew in her gut this was the rebel group Slaide hinted at. And yet, even with that knowledge, Hazel stared down death itself when she spied Wolf Mask charging straight for her.

So, she ran.

Hazel knew she wouldn't outrun a horse. She also knew she wouldn't outrun a man with superhuman speed. But she wasn't going to sit there and be taken captive by someone else with unknown intentions. Even if they were saving the witches. Who was to say they weren't transporting them to a worse fate?

Where the Hel is Slaide? He had a habit of swooping in when she needed him to, but the past two incidents he'd abandoned her. Maybe Magnus was right. She scowled at the thought. But he'd claimed Slaide was a self-serving bastard. And now that she wasn't playing the games his way anymore, he didn't care what became of her.

It was in that moment, mid-thought, that Hazel's foot struck a rock and she went sprawling to the ground.

The last thing she saw before her world went white was the boulder awaiting her face.

A BRAZIER CRACKLED in the corner. Hazel looked down at her hands. Something touched her shoulder, clasping it, turning her around…

It was the winged man. He stepped closer, their bodies almost touching. She balked, twisting away, stumbling over one of the infirmary cots. She slipped on the blood-slicked stone and crashed to the floor.

He stood over her, his menacing form blocking out light, his breaths seeming to suck the air out of her lungs. He reached out for her, his hand drawing closer… closer. Hazel held her arm out in an attempt to block herself from harm, tucking into herself on the floor.

A cold hand grasped hers, and she shuddered. When nothing else happened, she chanced a glance up at him. He tugged on her hand gently, as if to say "get up." It was clear her options were very *limited, so she leaned into his grip and allowed him to help her stand. He let go of her then.*

"We need to go. They're coming."

She recognized that voice. "Who? Who is coming?" she asked frantically.

"No time. We have to move." He stepped toward her then, grabbing her upper arm and tugging her into motion. She looked at him as they ran, and as the glow of the firelight danced across his features, she realized who she thought she'd been running from all this time.

Slaide.

Hazel awoke with a start, panting, heart pounding in her chest. She threw the covers off and raced over to her wardrobe, flipping through the contents within. "Phaedra!" she yelled. *What happened? How did I get here?*

In an instant, the angel was at her side, causing Hazel to jump. "Thank goodness you're here."

"Can I be of assistance, Mistress Hazel?" Phaedra bowed.

"I-I think you can. But Phaedra, what day is it? How long was I out?" Hazel stammered.

"Not long, Mistress," Phaedra replied, taking a seat in the writing chair. "The… incident… was just last night. You've slept most of the day, but it's not even been a full day since you hit your head."

Hazel reached up, feeling the bandage above her eyebrow for the first time. She winced.

"Phaedra, is the tournament over now?" Hazel asked. She had to assume after the events she'd witnessed, the King and his men would be more worried about damage control than crowning a new champion.

"I believe so, Mistress. Though, the ball is still this evening." The moment the words left her mouth, the angel pursed her lips.

"You're kidding me," Hazel said, kicking the covers off her legs. "That's tonight?"

Phaedra jumped to her feet, rushing to Hazel's side just as she tried to leave the bed.

"Mistress, please. Your head. You're in no condition to attend a ball. Please sit back down."

"I feel fine, really. There's no need to make so much fuss over a little cut. Besides, I have to talk to Slaide. Assuming he wants anything to do with me." Hazel frowned.

"As you wish, Mistress. Please mind that injury, though. Is there any way I can assist you in getting ready?" Phaedra asked, bowing her head.

"Yes, I believe you can. I know it's a bit early, but I need you to run and fetch Master Pimley for me, please. Tell him Hazel has urgent need of him."

"Right away, Hazel." And the angel was gone.

Belle of the Ball

NOBLEMEN and women filtered into the grand ballroom in a nauseating mixture of bold perfumes and obnoxious fabric choices. They soon found themselves indulging in food, drink, and conversation. Slaide stood still as a statue at King Magnus's side, a dog tethered to his master. Their circle consisted of Magnus's most ass-kissing noblemen from the most powerful houses in Aeos, his Hand, and Prince Tristan.

Conversation drifted to some attack on a Border patrol unit the night before. Slaide caught bits and pieces as they discussed the details in a hushed manner, all the while ignoring the very public crowd around them that could likely hear what they were saying. As if citizen morale wasn't low enough already, the last thing they needed to overhear was a discussion of the instability of the Border and the masked bandit making everyone's life a living Hel. Slaide smirked into his glass as they tried to mask the panic in their voices. Their discomfort was a drug, and he couldn't get enough.

Slaide noticed Prince Tristan ignoring most of the conversations around him, and he couldn't fault him for it. He was maturing into a handsome young man, and that was not lost on the ladies who practically crawled over him, vying for his attention. *He may be a prince*, Slaide thought, *but he is still a boy*.

"Slaide, what happened to your ward? I thought she was supposed to be attending at your side?" the King's Hand, Cyrus Goodwin, questioned.

"Yes, *indeed*, boy. Where is that pet of yours?" Magnus added, smiling into his drink. He knew damn well.

Slaide shifted uncomfortably. "She couldn't make it this evening. She suffered a head injury during last night's ambush." *Keep it short and sweet. No need for details, no need for emotions.*

"Ah, what a shame," Cyrus said.

"Yes, quite unfortunate, that," Magnus grumbled, sloshing his wine, "seeing as she's your responsibility, and you were nowhere to be found."

"She was a rare looking woman, that one." This time it was Lord Marsh who spoke. He was sporting an orange fox mask, where the King and his Hand wore none. Only the lords, ladies, and attendees without greater status would be wearing them this evening.

Slaide wasn't expected to, but being able to hide his face was a perk he wasn't going to let pass him by. Most people knew who he was by stature alone anyway, so it was merely just for fun. If you could call it that. He swirled his glass of whiskey, disinterested in the frivolous conversations around him. He tipped it back, draining every last burning drop of amber liquid.

As he wiped his mouth on the sleeve of his jacket, Slaide noticed the men around him had gone silent. Their eyes cast upward, toward the top of the staircase behind him.

"Who is that?" The man Slaide had marked as Lord Ambrose was practically drooling.

Slaide turned to see what the fuss was about and found himself staring into a daring pair of brown eyes flecked with gemstone hues of emerald and citrine.

Hazel eyes.

She wore a simple yet elegant black mask. Her hooded eyes were kohl-lined and dusted with a smoky-grey powder. His eyes made their way to her lips, plump and painted a deep, glossy red.

As his gaze trailed further down, he found her unruly chestnut hair had been tamed into loose, cascading waves, pinned to one side by an emerald brooch with silver embellishments. There, on a delicate silver chain, rested that pendant she was so obsessed with.

Her black dress was stunning, if not daring. She bore no sleeves nor straps, instead leaving her shoulders and decolletage bare, her curves accentuated by a sweetheart neckline that was split down the middle, creating a deep V down past her ribs, ending just above her stomach. A full skirt embroidered with leaves of silver gave the illusion she was gliding across the floor.

She was escorted by a man Slaide immediately recognized as Pimley, despite his mask and attire. Just behind them, he spotted Phaedra, trailing in the shadows. The two of them must have helped her get ready. And good gods, they'd nailed it.

Hazel released Pimley's arm at the top of the staircase and curtsied politely in thanks.

She turned, facing the gathering crowd, and began her descent alone. She was making a statement, Slaide realized. She came here because she chose to, alone. And she would descend these stairs, alone. Point taken.

All eyes were on her as she reached the main floor where she turned to face the King and curtsied once more. Slaide's feelings for her betrayed him, and he swallowed dryly.

"I don't know who *that* is," Tristan said, pushing away the two women hanging onto his arms, "But I *must* dance with her."

Slaide stiffened. *This is not happening. Not him.*

Magnus clapped Slaide on the shoulder, laughing heartily as they both watched his son walk up to the woman Slaide had let slip through his grasp. "That boy has tenacity," Magnus noted.

"He has *balls*, you mean. And he's acting as though he just discovered them." Slaide shrugged off Magnus's meaty paw, earning him a chagrined, sideways glance.

Prince Tristan met Hazel where she stood, bowing deeply and kissing her hand. She curtsied again, and a blush creeped into her skin. She looped her arm into the prince's, and they rejoined the group.

Hazel curtsied again in the presence of the King, bowing her head. "Your Majesty," she said by way of greeting. Slaide wondered if Magnus could tell who she was, or if he was as daft as the look on his face suggested.

"Father, start up the entertainment!" Tristan turned and commanded his father. "A woman this beautiful should be shown off on the dance floor."

King Magnus pulled one of the servants aside, telling him something Slaide couldn't hear over the din. He watched as the servant scurried off in the direction of the main stage. When he looked back at the group of men, they were dispersing, with Magnus retreating to the ballroom's seat of honor upon the dais. He turned, catching Slaide's eye, and beckoned for him to follow. Slaide groaned his annoyance but obeyed orders.

He took a seat on the dais beside the King, feeling royally uncomfortable in the spotlight. This was a most unnatural place for him to be. He had always been more at home, more secure, in the shadows. *Let's get this over with.*

Magnus stood and addressed the gathered crowd with a short speech, ending with two solid claps of his hands to start up the music.

Slaide watched as Tristan dragged Hazel to the dance floor. He glared as Tristan held her hand within his own and placed the other on her waist. Something snarled within him, an angered wolf coming out of its den. He shook his head. *No, you don't get to claim her, you fool. She's not yours.*

And besides that, Hazel was… smiling. She was grinning broadly at the prince as he spoke to her. Had he ever seen her eyes light up that way? Had she ever smiled at him like *that*? A servant boy walked by with a tray of drinks, and Slaide swiped a glass of whiskey, downed it in a single gulp, and replaced the glass before the boy had so much as taken a step. It didn't matter. She wasn't his. She was never meant to be his.

The opening song came to a close, and with its end, the end of Slaide's torment. Or so he thought. No sooner than Tristan had taken his leave of her, kissing her hand again and saying something that made her blush deeply, someone else approached through the parting crowd.

Ezekiel Bertram.

Slaide steeled himself against the jealousy-laden anger welling within, gripping the arm of his chair so fervently it creaked in his grasp. He wasn't even sure what he had to hold against the man. Was it the fact that he'd been in her life first? Was it the way he looked at her when she wasn't paying attention, like she was the only thing in the world that mattered? Or maybe the fact that each of those things was true, and it wouldn't be long before she caught on? Did that scare him?

He sat deep into his seat and crossed his arms. It would be over soon. Besides, she looked incredible and would probably get asked to the dance floor by several more men. He needed to get over that. *She. Isn't. Yours.*

Hazel smiled broadly at Zeke as he walked up to her, his tight onyx curls framing his tan face. As a member of the King's guard, he was not permitted to wear a mask to these events. Identification was crucial in case of an emergency where time could be of the essence.

He approached her with his arms open wide, scooping her into a full embrace and lifting her into the air. They hugged longer than two lovers kept apart for years. Zeke pulled away, looking her over. Slaide laughed to himself, wondering if Zeke thought he needed to check her over for damages. *She's fine, I assure you,* he thought.

Zeke leaned in and whispered something into Hazel's ear. She immediately blushed and slapped his arm. He laughed. She smiled. Slaide wondered why the fuck he was still sitting there.

As if on cue, the first notes of another song started to play. Zeke bowed to Hazel respectfully and offered his arm.

Two songs later, Slaide decided he'd had enough watching. He stood, rolling his shoulders and cracking his neck from one side to the other. He finished what was left in his current glass of whiskey and set it on the tray of the nearest servant. *My turn to play.*

He strode down the stairs from the dais, drawing attention from some of the nearer revelers, who stepped out of his way.

But when he arrived where she'd last been on the ballroom floor, Ezekiel was dancing with someone else, and Hazel was nowhere to be found.

Slaide scoped out the room, silently cursing himself for not making a move sooner. Now she was gone, and with her any chance he might have had to explain himself.

And then, through a break in the crowd, he caught a glimpse of her. She'd just crossed the threshold onto the balcony.

He raced through the crowd, parting the dancers as if they were merely obstacles to get past. Once outside, he slowed, running a hand through his hair as he approached her. She stood still as a statue near the railing, overlooking the moonlit gardens.

"Hazel," he said quietly, voice just above a whisper.

"Slaide," she replied, scowling, refusing to meet his eyes.

"I'm sorry." There was no ire in his voice, no sarcasm, no anger.

Hazel looked up at him, meeting his gaze, her eyes roaming, searching him. "How did you know it was me?"

He laughed, quietly and with such subtlety that passersby would miss it. "There's not a costume you could wear, no mask, no shroud, *nothing* could make it so that I wouldn't recognize you."

She swallowed hard, looking away as if it pained her to see him. "There's something I need to talk to you about."

He stepped beside her and leaned over the stone railing. "I'm listening."

"I don't know that here is the best place," she said. "Can we go somewhere more private?"

"Seeing as you hate me right now, I'm not sure it's safe for me to go anywhere secluded with you." A serious topic, but there was a playful ease in his voice.

"Cut the bullshit, Slaide. This is serious." She glanced around, looking for prying ears. "Do you have dreams?"

He raised an eyebrow. "That's kind of a philosophical question, and I've had far too much to drink for that kind of deep thinking."

"Not *those* kinds of dreams," she groaned in frustration. "Nightmares. I have them often, for quite a while now. But lately… lately you've been in them."

In the ballroom, the performers began another song.

He ignored what she'd said, pushing off the railing and offering his hand.

"Dance?" he asked.

"Slaide!" she hissed. "This is serious."

"What makes you think I'm not?" His smile faded.

Hazel sighed and continued. "Since I've been in the castle, these nightmares have been fewer… less frequent. There were several days this week when I didn't have any at all. But back home, every night was plagued with similar nightmares. One where I was walking through a dark corridor, hearing screams. Another where there was a dark, winged man stalking me through the halls, reaching out to touch me. And last night… last night he grabbed my hand. *You* grabbed my hand. All this time I thought I was being chased, but then you took my hand, and we were running. *Together.*"

The Gift

SLAIDE stared into Hazel's eyes, as if he were searching the depths of her soul.

"Yes," he spoke quietly.

"Yes, *what*?" She frowned.

Inside, the music built in its intensity and dancers moved with fervor. It was the same dance they'd practiced with Pimley, the one when Slaide had interrupted her training.

To her dismay, Slaide grabbed her hand and tugged her toward him, forcing her into a spin that brought her back flush with his body.

"The nightmares," he whispered into her ear. Slaide nudged her away, and Hazel danced in a circle around him, her eyes growing wide.

He pulled her to a bench beside the stone railing and helped her adjust her dress so she could sit. Slaide sat down beside her, running a hand down his face with closed eyes, and exhaled. His annoyingly self-assured demeanor fractured, replaced by something uncertain. His face was unreadable.

He cleared his throat. "So, tell me more about these nightmares."

And Hazel did. Slaide never interrupted, just nodded and asked the appropriate questions at the appropriate times. No snide remarks, no snark, no attitude. When she finished, he sat quietly, thoughtfully, as though mulling it all over.

"I have a few thoughts on this," he began, "and I'm not sure I like any of it, nor am I sure what it all means. One thing is for certain, though. We are somehow connected by these dreams."

Her breath hitched.

"There's something else I need to tell you." He looked down at his feet. "I don't exactly know how to explain it in a way it makes sense while also keeping you out of trouble."

Hazel arched a brow at that.

"I have some… personal work… that draws me away from here some nights. I have found that on those nights, when I'm away from the castle—away from *you*—the nightmares are relentless."

"So, I suppose that would explain why I've had a few horrible nights this week, and others I slept soundly. It was a difference of whether you were close or if you'd gone… wherever."

Slaide nodded. "It was the same for me. I found it strange, how one day it was like the nightmares just… disappeared. It was the same day you were brought here. I slept as well as I have in ages. Then, on my first night away since you were here, I woke up in a pool of sweat." He was fiddling with his fingers, a nervous habit. What was he so afraid to tell her? "It's part of the reason I fought against Gammen and his spineless pet Oriss. There was something about you I needed to figure out, and the only way I was going to do that was if I kept you out of their clutches."

"What was the other reason?" she inquired.

"Hmm?" He raised a brow.

"You said it was *part* of the reason you fought to keep me from the mages. Was there more to it than that?"

Slaide swallowed hard. "Yes. But I didn't realize what it was until I'd gotten to know you a little better. I had a strange feeling, call it intuition, instinct, whatever… but something was screaming at me not to let you go."

"And what was it that you discovered after we spent some time together?" She was treading dangerous water, her heart a war drum in her chest.

"That you were Aisling's daughter." He looked as though he wanted to shrink down to the size of an ant so he could scurry away and hide.

She started to pull away, but Slaide held her hands in his.

"Hazel, there's more to your mother's story. It didn't end with me."

She glared at him, her eyes glassy and steeped in hatred.

"Listen to me. I can't tell you whether or not she is still alive, but I can tell you she made it out of this castle that way."

She scrunched her face in apparent confusion.

"I got her out. It doesn't excuse what happened or my part in it, and it doesn't take away any horrors she probably experienced here. But Hazel, I swore I would get her out if it was the last thing I did. And I did."

"How?" She was nearly breathless.

"The slave tunnels," he said pointedly.

Everything came crashing down at once. "The nightmares," she gasped. "The woman… I… That wasn't me."

Slaide shook his head. "It was her. It had to be. I don't know how yet, but it's like you're reliving her memories in your dreams. Almost as though we both are."

Hazel's shock was visible as her power thrummed against the underside of her skin.

"I realize it's a bit of a stretch expecting you to trust me, even just this once," he said, bowing his head as if he's embarrassed by his actions.

"You really don't remember any of that night, do you?" He inclined his head.

"No," she said, "why would I?"

He sighed. "Because you were there the night I captured her. She let herself be captured in order to send you away. Powerful as she was, she couldn't both fend us off and open the portal for you. She chose you."

Hazel grew quiet, face twisting as his words landed. "So, you've known. All this time, you've known?"

"No, Hazel. I didn't. I won't lie to you; from day one there was something familiar about you. I felt certain I'd met you before. But I couldn't place it. I've come to realize, as strange as it sounds, that I recognized your scent. It just didn't occur to me where I recognized it from. That *was* twenty-five years ago, after all."

Hazel looked at him thoughtfully, with glassy eyes. "Why did you help her if you were just going to turn around and do the same thing to other women, witches or not? Let's pretend I believe you, which I'm not sure I do. How could you pick up where you left off like nothing happened?"

Slaide looked as though he'd prepared for that very question.

"I do what I must to survive, but for the most part, I don't… hurt them. You hear and see the same things as everyone else, so you know that word of mouth does wonders for a reputation, especially a bad one. Play the role of the bad guy, dress the part, get your hands dirty every now and then, and people stop questioning the validity of the rumors. Yes, I hunt magical creatures. I spend most of my days now hunting those monsters coming across the Border. When he commands me to arrest and execute a witch…" he paused, appearing to search for the right words. "He would be presented with a token representing their fate. A necklace. A wedding band. A lock of hair. Rarely a live witch, and never a body. The problem is, the charade has run its course. Magnus has started calling my bluff—or at the very least has grown suspicious—and is now having his Bloodseekers swoop in after me to tie up any loose ends. Which as you can imagine is undoing many years' worth of work."

"You mean to tell me that you, Slaide Elias, hunter of witches and monsters for the High King of Aeos, have actually been undermining His Majesty this entire time?"

Without acknowledging the truth, Slaide smiled. "Don't forget *Fallenborn whelp*."

Hazel smiled, but it was brief. A conflicted look overtook her features, and her hand rose to her pendant. Before she reached it, Slaide caught her hand.

"You don't need that, you know. You're safe with me."

Her eyes roamed his face expectantly. "I don't know if I want to slap you or kiss you," she blurted before covering her mouth.

"Do I have a say in the matter?" he asked, watching as her cheeks turned his favorite shade of pink, as her eyes dipped to his mouth before returning to his gaze. And he moved—cautiously in case she was planning on smacking him instead.

Someone nearby cleared their throat. "Master Elias, I do not mean to interrupt—"

"Then don't," Slaide growled as he pulled away from her to find a mousy, middle-aged servant standing a few paces away.

"Yes, sir, I apologize, but His Majesty is requesting your presence back in the ballroom for the presentation of the prince's gifts."

He rolled his eyes. "We'll be there shortly."

"Yes, Master Elias. Please see that you do," he said, his voice curter than it had any right to be.

"I said we'll be there *shortly*. You're dismissed." Slaide snipped.

"Yes, sir." The man bowed and took his leave. Slaide's spiteful gaze followed the poor servant until he was out of sight.

He sighed, looking Hazel over once more. She looked embarrassed, gaze averted and cheeks flushed.

Slaide stood, sighing, and offered Hazel his arm. "I guess we'd better be off. Wouldn't want to keep His Majesty and the princeling waiting. Besides, if you keep looking at me like that, I might just forget we're in public and take you here, for everyone to see."

Hazel's eyes grew wide at that. Slaide wondered if her body and mind protested as much as his did, tired of these moments being cut short just when they were getting *good,* but she accepted his offering and stood, allowing Slaide to pull her in close.

As they approached the archway leading back inside, they could see that Magnus had come down from his place of honor on the dais and was mingling with various lords. He hadn't made it to the stage yet.

Slaide grabbed Hazel with a force that made her squeal, causing him to clamp a hand down over her mouth. He shuffled her over to the shadows and pushed her through a door. Only then did he remove his hand as he pressed her up against the room's inner wall with the weight of his body.

"Slaide," she panted, "What are you doing?" Her voice was not quite a whisper.

He pulled back momentarily, placing his hands above her on the wall. "Correct me if I'm wrong, but after what happened just now, I think I speak for both of us when I say we have unfinished business." He searched her eyes for any indication he was wrong. "The princeling can wait."

In the span of a breath, she had her hands on him. She grappled for his shirt, pulling him against her body and wrapping her arms around his neck. She kissed him greedily as though he was the very thing sustaining her; the only thing that could keep her alive. And he was glad for it.

Slaide pulled away again, his absence met with a groan of protest from a rather flustered Hazel. He smirked at her, savoring the way she looked when she was coming undone.

She reached for him again, and he stepped back, wagging his finger at her. All around him, the shadows lengthened, and began to move on their own.

Slaide put his hands in his pockets as his shadows leaked off of him and made their way toward her, crawling across the ground and up the wall. With a flick of his fingers, his shadows had her arms secured above her head. One shadow curled lazily about her neck, its tendril drifting daringly close to the slit in her dress. Only then did Slaide step back into her space.

He leaned in, placing delicate kisses up her neck and cupping one breast in his hand. He rolled his thumb over the fabric of her bodice, feeling her nipple peak beneath it. He groaned as she arched her back off the wall, as if needing to feel more of him.

He pulled back for a moment and whispered into her ear. "Hazel, if at any point you want me to stop, you know you can say so, right? Just say the word and these are gone in an instant," he gestured to his shadows. "Don't get me wrong, I want to *ruin* you, but the last thing I want to do is to hurt or scare you. Just say the word."

"Don't…" She breathed heavily.

He pulled away further, waiting for the rest. Waiting for the command to back off, for the moment when it all came crashing down that this was too much, too fast and most certainly *not* the right time.

"Don't!" She hissed, "Don't stop."

So, he didn't.

Slaide came unleashed. He released Hazel from the wall and spun her so she was facing away from him. Without hesitation, he undid the corset back of the dress's bodice, his fingers moving furiously as he stifled the urge to rip the damned thing to shreds.

His hands grabbed desperately at the bodice as he kissed her, trying to pull it down. To access the woman before him without so much cumbersome fabric between them. But she stopped him from going any further.

"No," she panted between kisses up the column of her neck. "Leave it on. We can't stay in here all night."

Slaide groaned his displeasure but made no more attempts to remove the dress. Instead, he pushed her to the wall again.

And then he dropped to his knees, immediately grappling with her skirts.

"What in the name of the gods are you doing?" She reached for him, but with a snap of his fingers, her wrists were snatched by his shadows again and kept at bay.

He looked up at her with a devilish smirk.

"Tell me, Hazel. How does it feel to bring a witch hunter to his knees?"

She gasped, her mouth parting, but no words escaped.

"That's what I thought," he growled, his expression growing dark. "Now, be a good witch and let me *end* you the way you deserve." His voice was smooth as silk.

Hazel folded. She didn't balk when he uttered the word witch; didn't protest such slander. She also didn't resist when he found his way beneath her dress.

But before he could continue, the door crashed open.

And in the doorway stood Ezekiel Bertram.

"Hazel?" Zeke asked, his voice shaky with uncertainty.

She said nothing. Her mouth hung agape as she stared at him.

"Hazel, what're you… what the *fuck*?" Zeke's demeanor shifted as Slaide stood and brushed nonexistent dust from his clothes.

"I'm assuming," Slaide began, "you've got life-altering news to share? Otherwise, get the fuck out," he growled.

Hazel whirled on him. "Stop it, Slaide. Zeke… I—"

But Ezekiel cut her words off. "Save it. You two are *perfect* for each other. An accused witch and the King's dog." He shrugged his shoulders. "I do have something rather important to share. You would have heard for yourself, if you weren't preoccupied with fucking this trash." He spat on the floor, fists flexing at his sides.

Slaide made to step forward, but she placed her arm in front of him.

"Who I am with is *none* of your concern, Ezekiel Bertram. We are all adults, last time I checked. Free to make our own choices."

"Free?" Zeke's voice rose, sounding rattled. "You are *anything* but free, Hazel. Or did you forget? While he's been parading you around, feeding you pastries, and teaching you how to dance, you're still a prisoner. You're fucking your executioner."

"I've heard enough," Slaide interjected. "Unless you have something important to say, get out. I'm not going to ask again."

Zeke glowered at them both. He pursed his lips as though considering whether to reveal why he'd busted down the door in the first place.

"Fine." He relented. "I saw you head this way after our dance. Shortly after you disappeared, Magnus presented the prince's gifts. He was rather displeased that the two of you couldn't be bothered to join us," he sneered as Hazel adjusted the bust of her dress. "Tristan was gifted an Axian Destrier. A stallion."

Slaide laughed, rolling his eyes. "Well, congratu-fucking-lations to him."

"I wasn't finished, dog," Zeke snapped. "After they walked the horse back out of the ballroom, His Majesty revealed one more gift." He looked toward Hazel with sympathy in his eyes. "We're reinstating Court-sanctioned witch hunts. Instead of relying on *this* one to do his job, Magnus has decided to send his knights door-to-door, town-to-town, seeking out anyone with magic in their blood."

Hazel stiffened. Slaide's hand found the small of her back, steadying her—a small comfort.

"As part of the prince's birthday celebration, they're kicking off the hunts *tonight* and allowing regular citizens to join in. He's awarding a prize to anyone who brings the witch in alive."

No no no. This is not happening. Please, don't—

"Hazel, the hunts are starting in Larksridge."

Breaking Point

HAZEL could hear nothing over the thundering of her own heart. They were going to Larksridge. To her home. To her father and Agnes.

Agnes.

There was no doubt in her mind that she was the target. And the only thing she was guilty of was existing in a kingdom that didn't want her.

"They're gathering the mob now, Hazel. There's not much time." Zeke sighed and shook his head. "Don't say I never did anything for you."

With that, he turned his back on them and left the small room.

"Zeke, wait!" she shouted after him. But he didn't spare her a glance.

As he departed, the air left Hazel's lungs. She turned to Slaide.

"That look tells me he's not bluffing," Slaide observed. "You have witch friends back home?"

She shook her head. How could she explain Agnes? She sucked in a breath, preparing to speak, but only a squeaky, choked sound escaped her.

"I know, I know. Come with me, quickly, quietly. We're going to get there first." But he didn't know. Not really.

"Slaide, I…" She debated having this conversation now, but what choice did she have? "My aunt. My aunt is the witch." Her voice cracked. She would not break down here. Could not break down here. "She lives just outside of Larksridge in a cottage. She keeps her home warded but…" She faded off.

"It's not going to be enough." He acknowledged, turning with her and bolting inside.

Inside, the crowd had already transformed into an angry mob, many of the noblemen shaking their dueling swords in the air, raving on about killing the witch. The mentality was as contagious as any disease and left Hazel wondering how these people had fallen so low, how they'd left their humanity behind without a second thought.

Such was the reign of a King left unchecked, she supposed.

They left the room in haste, Slaide dragging Hazel by her wrist behind him. He strode to the carved marble bench and leapt onto it with feline grace. In no time at all, he discarded his jacket, leaving just a linen undershirt between Hazel and his solid, chiseled body. He faced Hazel with his arms outstretched. "I'm going to need you to trust me."

"What happened to needing only my compliance, not my trust?" Despite the circumstances, she had to smirk at the opportunity to use his own words against him.

He rolled his eyes, but a reluctant smile broke through.

"I'm glad your humor is still intact." He looked out to the sky, then back to her, reaching his arm out. "I won't let anything happen to you."

What strange, alternate reality had she stumbled into, where this man who was once her enemy, who could snap her neck without touching her if he wanted, was now the one offering to save her family? To save her?

Hazel reached up, accepting his hand. He pulled her up onto the bench and she stumbled, her gaze falling over the sheer drop off beyond the railing. She found herself diving back into the safety of Slaide's embrace. He hugged her, then held her away to look into her eyes.

"You might want to close your eyes." He pulled her tight to his body and launched them both from the balcony into a free fall. Hazel screamed, but the sound was torn from her throat by the speed of their dive. They plummeted together, Slaide waiting until they were just above the treetops to expand his glorious, feathered wings.

"You okay, sweets?" he spoke softly against her hair.

"I'm fine," she mumbled into his shirt. She was definitely not fine. Her stomach teetered on the edge of something disastrous, a twisting, swirling combination of exhilaration and soul crushing, debilitating anxiety.

His laugh rumbled deep in his chest. "You can open your eyes now, if you want. Usually, the initial fall is the worst part for first-timers."

Hazel thought about that, weighing his words. She had no desire to see the world from above... and yet... when would she ever get this chance again, to see everything the way a bird did? She turned her head and peeked one eye open, slamming it closed immediately upon glimpsing the ground below. Then she braved opening it again, working up to them both, taking in the scenery as it blew by them. It was both the scariest and most fantastic thing she'd ever witnessed. They flew over the trees at breakneck speeds, their shadow sending creatures scurrying on the forest floor.

A commotion behind them drew their attention. It was the mob. The glow of torches bobbed in the distance, warning of their approach.

"Hold on," Slaide said as they cleared the last row of trees. The royal stables came into view, and Hazel spotted Phillip and Nanna grazing in the moonlight. Slaide made a beeline descent, not for the barn itself but for the pasture. Phillip looked up as they approached, and Hazel found herself wondering how often Slaide made his entrance in this way, for neither of the horses worried themselves over a giant winged man in the sky.

The landing was gentler than Hazel expected, Slaide landing in a crouch with a soft thud. And then her hand was in his again and they were jogging to their mounts, who simply looked up as though this were an everyday occurrence. And maybe it was. After all, Hazel had no idea what Slaide got up to at night. She wasn't too keen on riding Nanna bareback but hoped and prayed to whatever gods cared to listen that the angsty pony would sense their urgency and mind her manners. Just this once.

But as soon as that thought crossed her mind, she was relieved to hear Slaide whistle softly in her direction. She jogged over to him where he crouched, interlacing his fingers and creating a step up for her. She placed her foot into his hands at a run, and Slaide launched her up to Phillip's back. Then he was behind her, urging Phillip on.

The gelding was soon at a gallop and headed straight for the pasture fence, with no gate in sight. She wasn't one to doubt the horse's abilities, but in this moment, they could not spare time for a misjudged jump. Could he even jump that high?

She received her answer a few moments later as Slaide wrapped his arm around her waist, instructing her to "squeeze with her legs like her life depends on it." Below her, the horse's muscles contracted, tension coiling, and then Phillip's feet left the ground, sending them soaring through the air.

Phillip cleared the fence as though it wasn't there, and they were galloping into the night, guided only by sheer will and the light of the moon.

They rode long and hard as time passed, the midnight sky giving way to the first purples of the pre-dawn hour. Hazel had commanded Slaide to bypass Larksridge. Her father may or may not have caught wind of this already; either way, she wasn't going to waste time dragging him into it. Agnes was priority number one.

As they approached the road leading to Agnes's stead, she could already tell something was off. There was no hum of the ward magic along her skin, no familiar buzz in her head. *It's nothing. Connall beat us here and got her to safety, that's all.*

But when they rounded the bend where the path faded into nothing but trees, Slaide brought Phillip to a screeching halt, the move sending dirt and debris flying. Hazel's throat plummeted into an abyss unlike anything she'd felt before.

They were greeted by an orange glow through the sparse, half-dead forest.

Agnes's cottage was engulfed in flames.

They were too late. Hazel made to scream, but the sound was drowned out by wails and shouts in the distance. They had to move.

Slaide pushed Phillip into a gallop once more, churning the ground into a cloud of dust in their wake. They'd been so close, had ridden so hard, and still it was not enough. They made it to Agnes's glade and the wards were, in fact, gone. The blaze roared with an unmatched intensity, making it impossible to get too close as it continued to feed on the thatched roof and many flammable materials within her home.

But what startled Hazel the most, perhaps even more than the fire, were the people. There were maybe a dozen townsfolk, bustling about, shouting orders to one another, attempting to save what they could. She recognized several faces from the tavern and the market as women and men alike fetched water from the nearby stream, tossing bucket after bucket onto the relentless fire.

Hazel froze in her panic. Where was Agnes? And where was Connall? If the townspeople were here, that meant he was, too. After all, Connall would have been the one to rally them from their beds at this late hour to save her. It was a small silver lining that the townspeople still came to Connall's aid despite the horrible rumors about him.

There was no sign of anyone who might have started the fire, but she was on high alert. The castle mob would be there in a matter of minutes to be sure. She spun to ask Slaide what to do, but he was gone, and Phillip too. She had no doubt that he'd probably sprung into action while she stood there gawking.

As her gaze darted about, searching for any sign of them, the cottage door burst open and a large figure came tumbling out, crashing to the ground and rolling into a heap. An angry, hungry fireball exploded behind them.

Connall.

And in his arms, he held Agnes's frail form.

No, she thought. *NO! This is not happening!*

She ran to them alongside several townspeople who'd seen the blast. Two large men rolled an unconscious Connall over and dragged him beyond the reach of the fire's fury. Hazel ran for Agnes, scooping underneath her arms and attempting to pull her away, but she was not strong enough. A rough hand landed on her shoulder and patted, gently telling her to move aside. Reluctantly, she did, and a third man dragged Agnes to safety beside Connall.

Breathing. They were both breathing, thank the gods. And they were out of immediate danger, though the growing blaze was putting off searing, singeing heat that threatened to melt the flesh from their bones if they stayed there much longer. She looked over her shoulder at the burning cottage in time to see part of the roof collapse, sending a column of smoke and ash and embers into the night sky.

Someone behind her broke into a fit of coughing, and Hazel turned to find Connall rolling to his side, trying to sit up. He was coughing fitfully, unable to catch his breath, reaching for her.

"Hazel," he rasped, "You came."

A sob escaped her throat as she ran to him, dropping to her knees and helping him sit up. "Of course I came, Pa. I came as soon as I could. Shh, don't speak." She turned, frantically looking for help. *Where is Slaide?* "Water! Please someone bring us some water!" she shouted to anyone who would listen.

A woman jogged over with a waterskin and offered it to them. "It's only about half full, but—"

"It's perfect. Thank you." Hazel cut her off, tipping the waterskin to Connall's mouth and pouring the water in a little at a time. He coughed and gagged at first but was able to take a few mouthfuls.

"Agnes…" he managed. Hazel looked over her shoulder at Agnes's unmoving form.

"She's going to be alright, but only if we get her out of here. There's a mob coming."

His eyes widened as if in realization, transforming into something hard and unmovable.

"Stay right here," she said, knowing he wasn't going anywhere fast, but understanding that Connall Callahan was not one to be deterred by much, not even a brush with death.

She rushed to Agnes, where a woman was tending to a gash on her cheek. Another laceration stretched the length of her left eyebrow, her bottom lip was blistered and split, her hair was singed, and her forearms were covered in blistering, bubbling burns, flesh completely lost in places. The amount of pain she had to be in was overwhelming to think about. But she was breathing, and she was being tended to. *Now to get everyone out of here before…*

Her planning was interrupted by thundering hooves and the shouting of men. She looked up to see torchlights glowing in the distance. It was too late. Agnes's burning home had served as a beacon for their exact location, and the mob had arrived. They would have to make a stand.

As the mob approached, the townspeople did something unexpected: they prepared to fight. Hazel had never seen this kind of mentality from them before. What was usually "every man for himself" had suddenly become "no man stands alone" as they set aside their water buckets for short swords, daggers, and pitchforks, abandoning the still-blazing cottage behind them.

Magnus brought the fight to one of their own, and they would go down swinging. Maybe the townspeople of Larksridge hadn't been as complacent as she'd thought. But more than likely, this was Connall's doing.

A grunt came from behind her, and Connall was climbing to his feet. He was remarkably unscathed, save for a few burns blistering his skin. His face was smeared with soot and ash, the corners of his eyes wet with tears from the heat and sting of the fire. But he was whole.

She sprinted for him, slamming into him as she wrapped her arms around his body as much as she could. He stutter-stepped sideways, catching her and hugging her tight.

"Oh, my girl," he said. "I thought I'd lost you."

She pressed her head into his chest, tears streaking down her cheeks. This was all she had wanted. *This* was home.

He looked down at her with warmth in his eyes, holding her away from him as though to look her over. "You're alright, then?"

"Yes, Pa. As well as I can be considering everything."

Concern overtook his face as he remembered where they were. The shouts of the mob grew closer.

"Pa, we need to get everyone out of here. They're coming for her." She glanced over to Agnes, who was still being tended to a safe enough distance from the blaze.

"Who are they? How did you know to come here?" he asked. *Right. He has no idea what I've been doing this past week. What I've been through and seen.*

"It's a long story, but I promise I will tell you everything. For now all you need to know is that the High King has re-initiated sanctioned witch hunts. And they're starting here, with her." She thought about it for a moment. "Pa, how did *you* know to come here?"

"She told me," he nodded toward Agnes. "Somehow she knew. I-I think she sees things we can't, Hazel. She came and got me. Said she was in trouble and if I thought anyone might help, to bring them along."

He faced the approaching mob. "So, they think they can take us out that easily, eh?" he growled. Turning to Hazel he commanded, "Get some of the others to help you get Agnes out of here. The Border isn't far and—"

"I am not leaving you here," she interrupted. "We all need to go. There's still time."

"There is no time." He put a hand on her shoulder. "I know you are strong, and I know you want to help, but sometimes the best thing we can do is get others to safety. I will hold them off with the other men to buy you time. Now go!" He gave her a gentle push, spinning her in Agnes's direction. She whirled around to protest, but Connall was gone, shouting orders and organizing the remaining men.

Right, then. Time to get Agnes out of here. Hazel sprinted to Agnes's side, and the woman caring for her looked up with fear in her eyes.

"How is she?" Hazel swallowed the lump in her throat from seeing Agnes in this state. She had to be strong. For Connall. For Agnes. For these people who needed saving.

The woman shook her head. "She's alive. Breathing fine. But she is still out of it. I cannot get her to wake." Hazel wished she had some of Slaide's hartshorn powder. *Damn it. Where is Slaide?* She'd crossed the paths of many of the same people repeatedly as they bustled about, and he had not been among them. But there was no time to concern herself with that now.

"We need a way to move her. There's a wagon over there and we can—"

She was interrupted by the clash of steel and angry shouting of men. *No! We need more time…* But it was too late. The mob was upon them, and they were bolstered by the sight of armed villagers prepared to fight.

Cheers arose followed by chants of "kill the witch," even though the King had commanded she be brought in alive.

There were so many of them. The burn of the locket stung against her skin.

Swords clanged against one another, men shouting insults and grunting as blades hit their mark. Hazel watched as one man from the mob swung a mace, crushing the skull of a Larksridge man whose name she didn't know, spraying blood and brain matter as he pulled the weapon free. And then he was charging toward the next.

To their right, a member of the mob was run through from behind by a blade, and he collapsed choking on his own blood.

She looked to their left to find a man heading straight for them with a dagger held high, screaming something inaudible as he ran. He was nearly upon them when his attention was drawn to something more pressing, and he let out a shout that was cut off as a hulking black horse and rider slammed into him. The man was sent flying, his body landing in a heap on the ground. A trickle of blood by his ear glimmered in the flickering firelight, and he did not get back up.

The horse and rider dashed into the woods behind what was left of Agnes's cottage, leaving her to take in the carnage around them.

The woman beside her screamed, and Hazel spun to find a man atop her with a dagger pressed to her throat. Before Hazel could move, he drew his blade across the woman's soft flesh, leaving a red rent in its wake. Her face twisted into a wordless scream as her life leaked out of her into a warm, dark pool on the ground.

He was standing over Hazel then, a malicious grin spread across his face as he took in the one thing standing between him and his prize.

Hazel reached for Sylvie's dagger, preparing to defend herself. The man's eyes darkened as he laughed at her. And then she understood why as he unsheathed a broadsword she hadn't noticed before. He was going to cut her down where she stood, and there was nothing she could do about it. He raised the weapon overhead in a two-handed grip, and despite herself, Hazel closed her eyes, preparing for the blow.

When it didn't come, she opened her eyes to find the man falling over, an arrow protruding from between his eyes, another through his heart. Hazel spun to find the assailant and was overwhelmed with relief when seven riders in black stepped out of the black smoke like the harbingers of chaos they were.

And one of them was Wolf Mask.

Wolf Mask, the man who had only just led an ambush at Ravenhold. Wolf Mask, who had continued to spread terror around the kingdom. Wolf Mask, who saved her life not just once now, but twice.

He nodded to her, and she returned the gesture. Then he and his masked men were moving, charging attackers from atop their mounts, cutting them down and effectively pushing the mob back. They weren't retreating, but it at least allowed her a moment to regroup. She'd made herself a target by protecting Agnes. She needed to grow a spine, or she wasn't getting out of here alive.

She backed up, keeping her distance from her next attacker while still protecting Agnes. Another step back and Hazel tripped, losing her footing and falling to the ground. The relentless man seized the opportunity to corner her, and he pounced.

Without warning, another man dove in front of Hazel, their swords clashing and parrying the blow. As she came to her senses, she discovered it wasn't just another man. It was Connall.

Connall and the large, broad-shouldered man were dangerously similar in strength and ability. The world slowed around them as sword connected with sword, steel sliding and grinding against steel over and over again.

But as quickly as it began, it was over. His opponent fell for a maneuver that proved Connall really was the superior fighter as he dodged a sloppy strike and sliced through the man with ease. When he pulled his sword free, Hazel was staring at him as though she was seeing Connall for the first time. Not in fear, but in awe.

He sheathed his sword and ran to her. "Are you alright?"

"Yes, but I can't do this on my own. I need help moving her." She faced Agnes and tried to pull the woman's arm up over her shoulder, hoping Connall would set his desire to fight aside and just help her. When it became clear he wasn't going to help, she turned on him with the intent of begging him to forget his pride long enough to drag Agnes to safety when the world was torn out from under her.

Connall was on his knees, an arrow protruding from his chest. The man was tough as an oaken battle shield, yet he'd been pierced as though he was no thicker than parchment.

Hazel screamed, though she heard nothing, felt nothing as she collapsed before him, her hands frantically trying to figure out how to fix what was not fixable. Nothing else mattered except her father's lifeblood as it dripped from the arrowhead.

Connall's face twisted in shock and agony as he fell to his hands and knees, gasping and clutching at the place he'd been struck.

She crawled to him, pulling him into her and cradling his head against her body. *This is not real. This is not fucking happening.*

"Pa, say something please! You're fine. You're going to be fine, you hear me? Everything is going to be fine!" She was beside herself. "Someone help us!" she screamed.

Somewhere in the distance, the fighting raged on. Wolf Mask and his vigilantes were putting up a good fight, but still grossly outnumbered. The remaining citizens of Larksridge were fighting for their lives and struggling to protect themselves. No one was coming to save her.

A hand reached up and caressed her face. She looked down to see Connall looking up at her, smiling, his teeth red with blood.

"Pa, please! We are going to get out of here. Everything will be fine." She sobbed, repeating herself.

"Shh," Connall whispered. "Don't you fuss over me, my girl." It was an effort for him to talk as he gasped between words. "Do you know… how proud you've made me? Do you know how lucky I am… that Fate brought us… together?"

"No, you are not allowed to talk like this. You are not leaving me!"

He closed his eyes, cringing against the pain racking his body. When he opened them again, his eyes were softer, full of sorrow. "I am… sorry… for not telling you… the truth… sooner. That was… never my intention. I hope… you will forgive… me."

Hazel couldn't think straight, she couldn't function because none of this was real. It couldn't be. "Please…" she whispered. "Please don't… I don't need to forgive you. There's nothing to forgive. You're mine, and I'm yours, and we are going back to Larksridge together, do you hear me?"

He blinked at her, a single tear rolling down his cheek as he reached for her hand. He didn't speak, he couldn't speak. He was fading.

"I forgive you," she cried. "There's nothing to forgive, but if that will make you stay then yes, I forgive you. I love you more than anyone in the world, and I need you. Please, just hang on."

He smiled at her, giving her hand a squeeze. And then the light was gone, his grip releasing her as his hand fell away. Connall Callahan was gone.

Overwhelmed by rage and unimaginable sorrow, Hazel screamed and dug down into that place deep within her soul. The endless well where her magic lied in wait, begging to be called upon. This time it was easy to access, boiling up within her with an ease that shocked her. This was power, and she would make them pay.

Hazel brought her power to the surface and set it free, exploding in a blinding light, wiping out every attacker in her vicinity and blasting apart trees. Her eruption shattered the ground and rattled the very stars in the sky.

And then she was nothing, and the world went black.

No Visitors

The iron lock slid out of place, followed by the sound of stone grinding on stone as the dungeon's main door pushed open. The armed guard entered and stepped aside, allowing Slaide to walk past him. As soon as he'd cleared the threshold, the guard pushed the door shut once more.

Slaide paused momentarily, his skin prickling at the sound of that door closing. He steeled himself against the unease. *It isn't like that this time. They'll never lock you in one of these cells again.*

He pushed through that feeling, ensuring no one noticed Slaide Elias balking at the thought of being locked in this dank, windowless, soul-rending dungeon again. He closed his eyes, rolling his neck from left to right and back again, and his resolve returned.

Focus on the task at hand.

He walked down the aisle, noting that most of the doors were propped open. Empty. He smirked, knowing the witches who'd been imprisoned here were likely somewhere safe. He thought of the things he'd read in that history book. The things Magnus himself had admitted to. The things Hazel could—would—face if she stayed there.

Slaide picked up his pace. Was she even still here? Was this all a waste of time? But then it came into view: the solid, iron door three times as thick as the others along the hall. It was closed and bolted shut. Likely warded as well. And if that was the case, he was going to need more help getting that door open, because the kind of chaos his magic drew on was far from the refined type that could be controlled with runes and glyphs. He drew his shadows and storms from the world around him, relying on the unrefined mana he could find below the ground.

In short, while he was impeccably strong, Slaide Elias could not make or break warding spells. There was no barging through them on sheer power or will alone. And if he knew the mages, which he unfortunately did, these wards would retaliate against anyone who either tried to break them with the wrong magical imprint or tried to force their way in.

And that spell would be written to kill.

He turned to the guard. "I need access to that prisoner."

The man raised a brow. "And I need a day off. No one is to go in or out of that cell. King's orders."

Slaide didn't let his frustration show, but he had to think fast. "While that may be true, I was sent here to interrogate her. King's orders." He smiled that charming, murderous smile that made most people back down in his presence.

This at least gave the guard pause. But it was clear he was thinking it over, considering his options. He was going to call Slaide's bluff.

"Master Elias, sir, I understand you're a man of great power and status, but I've received no official word from His Majesty in regard to solicitations of the prisoner. Might you have something with his signature or seal indicating such?"

Slaide roared internally. Of the few times he'd ever come across a guard who could think on his feet and hold a sword equally as well, this man had to be one of them. He examined the guard, who just stood there, arms folded and watching him with hawklike intensity.

"No, he didn't send me with anything official. Simply his words as you hear them coming out of my mouth. I'm not generally questioned on my authenticity. But no matter, if it's going to be an issue I can just return to him—"

The guard looked conflicted. "Ah, well, I'm sure we can work something out. No need to involve His Majesty if it can be avoided, sir." He eyed the door over Slaide's shoulder. "I can allow you a few minutes, but you'll need to be out before shift change."

"And when is that?"

The guard glanced over his shoulder at the short, mostly melted candle by the main door. "By the looks of it, less than ten minutes."

Slaide frowned at the candle and the guard. The guard shrugged dismissively.

"Primitive, maybe. But do you see any other ways to tell time down here? Magic doesn't work here, and there aren't any windows by which to see the sun or shadows cast throughout the day. So, we use what we have. You might be surprised at how well it works."

"I'll take your word for it."

"Right, well, better get moving." He worked past Slaide toward the ominous door. The guard removed a key from his pocket—no, not a key. A wardstone.

In the center of the door was a large inscription. There was a small circle within a larger one, and in the center of them both was a circle of glyphs. Slaide couldn't read them as they were inscribed in the ancient runic language. In the center of the glyphs, there was a recessed shape in the door.

As he expected, the guard pressed the wardstone into the hole, where it nestled perfectly with an audible click. Then, he turned the stone to the right by three glyphs, left by two, and then all the way around so that it was back in its original position. He pressed his palm into the stone, and it sank deeper into the door.

What happened next, Slaide had never seen before. The stone itself glowed with an eerie blue light, which flowed outward into the grooves connecting the glyphs, into the glyphs themselves, and then into and around both circles. It was like watching water flow after a dammed river was unclogged. *Fascinating.*

This was followed by several more clicks and the grinding of gears within the door. Slaide recognized the sound of steel against iron as the hidden bolts slid out of place. Finally, the sounds ceased, followed by a release of air as the prison cell decompressed. His hair rustled slightly as the breeze blew past them.

"You're sure about this?" The guard had grown uncertain in the moments it had taken the door to open, going from seasoned veteran to nervous novice. Perhaps he'd never witnessed this door in action. After all, there was an innate fear that came with this cell; once you went in, you weren't getting out.

Slaide leveled a look at the man which was enough to convey the message.

He let out a hefty breath in response. "Alright then. Best be on alert." He leaned into the door, and it groaned, moving inward.

What do these people think she is? A monster? The irony wasn't lost on him, that they let someone—something—like him walk around freely, while she was kept under the tightest security the kingdom had to offer. She was but a girl. A girl who might possess magic thought lost for almost a thousand years with not a clue how to control it, but a girl nonetheless.

And yet, hadn't they said the same thing when he was young and untested? *Just a boy.* He'd shown them, too. Shown them just what that *boy* they'd created was capable of.

The door opened into darkness. They were greeted by a whoosh of air that was cold and smelled of damp earth. He couldn't see her, but he could sense her presence. At the very least, she was still alive.

Behind him, the guard lit a torch and set it into a sconce on the wall.

In the shadows that danced in the flickering flamelight, Slaide could see the rest of the room with a little more clarity. A few feet in front of them was a wall of floor to ceiling iron bars, separating them from the cell proper. That part was new. Perhaps they'd added that after the difficulties they'd had containing him.

On the far wall was a stone bench with a threadbare blanket, a wooden tray with a plate of food on the edge, completely untouched. Hazel was nowhere to be seen in any of the visible portions of the cell. She must be hiding in the shadows. And who could blame her?

In his periphery, Slaide caught the guard reaching for the hilt of his blade.

"Watch yourself. She could be anywhere. I told you we shouldn't come in here."

Slaide almost laughed. "You're joking, right? What do you think she is, a snake? Going to strike at you from one of those dark corners? Please. She's just a scared girl."

"She's a witch. A monster."

"Right. Well, if you don't mind, I'd like a minute with her." He nodded toward the door.

The man recoiled as if Slaide had insulted his mother, then laughed hysterically. "You must be mad if you think I'm going to leave the two of you in here alone."

"Some would say I'm more than just mad. But I must know, would you be looking out for her safety, or mine?"

"Sir, I-I only meant that..." he stammered and took a step back.

"Save it." Slaide raised a dismissive hand. "Get out."

The man, to his credit, faltered, and Slaide thought he might actually put up a fight. But that moment passed and he came to his senses, sighing as he turned to leave.

"You've got two minutes. That's about all we have left before my shift is over, and I don't want to explain to the next guard why you're in here. At least give me that."

"Fair enough."

Reluctantly, the guard closed the door, leaving Slaide alone at last with Hazel. But would she trust him enough to come out?

"Hazel?" He took a deep breath. "It's Slaide. Can we talk?"

Silence.

"I'm not going to hurt you. I don't know what to say about... about everything that happened. I truly had no idea. The truth is, if it isn't already blatantly clear, Magus despises me. I have no idea why he keeps me around, despite my efforts to piss him off at every opportunity he gives me. I live to be a thorn in his side. I am an asshole. I am all the things everyone else says about me. But I am not a liar. I've never lied to you, and I will not hurt you."

Something shifted in the corner, but he still could not see her.

"Listen, Hazel. We don't have time for this. You can ignore me all you want, but I'm getting you out of here. I have mere minutes to discuss my plan. Please."

"I thought you didn't beg?"

Thank the fucking gods. He couldn't help it, he smiled. "Gods, I love that smart mouth of yours; I thought you were going to give me the silent treatment until I had no choice but to leave."

Hazel crept forward out of the shadows on her hands and knees. She was dirty and disheveled, her hair a matted mess and her face coated with dirt and blood.

"Don't know how to stay out of trouble do you?"

"Is this a joke to you?" Her face was twisted with rage, tears welling in her eyes. She scooted further forward on her knees. She was in a tunic, shredded and dirty, looking and smelling as though it had been worn by one hundred or more people before her. "I said, is this a joke to you?" Her voice trembled, the voice of a woman about to break. And this was not the place for her to shatter. Not again.

His eyes landed on the onyx shackles around her wrists. Her skin was chapped and torn where she'd obviously been fighting to break herself free. Good. That meant she still had a will to get out. To live. It also meant she wouldn't be able to explode as long as she wore them. Probably for the best.

"Slaide fucking Elias, answer me right now. Do you think this is all a big joke? My father is dead. He's fucking dead! And for what? To protect Agnes? To protect me? And now look at us both! He died for *nothing*. Nothing!"

Slaide was not prepared for this conversation. Not right here, not right now. That guard would be back any minute.

He got down on his knees and grabbed the bars between them. "Listen, Hazel," he pleaded softly, hoping that if he avoided pissing her off too much, she might listen. He had to get her out of this enraged state if he hoped to reason with her. "I know you're in pain, physically and emotionally. We don't have time for my traumatic backstory right now, so you'll have to trust me when I say I get it. I've been here, in this exact cell. But no one came for me."

She stared at him blankly, her eyes still threatening to overflow.

"I am here for you Hazel, but you have to let me help you. Hate me all you want, but love yourself enough to live. You owe yourself that. Hel, you owe your father and Agnes that much."

"You said before you weren't helping me, you were helping yourself. And you just told me you don't lie. So which is it then?"

Fuck me and my stupid mouth.

He sighed. *Well, no time like the present to really start being honest.* "Both. Because when I dove headfirst into this, into you, I had an agenda, and you didn't matter. I was going to do anything it took to keep you out of the Magistry's hands, and not because I cared about you or your safety. I despise the mages as much as Magnus despises me. So, keeping you out of their reach was priority number one. And yes, with that I bargained for my freedom. I was desperate, and you were no one to me. Discovering what you were capable of, and whether or not you really were a witch, was priority two.

"But the thing is, Hazel, things change. Plans change. People change. All of this was before I knew who you were. Who you really are. I don't have time to explain all of this to you right now because as I'm sure you heard, we have but a few moments until that shift change. But I swear to you, I will. Just help me get you out of here. I have a plan to—"

The door groaned and swung inward, the first guard poking his head in.

"Time's up. Let's go."

Slaide—master of storms and shadows and general calamity—began to panic internally. He leapt to his feet and stared wildly into Hazel's glossy eyes. She was completely unreadable. "Agnes lives for now," he whispered. "If you want to save her, get your shit together."

"I said, let's go." He moved to grab Slaide's forearm, and Slaide recoiled, a snake preparing to strike.

"Touch me, and it will be the last thing you do."

The guard withdrew his hand and stepped aside to let Slaide pass. As he closed the warded iron door, Slaide peered past him into the cell, but Hazel had disappeared back into the shadows. The guard pocketed the wardstone, and they returned back where they'd come from.

When at last they reached the end of the dungeon hall, they were greeted by the shift change guards. A new guard to take the place of the retiree, and one to oversee the swap and make sure there were no hiccups and nothing was removed from the prison. Especially no keys, and certainly no wardstones.

One was a middle-aged man of medium build, with sandy blonde hair and striking cobalt eyes. While he couldn't recall the guard's name, he remembered the man from his own time in the dungeons. The thought of him being left alone with Hazel was… unsettling.

The other man was much younger, closer in age to himself and lacking the confidence of a seasoned warrior. He had dark hair and dark eyes, and an expression dripping with concern and fear. And then it hit him. Ezekiel.

"It's about time, Breck. Not setting much of an example for this recruit, returning to your post this late," said the blonde man.

"Yes, sir. Apologies, sir. Just finishing up rounds. Won't happen again."

"I should expect not. You know the consequences for tardiness. I wouldn't want to have to use you to demonstrate to Bertram here how things work."

No. Fucking. Chance.

Breck bowed his head submissively.

"Anyway, moving on. This is Ezekiel Bertram, one of our newer members of the guard. He's been working shifts on the upper levels for a bit now, and has proved himself trustworthy and capable. So tonight, he's your relief."

Slaide noticed the subtle shift in Breck's expression, and knew they must be thinking the same thing. This was no place for a novice. The upper level dungeons were nothing in comparison to the monsters they kept down here. Lucky for Bertram, there was only one inmate, and she wasn't much of a threat.

"Ah, it's nice to meet you, Ezekiel. You've been the talk of the barracks the past few days. Nice to have some competent men joining the ranks, finally. As it stands, I've nothing to report. Our prisoner has remained quiet, though she refuses to touch her food."

Probably thinks it's poisoned. Who could blame her?

"Your goal this evening is just to ensure she remains quiet. If you can convince her to eat, even better. His Majesty plans on turning her over to the Magistry soon, and their testing will surely be rigorous. It would be a shame for her to starve to death before she makes it there."

Pardon? That bastard. Though he supposed his week was up, and that had been the deal. Slaide had kept his word, though none of this had gone as he'd expected or hoped. She didn't win the tournament. Granted, no winner had been announced. But in the eyes of those who mattered, she was no champion. He'd discovered that Hazel did, in fact, have the magic they were looking for, but it had been a complete and total disaster. And Slaide had broken his golden rule when interrogating and infiltrating the minds of his captives.

He'd gotten much, much too close.

With Friends Like These

HAZEL sat in a dark corner, knees pulled to her chest. *What an absolute fucking disaster.* How could someone's life be upended so drastically in just over a week's time? What had she done to deserve this, for *this* to be her fate?

She'd been out for hours. When she finally awoke, she'd laid there, wishing to disappear. Each time a guard entered, she'd feigned sleep, and they'd left her alone. After a while, she crawled to the darkest corner of her cell and stayed there. Guards came and went, offering food, drink. Probably making sure she was still alive. And unfortunately, she was. No one else who truly mattered to her could say the same. They were gone.

Her stomach growled audibly. She was hungry, despite her insistence that she wasn't. She crept out of her corner, chains scraping against the stone floor as she went. They'd left a small piece of bread and an even smaller chunk of cheese. Her stomach gurgled, and she eyed the plate suspiciously. *They'd be stupid to poison me, right?* Not that she actually cared. All she could think about was how she should have died right there alongside him. But no… that wasn't fair. She had to live. For Agnes.

She gnawed off a stale bite of bread and formed the beginnings of a plan.

HAZEL WAS AWOKEN later by the whirring, buzzing sound of the iron door being unlocked. Her skin tingled as the magic field changed. Someone was coming in. Some part of her hoped it was Slaide, hoped he had returned to discuss how he was getting her out of here. Since she'd started planning her next moves, she'd been kicking herself for not making the most of the time she'd had with him. But no, she'd chosen to be a brat instead.

Nothing could have prepared her for the very *not-Slaide* form that stepped through the door. Or the fact that anyone else would have made her feel a sense of ease. But there it was as Zeke entered the inner sanctum containing her cell. The way her shoulders dropped, releasing the tension she'd ignored. And she sighed the most generous sigh of relief.

"Hazel?" he asked, closing the door behind him without locking it. "It's Zeke. I'm on your security detail for this rotation. Just wanted to see if you were alright."

She immediately noticed his tone was off, a far cry from his jovial self. She second-guessed coming out of the safety of her shadows. He sounded uncaring… unfeeling. And her locket… it warmed.

"You should know," he began, "Agnes is… well, she's in a lot of trouble, Hazel. A lot of people got hurt last night, and they're saying you caused it. That you interfered with a lawful, court-sanctioned arrest, led a counter-riot, and then used your magic against the citizens of Aeos and several knights."

She said nothing, still trying to decide if he was fucking serious or not.

He sighed, sounding defeated. "They're planning to use her against you, so you know. Hurting her to punish you. Is that what you wanted? Do you understand how much of a mess you've made? If you had just let the arrest go down like it was intended to, none of this would have happened."

Hazel was boiling from the inside, her iron chains hissing against her skin as the magic neutralized.

"She would at least have had a chance to stand trial. But now… now they're putting her to the pyre. Day after tomorrow."

Hazel lunged toward him. "How *dare* you come in here and speak to me as though you have any gods-damned idea what happened out there!" she spat.

To Zeke's credit, he didn't step back from the bars. Didn't so much as flinch.

"Here I thought you were coming to me as a friend, to offer support and let me in on the plan to get me out of here. But no, you just had to rub salt in my wounds, didn't you? You've changed, Ezekiel, and not for the better."

A furrow formed between his dark brown brows. "Plan to get you… Hazel what are you talking about?"

She watched as realization smacked him in the face. And smiled. He actually had the audacity to smile at her, and it was the darkest expression she'd ever seen on his face.

"Oh, Hazel. Don't tell me your boyfriend said he was going to get you out of here?" He shook his head mockingly. Zeke stepped up to the cell and held the bars in his hands. An obsidian stone ring inlaid with onyx glinted upon his right ring finger. "I warned you. I told you Slaide was bad news back when you crossed his path in the market. But you just had to see for yourself, didn't you?" His eyes shone with a darkness she didn't recognize.

"What happened to you, Zeke?" she questioned, a sadness lacing her tone. A sharp pain stabbed through her as she accepted the friend she thought she knew was gone. Replaced by a brainwashed monster.

"What happened to *me*? That's rich, coming from you. You're a *witch* for fuck's sake. A witch in a kingdom sworn against magic. That's not the person I grew up with. How can you sit there and ask me how or why I've changed when you've changed most of all? Hazel, my family has suffered greatly by the presence of un-tithed magic wielders in this kingdom. They're supposed to report to the monolith on the Tithe day following their manifestation and give their magic over to power the Border. They get a tracker implanted that allows the Magistry to monitor their magic levels throughout their life, and terminate them remotely if necessary. To refuse to do so… Hazel, it's treason. It puts all of us at risk."

"Do you actually hear the bullshit running out of your mouth? You act like I chose this. You're insane."

"No, what's insane is you keeping this from me for so long. For evading the laws of this land. At one time I might have been able to help you, but now I can't."

"You can't, or you won't? Choose carefully," she snapped.

Zeke stared into her eyes, his expression blank. He was so cold. So unfeeling. So *not* Zeke.

"Goodbye, Hazel," he responded, turning his back on her for the last time. And just like that, she lost another loved one.

Zeke was dead to her.

Hazel returned to her corner with ambition after that. She wasn't going to die behind iron bars, and Agnes wasn't going to be put to the stake. Not without a fight, anyway.

The next time a guard appeared with a tray of scraps for her to eat, she cleaned her plate. It wasn't much, but it helped to settle the massive void that had developed within her. She gathered the old blanket and returned to her corner to rest. But her hunger for food was replaced by something deeper. She was hungry for vengeance.

She wasn't expecting any visitors the rest of the night, so she spent her quiet hours planning and plotting. There were no windows, so she had no idea whether it was night or day. Guards came and went, occasionally bringing food or a cup of water. Every now and then, someone would poke their head in, clearly making sure she was still there.

Sleep finally found her, dragging her down with it. She'd been asleep for mere minutes when she was startled awake by the familiar grate and groan of the cell door opening. She was instantly alert, wiping the sleep from her eyes and pulling back into her shadows.

The guard entered without a word and didn't so much as look for her. He didn't even glance toward the corner where Hazel hid. He simply came in, set her tray down, and left as quietly as he'd come, with only the groaning door to mark his exit.

Well, that was certainly unusual.

A flurry of movement—an orange blur—caught her eye. And to Hazel's surprise, someone else slipped in just before the door closed. Or rather, *something*. A big, orange cat. He slunk into the shadows and slipped between the bars of her cell, at last finding his place by her side, purring deeply.

"You poor thing. Probably wondering where I was, huh? Shh, it's alright."

Hazel waited a while before going to investigate, passing the time by scratching her companion's head and listening to his contented purrs. Whatever he'd left, it smelled… fresh. The fact that it had any smell at all was something in itself. But the fact that the smell was warm, buttery—and with a hint of honey—well, she was practically drooling.

When she could no longer stand it, she all but ran to the tray of food to find a steaming bowl of baked apples and a pastry. That must have been where the heavenly smell was coming from.

Gods, an outsider would have thought she'd been locked up for weeks as opposed to days, the way she stood over her meal. As loudly as her stomach protested, she wasn't entirely convinced of it herself.

Wanting to save the pastry for last, she dug into the piping hot apples and nearly melted into a puddle with how perfectly cooked they were. The caramelized sugar, the unbelievably soft yet still crunchy apples, and the perfect dash of cinnamon. She eyed the pastry, wondering if it would hold up to the decadent bowl of apples. Setting them aside, she picked up the flaky-crusted delicacy—still warm. She took a large bite, crunching through the layers of exquisite, rich dough, and her eyes rolled back in her head. It was filled with tart dragonberry.

She took another bite, flinching when her teeth met something inedible and hard.

"What in the name of the blustering damned gods?" Hazel hissed through aching teeth. The cat, who'd been weaving in and out of her legs impatiently, paused and looked up at her.

She broke the pastry in two and found a tiny glass vial had been baked into the dessert. After removing it, she pulled the cork stopper and retrieved the rolled parchment within. It was a note:

A little birdie told me you like pastries. Sorry they were out of chocolate in the kitchens. Best I could do given circumstances. Anyway, if you're reading this it means you didn't swallow the glass vial. Which is good news, as I've heard glass is an unpleasant thing to... you know. One should always pay attention to their food.

—S.

Hazel couldn't decide if she was elated or annoyed that he'd tampered with her food. She looked at the ruined pastry and rolled her eyes. Her appetite was spoiled by the idea of messages being hidden within and the prospect of accidentally eating them. It gave her way too much to think about, when all she'd wanted to do was enjoy a real meal. She groaned her frustration and sought out the security of her shadowy corner.

A few moments later, she scampered back out to the bench and snatched the bowl of apples before retreating to the darkness again. A tiny mouse crawled out of a gap in the stones and zig-zagged over to where Hazel's pastry crumbs had fallen. Hazel froze, waiting for the moment her cat would spring into action. His body tensed beside her, but he didn't budge beyond the irritated flick of his tail.

The mouse gobbled the crumbs greedily, and while she wasn't sure if a mouse could experience pure bliss, she was certain she witnessed the mouse equivalent. The cat remained unbothered. His body relaxed and he moved on to cleaning his paws. Hazel cocked her head at the strange behavior. He truly was the oddest cat she'd ever met.

Hazel waited eagerly for her meals after that, wondering what news or plans he would attempt to send via pastry-mail. The real task was figuring out which food item would contain the message; she quickly learned it wasn't just baked goods.

The thing that puzzled her though, was that none of them made sense. It didn't take long to understand that it was coded, but she hadn't been given the key. As time went on, panic seeped into her bones at the possibility she might have accidentally eaten the key to the coded letters, and he would have no way of knowing. He'd expect her to be carrying out whatever plan he was trying to inform her of, and she would be completely in the dark. It didn't help that the cat came and went as he pleased, giving her one more being to worry about. The longer he stayed away, the more concerned she grew, expecting at any moment a guard would stomp in, holding him by the scruff.

As if in answer, the cat appeared almost out of nowhere. It was when he started grooming his ears and back that caught a glimpse of something strange. Tied around his neck, a collar of red ribbon looped through a small piece of parchment with an inscription on it. There were random holes cut throughout the message, resulting in a note that once again made little sense. She'd need some time to mull it over and compare this holey note to the previous installments.

She thanked the cat for his help and scratched him behind his ears, assuming the gesture would express her feelings more than words alone. He accepted her offering, staring at her for just a moment longer than Hazel thought normal.

Immediately, she started comparing the notes, looking for nuances and patterns across the set. And that was when it hit her. The cat hadn't delivered any ordinary message; he'd delivered the key.

Later that day or evening or whatever time of whatever day it was, she was met with the familiar noise of her door being opened. But when the door swung away, it revealed an unsettling view: four fully armed and armored Raven Blade Knights. She watched them from the shadows, quickly noticing they were not bringing her refreshments. *What could these brutes want now?*

The last knight to enter pushed past the others and stepped to the front. He scanned the cell from behind his visor, clearly looking for Hazel. Maybe expecting her to lunge from the dark in her fury.

"Come now, girl. His Majesty wants you moved to a different cell. We've been sent to escort you."

Why would he want that? Surely there was a motive…

When she didn't respond, he lowered his tone, and she supposed it was meant to make him sound more threatening. But what he didn't understand was that once a girl had nothing left to lose, not a whole lot could scare her.

"I don't make a habit of asking twice," he glowered. She couldn't see his face, but his voice was indication enough of the annoyed scowl she'd find there.

Fine. Fine. But first, she needed to do something with Slaide's notes. She hadn't had a chance to decipher them and couldn't afford them falling into the wrong hands now that she had the key. Finding herself lacking options, she stuffed them into her underclothes. And then she stepped into the light, hoping her cat would find his way to safety.

The knights were a brutish bunch, but none of them laid a hand on her beyond what was necessary, so she had to give them some credit. Though that was where the pleasantries ended.

When they entered the main hallway of the upper-level dungeons, Hazel found herself filled with a sense of dread. The knights led her to the end of the hallway and pushed her into the last cell.

"Welcome to the top side, girl. Don't get too comfortable, and don't try anything stupid. Just because His Majesty moved you up here doesn't mean we're taking our eyes off you. Understood?" The group's faceless leader grumbled at her.

Hazel nodded, and the knights locked the cell, taking the key with them. She heard the door close at the end of the long hallway, followed by the jingle of keys and the click of a lock sliding into place. She was alone again.

Something shifted in the cell adjacent to hers. Hazel could just barely make out a form in the shadows. *Not alone, then.*

She approached the bars, hoping to get a closer look at her new neighbor.

"H-hello? Is someone there?" she asked, trying to mask the unease in her voice. She half expected the locket to warn her of danger, but it did not.

She was met with silence. Whoever it was clearly didn't want to socialize. And that was fine. It didn't make much sense to make new friends here, anyway. No telling how many days or hours either of them had left. She turned her back and went to sit down in the only corner of her cell that received enough fire light to read by. She needed to get to work deciphering those letters.

"Hazel?" The voice was quiet, but scratchy, strained. And familiar. *No…*

"Agnes? Is that you?" Hazel's voice was desperate; she couldn't help herself. She'd already written off ever seeing Agnes again, so this was a blessing. And at the same time, a curse. Now it was even more imperative that she figure out what their next move was. Now there really was a chance she could save Agnes, a chance she'd thought lost to her.

"Yes, dear. My goodness, it is so good to hear your voice, sweet Hazel. Are you… alright?" It was a loaded question, and they both knew it. No, she wasn't alright, and neither was Agnes. And they wouldn't be, as long as they were trapped in the dungeon, facing whatever cruel fate awaited them.

"I am as well as I can be. And you? I was told that… well… I thought you were gone. I am so glad you're here, Auntie. I was sick over it. This is all my fault and—"

"Nonsense. You did what you had to, according to what I've heard. And had you not been there to intervene, we wouldn't be having this conversation. No sense in dwelling on the past. We are both alive, aren't we?" By the tone of her voice, she'd made peace with whatever she thought would come next. That didn't sit well with Hazel.

Agnes shuffled closer to the bars between them, the light from the sconces casting her in a warm glow. Hazel noticed her severely burned arms had been wrapped and sent up a silent prayer of thanks to whoever had shown Agnes that kindness.

"Hazel, dear," she began, sadness lacing her voice, "We need to talk about what comes next."

Well, that sounded ominous.

"I need you to understand something and prepare for how this will play out in the end."

Okay, I'm uncomfortable…

"I have lived a long life. An extraordinary life filled with blessing after blessing. My life has been enriched by magic and all the things it has done for me. But most of all, my life's work was this…" She gestured to Hazel. "You. You were always the end goal, Hazel. The one who would bring us out of the darkness, back into the light. The Fated one. My job was only to get you to the point where you could stand on your own two feet." She looked over Hazel appraisingly. "Safe to say I've accomplished my task here. It is time for me to return home."

"Auntie, I don't mean to hurt your feelings, but your home is gone. There was a horrible fire and…" She faded off, unable to relive the searingly raw pain of the night that resulted in her father's death.

Agnes nodded. "Yes, dear. I know. I know." She reached through the bars and placed one calloused, time-worn hand on Hazel's arm. Their gazes met and Agnes's eyes were glistening, but not with sadness. No, instead, her eyes sparkled with hope.

"What are you not telling me?" Hazel's voice was shaky and uneven.

Agnes smiled mischievously then. "All will be revealed in time, my child. Fret not, for the future that awaits me was written in the blood of those who came before. You are a Moonwater daughter, and a special one at that. It has been my honor to serve as your guide. When tomorrow comes, shed no tears for me. Instead, know that I feel no pain as I take the ash road home to the Otherrealm. Rejoice in the knowledge that my life was well spent and that I have successfully completed the task I was sent here to do. I love you, Hazel, Moonwater witch."

The Shadows

THE world tilted as Hazel grappled with reality. As Agnes spoke, she might as well have been floating outside her body, a spectator to her own life. Her head swam with all the new information, but mostly, that Agnes was resigned to her fate. That she knew she would perish and was at peace with that fact. Hazel, however, was not.

Her eyes welled over, and she pulled Agnes into as much of an embrace as she could with the cold iron bars between them and the chains restraining their extremities. The other questions, though burning, could wait. She never wanted to let this moment go.

Agnes pulled out of the hug slightly to look at Hazel. She always had that knowing gaze about her. The one that wrapped around Hazel's soul like a warm wool cloak.

She sighed softly. "We all have a role to play in this life, my dear, and mine has been a higher honor than I ever could have asked for. When I looked upon you as a babe, it was difficult to imagine what you were to become. But looking at you now, it's unmistakable."

"I-I don't understand, Agnes. I am no one," she whimpered.

"You, my dear Hazel, are going to break the chains holding witches back. You will shatter the world as we know it, and you will reforge it into something better. The Thousand Years War occurred so that one day a descendant of Adelladonna Moonwater would rise and reclaim what was taken from us, restoring our people and our homeland, and repairing the broken bonds between us and other peoples. That descendant is you, Hazel." She paused abruptly. "Now, back to your side, over there. Someone comes." And with that Agnes retreated to the far side of her cell.

A lone guard entered the dungeon and removed his helm. Oswald One-eye. Hazel's locket heated as he entered.

"Heh, if it isn't the dog's pet, got herself caught in quite the mess. Where's mister dark and broody now, pet? Have you figured it out? Slaide is a dog, not just in name, but by nature. He uses a bitch while she's easy, and when the going gets rough, he moves on to the next. Face it, pet, you've been forgotten."

She wanted to grow talons just as Slaide did so she could claw Oswald's remaining eye out herself.

"Oh, don't you worry, pet. Oswald here is going to take good care of you, eh? And when I'm through with you, we can see if anyone else would like a turn. You'll never be lonely, and you can forget about that Fallenborn bastard whelp. How's that sound?"

Hazel backed away from the cell door, trying to create space between them. She would fight him if she had to, but she would likely lose. And then everyone would know she was a fraud, that she was not some prophesied hero.

Oswald palmed the cudgel at his side, unhooking it from the loop on his belt. He caught her eyeing the movement. "Oh, don't you worry your pretty little face about this here. Just a precaution. But you're gonna be a good girl and not make me use it, eh? That's right. Just be a good little witch whore, and you get out of here alive."

He stepped toward her, undoing his belt and the top button of his breeches.

Gods, give me strength. Goddesses, hear me. Agnes somehow knew Hazel made it out of here alive. If prophesies could be believed, maybe she did. But no one said anything about getting out unscathed. And no one, not even Agnes, could pull her from this living nightmare.

He stalked toward her, his demented, one-eyed gaze peeling the clothes from her body.

No. I will not be a victim today. But I will play one.

"Please, don't hurt me. I'll do anything you ask," Hazel whined.

"Now there's a good girl. Come to your senses at last. Be good and sit for me." He put his hands on her shoulders, pushing her down. She obliged, though her stomach roiled at the proximity of him. He stood over her, gesturing for her to lie back.

This better work, you idiot, she scolded herself, trying to keep the underlying panic from taking over. She feigned a whimper. "Please..."

His breeches dropped to the floor, and Hazel was thankful his guard's uniform was long enough to obscure the view. When he straddled her, trying to get her to look, she averted her eyes. She just had to hang on to her sanity a little longer.

But then he made an unexpected move, throttling Hazel's only plan to survive this encounter. He grabbed the chain between her manacled wrists and hooked it to an eyelet in the floor. *So much for strangling him with the chain,* she thought, arms pulled tight overhead.

Oswald tsked at her, wagging a finger. "Can't have you getting any ideas now, can we?" Then he pulled her shift up above her breasts, exposing them to the brisk dungeon air. Beneath her underclothes, her nipples peaked in response to the chill on her skin. A slimy grin crawled across his face as he mistook it for eagerness.

"My, my. You are a little witch whore, aren't you? No wonder Slaide kept you on a tight leash." He knelt over her then, and she could feel his breath on her skin. With his knee, he pushed hers apart, smiling down at his view as her knees fell to the side.

Hazel clamped her eyes shut. "Please. I am begging you. Don't..." She didn't want to fight him, didn't want to provoke more violence against herself, but she wasn't just going to put up with this.

"Ooh, beg more, pet. I like that," he sneered. His eyes landed between her breasts, at the secret notes she'd folded and hidden there. "What do we have here?" He snatched them, his rough, calloused fingers brushing against her soft, sensitive skin. He unfolded one and frowned, clearly unable to decipher the madness written there. "A coded message, eh? Well, now. Seems I have even more reason to punish you, don't I?"

His words were met with a knee to the groin. He bucked and fell to the side, writhing in pain and groaning curse words in her direction. Hazel knew she was going to regret that, but he was making an awful lot of noise. Maybe she'd bought herself enough time for someone to come investigate.

But no one came.

After a few minutes, Oswald was right as rain and royally pissed off. He slapped her across the face and threatened her with the cudgel.

"If you try something stupid like that again, I am going to paint this cell with your blood. Starting with that face of yours. Understand?"

She whimpered, the handprint on her cheek pulsing an angry red.

He lowered his body against hers, and his breath was suffocating as he spoke, sour with the stench of too much ale. "I am going to ruin you, you filthy—"

He was cut off. Hazel opened his eyes to see Oswald's face turning an ugly purple hue, his remaining eye turning red with bursting blood vessels. He was being choked to death.

By shadows.

The tendrils of darkness constricted, lifting him up and away from Hazel's exposed body. But they didn't release him, not even once he'd been dragged kicking and flailing a safe distance away. Only after he went limp did the shadows release their grip on the man, slinking back to their owner, who stood in the doorway, his ominous form silhouetted by the flickering brazier.

When she noticed him there, Hazel loosed a half-sigh, half-sob.

Slaide stepped into the cell, his wings and claws retracting as though they'd never existed. As he approached, there was a gleam in his onyx eyes as they returned to their normal, golden hue. He came. He came for her.

His face was expressionless, and yet she could feel the rage seething off him as he stepped over her to remove her chains from the iron eyelet.

"Did he hurt you?" His voice was flat but wavered with barely repressed anger.

She shook her head. "Not in any way that matters." Her voice was unsteady.

"Hazel, look at me. Did. He. Hurt. You?" Each word was ground out. He wasn't mad at her. No, he was looking for a reason to grind Oswald to a bloody pulp against the stone floor.

He reached for her chin, and she flinched away from him, throwing her arm up in front of her face. Slaide recoiled, his eyes going wide and nostrils flaring. Then he reached more slowly, gently cupping her chin between his thumb and finger and turned her face to his. When his gaze caught on the redness spreading across her cheek, he let go and looked over his shoulder where Oswald lie unconscious. A growl vibrated deep within his chest.

Hazel reached out and touched his hand. "Slaide."

He took a deep breath, turning to face her, and pulled her into a hug. "I'm going to fucking kill him," he whispered into her ear.

Slaide pulled back then, looking into her eyes.

"I-I really am okay, Slaide. He didn't… it wasn't… I kneed him in the balls before he could, and I…" She really thought she was alright, but a single tear ran down her face. The shock set in, the reality of what had just happened hitting her with a force. She tried and failed to choke down a sob.

He hugged her again. "Shh, shh. It's okay. You're safe now. You are so brave and strong, standing up to him. I am just sorry I was not here sooner." He stroked her hair. "I knew something was up as soon as I got wind of your transfer. They're intentionally keeping me out of the loop. I…" He faded off, shaking his head. "This is my fucking fault."

Hazel sniffled.

"Oswald," he began. "He didn't come here to hurt you. He came here to try and hurt me. He saw us that day before the throne room doors and probably assumed I was fucking you. I should have stayed away from you. Far, far away. You would have been better off."

She looked up at him in disbelief. "Except if you had done that, the Magistry would have received custody of me right off the bat. You said yourself that I might not even be alive." Hazel thought his actual words were something more along the lines of having *saved her ass*, but she wasn't going to throw that in his face right now. "I am just glad you got here when you did."

Oswald groaned behind them, and Slaide silenced him once more with the snap of his fingers.

"We don't have a lot of time. More guards will be coming around soon."

"More? What happened to the ones at the door?" she asked in earnest.

"They're dead," he answered flatly.

"Good."

Slaide couldn't help but laugh. "My, my. You've been hanging around me for too long, talking like that. I like this version of you." He mussed her hair.

She ignored the quip and looked at the floor. "Well, what are we waiting for, then? Let's go." Hazel stood, chains jangling.

Slaide stood and took her hands in his. "Did you get the key? And my letters?"

"I got them. But I haven't had a chance to make sense of any of it. They dragged me out of the other cell moments after my cat friend delivered the decoder."

He looked perplexed. "Did you just say *cat*? As in *the* cat? The weird one?"

"Hey, he's not weird. But yes… Did you not send it tied to my cat?"

"That sly girl." He shook his head. "It wasn't me. I asked Phaedra if she could figure out a way to get it to you. The slaves have tunnels all throughout this castle, and they keep interesting company. Hence the cat, I suppose."

"Gods, I love her!" Hazel exclaimed.

"Indeed. She really is something."

Hazel grabbed his arm, and Slaide shook his head knowingly. "We don't have time. Once I get you to a safe place, I will see what I can do. But I had a plan in place to get you out tomorrow, when…" He looked toward Agnes's dark cell. *When they put her to the stake.* He didn't have to say it, she knew. "That plan included getting them out, too."

"How were you going to do that?"

"I'm going to blow these dungeons to shit." He smirked.

A grunt sounded from the other cell. Not a grunt, a laugh.

"Agnes?" Hazel called.

"That one has a big mouth and a bigger ego," Agnes mumbled, smirking. "But, really, Dark One, I'd love to know how you plan to blow this heavily fortified dungeon to shit. As if that hasn't been tried in the past." She stepped into the firelight, a condescending scowl etched onto her face as she assessed Slaide.

Hazel noted her use of the phrase "Dark One" again and found it perplexing. Slaide visibly stiffened as she said it. The lighting was low, but there was no hiding the unease it caused him. However, unlike he had in the past, Slaide didn't correct her. Didn't demand she not call him that. Strange.

Slaide stared at Agnes, and she him. Something like recognition passed between them. Slaide looked at Hazel, then back at Agnes.

"No," Agnes replied. "I'll only slow you down." Hazel looked at both of them, confused. *Did I miss something?* "I appreciate the thought, even if it is just a bold attempt at making up for your past transgressions." She sighed then. "I'm tired. A sort of tired neither of you will understand for a long, long time. As I explained to Hazel, my time has come, and I am at peace with my fate."

Her heart broke all over again. Agnes was all she had left. Her mother, her father… and now the only matronly figure she'd ever known. It was all the more painful knowing in advance, as opposed to having it sprung on her. Her heart wanted nothing more than to drag Agnes with them against her wishes. But in her head, she knew it would never work.

Voices sounded down the hall, beyond the main dungeon doors.

"Shit," Slaide said. "Out of time. We have to go, now!"

Agnes gave them a curt nod, and Hazel stifled another sob, knowing she would never look upon Agnes's warm face again.

Slaide urged Hazel along gently but firmly, forcing her to leave Agnes to her fate.

Slaide and Hazel ran deeper into the dungeons. The main entrance was no longer an option, but as Hazel soon found, there was more to the old castle walls than their plain stone exterior led on. These walls held secrets.

They reached what she thought was a dead end. Slaide tapped on certain stones in a pattern she couldn't follow, and before she knew it, the stones were shifting, turning inwards on themselves, and revealing a crawlspace. He entered first. Once Hazel was within, Slaide tapped on the low ceiling twice, and the stone doorway returned to its unassuming state. She rubbed her eyes in disbelief.

It was dark. So dark that she swallowed deeply, desperately needing something to ground her.

Slaide remained statue-still for a few moments, which gave her eyes some time to adjust. It was hardly enough. Just beyond the wall, the voices of flustered guards grew louder, their shouts frantic and calling out the escape. Just as quickly, their voices faded into the distance. Without a doubt, they'd scurried from the dungeons to raise the alarm.

Urgency found them again. Slaide grasped her hand in the darkness.

"Here's the deal, sweets. You're going to do everything I say the very moment I say it, no hesitations. Got it? Good. From here on out, we don't talk unless it's urgent." There was something comforting in the return of strictly business Slaide. A sense of familiarity.

She nodded her agreement before mumbling "yes" when she reminded herself it was so dark he likely couldn't see her head movement.

He led her on then, winding through the dark tunnel for far too long. Did he know where he was going? *Of course he does. That sort of thinking is going to get you killed*, she thought.

At last, they reached another dead end. Slaide turned to her and spoke quietly.

"Now comes the fun part." She could hear the grin in his voice. Light was filtering in between the stones, not quite enough to see, but enough to suggest it was no longer night. Meaning there would be fewer shadows for them to hide in, and more people moving about the castle. This was suicide.

"Trust me." And she did… sort of. Maybe it was less trust and more of a lack of options. She'd have to revisit that when her life wasn't on the line.

Slaide repeated the same sequence as before, knocking on seemingly random stones. Once more, the stones rotated and rearranged themselves to form a small opening.

To Hazel's surprise, they stepped into someone's living quarters. There were three pallet beds on either side of the cramped space. Hand-sewn sheets appeared to be stuffed with straw, which by the smell of the room, was beginning to mold. A few of the beds had the luxury of a stained pillow or threadbare blanket. There was a community chamber pot in the far corner. Her cheeks reddened as she determined where they were. *Slave quarters.*

"All the resources and wealth the king has," she hissed, "and he forces them to sleep like this?"

"You're right to be angry, but understand this: these are the ones who are treated *well.* You don't want to see where the rest are forced to sleep." He rushed around while he spoke, and just as Hazel was about to ask what he was looking for, he held up a knapsack and a change of clothes for her.

She jangled the manacles. "How do you expect me to change like this?" Her voice was just above a whisper, a little too loud. This earned her a chastising glare. "Tell me you at least have the keys to these, or maybe you can tappy-tap on them like that little trick you did with the magic doorways back there? You know, wave your hand and make them fall off? Anything?"

But the look on his face was enough. Slaide Elias did not have the keys, and there was no magic trick to make the iron shackles fall from her wrists.

"Then how do you propose I change?" No sooner than she'd said it, Hazel became acutely aware of her mistake. Slaide was going to relish in the way she had phrased that.

But to her surprise, he held his tongue. There was no snide remark, no biting sarcasm about how he could "help her with that." And she was glad for it. Because while she'd recently found herself in some precarious, deliciously sinful situations with Slaide, her mind could not currently fathom the idea of a man's body pressed against hers. Not after… no, she wouldn't focus on that right now.

He truly looked stumped on how he could help her.

"It's okay," she said at last. "We don't have a choice. I need your help."

His movements were cautious and deliberate as he moved to help her remove the soiled shift. However, they quickly discovered her shackled hands posed an issue there as well.

"Just cut it off," she spoke flatly.

That caught him off guard. "What?"

"Tear it. Cut it. I don't care what you do. Get this disgusting thing off of me." Because maybe, just maybe, the shock was beginning to set in.

She was feeling panicked, losing control. And she was no risk to anyone as long as she wore the irons, but that didn't mean she couldn't break down into a useless, sobbing mess when she needed to stay strong.

So Slaide unsheathed his knife and went to work, the sharp blade slicing through the paper-thin fabric with ease.

At last, the dirty piece of cloth fell in a heap at Hazel's feet. She shivered as the air met her exposed flesh.

Hazel turned around, wearing nothing but her underclothes, and was surprised to find Slaide had averted his gaze. She was glad for it, unsure how she would feel to see the feral longing in his eyes knowing she did not currently return the sentiment.

"Slaide, we still have a problem." She could manage to shimmy into the reinforced, boiled leather pants of her fighting leathers well enough, but her bindings once again created a complication in putting on any sort of top.

She opened her mouth to explain just that when she was interrupted by a knock at the door.

Rap-tap. Rap-tap. Rap-tap.

Hazel froze.

Slaide moved to the small single door, hand hovering over the dagger on his hip. A curious tendril emerged from the shadow he cast on the floor, slithering like a snake toward the door. It spread so thin Hazel could hardly see it as it slipped beneath the door. A moment later, it retracted swiftly.

Whoever it was, they must have been expected. Slaide unlatched the door and cracked it open to confirm the visitor with his own eyes. Satisfied, he let them in.

It was Phaedra.

And in her hand, she held a key.

Lock and Key

"Phaedra!" Hazel exclaimed, causing the angel to jump. Slaide shot her a glare, a reminder to be quiet.

The angel—who had an uncanny way of being exactly where and when she was needed—blushed and looked at the floor. "I heard Mistress Hazel was in trouble. I wanted to help." She said it so matter of fact, as though it was the same choice anyone would have made in her position. But it wasn't, and they wouldn't. No, Phaedra had everything to lose and faced the risk of being severely punished if caught, and yet here she was… committing treason. Perhaps she was the bravest of them all.

Hazel wanted to hug her. Tried to hug her, but was deterred by the damn manacles again. *Right… that's why she's here, after all.*

"Reunions are great and all, but we—and I cannot stress this enough—we don't have time. Phaedra, you're incredible. I'll take those," Slaide said, reaching for the keys.

He inserted the key into the lock and with a *click*, the iron fell loose from her wrists. The lack of weight on her arms, the release of pressure… it was euphoric, something of a dream. But no, this was real, and they were all in real danger. She should be elated, but instead a pang of guilt ran through her at the realization that Phaedra was now an accessory to her escape.

The chains clattered to the floor and Hazel jumped over them, wrapping Phaedra in her arms. She wanted to scream and cry and laugh. She did not deserve such loyalty from someone who had likely seen her share of horrors as a slave in this castle. No one did.

She looked the angel in the eyes and found hope there. "Why?" Hazel asked.

"Mistress?" Phaedra looked confused.

"Why are you helping me? You're putting yourself in harm's way, and there's nothing I can give you in return."

Phaedra smiled and shook her head. "You have given me all I needed from the day you arrived." She looked forlorn. "Master Slaide has always treated us Lessers with respect, but the same cannot be said about the castle guests. They are above us and treat us as such. Until you. I saw the fear in your eyes, heard your screams at night when you had nightmares. And through it all, you were kind. You never asked for anything extra, and certainly never made demands. You never yelled at me and never struck me. Most people… their power over the slaves here is the only power they have in their lives. It makes them feel superior to belittle us, sometimes beat us."

"You're putting your life at risk because I never hit you?" She was heartbroken and flabbergasted at the thought.

"No, Mistress Hazel. I risk my life for you because I consider you a friend. And friends don't leave each other behind."

Hazel's heart sank into her stomach at that statement. Because wasn't that exactly what they were doing to Phaedra, leaving her behind?

Slaide put a hand on Hazel's arm. "I told you before, she's going to be fine." He addressed the angel then. "As you can see, plans have changed. The timeline has been moved up considerably, but everything else is still in place. When the phoenix burns bright, the world will shatter. Make sure everyone knows and is clear of the dungeons beforehand."

Phaedra nodded her understanding.

Hazel could not make heads or tails of what was said, but she understood the message all the same. Slaide was going to make good on his promises.

They'd said their goodbyes, Slaide insisting they were *really* out of time. And maybe they were, but was rushing going to change the outcome for any of them? Agnes was conscripted to her fate, Phaedra was putting herself in danger, and Slaide, well the fact that Slaide was helping her at all was a mystery. Yes, things had changed drastically for them in a short amount of time, but he appeared to have it pretty good as a member of the King's inner circle, even if he hated it and admonished the King's actions. He could play their game. After all, isn't that what he'd been doing all this time?

Hazel was concerned with getting out unseen now that the sun was rising and the castle inhabitants were beginning to roam about. Slaide, of course, had a plan for everything. They stuck to the walls and places where the natural shadows grew longest. His magic was incredible, the shadows enveloping both of them in darkness and allowing them to creep along unnoticed.

Outside, it was easier to stay hidden. The sun was just high enough to cast shadows from the ramparts and outbuildings. They kept to the walls where they could, taking advantage of every bit of shade they could find. Occasionally, they'd cause a shadow to fall at an improper angle or an unnatural length for the height of the sun. But no one in the castle bothered to pay attention, and if any of the slaves noticed, they certainly weren't saying so. A single pair of guards jogged by, headed back to where Slaide and Hazel had come from. Toward the dungeons. No doubt word had spread of her escape.

The exterior grounds were mostly vacant. The gardens were abandoned save for the lone gardener, trimming hedges as though nothing were amiss. On a normal day, ladies and noblewomen would mill about, chatting on the latest gossip while persistent young noblemen attempted to woo them.

Hazel took a moment to admire the well-kept space, so colorful with its rolling green grasses and endless rainbow of assorted floral species. It stood in stark contrast to the harsh, wilted landscape outside these castle walls. The irony was not lost on her, that the lush garden was likely cultivated and maintained with the very magic Magnus sought to eradicate.

Sticking to the shadows, Slaide and Hazel passed unseen through the gardens and into the courtyard. At its center was a large fountain with a statue at its center portraying the gods. Not just any gods. The Gods of Wind, the only ones left after the great divide, the abandonment of Aeos, when humankind was forsaken by the *other* gods. Notros, Boreos, Zephros, and Eureos.

She and Connall didn't pay the gods much attention, and didn't "play their games" as Connall used to say. They didn't dedicate their lives to prayer or worship, though he had taught her their names in passing.

Over time, she'd learned what each was known for and quite frankly wasn't sure why anyone would choose to give them a moment of their time. They were malevolent beings, generating chaos and causing harm when they were slighted.

There they were in all their sculpted glory, all that remained of the original pantheon. Hazel had an overwhelming urge to hurl the nearest rock at the hideous monument. No, four rocks—one for each ugly face. The pantheon had brought balance. Without balance, there was only destruction. Aeos was dying. And yet, Magnus was perfectly content with that.

A strong hand wrapped around her wrist and tugged, pulling her from the rage-fed stupor she'd fallen into. Right. They had to *move* and there was no time to dawdle. And yet, as they departed the statue, she couldn't help but feel the weight of their godly stares bearing down on her.

Two coaches rolled up, wheels and hooves clattering on the cobblestone paved drive in front of the carriage house. One was a late arrival to the *festivities*, a well-dressed man all but dragging his woman into the castle as she hefted the hem of her skirt as high as she could to avoid tripping on it.

The other appeared to be driven up by the carriage house valet, who dismounted the driver's seat and applied the locking brake to the wheel. He stood beside it, unbothered as he waited for the owner to arrive.

Someone was leaving.

Slaide elbowed Hazel, and she nearly cussed him out before catching herself.

"We are getting you on that wagon," Slaide whispered. "It might be your only chance to get out of here."

She whirled on him. "What are you saying? *My* only chance? You're coming with me."

He just stared at her.

Panic set in. Slaide was just barely tolerable, yes, but he'd saved her ass multiple times and she had admittedly grown comfortable with him around. On her own… she found she didn't know exactly *how* to be on her own. There had always been someone.

Connall.

Agnes.

Zeke.

Slaide.

One was dead. One would die. One was dead to her. And one was forcing her to leave him behind.

She sucked in air, unable to form words.

"I can't come with you."

Something within her was cracking. "I don't understand."

"There are things I have to take care of. People… there are people depending on me to protect them… to get them somewhere safe if I can." He looked ashamed. Embarrassed even.

It smacked her in the face then. Every half-truth, every absence came slamming down at once. "Y—you're smuggling refugees. You're getting them out. Not killing them." Merrill. Merrill the mirror had shown her this. But she'd written it off as a lie.

Slaide winked at her. "You're smarter than you let on."

She ignored the jab. "Why wouldn't you just tell me that, instead of letting me think you were the vilest creature ever to exist?"

He cocked his head. "You think so highly of me? I'm flattered, sweets."

Hazel shook her head. "Of the stupid things you've done, this tops them all."

Slaide raised a brow. "That might be a stretch, although you don't know half of what I've done in my short life. And *no one* knows what I'll do next. Hel, sometimes I surprise even myself. But let me remind you,

I *am* that awful creature. No amount of sacrifice will ever compensate for the people I've hurt and killed. The throats I've ripped out with my teeth, the still-beating hearts I've squeezed in the palm of my hand. I did those things, and I have no one to blame but myself." And he did. He did blame himself. Hazel could see it etched into his features.

On the surface, it was his fault. He was a monster who hunted his victims for sport. But wasn't that how he'd been designed? After all, his parents had been bred like prized horses hoping that Slaide would be the result. An unfeeling killing machine with superior strength, stamina, and a thirst for blood. That wasn't his fault.

A distant voice called out, a booming voice, too loud to be natural. Probably amplified by magic, because wouldn't that be the culmination of all the hypocrisy she'd seen in this kingdom? The use of magic at a magic-user's execution? It was just far enough away that she couldn't quite make out the words.

Slaide tilted his head, focused. His eyes met Hazel's. Clearly, he could hear what she could not, presumably another feature of his superhuman genetics. Not human. Angel. Nephilim. *Other.*

He closed his eyes.

"The sentencing has begun."

"Wait. You mean she gets an actual trial?" The hope in her voice was devastatingly palpable, and unfortunately misplaced.

He shook his head. "No. The sentencing is just a formality. It's an announcement of her crimes, no doubt embellished to work up the crowd. No trial, though. His mind is made up, and her fate is set."

Fates be damned. She was so tired of the Fates interfering in innocent people's lives.

"Hazel."

Her head snapped, her glossy-eyed gaze meeting his.

"Her fate was determined long ago." He grabbed her by her shoulders. "Yours was as well, and it isn't here with us. With me. It's out there, past the Border, beyond the reach of this kingdom."

"Where am I supposed to go then? I can't go home. I can't stay here. I have no family."

"My hope is that we can get you to someone who can handle your magic. Someone who can help you reel it in and hone that power into something usable."

"And who in the name of the gods is going to do that?"

"The witches," he spat, as though the words were poison on his tongue.

The Phoenix

SLAIDE hung his head in defeat.

"What? What is it?" Hazel asked, frantically grabbing him by his shirt.

"He just announced her sentence. They're…"

"Don't." Hazel held her hand up. "I get it." *Fuck. I should be there. I should be tied to a post right alongside Agnes.*

She certainly didn't need Slaide to give life to the words. If the King had announced her sentence, the only thing left to do would be to light the pyre. Her insides knotted.

"Hazel, I—"

"How long?" she interrupted, eyes shining.

"What?" He frowned.

"How long until…" She couldn't say it. Couldn't bring herself to ask what she wanted to know. How much time did Agnes have until the flames licking her skin were no longer bearable? How long until they heard her involuntary screams?

He sighed. "Minutes, maybe. Perhaps not at all. I don't know what she's capable of. She said something about going home. I don't think this is the end for her."

Hazel looked at her feet. "She said not to worry about her pain. Is there magic that can ward off the pain of such a death?"

"I don't know the answer to that, Hazel. But I need you to find out for me, okay? We need to get you clear of this castle before my plans come to fruition. I am going to have enough people to evacuate that I don't need to worry about whether or not you made it out alive. Which is why you're getting on this wagon. *Now.*"

The group's members were distracted with their departure preparations, and for that Hazel was grateful. It allowed Slaide and Hazel ample time to cross the carriage grounds to the wagon they'd chosen for her escape.

Multiple crates were stacked beside the wagon, along with several bulging burlap sacks that had yet to be crammed into the wagon they'd hitched to the coach. There would be plenty of places for her to hide among their belongings.

Slaide offered Hazel his hand to assist her into the wagon. She took it, and was hefted inside without any obvious effort on his part. But when their hands separated, Hazel found two vials in her grasp: one contained fine, black powder; the other contained larger black granules. She read the labels, and her eyes snapped up to Slaide.

Witchbane. Obsidian Salt.

And there was a note attached that was short and to the point.

One is for ingesting—to help disguise what you are during your travels. The other will get you across the Border without dying. Don't mix them up.

-S.

Hazel stashed the note and vials in a small knapsack and scooted back as far as she could, keeping her head ducked below the animal hide cover. As she squeezed in among the boxes and crates that had already been packed, the heel of Hazel's palm came down on something soft, and she was met with an angry, screeching yowl. *What?*

It was that gods-damned orange cat. He hissed.

"Cat!" she snapped in a scolding whisper. "Of all the places you decide to show up. Here? Shush!"

Though Hazel supposed it wouldn't be terrible to have a travel companion, so long as he could keep quiet and out of sight. And seeing how he hadn't made a sound until she'd landed on him, she figured it was more her than he who needed to worry about getting caught.

She sighed. "I'm sorry," she whispered to the cat. "I didn't mean to hurt you."

He eyed her suspiciously, tail flicking side to side. He didn't seem convinced.

Slaide's face popped up into view. "You good in there?"

"I suppose so." She grinned, hefting the giant orange feline up in her arms.

"Are you kidding me?" He smacked his palm against his forehead.

"To be honest, I'm starting to think he's… well…" She faded off, not wanting to say the stupid thing she was thinking out loud.

"Your familiar? Like one of those creatures that bond with witches?" Slaide finished for her.

She nodded. "It can't be that simple."

Slaide snorted. "I guess it makes sense. It is the same one, right? You don't just have a horde of weird orange cats following you around?"

Hazel looked at the beast in her arms, everything about him oversized. The too-large ears and giant furry paws.

He looked up at her with his eerie, emerald eyes. Those weren't normal either. Not compared to any cat she'd seen before, anyway.

"Yeah," she said. "It's him."

When Hazel looked from the cat to Slaide, the weight of his gaze warmed her cheeks. He reached a hand up, cupping her cheek gently. Hazel rested her hand atop his.

"I love it when you do that," he said softly.

"Do what?" Hazel asked, feeling as though the air had been stolen from her lungs.

"Blush for me."

The pinkish glow on her cheeks deepened and she looked away quickly.

Whatever this moment was they were sharing was shattered by the sound of voices calling up ahead, toward the front of the wagon.

"Just throw it in the back with the rest of our things!" a man's voice yelled. "We don't have room for your smelly socks and dirty underthings up here, Mutt!"

Another man groaned, grumbling something under his breath as his footsteps carried him in their direction.

A woman's voice said something inaudible, causing the first man to laugh at whatever she had said.

Hazel's eyes bugged. In a few moments, she'd find out if her hiding spot was as stupidly obvious as it felt.

Slaide disappeared into the shadow of the carriage house. Between the natural shadows and his own, he was nearly invisible.

Hazel pushed herself as far into the wagon as she could, pulling her feet behind a wooden crate with what appeared to be performance props sticking out of the top. She was out of sight, for now. Of course, if anyone decided to roll back the animal hide tarp over her head, she'd be completely exposed.

The footsteps grew closer and then the man, presumably the one they'd called Mutt, stepped up to the back of the wagon, grumbling something about how it was stupid that he couldn't keep his belongings close to him. Seemed a little paranoid about someone nabbing his things.

Reluctantly, Mutt tossed a burlap sack in, and it thumped next to Hazel, falling open on impact.

A few moments later, Hazel understood why the others had insisted he stow his belongings in the back. She was blasted with the awful stench of Mutt's unwashed clothes. It was a terrible mix of feet and sweat and body odor. She clamped her hands over her face in disgust.

Mutt crouched down, sniffing loudly. Hazel pulled the cat in close to her body.

And then he sneezed, causing the cat to jump violently. She managed to hang on so the startled animal wouldn't get them caught.

Mutt wiped his nose, sucking the snot back in audibly. "Cats… stupid castle cats," he grumbled, walking away.

Hazel loosed the breath she'd held in, releasing her grip on the orange cat.

The woman's voice called out again, harrying her party to get a move on.

"Roland! Bode! Bor'tuk! Drobak! Mutt! Fall in!" she shouted over the growing din. "We need to get a move on before this place gets any more chaotic."

Hazel could hear murmuring near the front of the wagon. Then footsteps came her way again, forcing her to pull her knees into her chest. Large, calloused hands lifted the edge of the tarp, causing Hazel's heart to skip a beat.

But instead of lifting it any further, he tossed a small sack into the wagon. It landed with a clink, sounding of metal. Against her better judgment, she peeked in the bag and found it full of about a half dozen throwing knives. She swallowed the lump forming in her throat.

They're performers, Hazel, not assassins, she reminded herself. *Just performers.*

The smell of smoke drifted over on a warm breeze. Somewhere through the castle archways, a few women were crying and someone shouted their disapproval. Someone might have screamed, but it wasn't the scream of someone suffering. No, it was just a reaction to the horror that had begun to unfold before them.

A whip cracked somewhere toward the front of the coach. The cart lurched as the lone horse abruptly pulled it into motion. As it pulled away, Slaide revealed himself, springing forth from the shadows, a wraith materializing in the night. His own shadows swirled around him as though they were alive.

Hazel noted his change in appearance: the addition of a chest plate and a flowing black cloak… and a darkened, glazed-over expression. This was not the Slaide she'd come to know, but the Slaide nightmares were made of. His wings were out, no longer glamored from sight. He had them folded tightly into his body. Under his arm, he held a helmet so reflective it looked almost white.

No, it *was* white.

Because it wasn't a helmet at all.

It was a skull. A wolf skull with horns.

Holy gods. Hazel reeled. She wanted to give up her hiding place and leap from the wagon. She wanted to run Slaide down and demand answers.

All this time. All. This. Time. Slaide had been disappearing at odd hours and without explanation because he was *the* traitorous Wolf Mask.

He'd saved her from the Striga, he'd led the ambush during the third trial… he'd killed many, many people.

But there was a whole host of things Wolf Mask had done that were admittedly good. According to circulating rumors, Wolf Mask and his bandits had taken down supply lines transporting crucial imports to the castle. He'd taken out a Border patrol unit that had supposedly allowed refugees to escape beyond the Border.

He'd saved her the night her father was slaughtered. Slaide was nowhere to be found when Wolf Mask appeared that night, leaping over bodies and through flames on his devilish black war steed. *Phillip.*

It was them the entire time.

The nights she'd had horrible nightmares, he wasn't on the castle grounds. He was out creating chaos and wreaking havoc against King Magnus.

The nightmares had been trying to show her something. Had been trying to show them both. She'd been dreaming through her mother's eyes, her memories, Slaide's memories. But there was something else.

It was as though the Fates were screaming something at them, but neither could hear it clearly. One thing struck Hazel for certain, though: the Fates wanted them to stay together.

The fated witch and the fallen bastard.

And here she was, hiding in the back of a wagon, headed *away* from him like a gods-damned fool.

No. No, she wasn't doing this. Every fiber of her being screamed this was wrong. In a split-second decision, Hazel threw herself from the wagon. To her surprise, the cat followed.

The dust cleared, revealing a dirty, coughing Hazel kneeling in the middle of the road.

"You there!" a man's voice called. "Are you alright?"

Hazel looked up to see a knight walking toward her. *Shit. Better move.* She ignored the man and scrambled to her feet.

"Hey! I'm talking to you!" the knight tried again.

Before he had time to process, Hazel was running, orange cat slung over her shoulder.

The knight detected what was going on a breath too late, and his hesitation was probably the one thing that allowed Hazel to get ahead of him.

"You! Guards, stop her!" he yelled, raising the alarm. Moments later, more voices joined the shouting and the giant bell tower bell rang out, alerting the entire castle to join the chase.

"Hazel! Gods!" Slaide called to her, sun-bleached wolf's skull concealing his identity.

She was almost to him, and even though her problems didn't end there, she knew it was where she needed to be.

With mere steps to go, another Raven Blade Knight stepped out from an alcove to her left. Hazel's boots slid on the dusty cobblestone, and her feet almost swept themselves out from under her. He blocked her path to Slaide as the other knights approached from behind.

Trapped again.

Almost instantly, a dagger burst through his throat, and he slumped to the ground, clawing at the wound and gurgling as he choked on his own blood. When he fell, he revealed a pissed off Slaide, who stepped forward and retrieved his dagger from the knight's neck before he was even dead.

He sidestepped the body and growing pool of blood, seizing Hazel by the wrist. And then they ran.

"I don't know what you were thinking, but that was one of the most stupid—" Slaide's words were cut off by the scene ahead. They were too late.

The road before them was blocked by a handful of knights and their commander, mounted on his pale steed.

"Well, would you look at what we've got here? The rebel witch and the thorn in our sides," he deadpanned.

Slaide pulled Hazel behind him. "I'm going to need you to trust me again," he murmured out of the corner of his mouth. "Can you do that?"

She could, couldn't she? He'd lied—at least omitted—more than she'd ever have guessed. But each of those times had apparently been to protect her or someone else. If she wasn't going to trust him, she should have stayed on that damn wagon.

"Yes." She squeezed his arm as she looked straight ahead. Something told her this wasn't going to be as simple as diving off of the balcony and trusting he wouldn't let her fall to her death.

Slaide's body tensed beneath her grip, the arm she was holding slipping into his pocket ever so slowly. The air shimmered, vibrating as though it was being pulled apart.

The next moments happened in the span of a breath as the world around them stood still. Hazel wondered if that was her imagination or yet another facet of Slaide's magic.

When Slaide removed his hand from his pocket, he released a handful of black powder, shrouding them in the fine dust—and giving them a moment to escape. But to where?

Slaide apparently had an answer for that, too. Moments later the air that was still vibrating sundered, creating a rift large enough to fit them both—a gaping maw of swirling smoke and glittering stars.

"Grab them!" the commander shouted, his urgency evident in his panicked voice.

"I'd say after you," Slaide said, voice low, "but I'm going to assume you've never rift-jumped?"

Hazel shook her head. Her stomach lurched prematurely.

"Right. Well, in that case, I suggest you hold on." He grabbed her hand and shot her a warning glance when she immediately squeezed it tightly. "And you might want to close your eyes. This is *much* worse than flying."

Without warning, he pulled her in tight, wrapping his muscular arms around her waist.

And the next thing Hazel knew, she was falling into an abyss.

The pair emerged from the rift in opposite fashions. Slaide stepped out of the vortex with a casual air befitting someone with a lifetime of practice under their belt.

Hazel, on the other hand, tumbled out into an ungraceful pile, scrambled to her hands and knees, and vomited.

She looked up at Slaide to find him assessing her with a discerning scowl, one brow lifted toward the heavens.

"That was…" Slaide's words trailed off as a stupid smirk tried to grace his cocky face.

"Shove it," Hazel grumbled. "What in the name of the gods was that? How are you even standing right now?" She continued hugging the grass. Her cat, seemingly unfazed, sauntered by as though showing off.

"That was a rift jump. It's a tear in space and time that allows me to travel to certain places quickly—and without being seen. As for that," he gestured toward Hazel and her apparent obsession with the ground, "you just get used to it. Like sailors and their sea legs. Time and practice, things you unfortunately do not have the luxury of. But at least you're not dead." He walked toward the cliff side jutting out beyond the trees.

As Hazel mulled that over, she came to a realization that pissed her off. "You mean to tell me you can jump to wherever you please, and yet when Agnes and my father were in grave danger we had to fly and take Philip?"

Slaide turned, looking as though he wouldn't waste his time responding to her. "No, smart ass. If you'd paid attention at all, you wouldn't dare ask me something like that. I would lay my life on the line for that horse. You think I wanted to ride him that hard? To run him down unfamiliar roads at night, where he could easily break a leg? We did that for *you*. Trust me, if I could have jumped there through a rift I would have. But I'd never been to Agnes's cottage. So it wasn't an option."

Hazel thought she was beginning to understand how this rift jumping thing worked, but it only made her stomach revolt more to ponder it.

She watched Slaide as he looked out over the horizon. They were atop a grassy knoll, a line of trees to their backs that thickened into dense forest. He stood at the highest point of the hill and looked out over the world, surveying the fallout.

Something had his attention, so she climbed up beside him.

A tower of heavy black smoke billowed into the sky, ash and embers falling like snow. She could hear echoes of shouts here and there, and there might have been someone screaming. But nothing indicated that what she heard was Agnes herself. There was no agony in the voices, just fear.

As she watched in horror, a column of flame shot into the air, rising above the ramparts and licking the sky. She could hear its roaring intensity even from their position. *Holy gods...*

The flames devoured themselves, giving way to something else entirely.

A *phoenix*. A phoenix made of fire.

Hazel thought she heard shouts from the awestruck spectators.

It spread its wings as wide as the courtyard itself, tilted its head back, and bellowed another jet of flame into the sky.

With a blood-curdling screech, the phoenix exploded into a ball of light, energy, and flame, shooting millions of scorching embers in a radius wider than the castle itself.

Those shouts of awe turned into screams of terror. Though she could not see from where they were, she had to assume fire was catching and beginning to spread through the courtyard and beyond.

Hazel watched in a gut-curdling mix of sadness and horror. The eruption of that phoenix could mean only one thing.

Agnes was gone.

She wanted to scream and cry, but the tears wouldn't come with the adrenaline coursing through her body after witnessing the chaos Agnes had started. She'd sparked a flame.

A revolution.

Ambush

As the chaos unfolded, Hazel heard the initial booms before the entire world shook as though it might break in two.

The accompanying shockwave rattled them, causing Hazel to grab Slaide's upper arm to steady herself.

From their vantage point on the hill, Hazel watched the eastern wing of the castle collapse into itself, leaving a cloud of dust and smoke in its wake. The sight stole her breath.

Slaide and his bandits were behind the destruction. He'd blown it all to Hel, just as he promised.

But when she looked up at him, Slaide didn't appear proud of what he'd done. A frown, deep and contemplating, marred his face.

"You did that," Hazel remarked with a smile in her voice.

He looked down as though he'd forgotten she was standing there. "Yep."

"What's wrong? I would have expected you to celebrate destroying those cells and everything they're associated with."

He stared out over the smoke-filled horizon again. "It's not something to celebrate. There's a good chance innocent people got wrapped up in those blasts, not to mention the aftermath. That's the cost of what we're doing, but…"

Hazel laid her hand on his arm. "Thank you."

His head snapped to hers. "The little witch is thanking me *now*? For what, exactly?"

What could she say? She should be thanking him for everything. For the way he hadn't given up on her, even when she gave up on herself. For refusing to let her die. For saving her from Oswald. She shuddered at the thought.

"He'll never hurt you again, you know," Slaide said, as if he'd heard her thoughts.

Hazel rubbed her arms and looked away. Even if she never saw Oswald again, she was certain he would haunt her nightmares.

"How? Something tells me I haven't seen the last of Ravenhold. And I'm sure he'll be waiting to give me a warm welcome if ever I return."

"Maybe not. I can't predict the future, and you have a knack for getting yourself into trouble." A sly smirk graced his face. "But I can assure you the bastard will not so much as look at you again."

"How do you know?" Hazel frowned, although she thought she knew the answer.

"Well for one, I cut out his remaining eye." He smiled at Hazel's grimace. "And two, I taught him a lesson before leaving him tied up in a sorry state in that dungeon. It's unlikely anyone ventured down there before the collapse." He stuffed his hands into his pockets and shrugged as though this was just another day for him.

But it was, wasn't it? Slaide Elias was a killer by nature. She shouldn't be surprised when he reacted in violent ways. And she should be grateful. She was grateful. Now Oswald One-eye would be a monster in her nightmares and her nightmares alone.

"We need to get going," Slaide reminded her as he turned his back on the sight. "Nightfall is coming, and I know you well enough to know you won't want to see the things that haunt these woods at night."

"You mean hunt?"

He leveled a glare at her. "No. I meant what I said. If you care to stay here and find out, be my guest."

Hazel scurried to his side again, not wanting to be left behind.

"Where are we going, anyway?" she wondered, keeping a close pace to his long strides.

"To see a friend. It's a long way to where we're going, and I prefer not to wear holes in these boots just yet. I happen to like them."

Hazel looked at Slaide's feet. His boots were nothing spectacular. Was that an attempt at a joke?

He stopped and stared at her, assessing. She wanted to shrink under his gaze for some reason.

"What? Is it something I said?"

"No. It's just… fucking Hel. This is all such a mess." He propped his hands on his hip. "Before we go there, I need to visit someone to fetch Phillip. They don't take kindly to strangers, and they're going to be completely sideways with me for bringing you."

"Then why are we going?" she countered, brows raised.

"I already told you. I'm not walking. And the only solution to not walking is by taking my horse, who is currently in the care of another *very* defensive friend," he explained. "And no, before you ask, I'm not flying us all the way there or rift-jumping. One of those would be far too exhausting for me, the other—"

"It's somewhere you've never been. I get it," Hazel interrupted.

"Wrong. I have been there. And I know for a fact that making an entrance via rift without being invited is a sure way to get us both killed."

Why were they going there again?

Something screeched in the woods, and Hazel's hair stood on end. She watched Slaide roll his eyes, because of course only he could be inconvenienced by monsters coming out to play in the night.

"And on that note, we're no longer walking," he concluded. Moments later, he'd opened a rift.

Hazel's stomach did a flip at the sight of it, every fiber of her being protesting.

"Come on," he huffed. "We don't have a lot of time here."

Hazel took one last look at the castle of horrors. With any luck, she would never lay eyes on it again. Then she stepped beside Slaide, who wrapped an arm around her as he stepped inside the rift. The last thing she witnessed before the darkness consumed her was the rift closing bit by bit, as though the world was stitching itself back together.

The ground rose up to meet Hazel quickly, folding her knees into her chest and forcing the air from her lungs. Slaide, as usual, stepped from the rift with practiced grace. Her cat, again, pranced out of the rift with veteran swagger. Slaide shook his head and laughed.

"At least one of you is getting it," he mocked.

It was darker there, wherever there was. The heart of a forest, no doubt, but who could say if it was even the same one they'd been in moments before?

Slaide sighed and ran his hand through his hair. "I don't suppose I can convince you to wait here while I fetch Phillip?"

Her face must have said exactly what she intended it to. *Absolutely not.*

"Fine. Let's go. But I'm warning you: keep your mouth shut. Do not speak unless spoken to. These are my people, but they're only my people because of trust. Trust that was hard earned, and I have no doubt easily broken. Understood?"

She nodded and Slaide spun on his heel, striding deeper into the forest.

She was unfortunately unprepared to see the makeshift encampment they walked up on, and a surprised gasp escaped her lips. Slaide whirled on her, but before he could tell her to be silent, she was looking past him, gripping her locket.

Behind Slaide stood four masked men, looking ready for a fight.

Slaide turned, releasing a relieved-sounding breath when he noticed who awaited them.

"Hazel, this is my crew," he explained, gesturing to the four men behind him. "Some of them, anyway. That's Ruin. To his right are Malice, Havoc, and Fury. Vex and Venom are… scouting, I'd imagine."

The one he'd called Ruin nodded.

Slaide introduced the men nonchalantly, as though it were normal to have such names. Hazel stared without blinking at the masked bandits before her, trying to remind herself that the people they murdered were the evil ones, not them… right? Easier said than done.

Despite their masked faces betraying nothing, their postures—crossed arms and hands on weapons—told her they weren't any happier to have an uninvited guest than she was to be there.

Slaide moved about, gathering supplies as though he owned the place. Perhaps he did. Havoc and Malice never took their eyes off her, eyeing her feline friend suspiciously.

Ruin followed Slaide around the encampment, berating him for bringing her there. He spoke as if she wasn't standing just paces from them.

"What are you thinking? Bringing her here? We just moved! Are you trying to bring the Raven Blade down on us again?" he rattled.

Slaide mostly ignored him, much to Ruin's chagrin. "If it bothers you so much, pretend she's not here. We aren't staying, anyway."

"Damn right you're not. You should've sent word, Venge. You've put this entire operation in jeopardy," Ruin spat.

Slaide appeared to have had enough, as he got into Ruin's face then, jabbing his index finger into the man's chest. "She is the operation, Ruin. What don't you get? It's her." They both looked at Hazel then.

"Anyway," Slaide began, "we'll be out of your hair now. Thanks for bringing Phillip."

"Yeah, whatever. Bastard gave me a Hel of a time getting here. You owe me."

They clasped forearms in what Hazel could only guess was some kind of brotherly handshake.

Slaide took Phillip's reins then, having packed his saddlebags full, and motioned for Hazel to hop up.

He aided her into the saddle, grabbing marginally less of her ass than the first time. After joining her, they left the encampment behind with little fanfare. Something told Hazel the bond between those men was tenuous at best.

They rode in silence for a while before Hazel spoke. "So, Venge, is it?" She tried to hide the smile in her voice.

He growled behind her, somewhere between pissed and annoyed. "Eavesdropping is going to get you killed, little witch."

She ignored that. "Is it short for something?"

Slaide said nothing for a beat, the only sound between them the thudding of Phillip's heavy footfalls on the loamy forest floor.

"Vengeance," he said at last. "It's short for Vengeance."

Vengeance. Ruin. Malice. Vex. Fury. Venom. Well, if they wanted to come off as dark, broody monsters, they nailed it on the naming. She found herself wondering what their real names were. An ill-timed chuckle escaped her as she imagined Ruin's not-so-scary real name being Terrence. Or William.

As Slaide bristled, she realized her mistake. "Ah, I wasn't—that laugh wasn't at you."

"I don't particularly care."

Was it just her, or was he extra crabby? Fine. She could be quiet.

The forest eventually grew thinner before giving way to an open field. It was at that point that Slaide proceeded to direct Phillip with obvious caution.

"Is something wrong?" Hazel drew in a breath, readying herself for whatever unseen thing troubled him.

"Other than this gigantic open field with nowhere to hide? No," Slaide responded.

Point taken.

"I don't want to get picked off crossing here, so you'd better hang on," he warned before spurring Phillip into motion.

It happened halfway across the field.

A rumble sounded somewhere behind them, reminiscent of an approaching storm. But one look at the sky indicated it wasn't a storm at all. Her locket warned her of what she already feared.

As Hazel turned to glance past Slaide, only to find riders approaching, churning dust in their wake. It was to her horror, then, she ascertained they were no ordinary bandits or bounty hunters.

Six Raven Blade Knights were hot on their trail.

And they'd come for her.

She could see the whites of the horses' eyes, the sheer frenzy they'd been worked into in their pursuit. The riders would be upon them in seconds.

And because the Fates were cruel beings, Phillip's foot found a divot mid-stride, tossing Hazel to the ground as he struggled to maintain his footing. Hazel tumbled and rolled while Slaide kept his seat and careened on by.

She scrambled to her feet, palming her dagger. The orange cat draped over her shoulder, an unwilling participant in the ensuing battle, but she wasn't leaving him behind to be slaughtered.

She didn't see the first assailant.

Someone grabbed Hazel by the hair and yanked her backwards. She landed on her back; the wind knocked out of her body. She rolled over, gasping for air. Hoofbeats thundered all around her.

She heard the approaching footfalls, the clink of metal armor as they approached.

The Raven Blade Knight stood over her, and in that moment, she knew his imposing figure marked the last thing she would see. This was it. Her time was finally up, and really, it was a gods-damned miracle she'd even made it this far. She was, after all, just a simple woman from a backwater town.

The commander hefted his broadsword high, the onyx eyes of the detailed raven-head hilt gleaming in the sunlight. And then the sword began its descent, falling in slow motion to end her. She closed her eyes and awaited the blow, hoping the sword was razor sharp and that the commander would strike true. A mercy that she wouldn't feel a thing. The world would just cease to exist.

The telltale whine of metal rang out, followed by a meaty squelch. Hazel was showered with hot blood, her eyes flying open to find the commander still standing above her, mouth agape as though he was frozen in time.

And then his head toppled off his shoulders, falling to the ground and rolling to a rest beside her. His lifeless eyes were wide in terror. Then the rest of him crumpled to the ground in a bloody heap, blood spurting from the remaining stump of his neck. She scrambled backwards, only to slam into another set of legs. But when she looked up, it wasn't another knight waiting to dismember her.

A gloved hand reached for her, and when she took it, Slaide hefted her onto her feet. He broke into a run, hauling her behind him.

Horse hooves thundered behind them, and Hazel stupidly chanced a glance over her shoulder, losing her footing and toppling to the ground once more.

Despite his firm grip, the force of her fall tore Hazel's hand from Slaide's. He spun to retrieve her, but the mounted knight was already upon her, blade poised to strike.

Hazel outstretched her hands before her, and her palms began to glow. But something was wrong. She grimaced, working far too hard to pull her magic forth.

The well of power was there, but the harder she pulled, the more it resisted. Instead of feeling empowered, the magic was sucking the life out of her. Perhaps she was too tired or too beat up… or just flat out too inexperienced.

Slaide raced to her, wiping out anyone and anything in his path.

He looked fierce, and she thought if Slaide in battle was the last thing she laid eyes on, she might be alright with that.

Before Slaide reached her, Hazel's hands went limp, and she slumped over, conscious, but unable to move.

"No. Hazel, no!" Slaide shouted. Why did he sound so far away?

Her mind raced. She couldn't have burned out that quickly. Could she?

Seemingly out of nowhere, her cat leaped through the air and latched onto the war horse's face. The beast reared, screaming in pain as the oversized feline sank its claws and teeth into the soft flesh of the horse's face.

The beast returned to its most basic instincts, bucking and rearing in an attempt to remove the furry assailant. But the cat was formidably latched on, and the only thing the horse succeeded in was unseating his rider.

The knight tucked and rolled as he hit the ground, righting himself with unnatural ease. He strode toward Hazel with the swagger of a man who knew he had the upper hand and was about to kill his enemy. However, he hadn't expected the cat would turn on him as well.

Just as he raised his sword to parry Slaide's blow, the feisty orange beast wrapped itself around his helmet, grappling for purchase against the hammered iron. The knight fought to peel the cat from his head but found that a nearly impossible task while wearing bulky iron gauntlets.

Hazel tried to call out, to do anything to save that damned cat. But she couldn't make a sound.

Slaide, on the other hand, was able to take advantage of the chaos the cat was causing. He leveled his blade and prepared to strike.

But Hazel's awe turned to horror as she watched him bring his sword down for a killing blow—only for the knight to deflect it by sheer dumb luck. In one seamless move, he spun, grabbing her cat by the scruff and throwing him to the ground, where he lay disoriented. He then angled his iron-plated sabaton and kicked the cat across the clearing.

He didn't get up.

No! She wanted to scream. To lash out. To do anything but lie there.

Slaide bellowed, drawing her attention again even as a warm tear ran down her cheek. He brought his sword down once more, dragging white-hot lightning from the sky as his shadows entwined with the metal of the blade.

He cleaved the man's chest from right shoulder to left hip, his lightning singeing the flesh as it cut, and the knight was dead before he hit the ground.

She couldn't see what went on around them, but it didn't feel like they were winning. Especially not after Slaide scooped her up in haste, whistled sharply, and tossed her onto Phillip's back before the horse had even come to a full stop. Slaide ran alongside Phillip for a few beats before vaulting behind her into the saddle.

But they couldn't leave yet. From her vantage point, she could see the cat, still lying on the blood-soaked earth, unmoving. Perhaps he was dead. But he'd been a faithful acquaintance to the very end if that was the case. Did he deserve to be forgotten on a bloody battlefield, picked apart by carrion birds? *No.*

Hazel managed a groan, but it went unnoticed. She tried again, and while it at least earned his attention, he still hadn't seen the cat.

"I know," he murmured between thunderous hoofbeats, "close your eyes. I can't help you, but I know someone who can. Just… stay with me."

"Noooo!" Hazel managed, feeling overcome by dizziness. "Caaaattt!"

She didn't know how, but Slaide evidently understood if the flash of realization on his face was any indication. He looked over his shoulder, eyes darting about. He locked in on something, and then they were moving again.

Phillip's gallop was jarring, and Hazel's consciousness slipped away with each bounce in the saddle. Slaide was going to save the cat. He'd saved her… perhaps she could rest.

Just for a little bit.

A sense of urgency emanated from both Phillip and Slaide. Despite losing consciousness, despite barely hanging on and the edges of her vision blurring, she could hear Slaide's voice urging Phillip to go faster. She was safe now. She closed her eyes and drifted away.

Life Debt

Hazel attempted to peel her eyes open, but her skull shuddered with pain. She turned onto her side and vomited violently onto the ground. As she rolled to her back, her mind raced, head feeling like it had been split in two. She grasped her head in her hands as though she could will the pounding headache away, but it was no use.

A cough racked her entire body, the pain almost unbearable. It was the aftermath of the tournament all over again. A terrifying thought consumed her, and she shot up, ignoring the wildfire of pain coursing through her body.

Had she dreamed all of it? She took in her surroundings. No, she was in a large canvas tent, appearing to be some sort of medical bay. She wasn't shackled or bound, and her external wounds had been tended to. Perhaps she was in good hands.

Memories flooded her, and she was overwhelmed with emotion. Her mind replayed the last scenes of her consciousness: the commander poised to end her life… her inability to pull her magic… Slaide coming to her rescue… the cat—*her* cat—launching into the fray. *No. No, please let him be okay.* That damn cat was a nuisance as much as he was a loyal companion. And if she didn't know better, she'd swear he was protecting her.

Where was Slaide? Where was she? She rolled over and vomited again. When she was finished, she noticed her necklace on the pillow beside her head.

The tent flap rustled, and a striking woman with cloud-like blond hair the color of pale moonlight and a silky, dark brown complexion entered, carrying a tray of what looked to be food, drink, and what were likely vials of medicine. She was dressed plainly and in very comfortable-looking clothing, not unlike the pants and tunics Hazel was used to at home. She startled when she discovered Hazel was awake, nearly dropping the tray. Hazel sat up, not knowing if this stranger meant to help her or harm her.

But as she got a good look at the woman, she noticed something strange. There was an aura about her, and she radiated magic, as though her entire body was overflowing with it. Seeing her essence flow so freely… it could only mean one thing. She would ask about that later. Being in the presence of someone who clearly had strong magical ties was soothing, disarming. Surely, a witch wouldn't harm one of her own, right? Assuming she was a witch. Hazel was more than aware there were many other magically inclined beings outside her own species. Perhaps she was a druid or a dryad, and not a witch at all. Would she still protect Hazel then?

When she spoke, Hazel thought this must be a goddess descended from Caelis, for surely no mortal could have such a spellbinding voice. The honeyed notes poured over her. It was music to Hazel's ears, and all she'd done was speak.

"I am Mori. You are safe here, for now. Mother will want to speak with you when you are feeling up to it, and from there, your fate will be decided. For now, please eat."

Hazel coughed, and the pain spasmed through her ribs, sending her spiraling into an unrelenting hacking fit.

Mori offered her a vial from the tray with an opaque liquid inside. She nodded toward it reassuringly as Hazel took it in her hand. Hazel's fingers shook with the memory of her time in the castle, when Nemsen had kept her drugged. He, too, had claimed it was for her own good.

But she'd do anything to shake this cough racking her body and to stave off the pain a while longer. So, she tipped the vial to her lips and downed it in a single swig.

Her throat was instantly ablaze, the burning sensation tracing all the way into her stomach, and Hazel was certain she would puke it all back up. She shot an accusatory glare at Mori, who only watched.

Poison. It was poison, and she's waiting for me to die. She pointed a finger at the woman, but before she could attempt to speak, the inferno receded. She was fine. Not dead nor dying. And her cough was gone. She lowered her finger, and Mori smiled.

"Think you were going to die?"

"I did. Why are you helping me? Who are you?" She wiped her mouth on the back of her sleeve.

"I already told you that. I am Mori. As for why I am helping you, you are a witch, are you not?" She cocked her head to the side as if observing a wild animal.

"I-I don't know what I am. I have powers, but I can rarely call on them when I need to and when I do…" She looked at her hands, betrayers of her own body and soul.

"You burn out," Mori finished for her.

"Is that what this was? Is that why I'm here? Everything went black and I…" Her mind raced. *Slaide.* "My friend. The man who was with me," she lurched to her feet, the pain stifled to a dull reminder she'd been injured. Mori jumped back from her in alarm, eyeing her from head to toe. "Where is he?"

She scoffed. "Friend? Hmph. The Dark One, yes? He is being held by our people until we can bring you both before Mother. He is fine, uninjured except for a few minor cuts and scrapes he suffered in battle. However, he is not free to move about as you are. Not yet." Her voice was stern.

She knew what that meant. They had Slaide in chains somewhere. She needed to get to him. "May I go to him?" She wasn't above begging. He'd saved her life. Again.

Mori frowned and shook her head softly. She took Hazel's hand in her own. "Mother was excited to hear a witch was brought to us alive, but when she realized who it was that delivered you, she almost killed him on the spot. The Dark One is not a friend of the witches."

Right. Okay, she would have to deal with that touchy subject later. Slaide was alive and they would not kill him… yet. She changed the subject. "So, this burnout. What happened to me? How do I avoid it? I wasn't even able to draw my magic up this time before I passed out."

Mori nodded thoughtfully. "This is normal in untrained witches. You've not mastered your gift yet, and that is to be expected. Now that you are here, you will learn. I cannot say you won't burn out again, but at least here we can fix the problem immediately before it kills you. To have it happen on the battlefield and live to tell the tale…

"Magic, specifically natural magic, is part of the balance of nature. Not to be confused with what the goddess-forsaken Magistry does," she spat. "Our magic pulls from the earth below us, the sky above, and every living thing in between. But there must be *give* in order for there to be *take*. One does not exist without the other. Trained witches prevent burnout by trading some of their life essence for the magic they wish to use, and they take only what they need."

"What if a witch doesn't want to forfeit pieces of herself?" Hazel asked, taking a bite out of a hunk of crusted bread from the tray of food. She was almost completely sidetracked by how good it was.

"They do not have a choice. As soon as you channel, as soon as you open your mind's eye and tug on that glowing string of power, nature will siphon what it wants. As I said, there is no take without give. And if you take without giving willingly, well, nature still rights the balance with her pound of flesh. Or your soul, in this case. You don't want to make a habit of over-channeling."

"So how does one prevent over-channeling while they learn? With witches being persecuted as it is, isn't it dangerous to risk losing even one in training?"

Mori smiled. "We are not so poorly numbered as your King wants you to believe. You'll see soon enough. As for your question," she pulled a jeweled pendant out of her pocket. It was a ruby gemstone set into silver. "We have these. These jewels are imbued to act as siphons, absorbing the magic at a rate that will not kill us. But we do not give them to witchlings, they must be earned. In the meantime, many will experience fainting spells. Occasionally one will die, but it has been many years since we have suffered that kind of loss."

Hazel found herself enraptured by the many-faceted gemstone until Mori returned it to her pocket. They locked eyes, and Mori raised a brow.

"Anyway, that is enough questioning for now. Finish eating and then bathe. Mother awaits." She turned to leave through the flaps of the tent.

"Mori, wait… uh, please," Hazel called after her. Mori paused, looking over her shoulder as though she had a much better place to be. Hazel shrank under her gaze. "Just one more question before you go."

Mori sighed and gestured for her to continue.

"When we were ambushed, I was traveling with a small companion. A, uh, well he's a cat. I know it seems stupid, but he actually saved my life back there and—"

The woman laughed. "Yes, yes, I know. I heard all about Roshi's exploits on the battlefield as a cat, of all goddess-forsaken things. She'll live. She's just… bruised. Now go, wash up."

She turned without another word, leaving Hazel alone and blinking in confusion.

Mori and another similarly dressed attendant, with darker, curlier hair and piercings about her nose and pointed ears, walked with Hazel between them. Where Mori had been the face of a kindly healer before, she now wore the mask of a devastating warrior, bedecked in jewelry that Hazel now knew was for siphoning and controlling magic. It was the most elegant, sophisticated form of weaponry she'd ever seen. Not to mention easy to transport and hide from unsuspecting eyes.

Hazel was taken aback by their home. It was a city among the trees, with tree homes scattered throughout the canopy and semi-permanent canvas tents along the forest floor. The atmosphere was cool and earthy, with moss carpeting the ground wherever there weren't walking paths.

Mori caught her gazing around in awe. "It is beautiful here, isn't it? Our own oasis," she preened.

"I am just shocked how all of this goes unnoticed and untouched by the King."

Mori laughed under her breath. "He cannot reach us here."

"And where is *here* exactly?" Hazel wondered.

Mori smiled down at her in a way that made her feel small. "Beyond the Border, of course."

Hazel stopped in her tracks, eyes bugging out of her head.

With a grin that encompassed her entire face, Mori asked, "First time?"

But before she could answer, they rounded a corner and almost smacked into another set of guards.

It took Hazel only a moment to realize the four guards walked Slaide between them, a dog on a leash. He had an iron collar around his neck, and his hands were bound in what Hazel could only assume were anti-magic cuffs. Seeing him in this state, still bloodied and bruised from battle, sucked the wind out of her. She reached for him, but his guards crossed their polearms before him, blocking her way. Mori placed her hand on Hazel's arm gently, but the message was clear: she could not touch him. He wouldn't even meet her gaze. *What did they do to you?*

Hazel, Mori, and the second guard walked in front of them down a long row of ancient ash trees. She wasn't able to look back, but Hazel could hear the forlorn shuffle of Slaide's boots against the dirt, the rattle of his chains as he walked. Her heart ached to free him from his restraints. This was a misunderstanding. Whoever *Mother* was would certainly see that. She had to.

That thought was ripped from Hazel's mind as they rounded the next bend. The ash trees opened wide into a throne room carved from the earth itself. Upon a dais carved from stone sat a woman unlike any Hazel had ever seen. Her hair was stark straight and black as night, with a strip of white framing her face. Her eyes were an ethereal green, the color of malachite. Uncertainty washed over Hazel, reinforced by the slightest warmth building where her locket rested.

She sat upon a throne of bones stacked with skulls of various sizes and species, long femur bones providing structural support. The gaps were filled with what appeared to be toe and finger bones, and… teeth. It would be incredible if not so morbid.

The woman held a goblet in one bony hand, her pale skin stretched taut. The other rested on the arm of her throne. Her thin body was draped in a dress made from layers of sheer fabric as fine as spider's silk. A slit ran up each side, exposing the flesh of her thighs, up and up until it met the crease of her hips, where the excess fabric pooled. Her demeanor was casual, but harsh, her unnaturally green eyes feeling as though they were peeling Hazel apart layer by layer.

Mother was not just the matron here. She was Queen.

She stood, the tawny owl behind her rustling about and finding a new position to perch in. Using an ashwood staff as a cane, the woman limped to the dais and made her way down the crumbling stone stairs to stand before Hazel, who averted her gaze and stared down at her feet.

Icy fingers cupped Hazel's chin, and then her face was tilted up. She had been so woefully unprepared to see what awaited her there. Where a hard, unrelenting Queen had been just moments before, she now found something else entirely. Something softer, warmer. Those green eyes were brimming with tears as she stood before Hazel and grabbed her by the shoulders, wanting, searching.

And then she choked back a sob and sputtered, "It's you. It's really you."

Before Hazel could so much as utter her confusion, the Queen pulled her into a tight embrace, letting the tears fall down Hazel's back.

"Welcome home, my Rhiannon. My daughter."

Hazel pulled out of her grip. She was familiar in all the right ways. And yet, her face was so sharp. Something about the softness in her eyes felt hollow, as though it was a mask over the cruelty hiding beneath. A sensation crawled over her, something screaming that there was more to this reunion than she understood.

"I'm not…." She couldn't form words. "That's not my name, Your Grace."

The Queen laughed softly, brushing off Hazel's discomfort. "I'm Queen Aisling to them. But as so many of them do, you can call me *Mother*." She stood there expectantly. "After all, you're the only one with a claim to me."

Mother. Mother. Mother.

Gods, she'd waited so long for this moment, hadn't she? Was this not the culmination of her hard-fought journey? She'd looked death in the eyes and kept pushing for this outcome. And yet, despite enduring so much, Hazel hadn't imagined she would face her mother so soon. Perhaps she needed time to process.

After all, this woman, a woman whose presence Hazel had craved her entire life… had been alive all this time. To make matters worse, she hadn't even been all that far away. They were, what, a short day or two ride from Larksridge? Just beyond the Border? But she'd never seen Aisling's face before. At least not that she could remember. And if this woman had ever bothered to check up on her… well, it wasn't a face she'd easily forget.

"I take it you have the locket? That you found the book I left you?" she asked.

"Yes," Hazel started, "but the locket was… empty."

The Queen met her gaze, eyes softening. "Dear child, it was never about what was inside the locket. All you ever needed was in here." She brought a finger to rest over Hazel's heart.

Hazel was stunned into silence at the profound statement. But before she could ask her next question, Queen Aisling turned her attention to Slaide. "Though I'm surprised it didn't warn you away from *that one.* Curious."

Slaide, who was finally looking at Hazel. *He knew. He knew she was alive, and he knew exactly where he was taking me.* But she couldn't decide if she wanted to hug him or kill him.

"And you, my dear," she crooned to Slaide, "You have a lot of nerve showing your face within my sanctuary. However, since you've delivered to me my long-lost daughter and heir, I at least owe you my thanks. So, thank you. Guards," she paused, leveling a murderous gaze at Slaide, "execute him and toss his body back to those dogs across the Border. Let it serve as a warning: the Moonwater Coven does not forgive the transgressions against our kind. The Cailleach will rise again."

Slaide was prodded in the back with a spear tip, forcing him to bend over further.

Too fast. This was all happening too fast.

A tall, broad-shouldered figure appeared as if out of thin air, their hooded cloak hiding their identity. But Hazel didn't need to know their name to know why they'd arrived. No, the gleaming executioner's axe told her plenty.

The cloaked figure stalked toward them, an Aetherial reaper from Hel, axe resting on their shoulder too casually.

Hazel's eyes darted from the executioner to Slaide to the Queen, chest heaving as panic gripped her. Mori's grip tightened slightly on her arm, as though sensing Hazel's unrest.

"You can't!" Hazel pushed away from the Queen and pulled free from Mori, who attempted to restrain her, baring her teeth. But Hazel dove atop Slaide, putting herself between him and the executioner's blade.

"Slaide saved me from the darkest pits of Hel by pulling me out of that dungeon. He didn't kill me, though he could have plenty of times. Instead, he rescued me from the mad King. Not to mention he saved *you*! That's right, I know all about your little escape from Ravenhold. You wouldn't have made it out if not for him." A few gasps went up in the gathered crowd.

"I don't owe that beast anything. He slaughters our kind without end. They *bred* him to destroy us. Did he tell you that bit? He's no more than an animal. A hunting dog. So what if he brought me one alive this time? I said *thank you*. I owe him nothing beyond that," the Queen snarled.

Hazel did not roll over. This woman held no power over her, mother or no. "I know exactly who and what he is, and I have moved past it. Slaide Elias is more than the High King's witch hunter. He's a slave just as much as you were. He has earned my trust, and I owe him my life several times over. So, if you're going to execute him, you might as well execute me, too." Hazel was feral. Her eyes glowed almost gold with rage as she hovered protectively over Slaide.

"Don't be ridiculous, child. He's an *animal*," the Queen repeated. "If he's kept you alive this long, it's more likely that he's getting something from you in return." Her gaze raked over Hazel accusingly.

"I don't know what you're trying to suggest, but—"

Aisling waved her hand in dismissal. "Save the dramatics for someone else. He is what he is. I don't care if you warmed his bed or he yours. After all, he *is* pretty to look at. But that changes nothing."

The Queen and Hazel locked eyes. Silence passed between them, tension mounting to an uncomfortable level. Two women, each fierce in their own regard, refusing to budge. Below her, Hazel could feel Slaide's shallow, tentative breathing, his anticipation palpable.

In the end, it was the Queen who broke first. With a huff that said *this is far from over*, she called her guards. "Change of plans. Take him back. Dump him across the Border and let the rutting Raven King come down from his perch to retrieve his trash."

The guards nodded wordlessly and took their leave, a dejected Slaide walking between the four of them.

"You can't mean to send him back there," Hazel interrupted.

"I can, and I do. You don't make the rules around here, Princess." She made a shooing motion at the court and her queensguard, who Hazel had completely overlooked. They blended into shadows.

Shadows.

She could not let Slaide be taken away.

"Do not mourn the half breed, Rhiannon. It is unbecoming of a princess to pine after a monster."

Hazel whirled on her. "I'm not pining. And the only monster here is you!" she spat. "You cannot turn him back over to Aeos. They'll kill him for what he's done. You owe him a life debt!"

"And I *didn't* kill him. I'm having him removed from here in one piece. Life debt fulfilled. What someone else does with him does not affect my end of the deal. Now, I understand this is all quite a shock. I'll have Mori take you to your rooms to cool down." With that, Queen Aisling turned on her heels, her deep purple cloak billowing behind her, leaving Mori to wrangle Hazel back to her own quarters.

THOUGH SHE HAD calmed down on the outside, her inner turmoil raged on, rocked by a sense of betrayal. And by someone claiming to be her own kin, no less. Her soul was a tempest of emotion, and she wanted nothing more than to unleash her anger on everyone around her. But she kept ahold of it, knowing she couldn't help Slaide if she blew her top now.

And she *would* rescue Slaide, no matter the cost.

A sharp whistle came from outside the tent, catching Mori's attention.

"I'll be right back, Princess." She bowed, backing out of the tent.

Hazel nodded, though she couldn't care less whether Mori came back or if they left her there to rot. To her dismay, Mori did, in fact, return momentarily.

She poked her head in between the tent flaps. "Princess, there's someone here who would like to see you. May she come in?"

Hazel shrugged. Why would she care what she thought? No one else did.

Mori opened the tent and let the visitor step in.

Hazel looked up, her gaze meeting eyes she'd seen before. The shape of them. The depth. The color. But she couldn't place *where*.

"Hello, Princess." She had light brown skin and freckled cheeks, with poofy bronze hair pulled into twin balls on either side of her head. But those eyes… they were so unnaturally green.

"Do I know you?" Hazel arched a brow.

She smiled. "Yes, and no. My name is Roshi, short for Roshiannagh. But you know me as…" In a burst of blinding light, Roshi transformed.

Hazel looked down to find Roshi was no longer herself, but someone else entirely. The orange cat. He—or rather, she—rubbed up against Hazel's shins and purred.

"Showoff," muttered Mori. "Roshi is a druid, specializing in animal likenesses."

"What in the name of the gods?" Hazel exclaimed. "You do not seriously expect me to believe… it was… he was *you*?"

The orange cat at her feet meowed.

In another flash, Roshi was standing before them again. "Yes," she said, "He was me. I was he. I can take the form of many creatures, male or female doesn't particularly matter."

"And you just never thought to tell me you're human? All this time?" Her shock was palpable.

Roshi made to answer but was cut off by Mori's soft touch.

"Perhaps it is best if I give you two some time. I'll be back when your accommodations are ready." Mori quickly left, leaving Hazel with so many questions.

When she was gone, Hazel found Roshi staring at her.

"A cat?" Hazel questioned. "All the times I was in trouble. All the creatures you could have been, and you chose a *cat.*" Her voice was thick with condescension.

Roshi laughed. "It's not that simple. Regretfully, I cannot take the form of something fierce like a wyvern or a were-cat. I'm limited to small animals and birds, mostly. Occasionally I can pull off the likeness of a pony or a stag. But… I was required to stay inconspicuous." She paused, looking contemplative. "I hung around your cottage for a while. I couldn't decide if I should stay or not. After all, you lived a quiet life. And I… seem to bring chaos wherever I go." She laughed, but then her face grew serious as she looked at Hazel's attentive stare. "Then, the night I was going to leave, you had a horrible fit in your sleep. So, I slipped into my cat form and hopped onto your bed. It seemed to comfort you, and somehow that was all the more reason I needed to stay."

Hazel thought about the times Roshi had comforted her without her knowledge. Every time she thought she had no one, Roshi—her cat—had been there.

"You want to know what's strange, Roshi? I knew there was something off about you from the beginning. But never in my wildest dreams would I have imagined that my cat companion was actually a druid."

"Surprise!" she exclaimed, grinning.

"Yeah, it was a surprise alright." Hazel shook her head. "Did you… did you know where I needed to go? What I needed to do? Or were you just along for the ride?"

"Ha! No, I was as clueless as they come. I just thought… well, I was lost and it seemed you were too."

Hazel looked at the floor, pondering her next words carefully. "Roshi, I have a lot of questions I need answers to. I don't even know where to start, but—"

Mori appeared at the tent's door, popping her head in as though she'd never left. "All questions that will be answered in time, once you've settled in. For now, though, your rooms are ready," she interjected with a stern look that held no room for negotiation.

Roshi bowed deeply. "Welcome home, Princess."

Hazel managed a soft smile that didn't reach her eyes. But deep down she knew she wasn't home. Not here. Not yet. And certainly not while Slaide, who'd sacrificed everything to get her where she'd thought she wanted—no, *needed*—to be, would face unimaginably severe consequences upon his return to Ravenhold. So, no, settling in would have to wait.

She may be a witch destined by Fate, but Fate had also shown her she was nothing without her Fallen. If she was to rewrite the future, she would do it with him by her side. She toyed with the locket, reminded of the irony that she had found it as empty as her heart upon finally meeting her mother.

I will find you, Slaide, even if it's the last thing I do.

Epilogue

Slaide glared at Magnus, his amber eyes ablaze. If looks alone could kill, the High King would be a pile of ash on the throne room floor.

"Well, well, well," Magnus began, "look what the cat dragged in. A filthy, lying, half-breed." He gestured to the Raven Blade Knight on Slaide's right. "Remove the gag. I'm curious to hear what he has to say for himself."

The knight did as he was told, unbuckling the muzzle-like contraption that kept Slaide's mouth shut. As it fell away, Slaide spat toward the King.

He took a swig of wine, the deep purple staining his upper lip and teeth. "Watch it, boy. I haven't killed you yet, but that doesn't mean I won't."

Slaide seethed. "You've been keeping me in the dark, Your *Majesty*," he growled. *For so long, and on so many things.*

Magnus only smirked, setting down his goblet. He stood and descended the dais. "On the contrary," he sneered as he approached the spot where Slaide kneeled, "I've been keeping you right where you belong. You're not my son. You're not my friend. You're my *weapon*, and it's past time you start acting like it. But I'll make you a deal. I have a task of utmost importance that, if completed, will earn you a spot back by my side."

As if I would want a spot by his side again. "Which is?"

"It's simple, really. Bring the girl back."

Slaide frowned. "Can you not just accept that she slipped out of your grasp? Why do you want her so badly?"

Magnus's expression darkened in a way even Slaide had never seen. He inhaled deeply, bringing his face close to Slaide's.

"She's my daughter."

TO BE CONTINUED…

Content Advisory

The Fated and the Fallen contains the following potentially triggering content:

- Depictions of violence and gore
- Slavery (specifically enslavement of those accused of practicing magic) and on-page abuse and mistreatment of the enslaved
- On-page torture and abuse (a man is tied to a post and whipped)
- On-page sexual assault and attempted rape
- Mental health struggles, mention of past suicide attempt (historical), feelings of hopelessness and being better off dead
- Addiction and substance abuse (fictional substance addiction & coping with alcohol)
- Loss of a close family member (on-page death)
- Off-page animal abuse (historical of a horse who was rescued)
- Mention of death in childbirth (historical)

Acknowledgements

As I stare at a blinking cursor on a page that reads "Acknowledgements," it's hard for me to fathom having made it this far. But here we are!

I have to start with the obvious: my readers. It is because of each of you that this dream can become a reality. Without readers, we don't have books. Or if we did, they'd serve no purpose. Thank you for taking a chance on me and for giving Hazel and Slaide's story a place on your shelf. I hope you'll stick around to see what happens next!

To my earliest readers, Tori and Justine: I cannot thank you enough for your feedback and selflessness in helping this story transform. You saw it at its worst, most basic form, and still didn't tell me to throw it in the trash. Justine, I cannot thank you enough for sharing your attention to detail in combing through the first draft. I still think you should pursue editing! Tori, I've enjoyed being a critique partner with you so much and cannot wait to see your book out in the world soon!

To my beta readers: I hope you know how much your feedback means. You are an invaluable part of the process and I am always grateful for readers who are willing to sacrifice their time to read a raw story.

To my friends and colleagues in the discord groups First Draft Mamas, Moms Who Write, and ARC Dragons: I don't know where this story would be without you. Thank you for sharing your experiences and knowledge on navigating the writing and publishing process (and everything in between).

To Aspin and Melody: you've been on this journey with me from the start and I know I've said more than once that this would not have happened had our paths not crossed. I'm forever grateful for your friendship, and infinitely thankful that Aspin's alpha reading group brought us together.

To my editor, Hannah: girl, you were a beacon of hope when I needed you. Thank you for letting me bounce my wild, reckless ideas off you at random hours of the day, for your humor and wit, your ability to yap about my characters, and of course, your editing excellence. I hope you find your way back to editing someday; I'll be waiting for you!

To my parents: you always told me I could. Never once, not even for a second, did you ever doubt me even if I doubted myself. Whether I was 13 or 33, you've always pushed me to keep writing. And in the years I didn't, I couldn't begin to count the times I heard "you really should have written a book." Well, after all this time, here it is. I love you!

Finally, and most importantly, to my husband and our kiddos: you are rockstars. Seriously. I know it's hard to hear "I'm almost finished," "just a few more minutes and then we can [insert fun activity here]," and "as soon as mommy is finished writing," repeatedly, but you took it better than you should have. I owe you endless pushes on the swing and many, many hours of playtime. You are the greatest gift I have in life! Hubs, thanks for putting up with me through this process. I know it wasn't easy and I know it drove you nuts at times, but your support means the world to me. Love you all so much!

About the Author

M. E. ALLQUIST is a lover of fantasy, science-fiction, and epic tales. As a creative soul in a nine-to-five world, she spends her quiet moments dreaming of vast worlds and sending her imaginary friends—er, characters—on epic, sometimes dangerous, journeys through hostile lands.

Residing in the Midwest, she finds joy in chasing around her two beautifully feral children and two rambunctious dogs. If she has a moment of peace, she enjoys relaxing with her husband and a good book. She believes magic can be found anywhere, you just have to know where to look. And if for some reason you can't find it, it might just be waiting for you to bring it to life.

Stay in Touch!

authormeallquist.com
authormeallquist@gmail.com
Instagram/Threads: author_meallquist
TikTok: author.m.e.allquist

Follow on Amazon: amazon.com/author/meallquis

www.ingramcontent.com/pod-product-compliance
Lightning Source LLC
Chambersburg PA
CBHW030044130726
47901CB00007BA/1841
9798994504918